# UNTIL ALEX

J. Nathan

Edited by Stephanie Elliot

Cover Design by L.J. Anderson, Mayhem Cover Creations

Manufactured in the United States of America

First Edition June 2014

ISBN-13: 978-1499707656 (print edition only)
ISBN-10: 1499707657 (print edition only)

*For my family, whose belief in everything I've ever attempted has inspired me to dream big.*

# PROLOGUE

## HAYDEN

*Alive.*

You learn early on it means living, breathing, undead.

But don't tell my mom that. She'd only hear the lyrics to her favorite Pearl Jam song. The one she'd been obsessed with since high school. The one that blared through the iPod dock on her dresser.

I couldn't remember the last time I'd seen her as happy as she was tossing shirts and shorts into the open suitcase on her bed. Her long brown curls bounced in time to the beat of the song.

Ten minutes before, she'd woken me up. And in the most angelic voice she uttered the words I'd longed to hear. "We're leaving, Hayden. We're finally leaving."

I jumped out of bed and stuffed my T-shirts, shorts, and hats into my backpack and joined her in her room. If I'd forgotten anything important, it could be replaced wherever we ended up.

With all the excitement and hasty packing, my mom shoved up her sleeves. Purple and yellow bruises covered her arms. Noticing my wide eyes from my spot on her bed, she shoved the sleeves back down, clearly forgetting what they concealed.

What they always concealed.

The last note of the song drifted through the speakers. I waited anxiously for the next song to begin—knowing her happiness and the twinkle in her eyes would continue.

But the song never played.

"What are you doing?" His emotionless voice traveled over my mom's shoulder, sucking the life right out of the room.

Goose bumps scattered up my arms.

My mom froze. Her face drained of color. And though her body blocked me from seeing the doorway, the terror in her eyes told me what I already knew. We weren't leaving. We weren't getting our fresh start.

She turned around slowly, her shoulders slumped. Even at ten, I could tell she was defeated. We both were.

I wanted to make a move, to tell him to leave us alone, but I sat frozen to the bed. It's what always happened when he took that tone with her. I was so small, the smallest in the fifth grade. And weak. So very weak.

And as much as I tried to be strong, tried to defend my mom when he became violent, he just tossed my feeble body to the side, oftentimes locking me in a closet to keep me out of the way. I was a nuisance. It's all I'd ever been for him.

"Hayden and I were just getting away for the night—"

*Whack.*

"Liar." The word dripped with hate as he lowered his hand.

My mother cupped her cheek as she twisted around, checking to be sure I remained safely behind her. Her icy blue eyes misted over. Not from the slap. She'd endured worse and never cried. Her tears were for our missed opportunity. Our foiled chance to escape once and for all.

"Please let us go," she whispered.

He leaned in closely. Now I could see him and the anger in his dark eyes. "Go? Go where?" The overhead light reflected off the shiny gold badge on the front of his uniform. The one that earned him respect from everyone in town. Everyone who didn't really know him. "Who'll want you?"

My mom sniffled. Or it could've been me. At that point, we both wept.

Needing to be closer to her, and wanting to keep him in my sights, I crawled to the foot of the bed. If I could see him, maybe I could protect her.

His white knuckles gripped her wrist like a vice. No wonder she hadn't moved away from him.

"Please." My voice came out low. Or was it that I just couldn't hear it with my heartbeat pounding in my ears? "I have a game in Austin tomorrow. Mom thought you were working late so we were going to make a trip out of it." I prayed my lie deflected the attention off of her. Because given his cold empty glare, she needed me.

*Whoosh.*

His fist slammed into my stomach. The wind knocked right out of me as my body folded and I toppled back onto the bed.

"Hayden!" my mom screamed, breaking free of his grasp and rushing toward me. She braced me in her arms as I gasped for breath. "It's okay, baby. Mommy's here. It's going to be okay."

It wasn't. But I let her soothing words wash over me as I struggled to catch my breath and regain what little strength I had.

And then she was gone. Ripped off me like she'd been caught up in a tornado. Perfume bottles crashed to the floor as her body slammed into the dresser. Her scream echoed as glass from the mirror shattered over her.

My eyes shot to the monster.

His big hands were braced on his knees, his breaths deep like he'd run a marathon. He watched through beady eyes as my mother steadied herself to her feet.

I wanted to hit him. To knock him back. To *kill* him.

I jumped down from the bed and lunged at him. A vicious backhand to the face propelled me onto the floor. Black spots clouded my vision. My head spun. My nose was surely broken, but none of that mattered. I needed to get to the phone on the nightstand. If I could just call—

*Click.*

My head whipped around.

He held something black in his right hand. He lifted it, extending it out in front of him.

Shock seized every part of me. It couldn't be real. It couldn't be happening like this.

"Please," my mother begged as he aimed the barrel of his weapon at her. She edged as far away from me as possible. She always kept his attention off of me. Always protected me. "I'll do whatever you want."

A calculated laugh escaped his lips. "*Now*, you'll do whatever I want? Weren't those the vows you promised me ten years ago?"

She didn't dare answer. She just took another step toward the bedroom door, stretching the distance between us.

"Then *he* came into the picture." He spun around with his gun aimed at me. "He ruined everything. He took you away from me."

I cowered to the carpet, preparing for the pain. For the nothingness. "Mom, run."

"*Noooo!*" she screamed, racing across the room and throwing her body over mine.

"He got your time. Your affection. Your love. It was all supposed to be *mine!*"

Three shots crackled through the air.

Three times my body jolted. I opened my mouth to scream, but the sound got cut off by the sight of blood spreading like a rush of ink through my mom's shirt. Within seconds, her grip loosened and her body peeled away from me, sinking to the floor.

Sobs ripped through me as I scrambled to my knees, slipping on the pool of blood surrounding her lifeless body. "Mom, wake up." I draped myself over her stomach, unable to look at her head where one of the bullets hit. "I'm here. I'm right here." With trembling arms, I tightened my grip, burying my face in her blood-soaked shirt. A putrid metallic smell replaced her floral scent.

*God, please help her. Please.*

"You're gonna be alright, Mom. Just stay with me." I couldn't hold her tight enough to stop her from hurting. To stop her from slipping away. To stop her from leaving me all alone. "I love you so much."

Guttural, unable-to-catch-my-breath, sobs poured out of me. And still, as my world crumbled around me and pain overwhelmed my being, I needed to get to a phone.

*Click.*

A quiver rocked through me.

I closed my eyes with my arms still wrapped around my mom, the woman I loved more than anything in the world. The woman who'd carry me over to the other side. To the light.

I braced myself for the impact of the bullet, praying for a quick death. Praying to be far away from him and the nightmare we'd been living.

But the impact didn't come.

I cracked one eye.

The monster stood over us with his gun to his temple and his eyes locked on mine. "This is all your fault."

When he was certain I heard him, he fired once.

# CHAPTER ONE

## HAYDEN

### *ELEVEN YEARS LATER*

My eyes snapped open. I wished I could blame the mid-afternoon sunlight seeping into my living room for the sweat dripping down my face and my heaving chest. But I couldn't.

Most people endured a rare nightmare. One that rocked them to the core. But not me. The same two plagued every one of my dreams. Unfortunately, they weren't strange figments of my imagination. Explorations into the deep recesses of my psyche. They were real memories. The worst I possessed.

I would've given anything to erase the horrid images from my mind, but they were my penance. My cross to bear.

I sat up from my black leather sectional, the focal point of my living room. It's the one place I normally fell asleep, *if* I fell asleep. Running my hands through my unruly hair, I scanned my apartment. For a guy, I kept it pretty clean. Of course I only cared about my flat screen. Without the white noise it provided, my bare walls closed in on me.

I stood up, working the kinks out of my neck. I should've grabbed my bag and headed to the gym, but I walked to the window at the rear of my apartment instead.

Late August in Texas didn't see many trade winds, so the trees and flowers surrounding the building sat idle in the balmy afternoon air. Luckily, a well-maintained pool flanked the rear of the property. And since most of the residents were elderly and rarely left the building, I was the only one who ever used it.

*Walk away, man. Walk away.*

I should've gotten something to eat. Taken a shower. Met up with Remy and the guys. But my damn eyes had a mind of their own. And they sought the sole picnic table. The reason I stood at the window in the first place.

Since moving in three years ago, it had been an ordinary picnic table. But for the last four days, it had become the very bane of my existence. Maybe not the actual piece of lawn furniture, but the unfamiliar girl seated on top of it. The one with her head buried in her knees and the coffee-colored waves of hair spilling over her body, bawling her eyes out.

Four days ago, she rolled into the parking lot in a killer black BMW sports edition. She lugged an oversized brand-name suitcase up the flight of stairs to the second floor, clearly not realizing the building had an elevator.

From my peephole, I watched her pull the suitcase down the carpeted hallway and approach the door diagonal to mine. Katherine, the owner of the building and a total babe for an older chick, greeted her with a sympathetic smile before stepping aside to let her in. Though they didn't hug, the girl was obviously staying with her, and not renting an apartment.

Sure, I looked like a creepy stalker staring out my second floor window, but I wasn't. At least that's what I kept telling myself. I just couldn't ignore the fact that the girl hadn't stopped crying in four days. Nor the fact that I felt like shit for not going down to check on her.

Don't get me wrong. My apartment was a revolving door of one-night stands, each convinced they'd be the one to change my ways. And never once did I feel bad for tossing them out after I screwed them. They knew exactly what they were getting when they agreed to go home with me.

I didn't do relationships. Too much trouble. I didn't care about other people's problems. Got enough of my own. And I didn't do kindness to strangers. Strangers didn't care about me.

Bottom line. I kept people at arm's length.

A shrink would attribute my aversion to relationships to the trauma I suffered when I was ten. But I'd been left to self-diagnose since I never saw a shrink. Bouncing around foster homes left little time for that. And truthfully, I wanted no part of baring my soul to some stranger. Fuck that.

If I learned one thing from my messed up life, it was that you didn't let people in, and you didn't let your emotions out. You couldn't. I wondered if I even had any. Emotions that is. Because if you asked me, life had hardened me beyond repair.

And just because I felt like a total dick watching the girl on the picnic table bawl her eyes out, it didn't mean I'd gone soft. Not by a long shot.

Maybe it was her shoulder-shaking sobs that kept my feet firmly planted by the window. Maybe it was the fact that she didn't seem much younger than me. Nineteen. Maybe twenty. Or perhaps it was the way her body scrunched into a ball that made her appear so small. So fragile. So broken. Like she needed someone to take care of her.

Jesus Christ. Listen to me.

I was one step away from playing sappy love songs and watching fucking chick flicks. I dragged my fingers through my hair and drew a deep breath. I needed to get the hell away from the window.

## ALEX

I'd been outside all day, hoping the fresh air would give me some relief. Some solace. Some reprieve from my broken world. But it hadn't. Not even close. The tears slipping from my eyes and sizzling on the wooden picnic table could attest to that.

What had I been thinking wearing a jean skirt? If I didn't have red welts on my rear end and the back of my thighs when I finally got up, it'd be a miracle.

At least my bowed head shielded my fair skin from the sun. Because I needed more pain in my life like I needed the proverbial hole in the head. Actually, a hole in the head would've been nothing compared to the hell I'd been through.

I swiped at my tears.

It didn't shock me that they hadn't stopped. I'd more or less been gutted. Stripped of everything in my life. Everything I'd ever known. Everything I'd ever loved.

My life was a complete mess. *I* was a complete mess.

Footsteps crunched over the dry grass.

My head shot up. My watery eyes, swollen from weeks of sobbing, squinted up at the shadowed figure before me. With the sun blaring directly behind the person, I could only distinguish a large build and towering height.

"You okay?" a deep voice asked.

I hadn't even spoken to my aunt about what happened in Austin, so I had no intention of sharing my sob story with a stranger I couldn't even see. "Not really."

I assumed he got his answer. Completed his good deed for the day. Paid it forward. Because he stepped away, leaving the sun shining in my eyes. But instead of walking away, the wood creaked under his weight as he sat down beside me.

*Alrighty, then.*

I rubbed my palms into my eyes, knowing the attempt to clear the tears would be futile. But really? What did I have left to lose?

I chanced a peek. But my blurry eyes, and the way the stranger stared down at the strategically placed rips in the knees of his faded jeans, hindered me from seeing his face. His body was lean, and he loomed over me by almost a head. His messy dark hair resembled that of the guys at my old school. Like he'd rolled out of bed and didn't care how he looked trudging across campus.

Long moments slipped by. Neither of us spoke.

I watched as he twisted and knotted his hands together like his life depended on it. He sported some serious muscles under the white T-shirt that clung to his impressive arms. He didn't look much older than me, twenty-one. Maybe twenty-two.

Despite his presence, my tears continued to drop as the silent minutes stretched on. My soft sniffles became lost in both the melody of chirping birds in nearby trees and the stranger's even breathing. I'd been surrounded by so much heartache over the past month that the in-and-out whoosh of his steady breaths soothed me. Cleared my mind. Gave me something new to focus on.

I wondered what he thought. What ran through his head as he sat beside a strange girl with a constant stream of tears flowing from—

A disbelieving laugh burst from my lips.

He glanced over. *Oh my.* His icy blue eyes, enclosed by gorgeous dark lashes, locked onto mine. Though they were confused and contemplative, they took my breath away. Was that even possible after everything I'd endured?

I flashed a half grin. The best I could manage under the circumstances that brought me to this town. "You must be some kind of miracle worker."

His eyes narrowed.

I rubbed away the remaining tears from my cheeks as another incredulous laugh slipped out. "I haven't been able to stop crying for days."

He nodded. "Four days." His pretty eyes flashed back to his jeans as if he'd said too much.

I didn't bother to mention my crying had lasted for almost a month. Instead, I shook off the unsettling thought and drew in a deep cleansing breath, actually feeling my lungs expand. "But then you sat down, and poof. They all but disappeared."

He made no attempt to respond. His eyes stayed lowered.

Had I made him uncomfortable? Had my honesty embarrassed him?

I stared down at his twisting fingers, his short clean nails, his knuckles covered with faded bruises and crisscrossed scars. Did he play sports? Work manual labor? Both?

Without even thinking, I placed my hand on his bare forearm. *Good Lord.* It was hard as a rock. "Thank you."

His arm stiffened. His eyes shot to my fingers wrapped around it.

I'd crossed some invisible boundary line. But what could I do? To remove my hand at that point would've made it even more awkward.

His eyes lifted to mine for a brief moment. And though it was brief, I caught the regret that flashed in them. It wasn't regret *for* me. More like regret he sat down next to me. Regret he crossed my path.

Without a word, he hopped to his feet.

My hand dropped unceremoniously to my side as I watched him tear off toward the building. When he reached the door, I expected him to turn around. To say something. But he didn't. He threw open the heavy door and disappeared inside.

## HAYDEN

I dropped onto the edge of my bed, burying my face in my hands. I *knew* I shouldn't have gone out there.

Miracle worker?

On what fucking planet? The girl clearly had me confused with someone who cared about other people. If she knew me—knew the truth about me—she'd see I was the complete opposite.

But man, after sitting beside her in that tight red tank top and ripped jean skirt showing off her incredible legs, I couldn't ignore the obvious. Very few could pull off the model body with girl-next-door face. She could. And did. Tenfold.

Even with the tears flooding her emerald eyes, a color I'd only ever seen in a tropical fish tank, she had the most flawless pale skin. Tiny freckles, unnoticeable from a distance, speckled her little nose. Pouty lips any guy would die to kiss, or enjoy in other creative ways, sat perfectly perched on her face. And the scent of vanilla rolled off her body like she bathed in it.

*Jesus.* Just thinking about her heated me in all the wrong places.

I fell back onto my bed, growling out my frustration. Since when did I start daydreaming about girls? That shit didn't happen to me. Hot girls surrounded me on a nightly basis. I had my pick. No need to think about them when they weren't around. I'd just replace them with the next.

Sure, this girl's looks might've caused my boxers to stand at attention, but something else wound me tightly, irritated me, fucked with my head. Something I sensed watching her. Sitting next to her. Having her frail hand on my arm.

Pain.

It *had* to be the pain. Pain so prominent in her eyes it put me on edge. Made me jittery. Made me uneasy. Because I'd been there. I'd felt pain so severe, so intense, so relentless, I thought I'd die from it.

She was obviously dealing with some major shit. Major shit I was *not* equipped to deal with.

I gripped the sides of my head, digging my fingertips into my scalp just enough to cause a sting. And then, like clockwork, my anger kicked in. It never ventured too far, always lurking right below the surface, ready to erupt. It was the only emotion that came naturally. The only one I could rely on. The only one I could trust.

Who the hell did this girl think she was worming her way into my head? What gave her the right to make me concerned like the pussy I'd been for the past four days?

Maybe I didn't know her name, but I knew her type. Girls like her only slummed it with guys like me to piss off their daddies. Their twisted way of getting them to fork over cash for jewelry, shopping sprees, and fancy cars.

I needed to snap the hell out of it. I lived in reality. And my reality didn't include expensive gifts or happy endings.

## ALEX

Twelve hours had passed since the stranger left me sitting alone on the picnic table. The same amount of time since I'd shed my last tear.

Footsteps sounded in the hallway causing me to spring from my aunt's loveseat and hurry to the front door. I lowered my eye to the peephole and instantly my cheeks heated and my heart thundered in my chest. It was refreshing to know it still worked. To know I was capable of feeling more than just anger, sadness, and guilt.

The stranger's eyes focused on the floor as he passed by with his head tucked down, stopping at the apartment diagonal to my aunt's. His dark hair flipped at his ears and the back of his neck like he'd worn a ball cap all day and just removed it.

A blonde in her early twenties stepped up beside him, hanging sloppily on his arm. Her barely-there skirt and too-tight black halter top left little to the imagination. Then, like a cat on a scratching post, she rubbed her overexposed body up his side as he unlocked the door.

*Classy.*

Her seductive eyes never left his as she slipped inside his apartment. Oh, he was definitely getting some. And he totally knew it. By the looks of the girl, the whole building knew it.

"Watch out for that one."

My entire body jolted before I spun around.

My aunt sat on the sofa with her eyes on her iPad. It had only been a month since our initial meeting, but her shoulder length dark hair, pouty lips, and green eyes still struck me speechless. She was the spitting image of my mother.

I walked back to the loveseat and dropped down across from her, crossing my legs beneath me. "What do you mean?" I settled in, hoping she'd elaborate. Divulge information. Shed some light on the mysterious guy across the hall.

"Hayden."

*Hayden.* I let the name and his image mesh in my mind. Yeah. I could see it.

She lowered her iPad and lifted an all-knowing eyebrow. "It's who you've been looking for, isn't it?"

Having no desire to deny it or explain it, I shrugged. *Plus*, I wasn't really sure how to explain it. Hayden was a stranger. Someone I'd barely spoken to. Someone I knew nothing about. Someone whose mere presence comforted me in ways no one else's had.

See? I was a mess.

"Well, allow me to tell you a little something about Hayden."

I leaned in, ready to absorb it all.

"In the three years he's lived here, I've never seen him bring home the same girl twice. It's a different one all the time. And he never lets them stay. They're always sneaking out an hour or two after they arrive."

A rush of disappointment washed over me. It was inexplicable. I didn't even know him. "So why do you let him live here?"

My aunt lifted a shoulder. "He pays his rent on time and doesn't make any noise. That's all I care about."

"I bet if he lived next door, you'd hear some noise." I gasped as the words left my mouth. It had been a month. A long trying month since I felt the urge to spew sarcasm. And though it wasn't delivered with the same *oomph* I normally used, it felt amazing to just exist in the moment with nothing else weighing me down. Not my sadness. Not my anger. Not my guilt.

My aunt smiled.

Fighting back my own smile, I glanced around her living room. As if I'd been living in an unfocused microscope since arriving, everything twisted into focus. *Holy red plaid.* Sofas. Ottoman. Curtains.

How had I not noticed that my young attractive aunt lived like a country bumpkin?

Little wooden trinkets sat atop her weathered maple furniture. Doilies rested below the light fixtures, fitting into the country motif. Our housekeeper back home would've been appalled by the fine layer of dust coating the furniture, but it worked for my aunt. And her taking me in when I had nowhere else to go, worked for me.

"So he lives alone?" I looked back to Katherine, hoping she'd reveal more than just the specifics of Hayden's sex life. But she only nodded. "Where's his family?"

She lifted her iPad. "Sorry, sweetie, that's his story to tell. Not mine."

I definitely wasn't surprised he had a story.

"Just don't go falling under his spell," she warned.

"His spell?"

She lowered her device, letting her eyes fall upon me. "I may be closing in on forty, but it doesn't mean I'm blind. He's gorgeous and brooding. Doesn't get more tempting than that."

This time I did smile. And it felt good.

The fact that I was in so much trouble…not so much.

# CHAPTER TWO

## HAYDEN

"Dude, can't you go any faster?" Remy asked from the passenger side of my truck.

I glanced over, cursing under my breath. His damn boot was planted on my dashboard. I'd given up asking him to move it, but it still pissed me off to no end. Especially when he laughed it off, leaving it there like he owned the truck.

That was Remy. He did whatever the hell he wanted. Including inking up his body and piercing his face and tongue.

"Once we get there," he said. "I hope the asshole says he ain't paying. I'd really like to beat a deadbeat's ass tonight."

I shook my head. Remy lived for the shit we did for cash. I just hoped they paid so we could get the hell out of dodge.

Remy dropped his foot and leaned forward, pointing to a single-level house coming up on our left. Except for the television flickering inside what I assumed to be the living room, the house sat draped in darkness. My eyes shot to the truck in the driveway. Good. He was home. Hopefully he'd just fork over the cash.

I steered clear of any street lights as I pulled my black F150 to a stop across the street and a few houses away from our target. I didn't own much, so I tried to keep it out of harm's way.

Before I even shifted into park, Remy jumped out. He jogged down the deserted street and crossed the lawn with wide strides. Apparently he planned to fly solo. He'd been doing that a lot lately. Which was fine by me. I'd lost the desire to join him three years ago. That's when we stopped running money and started hitting up guys who didn't pay their bookie.

There was nothing I hated more than laying my hands on someone. But I never let on, always showing up for Remy. He needed me. And I always had his back. No questions asked.

I killed the engine, taking in the lower-class neighborhood, with its similar houses tightly lining the street.

Remy pounded on our target's front door. He impatiently twisted to scour the neighborhood, searching the shadows for any sign of trouble. He was paranoid. Always had been. Just like he'd always been scrawny.

But his gaunt looks were deceiving. They gave no indication of the power a blow from him could pack. Juvie made Remy stronger. But life made him harder. I guess it's what brought us together in the first place. Both foster kids. Both angry at the world.

The door to the house cracked open. Remy spun around, jamming the toe of his boot in the gap. Good thing. The asshole tried to slam the door in his face. Remy's palm flew out, shoving it open and forcing his way inside.

I gripped my door handle, ready to assist if I got the sign or he'd been in there too long. It happened more often than not. Not because Remy and I sucked at our job. Because we didn't. We always delivered. But deadbeats had no intention of paying the money they owed. And most didn't owe chump change. They owed thousands.

I snagged the gun stowed under my seat and tucked it into the back of my jeans. These guys weren't just gambling addicts. They suffered other addictions, too. None of which I wanted to get caught in the middle of unarmed. Especially when demanding money they'd already stiffed our boss on.

The television inside the house flicked off, shrouding the house in complete darkness.

I flew out of the truck and across the lawn, unsure if I even shut my door. I reached the house and pushed the door open slightly, uncertain what I'd find.

The house sat unnervingly silent as I slipped inside the empty living room. Luckily, the moonlight squeezed through the window blinds and guided my route as I glided against the wall, careful not to bump any of the worn furniture and make my presence known.

Gripping the gun in the back of my belt, and hoping to God I didn't have to use it, I turned the corner into the small kitchen.

An angry shudder rolled through me.

A house-of-a-guy with a long gray ponytail and soiled wife-beater held Remy against the wall by his neck. By the looks of his huge biceps, he squeezed not only to silence Remy, but to kill him.

I drew my gun, aiming it at the back of the guy's head as I moved toward him.

"Let him down," I ordered, my teeth clenched in hate.

The guy didn't move, not even to readjust his grasp on Remy, now breathless and turning blue.

Beads of sweat rolled down the back my neck, kicking my adrenaline into gear. I jammed the gun into the back of his head, shoving it forward. "I don't think you heard me. I said, 'Let him down.'"

The guy must've had a death wish because he didn't acknowledge the fact that I'd spoken.

I released the gun's safety sending the ominous *click* echoing off the outdated metal cabinets.

"*Noooo*," my mother's scream broke through my subconscious.

I shook off the vision just as the guy's shoulders finally dropped. His grip loosened, and he lowered Remy to his feet.

Remy bent at the waist, gasping for air and massaging his aching neck. I didn't dare go to him. He wouldn't want me to. Instead I kept my gun on the guy.

Within seconds, Remy straightened up. He cracked his neck to the left then right. Then his fist flew out from his side, slamming repeatedly into the guy's face. Blow after blow. Blood sprayed from the guy's nose as he staggered back, his arms flapping in front of him in an attempt to ward off Remy's attack.

If he thought he could manhandle Remy without recourse, he had another thing coming.

I lowered my gun. It was time for the Remy show. When he was in the zone, no one could stop him.

It only took a few more powerful blows to the face to send the guy flying on his ass. But even then, Remy inundated his sides with full-blown soccer kicks, garnering grunts and groans as he struggled to shield his body. Knowing Remy, the guy's noises only added more fuel to his fire.

For me, the sounds elicited an immediate flashback. One so strong it yanked me by the collar and shoved me barreling back to the alley three years ago.

*With swollen eyes and a bloody face, the guy writhing on the filthy pavement shielded his head with his arms. I didn't matter to me. I didn't ease up my attack. My fists slammed mercilessly into any part of his solid flesh I could get a shot at.*

*I clenched my throbbing jaw, spitting out a mouthful of blood on the pavement as I stood. He'd gotten in a cheap shot before Remy and I took him down. That rarely happened. The mere thought brought the toe of my boot to the side of his head one last time before his body fell limp.*

*Remy heaved me back. "Fuck, Hayden. You probably killed him."*

"Get us the money!" Remy's voice snapped me out of my head and back to the here and now. His tone left no room for confusion. We weren't leaving until we collected what the guy owed our boss.

Bloody and woozy, he rolled to his knees on the kitchen floor, gasping for breath. Finally, he staggered to his feet.

Prepared for the stunts these deadbeats pulled when they felt desperate, Remy freed his gun from his boot. "Keep your hands where I can see them." He shoved the gun into the guy's back as he pushed his beaten body down the dark hallway.

Chances were the guy didn't have all the money. He wouldn't have stiffed our boss if he did. But Remy was good at getting some of it, then finding valuables as collateral until the balance got paid.

I leaned against the kitchen counter, giving my body a minute to recover. My chest heaved like I'd run a marathon and a shrill piercing rang in my ears. Nights like these, coupled with my walking nightmares, were taking a toll on my sanity.

I just kept telling myself this job—this life—paid better than any minimum wage job I could get. And since I had bills most guys my age didn't, and no parents to help out, I couldn't afford not to help Remy.

But that wasn't the truth.

The truth was I wanted out. No, I *needed* out.

But I owed Remy.

I'd always owe him.

Minutes passed before Remy emerged from the room alone.

I followed him outside, quickening my pace in case the guy came running after us. It wouldn't have been the first time. But Remy was in no rush as we crossed the lawn. "You think he called the cops?"

"Nope." Remy flashed a devious grin. "He'd have a hell of a time calling anyone right about now."

## ALEX

I padded down the dark hallway en route to the kitchen, careful not to slip on the hardwood floor or wake my aunt who'd fallen asleep on the sofa.

I poured myself a tall glass of water. The cool liquid refreshed my sour mouth, but it didn't help my insomnia. Nothing did. Twenty years old and dark circles already beset my eyes. *Fan-freaking-tastic.*

Insomnia for me wasn't like other people's. It was self-inflicted. I mean, how could it not be? The second I closed my eyes, my mind whirled like a carousel of memories. Memories I wasn't ready to revisit. Memories that reminded me I was broken.

And it was all my fault.

I finished my drink and turned back toward my room, considering the next book I'd read. Would it be my favorite Chelsea Fine or the new one by Stephanie Elliot? Before I could decide, a shuffling came from the main hallway.

I stopped dead in my tracks.

Pivoting, I tip-toed quickly by my aunt to the front door. I grabbed the handle and pulled it open.

Hayden twisted from his door, catching me in his fierce gaze. His eyes drifted down, sweeping over my pink camisole and white polka-dot shorts. Okay, so maybe whipping open the door hadn't been a brilliant idea.

"Hey." Could I get any lamer?

His eyes lifted to mine. But he didn't say a word. He just turned back to his door and inserted his key into the lock.

I held my tongue. Because the truth was, he owed me nothing. On an exhale, I turned back to my aunt's apartment.

"You still think I'm some kind of miracle worker?" His sexy raspy voice caught me off guard.

My body stilled. Prior to that moment, he'd said a total of four words to me. I hadn't expected the words to roll off his tongue so smooth. So confident. So masculine.

I spun back around, taking a small step into the hallway so I wouldn't wake my aunt.

With his hands buried in the pockets of his jeans, he made no attempt to disguise his wandering eyes still slowly raking over my pajamas.

Vulnerable under his gaze, and quickly remembering I wasn't wearing a bra, I crossed my arms over my chest. "Any chance you can cure insomnia, too?"

He flashed a faint smile, one I would've missed if my eyes weren't fixated on his lush lips. "Have you tried warm milk?"

I blinked, forcing my eyes back to his. "Every couple hours."

He pushed open his door, but remained in the hallway. "Reading?"

"Just finished book number five."

He raised a brow. "TV?"

I nodded. "Already ordered three infomercial products. If you need a body pillow, vegetable peeler, or lifetime supply of floss, I'm your girl."

The corners of his mouth twitched, but he suppressed a smile.

I wondered why.

"A bottle of Jack usually does the trick for me," he offered, before stepping into his apartment.

My heart dropped at his sudden retreat.

But then he stopped in his doorway and shot me one last look over his shoulder. "Goodnight."

Before I could say a word, he closed the door behind him, leaving me alone.

Again.

# CHAPTER THREE

## ALEX

The following morning I threw on my black bikini, the cute one with the pink hearts. I spread my aunt's floral beach towel on one of the lounge chairs surrounding the pool. Luckily, I had the pool all to myself.

I crept into the water. It was just the right temperature. Refreshing yet warm once submerged. I dipped my head under to cool my body while swimming leisurely toward the far wall. I grabbed onto the cement edge and gauged the length of the pool, wondering how many laps I could manage before needing to stop. Twenty? Maybe thirty? Either way, I'd be exhausted. And exhaustion equaled dreamless sleep. At least I hoped it did.

I pulled in a deep breath, then pushed off the wall with both feet. I made nice long strides, spearing the water like the swimmers in the Olympics. By lap three, I amped it up, kicking my legs as if a madman pursued me. If I kept up the pace, my legs would tire before my arms. I wasn't an athlete. I'd never claim to be anything even close, but I—

*Splash!*

Stopping mid-stride, I spun around in the center of the pool, circling my arms and legs to stay afloat. I didn't know what I expected to find. An animal. A small child. The pool man. But Hayden breaking through the water at the low end definitely wasn't it.

I tried not to gawk as he stood waist-high in the water. But I found myself smack-dab in the middle of every teenage girl *and* desperate housewife's most vivid fantasy.

The water dripped like honey down his face, over his broad shoulders, and onto his sculpted torso. His wet dark hair and bare chest practically glistened in the bright morning sun.

I tried to appear unfazed, but seriously? I was so far from it, it wasn't even funny.

"I'm not used to sharing my pool," he said, lowering himself so the water met his chin.

"*Your* pool? That'd be news to my aunt. She claims to own this place." I shot him a smug smirk.

He moved toward the center of the pool—toward me—wading water effortlessly while concealing a smile.

I couldn't fathom why someone so breathtakingly gorgeous would deny girls everywhere something as small as a smile. Wait. Maybe he wasn't denying other girls. Maybe just me.

Fully cognizant that the awkward way I circled my arms wouldn't keep me afloat much longer, I moved to the side of the pool. Grabbing onto the side wall, I spun around to face Hayden, extending my arms over the edge for balance.

*Your move.*

Hayden backed away, somehow keeping his eyes locked on mine. "I didn't catch your name."

"You didn't ask," I deadpanned.

For the first time since laying eyes on him, he flashed a grin. A wide grin.

Oh, sweet Jesus. Dimples sank into his cheeks. Of course he had dimples. Why wouldn't he?

"How 'bout we try this again." His eyes studied mine. "I'm Hayden."

"I know." I played his words off indifferently, but my entire body hummed. If the mere sight of him and those to-die-for dimples could affect me so intensely, I could only imagine what his touch would do. *Oh, my God. Who said anything about touching?*

His head retracted. "You know?"

I gulped down the fairly noticeable knot in my throat. "My aunt already warned me about you."

He laughed softly, an edge to the sound. "Did she now?"

I nodded, trying to keep the nervous ripples swelling inside my stomach at bay.

One side of his mouth lifted into a cocky grin, like he could somehow sense my nerves.

*Damn him.*

"So, what'd she say about the hottie in 2C?"

I furrowed my brows, pretending he'd asked a serious question. "There's a hottie in 2C?"

His voice lowered. "So I've been told."

Okay, so cocky and confident. Usually an obnoxious blend, but somehow he worked it. How utterly frustrating. And oddly delicious. "Maybe you could introduce us. I'm new here, and a hot friend might make things bearable."

Hayden suppressed another smile as he mimicked my move, resting his arms on the edge of the pool directly across from me. *Great.* Now I couldn't escape the finely chiseled muscles rippling in his biceps and forearms.

"You still haven't answered my question."

My eyes snapped from his muscles to his grinning face. Okay. So he caught me staring. So what? "What question?"

"You got a name?"

I swallowed. What was up with the swallowing thing? "Alexandra. Alex."

"You living here now, Alex, or just passing through?"

Why did I like that given the choice, he opted for my nickname? "Nope. I'm here 'til I graduate college in May." As the words left my lips, a rush of sadness swept over me. I tried to conceal it with a small smile. But given Hayden's intense gaze, he saw through my façade.

Thankfully, he didn't say a word. He just nodded, seemingly understanding there were things I had no intention of disclosing.

Without another word, he lifted his face to the morning sun and closed his eyes. Mimicking his move, I let the sun's rays spread over me, heating my body to the core. At least I assumed it was the sun's effects.

As the sun moved in and out of the wispy clouds fluctuating the air's temperature, we relaxed in comfortable silence. It gave me time to think. *More* time to think. The doctor said my mind would settle down, but it would take time. My pain ran deep. It was raw and intense.

The anti-depressants he prescribed didn't work. Hence me swallowing the entire bottle in need of sleep and a clear mind. But that just got me a hospital stay and a one-way ticket to my aunt's.

Not my finest hour.

Being hundreds of miles away from my old life was supposed to help. So far, it hadn't.

Grief overwhelmed me.

Guilt and anger ate away at my soul.

Except when I was around Hayden.

I didn't understand it. I couldn't explain it. But I'd take it. Because here in the pool, I could smile. I could laugh. I could breathe.

It took no time for the sun to sting my cheeks. Since I'd forgotten sunscreen, and my fair skin burned so easily, I needed to move into the shade.

When I opened my eyes, Hayden's gaze was locked on mine from across the pool. I expected his eyes to jump away, to pretend they'd been staring at something else, but they didn't.

"Is sharing your pool as bad as you thought it would be?"

A slow smile slid across his lips. "Could be worse."

I smiled back. "Worse, huh?"

He nodded.

"Like 'swimming with sharks with a big gouge in your leg' worse?"

He considered my question before shaking his head. "Like 'getting ready to bang a hot chick and realizing you don't have a condom' worse."

I choked out a laugh, completely blindsided by his response. But given the devious twinkle in his eyes, he was trying to get a rise out of me. Looking for a reaction. Testing me.

Giving nothing else away, I lowered myself into the water, allowing the coolness to soothe my tender sun-kissed shoulders and cheeks.

"You a swimmer?"

I pushed my wet hair out of my eyes. "Hardly."

He lowered his body into the water, submerging himself underneath. When he resurfaced, he raked his fingers through his dark hair pushing the wet locks off his forehead. "So if I challenge you to a race—"

"You'd kick my ass."

His lips tipped into a grin before he moved away from the wall and swam to the far end of the pool. I caught a glimpse of a tattoo on his right shoulder, but he spun toward me before I could determine what it was. "What makes you so sure?"

"I've seen the muscles." Once the words were out, I wanted to swallow them back. Not because I was embarrassed. But because of the sly, cocky grin that swept across his face. I desperately needed to save face. To regain the upper hand. To humble him. "You're not one of those guys, are you? The ones at the gym who gawk at themselves in the mirror while they lift? The ones grunting and groaning?"

Hayden's eyes darkened as he peered across the water at me. "The only time I'm grunting and groaning is in the bedroom."

I could feel myself morphing into a cherry-cheeked little girl. So much for saving face.

Hayden took pity on me. "I'm up for a race if you are."

Never one to back down from a challenge—and desperately needing to end our conversation—I nodded. "Sure."

I swam over to the spot beside him, staying a good six feet away. Not being overly athletic, chances were high I'd crash into him while swimming. I grasped the wall with one hand. My feet pressed flush against it under the water.

Hayden held on to the edge with both hands behind him, preparing for something fancy like the butterfly stroke.

*Show off.*

Okay. So maybe he had every reason to be. Because if I thought his muscles were impressive from afar, seeing the deep ridges flex and roll as he gripped the wall beside me gave the term *wet dream* a whole new meaning.

"Ready?"

I nodded.

"Go," he called.

We pushed off the wall at the same time, kicking and splashing like contenders for the gold medal. Clearly, I wasn't the only competitive one.

My arms flew through the water, using every bit of strength I had to slice the water and reach the opposite side before him. With the wall a mere yard away, I threw my hand out, slamming into it with a *splat.*

The water lapped against the side of the pool as I grabbed on and looked to Hayden. He hadn't gone easy on me. His chest heaved like mine. "Was it a tie?"

Water droplets hung from his impossibly long eyelashes as his gaze captured mine. "Yup."

I shook my head and laughed, knowing it was a total lie. A lie intended to spare my feelings. There was definitely more to Hayden than met the eye. And even though what met the eye was seriously intoxicating, I wanted to know more. "Bullshit."

He laughed a hearty laugh, throwing back his head so young and carefree. So unlike him.

Or was it?

"You callin' me a liar?"

I bit my lip to stop from grinning. "I wouldn't dare."

He lifted his brows. "No?"

Aware of his scrutiny, I shook my head, keeping my face composed. "I need you to introduce me to that hottie in 2C."

He laughed again, softer this time, as if trying to rein it back.

"How about a rematch?"

Instead of agreeing, like I hoped he would, his mouth became a tight line I couldn't decipher. His conflicted eyes lifted to the clouds for what felt like forever. And despite his apparent reluctance, his eyes slid back to mine and he nodded. "Yeah. Okay."

Exhaling the breath I'd unconsciously been holding, I leveled him with my eyes. "This time no lying."

His lips lifted into a crooked smile, and a tiny piece of my shattered heart shifted back into place.

After four or five more races, Hayden lifted himself out of the pool. "I've gotta take care of my laundry."

I tried not to stare as he grabbed his towel off the lounge chair, but I wanted to get a closer look at his tattoo.

He must've realized what I was doing from my spot in the pool, *or* he wanted to give me a better angle of his six-pack, because he turned toward me and draped the towel around his neck.

"Same time tomorrow?"

He shook his head. "I've got plans."

"Oh. Yeah. I totally understand." Heat pulsed in my cheeks. Talk about being shot down. How mortifying.

Hayden stared down at me for a long moment. He wanted to say something. I could see it in his pensive eyes. But in the end he headed toward the gate. "See you 'round."

I watched as he made his way toward the building.

Once I could no longer see him, I dropped my head in humiliation. *Stupid. Stupid. Stupid.*

The sun had already set and taken the intense morning heat with it when I stepped onto the lawn with my old green comforter in my arms. I maneuvered around excited residents seated in lawn chairs facing the windowless side of the three-story building eager for the "drive-in" movie to begin.

I said a quick hello to my aunt who was busy setting up the projector, then searched for the perfect spot in the back.

As I spread my comforter on the dry grass, tears prickled the backs of my eyes.

*Here we go again.*

I sat down, running my hand over the worn fabric beneath me. It had accompanied me to star-filled nights on the beach with my ex Preston. To concerts in the park with my girlfriends. To football games on cold December nights with my parents. Avoiding the memories was impossible. My mind rendered me helpless. I was an unwilling participant. A slave to whatever images invaded my mind.

Sure, those were good memories, but they still wounded me just as deeply as the bad ones. They were now part of my past. Part of a time that would never be recaptured.

I fell back onto the comforter and draped my arm across my eyes. I needed a moment to compartmentalize. To keep my parents, Preston, and my friends out of my head. It wasn't like I wanted to forget them since leaving Austin. I just needed them to take a vacation from my thoughts for a while. How else could I pick up the pieces and move forward?

The movie began with applause from the residents. Although my arm covered my eyes, I could hear the actors' voices. *Fantastic.* The comedy I'd seen with Preston last year.

A soft rustling moments later caused me to lift my arm and crack open my eyes.

Hayden sat beside me on my comforter, holding a bag of microwave popcorn. He lifted his chin to the movie projected on the side of the building. "You're gonna miss it if you don't sit up." He tossed a handful of popcorn into his mouth like watching a movie with me was the most normal thing in the world.

"I've already seen it."

His voice dropped to a lower register. "Not with me you haven't."

Tiny tingles fluttered in my belly. He definitely had me there.

Feeling foolish laying there while he hovered beside me, I pushed myself up. My head spun for a moment as the blood flowed down. Hayden's lips twitched, probably assuming his presence brought on the lightheadedness.

I reached over and snatched a handful of popcorn from his bag, popping one piece into my mouth at a time. "Extra butter? Nice."

Hayden grinned. In sank the dimples. Seriously? What girl could resist dimples?

He turned back to the movie, laughing at the scene unfolding between the main characters.

I couldn't help but be drawn to the hearty sound of his laughter. It was so refreshing. So real.

"Was it this funny the first time?"

Truthfully, I couldn't remember laughing at all. Probably because I hadn't. Laughing at the raunchy parts would've made Preston think I was immature.

Strange.

I hadn't realized I worried about things like that before.

"Too busy sucking face with the quarterback in the back row?" Hayden asked, interrupting my small epiphany.

"Actually it was the middle. The back row is so cliché."

A swoon-worthy smile flashed across his face. I wondered if he knew he even possessed a swoon-worthy smile. Or how accurate he'd been about Preston being the quarterback at UT and us making out in the dark movie theater.

Thankfully, that's all we'd ever done. I could say that now because we weren't together. Back then, it sucked. Most times it's the boyfriend pressuring the girlfriend to give it up. In my situation, it was me pressuring Preston. He came from a very religious family, one that brainwashed him into believing waiting until marriage was the norm. My response to that had always been *On what planet?*

An hour into the movie, exhaustion seeped in. I knew those laps in the pool—and unexpected races with Hayden—would pay off. My heavy eyelids sank to nothing more than a tiny slit, making it impossible to stay awake.

I reclined on the comforter, linking my hands behind my head and closing my eyes for a brief moment.

Before I knew it, silence surrounded me and I drifted off into a much-needed slumber.

A cool breeze drifted over me, prickling the skin on my face and the wisps of hair on my arms. The sounds of the movie had been replaced by chirping crickets and the hum of a distant car buzzing by. I wondered how long I'd been out.

Reluctantly, I opened my eyes. Darkness surrounded me. The moon and stars speckling the ebony sky provided the only source of light.

I jolted up, my eyes scanning the empty lawn and building cloaked in blackness.

I glanced down beside me. Ease instantly settled in. Hayden slept peacefully on his side along ▮▮▮. Moonlight cast a glow over his sleeping form, shadowing his strong jawline and perfect nose. Was that a day ▮▮▮▮▮▮▮▮▮▮▮ of his ▮▮▮? I hadn't noticed that before.

His freakishly long eyelashes fanned out, skimming the tops of his cheeks. His flawless skin, with a dusting of early morning stubble, made him appear older than he normally did. I wondered how old he really was. And why he stayed outside with me when he could've ▮▮▮▮ ▮▮▮ up. Or left me alone. It wouldn't have been the first time.

I shifted my focus to the ▮▮▮▮▮▮▮▮▮▮▮. Tyler ▮▮▮▮▮▮▮▮▮▮▮ me? Had she forgotten about me? It's not like she was used to having a roommate.

My hands shot to my pockets. *Great. No key.*

"Hey, Hayden," I ▮▮▮▮▮ ▮▮▮▮▮▮▮▮▮.

My eyes shot to ▮▮▮▮. His head rested on his palm as he looked up at me with tired eyes. "Sorry. I didn't mean to wake you."

He ▮▮▮▮▮▮▮▮, slipping his phone from his pocket. Probably checking

My hand shot to my mouth, covering a wide yawn. "Glad to see you're not slacking on the job."

Hayden pushed himself up to a sitting position, working the kinks out of his neck. "Well since you're up, I guess I'm no good after all."

"You're admitting you're not good at something?"

He lowered his voice, his hooded eyes luring me in. "Oh, I'm good at lots of things."

I stared at his cocky grin, grasping his intent and liking it way too much.

He jumped to his feet and extended his hand down to me. "Come on. Let's get you inside."

I reached up and grabbed hold of it. A wave of charged energy buzzed through me as he pulled me to my feet. *Holy hell.* I looked for a reaction, a confirmation he'd felt it too. But his eyes stared down at my feet.

Once I was steady, he released my hand, leaving me utterly bereft. But how could that be? I'd only known him for a couple days. And really, what did I know?

These feelings I felt couldn't be normal. Rational. Healthy. Especially after all I'd been through.

Hayden seized my comforter from the grass and led me into the building, guiding me with his free hand on the small of my back. Oh. I liked that. Especially the tingling sensation accompanying his touch.

We stepped onto the second floor and the stairwell door clicked behind us. I paused, cringing at the thought of waking my aunt to get into her apartment.

Hayden walked by his apartment and stopped in front of my aunt's. He didn't say a word as I stepped beside him. He just gazed down at me, his eyes unexpectedly gentle.

My heart jumped to my throat. I couldn't remember the last time a guy made me that nervous.

"Your aunt gave it to me."

Oblivious to anything but the flecks of silver in his blue eyes, my voice came out a whisper. "Huh?"

He held up his index finger in the space between us.

I blinked away the Hayden-induced haze to find a shiny gold key dangling from it. "Tonight?"

Hayden's forehead creased.

"The key. Did she give it to you tonight or did you already have it?"

His eyes narrowed. "Why would I have her key?"

I shrugged. "Maybe you two have a little thing going on. An arrangement."

Hayden's eyes gave no indication of what he thought. He simply turned to the door and unlocked it.

Had I gotten it right? Were they hooking up? My aunt was thirty-seven, but she could easily pass for late twenties. And God only knew how old Hayden was. It's not like he divulged anything willingly.

He turned back to me and held out the key. I reached for it, but he closed his fingers over mine. "You figured it out," he lowered his voice, his gaze holding mine. "We've been going at it for months now." He tightened his grip as he leaned closer. My breath caught in my throat. My palms dampened. "And it's been hot. Unbelievably hot."

I sucked in a silent breath, his words flustering me beyond reason. Maybe it wasn't his words. Maybe it was the way his eyes held mine, caressing them with a deep penetrating intensity. Or the way he inched closer to my face, like he had other intentions, a hidden agenda I wasn't privy to.

One thing I did know for sure. I was in over my head.

I kept my eyes on his as I wiggled my fingers, attempting to tug on the key. But he didn't let up. "So you're into older women?"

A muscle in Hayden's jaw twitched. Dark cobalt replaced his clear eyes. I'd overstepped that invisible line again. "You being here…"

I couldn't look away. I waited for whatever morsel he planned to share. Like any little crumb would be worth it.

He blinked a couple long drawn-out blinks until clarity returned. "…Is really cramping my style." He let go of my hand, relinquishing the key and taking a step back.

A giant breath left me. That's what I got for thinking we might've been getting somewhere. "Don't let me stop you. I don't take my aunt for much of a screamer, but I can just slip on my head phones. I won't hear a thing."

Hayden laughed a real authentic laugh, bringing out the dimples.

There was something victorious in knowing I caused his reaction. And with that, I turned the knob and opened the door, but not before glancing back to him. "Thank you."

The smile slipped from his face, and he shrugged like it was no big deal.

But it was a big deal. And it meant something to me.

# CHAPTER FOUR

## HAYDEN

*I glared down at the guy's lifeless body, bloody and unrecognizable. I should've felt remorse. I should've felt disgusted by what I'd done to him. I should've felt something. But as usual, I didn't.*

*Someone inside the club screamed and chaos erupted. No doubt the cops arrived with guns blazing.*

*My head twisted around, searching the windowless alley for an exit. With little time to get creative, I eyeballed our only option. The wall surrounding the alley.*

*Remy was a step ahead of me. "Over here," he yelled from the base of it.*

*I jogged over, my eyes drifting up the menacing structure. Even though I stood at a solid six feet, the wall towered over me by at least four. And forget Remy. I had him by half a foot.*

*My eyes flashed around, searching for something to stand on. Alleys were supposed to have rats and dumpsters. I'd seen the rats. Where the hell were the dumpsters? I glanced back to Remy, but he no longer stood beside me. He'd bent down, his fingers joined together.*

*I shook my head. "No way, man. We got into this together. We're getting out of it together."*

*"Hate to break it to you, bro, but we're about to go down together."*

*Remy shook me off. "This one's on me, bro. Now get the hell outta here."*

*I stared down at my scrawny friend. My partner in crime. My comrade. Could I really leave him down there to take the fall?*

*Frantic sounds from the club emptied into the alley. If I waited any longer, the cops would find me perched on top of the wall. And innocent men didn't run.*

*I sucked in a breath and nodded to Remy.*

*Then I did what only a coward would do.*

*I dropped to the darkness on the opposite side of the wall and left my friend alone with the body of the man I killed.*

Though I was in bed tossing and turning, it hadn't been a nightmare. I wasn't asleep. Not since sleeping outside next to Alex.

I knew I wasn't the miracle worker she claimed me to be, but I affected her. She stopped crying. She slept after admitting she couldn't. She smiled.

I scrubbed my hands over my face. *What the hell was I doing?*

"Fooling yourself," the voice inside my head answered.

All hell broke loose.

## ALEX

Hayden's door swung open. He stood before me in nothing but black boxer-briefs low on his hips. Seeing him by the pool was one thing. But having him a foot away looking all sexy with his messy hair, sleepy eyes, and rock hard abs was more than I could handle. Hence, my eyes shamelessly raking over his body.

"See something you like?"

My eyes flew up, catching his slow sexy smile. It took all the restraint I could muster not to nod. "Sorry. I didn't want to bother you since you said you'd be busy, but I just...I just wanted to thank you."

He lifted his arms and gripped the top of the door frame.

*There go the damn muscles.*

"You already did."

"Right. But I meant..." My pulse hastened, pounding in my temples. "I wanted to *do* something to thank you."

His eyes widened, his brows shooting to the center of his forehead. "What'd you have in mind?"

I swallowed hard. He made me so flustered it was ridiculous. "Well, I...*Shoot*. That's not what I meant."

He broke into a deep laugh, one that pulled his lips wide and rumbled in his chest.

Under normal circumstances, I would've tried to prolong the moment, enjoying his liveliness way too much. But knowing he laughed *at* me and not *with* me embarrassed me. I crossed my arms, the ones that had been uselessly dangling at my sides. "I meant what do people do around here for fun?"

He studied my eyes long and hard, like I'd asked a difficult question. Then, without warning, he dropped his arms and crossed them over his bare chest. "Okay."

My head shot back. "Okay?"

He nodded, his scheming eyes dancing. "I'll let you thank me."

"Good." I think. "Where am I taking you?"

His lips quirked into a sly smile. "It's a surprise."

I tilted my head. "Well, what time am I picking you up?"

His smile remained in place, but I could see the wheels at work. "Seven. Don't be late." He stepped back into his apartment and closed the door.

I might've been left standing alone. But this time I knew I'd be seeing him again very soon.

At two minutes to seven I stood outside Hayden's door, seriously rethinking my decision to ask him out. I lifted my hand to knock, but his door swung open before I touched the surface.

My eyes glided over the faded jeans hanging low on his hips and the navy blue shirt clinging to his chest. His tousled hair screamed he'd just rolled around with one of his one-nighters. But even still, he owned the look.

My eyes weren't the only ones perusing. Hayden's made a slow ascent, sweeping leisurely up from my knee-high brown boots over my favorite skinny jeans to my hunter green off-the-shoulder top. The one I'd been told matched my eyes.

I should've felt uncomfortable with his unapologetic inspection, but I didn't. I actually awaited his judgment when his eyes reached mine.

As usual, he gave nothing away.

Why would he? It wasn't a date.

Still, I wondered if I should have gone with more than the minimal blush, mascara, and pale pink gloss I brushed on. Or if I should have pulled my hair back instead of letting my natural waves hang loose.

"Ready?" he asked.

I nodded, wondering why I felt so let down that he didn't compliment me.

Hayden placed his hand on the small of my back and guided me toward the stairwell. Tiny tingles resonated in the spot. Geez. Did his touch need to feel so electric? Like I was special. Like he needed to take care of me.

I hadn't seen his hand on that girl's back he took home the other night.

"Are you letting me drive?"

"Nope," he answered as we descended the stairs.

Outside, the heat assailed us like a wall of glass. Being inside an air-conditioned building made it easy to forget how painstakingly hot Texas summers were. Even for a coastal town, the thick heat clung heavily to the air and snatched your breath away.

Hayden guided me to a big black truck in the corner of the lot, so masculine and conspicuous. Just like him. Catching me by surprise, he stopped on the passenger side and opened the door.

I grabbed hold of the interior handle and lifted myself inside. As he rounded the front of his truck, I tried to make sense of his actions. His quiet appraisal. His hand on my back. Him opening the door.

Did he consider it a date?

Did he think I'd be one of those girls who'd go back to his apartment at the end of the night?

Did he feel sorry for the girl who couldn't sleep or stop crying for four days?

If I were a betting girl, I'd take the latter.

## HAYDEN

I could barely focus on the dark road in front of me. Where was I supposed to take Alex looking all sexy like that? If I took her to Baxter's, the guys would be all over her. And I was in no mood to throw down. I also risked running into girls I'd slept with. Definitely not something I wanted to happen in front of Alex. If I took her to dinner, she'd think it was a date.

It definitely wasn't a date.

I chanced a quick peek over at her nestled in the passenger side of my truck. She stared out her window at the passing stores and restaurants, spinning a silver ring on her middle finger. I clearly made her nervous. Especially in such tight quarters.

I wondered why she hadn't mentioned the nineties' rock blaring from my speakers. Other girls complained the second they got into my truck. Either it was too outdated, too loud, or not country. But not Alex.

"So where you from?" I asked, needing to break the awkward silence between us.

Her eyes shot to mine, an unfathomable expression on her face. "I didn't tell you?"

I turned down the music and shook my head. Why was she so surprised? She hadn't told me anything.

"Austin."

I spotted Remy's truck in Baxter's parking lot. *Nope. Not going there.* He'd have Alex in tears in seconds with his vulgar mouth, blunt assertions, and foul sense of humor. "You like it there?"

I shot her a side-long glance, instantly noticing her moist eyes. *Shit.* My attention flew back to the road, unequipped to deal with whatever the hell this was.

"I did," her voice was soft, sad.

Even with the weight of her stare, and the underlying meaning of her words, I didn't dare look back. I knew how it felt to harbor secrets, ones you didn't want anyone else knowing. But I also knew how it felt to have people around who didn't give a damn.

*Fuuuuck.*

"So whatever brought you here sucked pretty bad, huh?" I peeked over to gauge her response.

Her eyes dropped to her lap and she nodded.

"Well then tonight's exactly what you need."

She didn't look at me, but a small smile tipped her lips. "I sure hope so."

*Great.* I still had no clue where to take her.

The further I drove, the further away from town we got. Maybe that had been my plan all along. Get her away from my demons.

## ALEX

I glanced over at Hayden. His left hand relaxed on the steering wheel while his right hand played the beat of an old Pearl Jam song on the seat between us. God. I wished the old song didn't send me into such a tailspin. I'd been lost in my head for most of the ride, memories of my dad overtaking my thoughts from the first note.

I wondered how Hayden did it. How he always appeared so cool and collected. Was he really? Or was it just a front to keep others out?

Without warning, he whipped the steering wheel to the left. My body slammed into the passenger door with an unceremonious thud as he pulled to an abrupt stop in the gravel parking lot—the one that appeared out of nowhere. "*Christ.* Who taught you to drive?"

Hayden's laughter filled the cab as dust billowed around us. But I wasn't laughing. Especially once he killed the engine and the dust settled. Because outside the window, I stared at a building with the neon signs in the windows.

He turned his body to face me, his dark brows bouncing. "So, you ready?"

"I probably should've mentioned this before…" According to the parking lot sign with the unlit E, we were at Jake's Pub. "I'm only twenty."

One corner of his mouth tipped up. "Yeah. I figured."

"You figured?" I crossed my arms. "Well how old are *you*?"

Genuine interest flickered in his eyes. "How old do you think I am?"

"If we're here, at least twenty-one."

Hayden smiled, neither confirming nor denying.

I glanced out at the old pickup trucks and motorcycles occupying the parking lot. "Well, I don't have my fake ID. I left it in Austin figuring I…" My voice trailed off, realizing what I almost divulged. I met his eyes. "Do you have one for me?"

He shook his head.

"Is it eighteen-and-over night?"

Again, he shook his head.

I heaved a sigh. "I didn't realize I signed up for charades when I asked you out."

Hayden threw open his door with quiet laughter. I took that as my cue, pushing open my door. Before I could step out, Hayden blocked my way, his proximity overwhelming me.

He leaned in closely, hovering by my ear. His warm breath tickled my neck. His crisp aloe scent invaded my senses. "They don't card," he whispered, sending shivers rushing through me.

Then, as if he hadn't just purposely sent my body buzzing, he stepped back.

*Bastard.*

Stale beer and badly sung music assaulted us upon entering the crowded bar. High-top tables filled the area between the door and the glossy oak bar that ran the length of the back wall. Though the room was small, the mirror behind the bar gave it a larger feel.

To the right of the entrance, a pair of older women sang Bon Jovi's "Wanted Dead or Alive" on a small stage. They laughed and fell all over each other while squinting at the scrolling lyrics on the screen.

Hayden wove us through the crowd to the only empty table as far from the stage as you could get. I scooted up onto the stool across from him, hooking my handbag on the back and pushing the condiment tray to the far side of the table.

Hayden's eyes scanned the room. My head whirled around, wondering who he searched for. Based on the clientele, his mother would be a good guess. Because the butchered song, the people filling the room, and the duet's teased hair, black jeans, and rock band T-shirts, were a total throwback to the nineteen eighties.

A blonde waitress, in a low-cut black T-shirt that didn't reach her belly button, slid a songbook and two coasters onto our table. "What can I get ya?" Her hazel eyes locked on Hayden, widening on contact.

"I'll have a Bud." Hayden flashed her a sexy grin before turning to me. "How 'bout you, sweetheart? What'll it be?"

Sweetheart?

The waitress' eyes remained fixed on Hayden, while her tongue managed to stay tucked inside her mouth.

I cocked my head. "I'll have whatever you're having, babe."

It visibly pained the waitress to pull her attention away from him. "Be back in a second." I didn't doubt her breathy words as she practically ran to the bar to retrieve our drinks.

Hayden arched a brow. "Babe?"

I arched my own. "Sweetheart?"

He chuckled under his breath while his eyes searched the room over my shoulder.

A twinge of jealousy clutched my chest. "Expecting someone?"

Hayden's eyes slid back to mine. This time guarded. "What?"

"You look like you're expecting someone to be here."

He shook his head, a lazy smile sliding into place. "Only you, sweetheart."

Something could definitely be said for his inviting glances and concise retorts. No wonder waitresses became speechless and girls willingly went home with him.

I lifted my chin toward our waitress. Her eyes jumped impatiently between the bartender and Hayden. "So, is it always like that for you?"

Hayden caught me in his mesmerizing gaze. "Like what?"

"Oh, please. She was practically panting."

He leaned in, his amused eyes creasing in the corners. "So is this where you admit the guy in 2C is a hottie?"

I leaned back and crossed my arms, putting as much distance between us as possible. His mere gaze could entice even the most unwilling catch. And I was in no way immune to his charm. But I'd fake it like no one's business. "First of all, I've never been introduced to Mr. 2C. And second, I hate to break it to you, but I don't think anyone actually uses the word *hottie* anymore."

Hayden laughed, but it could have been a reaction to the women on stage who finished their song with a locked-arm bow. The one on the right nearly toppled over, taking her friend with her. The few people in the bar who applauded drowned out the refreshing sound of Hayden's laughter.

"I guess I'm just surprised."

Hayden's eyes narrowed.

I lifted my chin toward our waitress whose eyes were still on him. "That girls act that way." He didn't follow my eyes, just stared across the table at me, forcing me to spit it out. "Our waitress. She was shoving her chest in your face and staring at you like she wanted to eat you. That just isn't my style."

His brows inverted as he leaned closer, his eyes focusing on my lips. "What is your style?" His seductive tone almost had *me* panting.

The waitress returned with our drinks, pulling our attention from each other. *Thank God.* The icy bottles landed on our coasters, and her hungry eyes landed on Hayden. "Can I get you anything else? Anything at all?"

He looked to me for a brief instant before flashing her a smile. "Not right now. But I'll let you know when you can."

Thankfully, she moved on to another table.

I lifted my bottle to my lips and took a nice long swig as a middle-aged man in cowboy boots took his spot behind the microphone. The music to "She's a Hottie" exploded through the speakers and people in the bar hooted like the real Toby Keith had entered the building.

Hayden smirked. "Well that answers that."

*Bastard.*

I lifted my middle finger to the side of my nose and scratched.

His smile widened. "You know…I would've taken you for more of a fruity drink kind of girl."

"And I would've taken you for more of a body shots kind of guy."

He held my gaze, his eyes unwavering as he leaned toward me. "I am definitely a body shots kind of guy. But I don't discriminate. Honey, whipped cream, chocolate. They all work just as well."

I took another swig of my beer, trying to swallow around the massive lump in my throat.

"How about you?"

"I like honey." I answered too quickly to be casual.

Skepticism shone in his eyes as he shook his head slowly. "You're too classy for that."

"Am not." A flush spread over my whole body. I needed to shut up.

He tilted his head. "I've seen the car, the clothes, the luggage. You're high-maintenance."

I leaned back in my seat and crossed my arms across my chest. "I didn't take you for someone who judges a book by its cover."

He dismissed my comment with the roll of his eyes. "Oh, come on. It doesn't take a genius to see you're the type of girl who needs to be wined and dined. Not treated like the main course."

"Well, it's a good thing you didn't request a bowl of nuts." I tilted my head and raised a brow. "I might've thought you were wining and dining me."

The corners of his lips twitched, but he suppressed a smile. "I guess we don't know much about each other, do we?"

"Is that such a bad thing?" I sipped my drink.

"Not if you're lookin' for a one night stand," he drawled slow and sexy.

I choked on my beer like a flippin' teenager. *Nice, Alex.*

Hayden sipped his beer behind a smile.

Feeling too vulnerable for my own good, I tossed open the song book and skimmed the endless songs. Some would surely get people on their feet. Others would clear the room.

When I glanced up, Hayden's eyes studied my face. Just like in the pool, they didn't jump away when I caught him. And seriously? Did they need to be so damn hypnotic? I held up the book. "So, did you bring me here to show me what you've got, or what?"

His dimples popped and his straight teeth gleamed. "Sweetheart, if I get up there, there's no doubt in my mind, I'll clear the room."

"You could always just take off your shirt."

He glanced down in contemplation, before shooting me a smirk. "You've seen the merchandise. What's the verdict?"

I ignored his attempt to elicit a compliment. "Your voice can't be that bad."

He nodded adamantly. "It can and it is."

"So, no duet?"

He shook his head. "No chance in hell I'd get up there and sing."

The waitress returned, claiming the spot beside him. The tables in the bar were close, but not close enough to warrant her cushy body pressed into his side. But, alas, there it was. "Decide if you want anything yet?"

Hayden peeked at me before his gaze fell to the waitress, his eyes roaming over her face for far longer than necessary. "Any chance we could do some body shots?"

She definitely groaned as her eyes squeezed shut for a long moment. Someone needed to save her. I gripped her arm. "He's kidding. We'll have another round and two tequila shots."

The waitress shook her head slightly, undoubtedly clearing away the Hayden-induced haze. Then with a quick nod, she hurried off.

"That was cruel."

Hayden lifted a shoulder. "What? You gave me the idea."

I brushed a wave of hair away from my face, tucking it behind my ear. "Yeah, well, she was about to take you up on the offer."

"You think?" He glanced over his shoulder to where she stood. He couldn't be that oblivious to his charm. When he looked back with a giant grin, I knew he wasn't. "Would that have embarrassed you?"

"You taking shots from her belly button?"

He nodded.

"You said it yourself. We barely know each other." It came out nonchalantly, but the truth created heaviness in my chest and disappointment in my heart. But why? We *didn't* know each other.

Hayden lifted his bottle to his lips. "Just so you know, I never said I wanted to do body shots with her."

A vicious quiver rocked through me, rattling my bones. Keeping my unaffected mask in place, I turned toward the man on stage, needing to collect myself and get my muddled emotions in check.

Out of the corner of my eye, I noticed a guy enter the bar. What held my attention were his sunken dark eyes, shaved head, piercings in his face, and sleeves of tattoos. The guy was downright creepy.

His eyes jetted around the crowded room with purpose. Then they landed on Hayden. Since Hayden was busy watching the man on stage, the guy's eyes shifted to me. They narrowed for a long moment while he clearly tried to place me. To no avail.

Then as if he'd never been there, he turned around and walked back outside.

Applause for the man on stage and our waitress returning with our drinks pulled my attention from the door. Once she moved to another table, I pushed Hayden a shot. "I want to make a toast."

His eyebrows bunched together. "A toast?"

I lifted my glass a few inches from the table. "People do make toasts, don't they?"

He shot me one of those shrug-nods.

"Okay, so it might sound kind of cheesy. But I swear, it's the truth."

Hayden tilted his head, eyeing me in both amusement and intrigue. He lifted his shot. "Well, let's hear this cheesy truth."

I'd never felt so inclined to throw up in my entire life. And not from the alcohol. From the words I was about to utter. "Obviously, I brought you here—or you brought me—to thank you. And I don't think you understand why."

He stared at me across the table, his narrowed eyes giving nothing away.

I inhaled a deep breath, letting it out slowly. "Clearly I've been going through a really tough time."

Hayden nodded, even though he had no idea what happened back in Austin.

"And then out of nowhere, you show up. Not once, but multiple times. And every time, you help me in some way. And I've got to tell you. I've thought about it a lot, and I don't think it's a coincidence…It's like you were sent to me or something."

Hayden stilled. His shot dangled in the air. And though his eyes remained fixed on mine, he wasn't seeing me. He was seeing anything *but* me.

*Ah, crap.*

The room suddenly felt too small, like the walls were squeezing in on the two of us. "To you," I mumbled, before throwing back my shot and wincing as it burned a prickly path down my throat. I chased it with my beer, finishing the entire bottle in a few solid gulps.

Hayden still hadn't downed his shot when I jumped to my feet.

But I didn't care. I needed to get away from him. Far away.

# CHAPTER FIVE

## HAYDEN

As if being chased by a chainsaw toting murderer, Alex wove her way through the tables. She clearly felt embarrassed by her toast. Her words. Her feelings. It took guts to be so open. So truthful. I admired her honesty. But it didn't mean I agreed with her.

Because the only people I got sent to ended up broke, wounded, or dead.

But, man, I'd be an idiot not to be affected by her words. They stole the air right out of my lungs. She saw me as someone worthy of her friendship. Someone she sought comfort in. Someone she could rely on.

Except for Remy, no one had seen me that way before.

Heads turned as Alex passed by. Her gorgeous face. Her hot body. Her innocence. It was all there for the entire bar to see. And they saw. How could they not?

She stopped at the DJ table beside the stage. Her eyes finally snagged mine from a safe distance away. Before I could acknowledge her, her attention shot to the DJ. They exchanged a few words before he handed her a microphone.

*Oh, shit.*

Alex climbed up onto the stage.

Center. Fucking. Stage.

She leaned against the wooden stool, her right foot resting on the lower rung like a rock star ready to belt out a ballad. She grasped the microphone stand, popped the microphone in, and lowered it to her height like she did it for a living.

I prayed it wasn't the alcohol making her brave. Because for a tiny thing, she'd just downed two beers and a shot of tequila.

Music to the eighties scorned girl's anthem "I Will Survive" filled the bar. The women broke into wild cheers. I sensed a fucking sing-along. Maybe their voices would drown out Alex's.

She lifted her head, her green gaze holding mine like we were the only two people in the bar. Even across a congested room, I sat captivated by not only those amazing eyes, but by the owner of those eyes. Her lusty expression made my body twitch. I couldn't look away even if I wanted to.

The lyrics tumbled out of her pouty little mouth slow and sexy as she explained she was afraid and petrified.

I sucked in a breath. Her words flowed out in tune. The girl could sing. She could really sing. I raked both hands through my hair, letting the relief wash over me. *Thank Christ.*

When the beat of the song picked up, Alex jumped to her feet, ripped the microphone from its stand, and worked the stage from left to right and back again.

That little vixen.

She knew exactly what she was doing, swaying her ass around up there in those tight jeans and knee high boots like a fucking rock star.

She threw her arm into the air declaring she'd survive, and the women in the bar jumped to their feet and sang along. Even the men whistled and cheered, hanging onto every raspy note and intentional swing of her hips.

Watching her up there, exuding confidence and sex appeal, struck me speechless. There was definitely more to Alex than met the eye.

It made me wonder. What "tough times" had she been through? What was she surviving? I wished I didn't want to know. I wished I didn't *need* to know.

As the final note drifted through the speakers, those who weren't already up jumped to their feet. The wild noise reverberated throughout the room like a full-blown concert. I rose to my feet wearing a big dopey grin, awed by Alex. A girl I hardly even knew.

She looked out over the crowd from her spot on stage. Her lips split into a giant grin as if the shit she'd been carrying just vanished. And if it only lasted for a fleeting moment, the moment had been worth it. For her. For me. For everyone in that damn room.

She stepped down into the crowd with the help of two guys at the front of the stage who were more than willing to put their hands on her. As she maneuvered through the room, she laughed as people reached out and slapped her hand.

When she finally reached our table, her eyes were alight, her face filled with joy. Without warning, she threw her arms around my waist with an adorable giggle and buried her face in my chest.

Instantly, my body stiffened. I didn't speak. I didn't breathe.

Sensing my discomfort, Alex dropped her arms and stepped back, plastering on an insincere smile and sliding into her seat.

I hated myself in that moment for not being able to control that part of me. The fucked-up part that kept people at a distance. It was a defense mechanism. My very own alarm system that kicked in when things got too uncomfortable, or in this case, too close to being normal.

Alex picked up the beer the waitress delivered while she was on stage and finished it off in a few long chugs.

"That was amazing," I said, trying to salvage the night.

Alex shrugged, her eyes landing on everything but me. "Keg stand champ back home. Two years running."

Though she didn't laugh, I did. Her sense of humor always surprised me. Pretty girls weren't usually funny. I mean, the ones I took home weren't there because of their wit. Alex's was a breath of fresh air. It became more apparent with every moment I spent with her. Whether I ruined the moment or not.

But being able to chug a beer wasn't what I meant. And she knew it. "Your *voice* is amazing."

She kept her eyes glued on the two girls taking the stage. "It's just something I can do."

"Have you tried out for one of those singing shows?"

She glanced at me like I'd said the most ridiculous thing she'd ever heard. "I only do it for fun. I'm not going to be a singer or anything."

I rested my elbows on the table and leaned in a little closer. "What *do* you want to be?"

Alex shrugged, her eyes suddenly uneasy. I wasn't sure if it was my question or the alcohol, but her gaze fell distant.

"You're not gonna tell me?"

Her eyes transformed from uneasy to irritated in a matter of seconds. "You know, Hayden, you have all these questions for me, but you haven't told me one thing about you."

"You haven't asked."

She sat back and crossed her arms. "How old are you?"

"Older than you."

Her lips pinched like she downed something sour. "Why do you live alone?"

"I choose to."

Her frown deepened. "How do you afford it? What do you do for work?"

I shrugged a shoulder. "You know, this and that."

Most girls found my evasiveness charming, practically begging me to take them home with me. But Alex looked about ready to kill me. "Seriously?"

No. But I couldn't tell her I beat down people for a living. I tipped back my bottle and chugged down my beer, allowing the coolness to penetrate my body. "So you're a senior?"

Alex paused for a long moment, obviously debating whether or not to answer my question.

I waited her out.

"Three days 'til senior year. At a new school. With no friends. Can't wait."

My lips pulled to the side regrettably. That sucked.

Her head tilted to the side. "So, are you a senior, too?"

I shook my head. I knew you were expected to offer more than what was asked. But the more I said, the more I risked letting people in. Letting them see the real me.

"Oh, that's right," she said, shooting me attitude. "You're too busy with this and that."

I didn't even try to hide my amusement as I swallowed the last of my beer behind a grin.

## ALEX

I sat back in my seat and watched the next few singers without another word. Hayden might've been amused by his evasiveness, but I wasn't.

Okay, so maybe it wasn't Hayden.

Maybe it was my own humiliation. I had no clue what possessed me to throw myself into his arms in the first place. I guess the excitement of the moment, and the fact that I hadn't felt that alive since leaving Austin, overwhelmed me.

But the way he stood there, stiff beneath my touch like I carried some kind of disease, mortified me.

I tried to play it off with indifference, but truthfully, I just wanted to get back to my aunt's apartment and lock out the outside world.

As if reading my mind, Hayden spoke over the music. "You ready to hit the road?"

I didn't answer, just grabbed my handbag from the back of my stool and rummaged through it in search of my wallet.

"Don't even think about it," he warned.

My eyes lifted to his. "This was on me, remember?"

"Yeah, I remember. Now put your cash away. I'm paying." His stern look and chilly tone left no room for an argument.

Five minutes later, Eddie Vedder blared through Hayden's speakers, preventing our drive home from being unnervingly quiet. I wondered if the other girls he had in his truck minded the nineties' music. My dad couldn't leave the driveway without Pearl Jam on, so I knew the songs and didn't mind them. If anything, they just made me sad.

But these days, what didn't?

I glanced over at Hayden's shadowed profile lit only by the sporadic headlights of passing cars. I wondered what made him so reticent. His past? His current situation? Me?

He hit the nail on the head when he said we knew so little about each other. But he wasn't the only one to blame. I didn't offer much in regards to me or my past either. "My favorite's 'Black.'"

Hayden's eyes remained on the dark road, but a little smirk tipped his lips.

I waited him out.

"Mine's 'Nothingman.'"

I nodded, recognizing the song. "Walking on your own with thoughts you'd rather not think?"

His eyes shot to mine, blinking hard. It made me wonder. Maybe we weren't so different after all. Both on our own. Both with heads full of memories that brought nothing but sadness.

Without a word, Hayden's attention turned back to the road. That was all I'd get.

Parking in the darkest corner of the parking lot, Hayden jumped out and circled to my side before I could even gather my handbag into my lap. He pulled open my door, but unlike the scene outside the bar, he didn't lean in and whisper in my ear. He waited for me to step out with one hand in his pocket and the other on the door.

As we crossed the parking lot, a spring peeper croaked its high-pitched call in the distance, making our silence in the balmy night even more prominent. Like things weren't awkward enough.

Inside, the blast of air conditioning sent chills scurrying up my arms. Or, it could've been Hayden's arm brushing mine as we took the silent ascent to the second floor.

I wondered why he never used the elevator. Scratch that. I wondered lots of things about him. Things, after the night's unfortunate turn of events, I'd probably never find out.

He stopped outside his door, running his hand up and down the back of his head, messing up his already tousled hair.

Saving him the inner struggle of what to say, I continued to my aunt's apartment and unlocked the door. I glanced over my bare shoulder.

With his hands buried in his pockets, he faced me.

"Thanks for tonight. You really helped me forget. At least for a little while."

Taking a page from his book, I pushed open the door and slipped inside without another glance.

## HAYDEN

I turned onto my side, checking the alarm clock for the hundredth time.

Seven thirty.

I hadn't slept at all. Not because of the usual nightmares. Because Alex's comments played through my head on a constant loop.

What did she need to forget? And why the hell did I only help for a little while? Did I really fuck everything up by blowing off her hug? Disregarding her toast? Dodging her questions? Not explaining my song choice?

Man. I was such a douchebag.

A loud pounding on my front door snapped me out of my head.

I rolled out of bed and moved through my living room. The pounding continued like the person didn't think they'd been loud enough the first time. I didn't even bother throwing on a shirt or checking the peephole. Whoever showed up at my door that early on a Friday morning deserved my wrath.

I yanked open the door, stepping back as Remy pushed by me. "Get packed." He landed his ass on my sofa and kicked his black boots onto my coffee table like he owned the place. "We're taking a road trip."

I rubbed my palms into my scratchy eyes. "What the hell, man? It's not even eight."

"Cooper needs us up in Houston." His brows bounced. "All expenses paid."

As much as I needed the money, Cooper expected us to drop everything to take care of his shit. Excuses were unacceptable. And since Remy was always game, it meant I was, too. We were a team and Cooper knew it. Hell, everyone knew it.

And even though I wanted out of this job—this life—I couldn't let Remy down. Not after everything he'd done for me. "I need to be back for Monday."

"Don't be such a bitch, Hayden. The sooner we get outta here, the sooner we'll be back."

# CHAPTER SIX

## ALEX

Back at the University of Texas, I loved the first day of a new year. Seeing everyone after a long summer apart. The new off-campus house. The new couples. The new classes. But as I pulled into the crowded parking lot of Southern State College, I could hardly swallow down the gigantic knot in my throat.

I wanted to stay at UT. But being alone in that huge empty house, waiting for the semester to begin, wasn't healthy. My stint in the hospital could attest to that. So when my aunt enrolled me at SSC, I didn't have a choice.

I'd heard about small colleges. The gossip. The drama. The cliques. I just hoped I could avoid all the nonsense and graduate on time.

I circled the parking lot in my dad's BMW. If the campus wasn't ten miles away, I would've walked. I had no desire to give off a false first impression that I was some rich snob.

But I hadn't been given much of a choice. A month ago, when I received the news that devastated my world, I totaled my Jeep with me in it. Preston thought it was a brilliant idea to break the news to me *while* I was behind the wheel. I guess I couldn't fault him. He'd just learned he'd been dealt the same unfair hand by fate.

Unfortunately, he hadn't called to comfort me. He called because he needed someone to blame. Someone to hate. After two years of dating, I never expected his parting words to be, "This is all your fault." Yet they were. And I still hadn't heard from him.

Tears welled in my eyes as I located a spot at the far end of the lot. Before I could even consider stepping outside, I rummaged through my handbag and found a crumpled tissue at the bottom. I dabbed below my eyes as people passed by, shooting quick glances my way.

I took deep breaths, filling my lungs before exhaling. Anything to ward off the tears.

Once I pulled it together, I stepped outside. The sweltering heat was such a bitter contrast to my air-conditioned car. I tossed my bag over my shoulder, smoothed my pink peasant top, and straightened my faded jeans. *Here goes nothing.*

I freed the trapped pieces of hair from my bag's strap as I walked to the path that led to the small quad. My head whipped around, taking in the four brick buildings surrounding the grassy area. From the looks of their modern décor, they couldn't have been more than a decade old.

Having no idea where I needed to go, I pulled up the campus map on my phone. Ten minutes and two wrong turns later, I sat in the back of Lit 350. No one even noticed me tucked in the back corner as the professor ran through her class syllabus.

Calculus followed and was definitely not my strong suit. It's why I'd put off taking it. The teacher spoke a mile a minute and his syllabus looked like a different language. Again, I sat in the back remaining unnoticed, until the girl beside me with the retro glasses and severe black bangs shared a smile.

I had an hour before Adolescent Psychology, so I located the Social Sciences building on the opposite side of campus, then stopped for an iced latte at a coffee shop I'd noticed on my walk in. After grabbing my drink, I stepped back into the bright sunlight, searching my bag for my sunglasses.

"Nice legs, babe," a guy called out.

My head flew up. Three guys occupied a patio table calling out to the girls passing by. With their devilish good looks and tattoos peeking from the sleeves of their fitted T-shirts, two of them clearly had no trouble getting girls.

My head withdrew.

The third sent a shiver up my spine. He was the guy from Jake's. The one with the piercings and tattoos who stared at Hayden and me then left. With his major drug-induced glare, he was downright creepy and likely struggled with the girls.

Giving up on my sunglasses, I took another step, but my body stilled.

Leaned up against the wall, behind the cat-calling trio, stood the last person I expected to find on campus. A guy with his hands buried in the pockets of his khaki cargo shorts. A guy who disappeared from the face of the earth three days ago. A guy whose crystal blue eyes were locked on mine.

Unexpected relief flooded my body. The tension I'd been feeling released in one fell swoop. I couldn't hide my smile at the sight of a familiar face. I practically floated over to him.

Brushing by the trio, I planted myself at Hayden's feet. It was ridiculous how quickly his presence comforted me. And though I had a strong desire to, I refrained from throwing my arms around him again. "Hey."

Given his deer in headlights expression, he was equally surprised to see me.

"What happened?" I lifted my hand, indicating the black and yellow bruise under his left eye.

"What's this?" Creepy guy pushed his wrought iron chair noisily back and stood. His dark sunken eyes crept over my body, putting me on edge. "Oh, I guess you didn't get the memo. Our boy Hayden never calls. One night's all you're ever gonna get. Hope it was memorable."

He and the other two burst into laughter. Hayden didn't. It was like he couldn't fathom why I stood before him. Like he didn't know I'd be there. Like he didn't know me at all.

I glared into his distant eyes, mine narrowing in frustration. "Are you gonna speak?"

The muscles in Hayden's jaw clenched. His eyes grew darker, colder. "Sorry, darlin'." The deep voice that came out of his mouth didn't even sound like his. He averted his gaze, his eyes scanning the flow of human traffic behind me. "I think you're confusing me with someone else."

I stared up at him, my eyes flaring. Was he freaking serious?

I spun around, hoping his comment was directed at someone behind me. But the only people there were girls who'd slowed to witness the bizarre scene unfolding between us.

I shook my head, both in bewilderment and total disgust. Screw this. I took off without turning back, walking away with as much of my pride as I could muster. I didn't need that from him. I didn't need it from anyone. He knew who I was. He was the one who neglected to mention *he* was still in college. The same college I'd be attending where I didn't know a single soul.

I'd been honest when I told him I didn't believe our first meeting had been a mere coincidence. That he'd been placed in my life for a reason. But as I raced away from the humiliating scene, with shaking hands and heated cheeks, I realized I'd never been so wrong about anything in my entire life.

I entered the sunlit dining hall, needing to grab something to eat before my fourth and final class of the day. Its floor to ceiling windows provided a beautiful panoramic view of the campus. But the view inside is what stopped me in my tracks. Until that moment, I had no idea what being in a room full of strangers felt like. Sure I attended UT with fifty thousand other students. But never once did I feel alone when I had my girls and Preston there.

But now, with only three thousand students, I felt daunted by the unfamiliar faces. The tables already occupied. The friendships previously established.

My head whipped around, trying to locate a vacant table in the corner. A leggy blonde in a pink top and short jean skirt stopped in front of me. "I've been dying to meet you all day."

"Me?" My skeptical eyes widened as she linked her arm with mine and tugged me to a table in the front of the room.

"Yeah, you." She flashed a huge smile accentuating her perfect white teeth. "You're all anyone can talk about."

"What? Why?" Leaving me no other option, I sat down on the seat beside her.

"Well, honey, first off, you're hot. Second, you drive an amazing car. And third, that scene with Hayden. Did you get him confused with someone else?"

I thought back to our encounter. The distance in his eyes. The hasty way he dismissed me. The way he allowed his friend to talk to me. "Yeah. I definitely thought he was someone else."

# CHAPTER SEVEN

## ALEX

The only thing I wanted to do after my exhausting day was curl up in bed and forget it. Hence my spot under my paisley purple comforter. The one that matched my purple walls still smelling of fresh paint. I knew my aunt wanted to make me feel at home. And I appreciated it.

What I didn't appreciate was feeling like a rag doll pulled in a million different directions. From the people who wanted to show me to my history class to the questions about UT and why I transferred, I felt suffocated.

I knew I didn't have to hide my past. But if people knew the truth— knew the real reason I'd come to town with nothing more than my dad's car and a suitcase—I'd be forced to deal with the pity in their eyes and their empty sympathies when they had no clue how it felt to be me.

A knock on the living room door pulled me from my thoughts. I threw the comforter off my head and listened for my aunt's footsteps. The infinite silence indicated I was alone.

*Ironic.*

I dropped my bare feet to the hardwood floor and waited, hoping they'd give up and go away. But the knocking continued.

I glanced down at my wrinkled clothes, the ones I didn't bother to change out of before jumping into bed. *Ah well.* I marched into the living room and peeked out the peephole, expecting to find a tenant with a leaky faucet.

But it wasn't a tenant with a leak.

Not even close.

Anger bubbled in the pit of my stomach.

Standing in the hall with his head hanging low was the cause of my latest grief. At least he had the good sense to feign remorse.

But did he honestly expect to blow me off then show up at my door like nothing happened?

My head twisted, my eyes sweeping over my aunt's empty living room. I needed time to think. Time to rein in my anger. Time to consider my options.

I had two.

Open the door and let him explain why he turned into a prick over the weekend. Or take a page from his handbook and blow him off like he was nothing more than a passing distraction.

I inhaled a deep cleansing breath, feeling stronger than I had in days. Then, secure in my decision, I turned on my heels and headed back to my room eager to bury myself under a heap of blankets.

Screw him.

Hayden's deep voice trailed in from the hallway stopping me mid-stride. "I could see your shadow."

## HAYDEN

I slammed my door, rattling the entire wall.

I hoped Alex heard. She needed to know I was pissed. At her. At me. At Remy for showing up at school. At the world.

I dropped down onto my sofa, letting my head fall back and my eyes squeeze shut. She didn't even give me a chance to explain. She made up her mind about what happened on her own.

I heaved a sigh.

Who could blame her? I was a total dick.

And any notion of us hanging out at school got shot to hell the second Remy showed up on campus.

He'd dropped out of high school, so college wasn't even an option for him. But it didn't stop him from tracking me down and showing up whenever he damn well pleased. I wouldn't be surprised if he had a tracker on my phone. He always found me. Whether I wanted to be found or not.

And while he might've been my friend, he was still a tornado dragging me into all sorts of shit, not caring where it all ended up.

That's why Alex needed to stay out of my world. She couldn't know the other side of my life. The side I wished I didn't have to live when Remy and I took our weekend trips or rolled up outside suburban homes late at night. And no way in hell could she find out about what happened three years ago. No one knew the truth about that.

No one except Remy.

I knew she couldn't see me tucked away in the corner of the dining hall at lunch, but I saw her. She seemed happy with Taylor and her crew. The way she'd been when she left the stage at Jake's. Before I fucked everything up.

Being at school put everything into perspective. Alex needed to be with people who'd take her to football games and frat parties. Shopping and out to eat. Clubs and formals. She'd get the true college experience with them. She'd never fit in my world, with my crowd. We didn't play sports, we didn't join frats, and we didn't give a damn what anyone thought of us.

If it wasn't for my mother, I would've never even been enrolled at SSC. As it was, I wasn't even full-time. More like on the eight-year plan, getting credits here and there with no real direction.

Being around Alex made me forget who I was and what I was. I started believing things I had no business believing.

My phone vibrated in my pocket, yanking me out of my head.

Before I could say a word, Remy's voice burst through the phone. "Baxter's at nine."

A night at Baxter's was exactly what I needed to get my head screwed back on straight. Everything that went down with Alex had me feeling all messed up. Like I wasn't myself. Like I'd grown a vagina. I needed a major dose of reality. *My* reality. "I'll be there."

I tossed my phone onto the countertop and grabbed a bottle of Jack from my kitchen cabinet. Forgoing the glass, I leaned against my counter and took a nice long swig, letting the whiskey burn down my throat and take me to another place. A place I didn't need to think. A place I didn't need to justify my behavior. A place where Alex couldn't turn me into a full-fledged bitch.

At nine-thirty, I pulled into Baxter's parking lot already feeling good. Harleys and trucks filled the lot, which meant a rowdy, shit-faced crowd playing pool and darts awaited me inside.

I strolled through the door, scanning the room for Remy. The Monday night football game flashed on the flat screens around the room, making it jammed for a weeknight.

Girls scoped me out from every corner. Their none-too-subtle gaping and lip-licking told me one thing. I had my pick. Sorority girl or bored housewife, I didn't discriminate.

Alex was shocked by the waitress at Jake's. That was nothing. She would've been stunned by the methods girls used to get my attention.

I hated to sound conceited because I wasn't. I was a piece of trash with an attractive face and body. The face was all genetics. My mom had been gorgeous. But the body, I worked for. Lifting at the gym kept my pent-up aggression in check. And no, I didn't grunt and groan at myself in the mirror.

Before I even spotted Remy, two bottle blondes in tight shirts, painted-on jeans, and hooker heels made their way over to me, latching on to both my arms.

"Hey, Hayden," one purred.

"Hey." I glanced between the two, only seeing the orange lines around their necks where they didn't blend in their makeup all the way. They must've had some hefty imperfections to cake on so much shit. Alex barely wore any. Her perfect face didn't need it.

*Fuuuuck.*

I shook off the thought. Alex was not going to screw this up for me. By the time I got one or both of the girls home, makeup would be the last thing on my mind.

"We were hoping you'd be here tonight," one of them admitted, running her finger down my chest.

I hated being touched. Not just because of my own fucked up reaction to it, but also the reminder of the cause of the reaction.

But if the touching meant the girl would go home with me, I let it slide—gritting my teeth and bearing it. Besides, I was well on my way to utter oblivion. When that happened, the touching didn't bother me as much.

I flashed a lazy smile, the one that made my dimples dig in. "Oh, yeah?"

Both girls nodded, using their come-hither gazes. I'd give them a C for effort.

I spotted Remy by the bar, chatting up some of our boys. I headed over to him with the blondes on my tail.

"What's up?" I greeted them.

Remy swiveled on his stool, eying the blondes then me. "No puppy tonight?"

My brows pinched together. What the hell was he talking about?

"The brunette. She was different. Not your usual type."

I didn't lie to Remy. We both knew it. "No clue what you're talking about."

Remy's crooked smirk told me he didn't buy it. "Then I guess you won't care if I have a go at her." Remy watched me for a reaction. I kept my face composed, giving nothing away. He finally nodded, telling me he'd drop it. At least for the time being.

But the fact that he had Alex on his radar made me anxious. I needed him to forget she existed. *I* needed to forget she existed.

We spent the night playing pool and getting wasted while the blondes looked on, getting us drinks when our bottles ran dry. *This* was my life. Partying and getting hammered with no questions asked. Taking girls home and doing whatever the hell I wanted. No stressing over some chick I'd never be with.

Remy left with one of the blondes just before one. I walked the other to my truck. I hated bringing girls home in my truck. Since I had no intention of carting their asses home at three in the morning, I got stuck footing the bill for a taxi. I knew I didn't need to. But I wasn't a complete asshole.

My engine roared to life and music blared from the speakers. Maggie, or maybe it was Maddie, lifted herself up into the passenger seat, instantly reaching for the radio.

*Oh, no way in hell.*

I grabbed her hand and held on to it. Her heavy-lidded eyes told me she totally misread my intentions. But I went with it. Whatever worked.

"It's really loud," she whined, pulling the passenger door closed.

I smiled over at her, nodding my head to the beat, pretending to be into the song. I couldn't help thinking Alex would've never touched my radio.

I pushed the senseless thought aside.

The chick pointed her long red fingernail to her ear. "Don't you want to talk or something?"

*Something.*

I sent her a wink. That would keep her quiet. I guess I did that a lot. Ignored the annoying habits and inadequacies of the girls I brought home. So long as they came home with me and gave it up, what did I care?

By the time we made it to the second floor, it was after one. Since most of the residents called it a night by eight, the hallway sat disconcertingly quiet.

"Shit!" she cried out, tripping on her hooker heels and nearly face planting on the hallway rug.

I caught her arm, steadying her back to her feet. Unfortunately, she found her little mishap amusing because an obnoxious snort spewed from her nose.

*Attractive.*

Worried she'd topple over again, I pushed her toward my apartment with my hand on her back. I glanced to Alex's door for a brief moment. *Big mistake.* A shadow lingered underneath.

Fuck.

We may not have been on speaking terms, but I didn't want her to see me with another girl. I didn't know why. I just knew I wanted her to see me differently than other people did. And she had, up until I blew it that morning.

Since there wasn't a damn thing I could do about it, I unlocked my door and shoved the girl inside, holding out hope it had been my landlord and not Alex at the door.

# CHAPTER EIGHT

## ALEX

Friday couldn't arrive quickly enough. I'd finally gotten comfortable with the layout of the campus and come to terms with my crazy schedule. I'd also avoided the coffee shop at all costs. After the way Hayden treated me and seeing him bring home that skanky girl Monday night—with his hand on her back—I had nothing left to say to him.

I stepped into the busy dining hall and made a beeline for Taylor's table.

"So what time are you picking us up?" she asked as I sat down beside her. Taylor was one of those southern girls. The ones whose words came out sweet as pie even if they were telling you to screw.

"You want *me* to drive?"

"Honey, with a car like that, you've got to flaunt it."

Giggles erupted from her BFF Chloe who, like Taylor, had accepted me as one of their own. With a perky up-turned nose, shoulder length strawberry blonde hair, and slow Southern drawl, she was exactly what you'd expect in Texas.

"Sure." I smiled, knowing it didn't even come close to reaching my eyes. "I can drive."

The past month had made me cautious. Never quite sure who to trust. If Taylor was just using me to be her designated driver, I'd rather her be up front with me, as opposed to faking our friendship.

"So how's your first week been?" Chloe asked.

"Good." I glanced over her shoulder at the packed room behind her. Only Monday I'd entered the same room filled with unfamiliar faces. Now I sat with two girls who'd embraced me.

My eyes shifted to the corner of the room where Hayden sat with his tattooed friends and a harem of girls in tight fitting tops. The girls talked, he nodded. Then, as if he could somehow sense me, his eyes flashed up, locking on mine from across the room.

I quickly looked away, trying to lose myself in the conversation at my table. But I couldn't ignore the feel of his stare. Even fifty yards away, his presence affected me. But why? He was just some guy I met. A guy who befriended me, only to blow me off like I was nothing more than a momentary diversion. Something to use when he was bored.

As much as I wanted to shake off the infuriating thoughts, they were the truth. And the truth kept me sensible.

Taylor's voice cut through my inner dialogue. "You'll meet our friends from TSU tonight."

"They're football players," Chloe added.

"I can't wait to introduce you to Cameron," Taylor chimed in while reapplying her lip gloss in a blinged-out compact. "You'll love him—you don't have a boyfriend, do you?"

Not the time to drudge up Preston, I shook my head.

"So, what's your plan?" Chloe asked. "Join a sorority? Play a sport?"

I shook my head. "I'm still trying to get through a day without getting lost. It may be small, but it's still a maze to me."

The two of them laughed. "Girl, we've been there," Taylor assured me. "It took Chloe a year to find a restroom."

"You try holding it every day," Chloe challenged. "I ended up with a massive bladder infection."

Taylor burst into laughter. I held back my own, until Chloe joined in.

"How 'bout you?" I asked, deflecting the attention off me.

Taylor held up her palms. "No bladder infection here."

All three of us burst into laughter. I almost felt normal again sitting there joking around with other girls.

"Chloe cheers for the football team," Taylor offered.

I didn't need her to tell me that. Chloe's perky personality, toned body, and mischievous smile gave her away the first day.

"And Taylor's our very own Beyoncé," Chloe added. "She's won the talent competition every year. She's amazing. Wait 'til you hear her."

I turned to Taylor with a lifted brow.

She shrugged, tucking her gloss into her handbag. "It's nothing."

"Nothing?" Chloe asked in disbelief. "Don't be so modest, Tay. You're gonna win a Grammy someday."

Taylor laughed. "From your lips to God's ears."

While Chloe continued singing Taylor's praises, my eyes betrayed me, drifting toward Hayden's table.

*What the hell?*

He stared directly at me, studying me from half a football field away.

It made no sense. He wanted nothing to do with me, yet he wouldn't let me be.

Well, two could play that game.

I latched onto his eyes, hoping my anger transcended the distance. But even across the congested room, electricity zapped between us.

The corners of his lips turned up slightly.

*Damn him.*

The seconds ticked by, but neither of us moved. My foot bounced with nervous energy. What was I doing? He wasn't even worth it. And soon, the girls would ask a question I'd have to look to them to answer. Hadn't considered that in my quest to push Hayden's buttons. All I knew was I wouldn't be the first to look away. He wouldn't get that.

Out on the quad, the bell in the bell tower rang, jolting my body. But my eyes remained in place as the twelve rings sounded. Other students jumped to their feet, getting an early start to their twelve-fifteen classes. In doing so, they blocked our connection. But I wasn't going anywhere. I'd sit there all day if I had to.

"You coming, Alex?" Taylor asked.

"I'll catch you later," I said, staring at the muddled crowd. I didn't see her reaction or hear them walk away, but they must've thought I was nuts.

Once everyone between us finally cleared out of the way, I had a perfect view across the room.

And I stared at an empty seat.

The coastal breeze blew lazily in when Taylor, Chloe, and I arrived at the beach a little after nine. Good call on the flip flops, jeans, and white hoodie. I'd also swept my hair up in a high ponytail so the wind wouldn't whip it in my face all night.

Back at UT, we spent our Friday nights at frat parties, clubs, or bars. Apparently when you attended a southern college, you took advantage of the local beaches. They didn't card or charge a cover. Win. Win.

A large crowd surrounded the fierce bonfire, soaking up the circle of heat the six-foot flames created. The girls circulated, making their way over to people I didn't know. But I didn't mind. The whooshing of the ocean waves immediately drew my attention away from everything else.

I stood captivated by the peaceful ebb and flow of the waves, and the white-caps crashing on the smooth shore. It had been a while since I'd been to the beach. I welcomed the salty smell and briny air washing over me and seeping into my pores.

"Here." Taylor appeared out of nowhere, shoving a red plastic cup into my hand. "The driver gets one, as long as it's at the beginning of the night."

I glanced inside the foamy cup. I'd be lucky if I even had half a cup. "Thanks?"

She laughed, her ponytail bouncing. "Hope you don't think I'm a bitch. It's just our rule to keep everyone safe."

I dismissed her comment with the shake of my head, then followed her beyond the fire to where Chloe sat on a surfboard with a group of guys in maroon jerseys. Their shaggy wind-blown hair made them look more like surfers than football players.

"Guys, this is Alex," Taylor announced, dropping down onto a blanket between two linebackers who clearly liked the idea of her slender body squeezed between theirs. "She just transferred from UT."

"Hi." I smiled as they eyed me up and down, throwing *heys* and *what's up* my way.

On the ride over, Taylor had been adamant I meet her friend Cameron. Thankfully, as she rattled off names, he wasn't one of them. I didn't bother mentioning that I'd heard enough about two-point conversions, safeties, and quarterback sneaks from Preston to last me a lifetime. It just opened me up for questions I wasn't ready to answer.

An hour into our night, I sat painfully sober on a surfboard beside Chloe.

"Alex," Chloe slurred. "You're so peeertty." She stroked the top of my head like a little puppy.

"Thanks."

"No, I'm serious. You're veeerrry peeertty."

"Leave her alone, Chlo. Ryan's looking for you." Taylor pulled Chloe to her feet and sent her on her way down the beach. "Yeah, probably should've warned you," she said, taking Chloe's vacated seat. "She has trouble handling her liquor."

Chloe staggered down the beach until she was devoured by the night.

"I'm sure Ryan isn't complaining."

Taylor laughed. "You're probably right."

We both gazed out at the water for a long while. I wondered if Taylor knew what it was like to have her entire world turned upside down. To have everything she ever knew or loved taken away from her. She seemed so put together, so full of life, so adored by everyone. Did she wear a mask like me?

"So, next time. I'm driving."

"I'm holding you to it."

She smiled. "That's if there is a next time. Are you having fun?"

No. "Sure."

"Yeah, until Chloe throws up in your backseat." I must've grimaced because she bumped her shoulder to mine. "Don't worry. I'll help you clean it. Actually, that's a lie. But I'll hire someone to do it."

We both smiled.

A football player the size of a shed jogged over, kicking sand all over us.

"*Robbie*," Taylor whined.

Her complaining didn't faze him. He leaned down and yanked her up, tossing her over his shoulder. She squealed as he charged toward the water, sand kicking up behind them. Soon they were swallowed up by the darkness. And I'd been left alone. Alone on a surfboard in the middle of a party where I knew no one.

I would *not* feel sorry for myself. I would *not*.

When I pulled into my parking lot a little after one, my eyes flashed around. I'd like to say I sought a closer space, but that wasn't the truth. I searched for Hayden's truck which wasn't there.

I blew out a disappointed breath, taking windblown pieces of hair with it. I had that same let down feeling in the pit of my stomach. The one I got at the beach every time someone new showed up and it wasn't him.

I know.

*Stupid.*

# CHAPTER NINE

## ALEX

Taylor waltzed into the dining hall, totally owning her plaid shirt, almost nonexistent jean shorts, and cowboy boots. Only a girl as stunning as her could pull off the cowgirl look. Even in Texas.

"Hey, Tay," Chloe greeted her with a smile.

Ignoring Chloe all together, Taylor slid into the seat beside her and across from me. Her eyes moved over the features of my face, inspecting every inch, every line, every imperfection.

I could feel my brows furrow. "What's up?"

She didn't answer. Her eyes continued their scrutiny. I couldn't decide if she thought I plumped my lips or shaved down my nose. She couldn't think I had implants. C cups were pushing it for me.

"Seriously, Taylor, you're starting to freak me out."

Her eyes landed on mine, her glossy lips in a tight line. "Is there something you want to tell me?"

All conversations within a twenty-foot radius ceased.

My head shot around. Everyone stared. "I don't think so."

Taylor's perfectly waxed brow arched. "Does SSC Voice ring a bell?"

My frantic eyes searched for posters on the walls, signs on the cluttered bulletin boards, anything to explain what the hell she was talking about. "What's that?"

Chloe chimed in. "It's SSC's version of *The Voice*. This year the winner gets an invite to try out for the real television show."

Taylor crossed her arms, her accusatory eyes narrowed. "Strange you don't know since your name's right below mine on the audition sheet."

I gasped. "What?"

"My question exactly."

Heat radiated in my cheeks. My waves shook back and forth slapping me in the face. "I have no idea. Maybe it's someone's idea of a joke. A very bad joke."

Taylor's face softened. A smile stretched across her lips. "I sure hope not. I'd love for you to be in it with me."

"You would?" My voice dropped at her sudden one-eighty.

"Of course, silly. Did you really think I was mad?"

Yes. "Well—"

"It's not like I'm worried. I've won the competition three years in a row." Conversations around us resumed. "Can you even sing?"

I paused, wondering if I should've been insulted by how easily she dismissed me as a worthy opponent. I shrugged it off, more interested in how my name ended up on the audition sheet in the first place.

"Promise me you'll do it," Taylor pleaded.

"I don't think so. I sing in the shower."

"Honey, I *need* competition. And who better than my new friend."

I wanted no part of it. I'd only ever sung in front of an audience once before. At Jake's.

*Jake's.*

My eyes shot across the crowded dining hall seeking the one person I knew had everything to do with my name on that sheet.

The problem was…he wasn't there.

## HAYDEN

I stood hidden within the shadows in the back of the dark theater. The bright spotlight shined on center stage, right down on Alex like a halo as she belted out a Taylor Swift song.

With the bright light shining, I doubted Alex could even see the professor in charge of the competition, or Taylor seated beside her. Having been the school's star for the past three years, Taylor was used to having it all. There was no way in hell she appreciated the fact that Alex was hotter *and* sported some major pipes.

Alex's voice floated flawlessly through the theater speakers, but she didn't seem as comfortable and confident as she did at Jake's. Still, it didn't stop her from working the stage. Her cute little blue dress with knee high brown boots flattered her slender body, showing off the curves I'd witnessed up close in that tiny bikini.

Christ.

I needed to get the hell out of there.

### ALEX

The door in the rear of the theater slammed shut. I squinted to see who it was, but the blinding spotlight obscured my view.

And though I only knew three people in the entire college, I knew who it had been. I felt it in every fiber of my being. Hayden had signed me up for the audition. He'd see it through to the end. No matter how it turned out.

It had been days since I'd seen him coming or going from his apartment. But the morning following my audition, I headed toward the English building making sure to stop by the coffee shop. I wanted to confront him. Force him to explain himself. Explain why he'd avoided me. Claimed not to know me. Signed me up for the stupid competition. Was it a joke? Did he want to embarrass me?

My senses were bombarded with cinnamon hazelnut the moment I stepped inside the busy shop. I scanned the faces of those filling the room, but Hayden wasn't there.

"Hi, honey."

I spun to find Taylor texting at one of the tables. We didn't share any of the same classes, so I usually didn't run into her until lunch. "Hey."

"I was gonna call you last night." She stood up and tucked her phone into her handbag. "But I decided I needed to say this in person."

"Are you breaking up with me?" I deadpanned.

She laughed, throwing her skinny arms around me and pulling me into a tight embrace. "You nailed your audition yesterday."

I stilled, pulling back slowly from her grasp. "How do you know?"

"I'm tight with Professor Smith. She let me sit in on all the auditions."

"You were there?" I started toward the exit, feeling suddenly embarrassed.

Taylor followed. "Seriously, girl. You can really sing."

She continued talking as we made our way across the quad, but the hum of a jet stole my attention. My eyes followed it across the sky until it disappeared into the clouds. The memory of Preston's frantic voice cut through my daze. *Oh, my God, Alex! Oh, my God!* I shook my head, clearing away the memory, the horror.

Chloe approached. "Hey, y'all."

I forced a smile. "Hey."

"So, tomorrow's the big day?"

I nodded.

"We should look at the top-ten list together," Taylor said, totally ignoring Chloe.

Chloe balked. "Are you worried, Tay? You never look."

If glares could kill, Taylor's would've taken out the entire campus. "Of course not. I just want to be there for Alex."

"Of course I'll look with you," I said, trying to dissipate the sudden tension. "When will it be posted?"

"First thing in the morning," Taylor grinned, as if she hadn't just turned into a terrifying version of herself.

I'd been sprawled out on the sofa in black sweats and an old T-shirt for hours. Too bad comfort didn't equal understanding because I'd done nothing but struggle with my calculus homework all night. The click of a door in the hallway pulled my attention from my books.

Still unsuccessful in my quest to confront Hayden, I hurried to the peephole and peered out.

*Finally.*

But why was he dressed from head to toe in black and headed toward the stairwell?

I couldn't stop myself. I grabbed my keys from the table beside the door, slipped on my flip flops, and snuck out of the apartment.

I crept to the stairwell, waiting until the first floor door slammed shut below. When it did, I hurried down the steps and peered out the exit, spotting Hayden sliding into his truck. I eyeballed the dark grounds, wondering if he'd see me if I made a mad dash for my car.

His headlights flicked on, casting two bright strobes across the lawn. I crouched to the ground, my heartbeat echoing in my ears. If he'd seen me, it didn't stop him from pulling out of the lot.

I jumped to my feet and ran to my car. Once inside, I gripped the steering wheel and hesitated. What was I doing? Why did I care where he was going? Had his erratic behavior just pushed me over the edge?

Despite my questions, and reluctance to actually follow someone, I started my engine and pulled out onto the road. I glimpsed my dashboard clock. Half past twelve. No wonder why the roads were deserted.

Hayden's lights glowed a good distance ahead of me. But, in an effort to remain undetected, I kept plenty of space between us. Him finding me trailing him was all I needed.

Up ahead, Hayden didn't signal. He just took a sharp right. Once I reached the road, I turned onto it.

His distant headlights illuminated the winding stretch of road. I glanced in my rearview mirror, but no one drove behind me. Not really shocking. I'd yet to see a single house as we travelled deeper into the woods.

Up ahead, Hayden turned right again without signaling. I slowed, so not to miss the turn. But when I came upon it, panic set in. He hadn't turned onto a road. He'd turned into a parking lot. A church parking lot. And except for his headlights, it was pitch black and empty.

Having limited options, I crouched in my seat and continued on the deserted road.

What was he up to? Was he meeting someone? A priest? A girl? A drug dealer? Or, had he taken a wrong turn and picked that spot to turn around?

Houses sprung up set back from the road, but I couldn't find any businesses where I could park or turn around. Making a split decision, I pulled a U-turn in the middle of the road.

I needed to see this through.

I spotted a dirt area to the right where a homeowner cleared out brush for guest parking. I pulled into the spot, tucking my car in as far as possible without being too badly scratched by the natural landscape. Satisfied I'd concealed it, I took a deep breath, locked up, and set off on foot.

My trek through the shadowy woods definitely wasn't well planned. I'd never been one for hiking, so the uneven terrain in my flip flops proved a challenge. Especially in the dark. The crescent moon provided some light. But the towering trees blocked it from cascading down. They also added eerie sound effects to the already unnerving night.

*Fantastic.*

I knew I could've used my phone for light, but then why not just announce my arrival with a bullhorn? I could only imagine what Hayden would think if he spotted me. After all, we weren't even friends.

But he'd left me no choice. His strange behavior. His wishy-washy attitude toward me. His intrusion into my life. They were enough to make anyone crazy. And sneaking through the woods alone at night was definitely crazy.

As the denseness of the woods tapered, a small white church appeared. In the light of day it would've been quaint. But late at night, set back from the road with a massive steeple ill-fitting of the diminutive structure, it looked like something out of a horror movie. It was just a matter of time before the zombies encased by thick fog crept out from behind it.

Luckily, the trees surrounding the parking lot kept me veiled, making it easier to remain hidden as I traipsed closer to the church.

Hayden's empty truck sat at the foot of the church's cement steps. From the edge of the woods, I scanned the area, wondering where he could've gone. The church would've been locked, so aside from breaking in, he couldn't have entered it. And since there were no other cars in the lot, he didn't appear to be meeting anyone.

A small light shining at the rear of the church caught my eye. I inched closer, staying to the outskirts of the woods. When I got as close as I could without being detected, I spotted Hayden in the church's small cemetery pointing his phone's light at a gravestone. He stood for a long time, doing nothing but staring down at it.

I didn't know what I expected to find, but this definitely wasn't it.

Something snapped in the woods behind me.

The hair on my arms stood on end. Every part of my body froze. Not because of the animal lurking behind me, but because I was seconds away from being discovered.

Hayden's head whipped around. The light to his cell switched off. I could no longer see him. But it didn't mean he hadn't seen me.

I backed into the woods, stumbling over fallen branches and clumps of leaves in the complete darkness. My heart pounded in my chest. In my ears. In my fingertips. When I could no longer see the church or the cemetery, I stopped and crouched behind the thick trunk of a mammoth tree, hoping my spot hid me.

I listened for footsteps crushing leaves. For the engine to Hayden's truck. For Hayden's voice. For a hungry animal. For a zombie.

Dammit. Now I was just scaring myself.

The silence dragged on for far too long, taunting me with the unknown ramifications of my hasty actions. Not even a lousy cricket chirped.

It was inevitable. Hayden would find me hiding in the shadows in the middle of the night because I'd followed him.

When had I become so pathetic? So psychotic? And why in the world was I so damn curious about Hayden to begin with? He humiliated me. Deserted me. Played me for a fool. What more did I need to know?

My body jolted as his truck's engine roared to life. I held my breath as his headlights broke through the brush, lighting up a vast portion of the woods between the parking lot and me. Thankfully, I was just out of reach from their revealing beams.

It didn't take long for him to pull away and his lights to disappear with him.

And even as the sound of his engine became a distant hum, I didn't dare move a muscle. It could've been a trick. A ruse to lure me out of the woods. A ploy to bring me face to face with him.

But after more long minutes passed, it was clear Hayden had gone.

I hurried to the edge of the woods, stopping when the church reappeared. My eyes flashed to the cemetery, then the road. A sane person would've turned on their phone's light, fled to their car, and gotten the hell out of there. But *sane* and me weren't necessarily synonymous lately.

I jogged across the paved parking lot to the cemetery entrance. I stopped at the rusted cast iron fence. My heart rate spiked at the sudden realization that I stood alone. In the middle of nowhere. Surrounded by darkness and the dead. And no one knew where I'd gone.

I hadn't realized it until that moment. But having Hayden nearby, if a zombie or masked murder stumbled upon me, had put me at ease. But now. Alone. With nothing but my thoughts to mock me for my rash decision, the whole situation frightened the hell out of me.

But it was too late to turn back. I'd made it that far.

I scrambled through the creaky gate, pulling out my phone to light a path. I flashed my beam around, searching the gravestones for the one that captivated Hayden.

Most of the stones were old, dates long passed. But one stood out. A newer one, set between stones that had begun to crumble. One with matted down leaves in front of it, where someone had recently stood.

I moved closer, shining my light on the front where *Victor Zane* was etched into the stone. Zane? How was it I didn't even know Hayden's last name? The dates indicated Victor died three years ago at the age of forty. Could he have been Hayden's father?

Hayden's car wasn't in the parking lot when I returned. I hadn't seen him bring home any girls recently. But then again I hadn't seen him period. Maybe he was servicing them at their homes. With that pleasant thought in mind, I settled on my bed with my iPad in search of anything I could find on Victor Zane.

An obituary popped up first. I read through the brief epitaph, which strangely didn't mention a wife, sibling, child, or Hayden. If Victor Zane wasn't Hayden's relative, who was he?

A series of news articles popped up next, each reporting the same story. Victor had been murdered. Beaten to death by a minor in an alley. The minor's name had been withheld from the articles. But he had been sentenced to ten months in a juvenile detention center for involuntary manslaughter.

Ten months for taking a man's life seemed awfully lenient.

I sat back and drew a breath. Could Hayden be the minor? Had he been detained for ten months for manslaughter? Is that what my aunt had been reluctant to tell me?

I knew Hayden harbored secrets. And while he was a lot of things, a murderer just didn't seem like one of them.

# CHAPTER TEN

## ALEX

"There must be a mistake," I whispered.

Taylor's eyes were about to pop from her head. But when she turned toward me, she plastered on a full-blown, mega-watt smile. I'd never seen anything more fake in my life. "Don't worry, honey. We'll get this fixed before the others even see it."

I followed her through the deserted halls of the theater arts building. The rapid clicking of her heels did nothing to ease the impermeable silence between us. We'd arrived so much earlier than the rest of the students, if she shoved me into a broom closet and locked the door, no one would find me for hours, possibly days.

Taylor stopped abruptly at a door with *Gail Smith* on the gold nameplate. She pounded on it like a woman possessed.

Then we waited.

Silently.

There was no shuffle inside Professor's Smith's office and no click of the lock signifying occupancy. So, without a word, Taylor turned on her heels and headed down the hallway to the professors' lounge. Again she pounded on the door. This time a shuffling behind the door ensued.

*Thank God.*

The door swung open. Professor Smith, a portly woman with gray hair and dark eyes, appeared. Once she spotted us, her grin slipped from her face. "Before you say anything…" She stepped out and joined us in the hallway. Her eyes focused on Taylor. "This decision took me a long time to make. But in the end, I felt some fresh blood could help rejuvenate the competition."

You could've heard a pin drop as we both stared at Professor Smith.

"You were there. We had amazing freshmen audition, and some great transfers, like Alex."

I closed my gaping mouth and pled to her good senses. "But I don't even want to be in the competition. Let Taylor. I never would've auditioned if I thought it would've affected her—"

Professor Smith's erect palm silenced me. "I've made my decision." She looked into Taylor's angry eyes. "I'm sorry if you don't like it. But with our stellar line up, you should feel lucky you're our alternate." She turned on her flats and walked back into the lounge, leaving us standing alone in the empty hallway.

Fear seized my tongue. Visions of a vicious cat fight flooded my frazzled brain.

When I finally worked up the courage to peek at Taylor, a grin pulled at her lips. "Oh well, I guess these things happen."

I turned my entire body toward her, desperate not to lose one of my only friends. "I don't want to be in the competition. I'm sure if we give her time to reconsider, she'll let us switch. I only auditioned because you asked me to. I'm serious. I not gonna do it."

Taylor nodded. "Yes, you are. You won the spot fair and square. If I can't win the competition, you damn well better."

I wanted to cry. Sure, over the past month and a half I'd cried enough for a lifetime, but the tears sat at the ready. I'd only been in school for two weeks, and I'd already ruined everything.

Wait a minute.

I didn't sign up for the competition.

"I've gotta go." I gave Taylor no time to respond. I spun on my heels and bolted out of the building.

I threw open the doors to the coffee shop, my eyes scanning the busy room. Of course, Hayden wasn't there. That wouldn't deter me. I took a seat at the front window. It provided a perfect view of the entire quad. From there, I'd see him before he saw me. What I planned to say warranted a face-to-face, no-holds-barred conversation. One that should have happened two weeks ago.

The two good-looking guys I'd seen Hayden with on the first day walked in and sauntered to the register. They spent a few minutes flirting with the barista then grabbed their coffees and headed to the door. When they noticed me, they shot me looks of pity. Did they really think I was waiting for Hayden?

Okay, so maybe I was. But not to grovel like they clearly assumed. It'd be a cold day in hell before that happened.

At lunch, Taylor still acted like her happy social-butterfly self, even after she had time to digest the morning's turn of events. My ears followed the conversation at my table, but my eyes searched the crowded room. Yet again, Hayden was nowhere to be found.

Did he have any idea what he'd done? Did he realize he almost sabotaged one of the only friendships I had?

"So as promised, I'm driving to the bonfire tonight," Taylor informed Chloe and me.

"I'll have to meet up with you there," Chloe explained. "I've got practice then a unity-building activity afterwards."

"No worries," Taylor assured her with a smile in her voice. "Alex and I will get the party started on our own."

We pulled up at the beach in Taylor's sporty red convertible just after nine. I had no clue why she'd been so eager to take my car last time. Hers put all others to shame.

I planned to tell her I was dropping out of the competition since it meant nothing to me and everything to her. But since she hadn't brought it up, I didn't want to spoil our night by reminding her she didn't make it.

We walked through the cool sand, skirting around groups of people surrounding the crimson flames.

"Look, there's Cameron." Taylor pointed to a white truck parked on the beach just past the fire. Music blared from its opened doors, and a keg sat in the bed. People with red cups hung around it.

A shaggy blonde in green board shorts and a black hoodie made his way over to us. He wore a giant grin and carried two cups.

"I hear a celebration's in order." He handed one of the cups to Taylor before handing the other to me.

I took the cup, eyeing him curiously.

"SSC Voice," he explained. "Taylor said you're gonna steal the show."

I gulped down half the cup of beer so I didn't have to respond.

He bumped my shoulder playfully. "It's okay to admit you're gonna kill it."

My cheeks burned and my face fell into a grimace. I needed him to stop talking about the competition. It only reminded Taylor why she should hate me.

"I'm Cameron," he offered, misinterpreting my expression as confusion.

"Right." I flashed him a regrettable smile.

"What do you say we take a walk? You know, get to know each other, see the sights," he offered lightheartedly.

I glanced beside me. Taylor had disappeared. "Where'd she go?"

He shot me a crooked smile, the kind that said I'd been set up. For some reason, it didn't feel like such a bad thing. He didn't have dimples like Hayden, but he possessed that cute surfer swag that turned girls' heads. "Does it really matter?"

"Only if you want her to walk with us." Feeling immediately embarrassed by my blatant flirting, I chugged more of my beer.

A smile dragged across his sun-chapped lips as he shook his head. "Did you?"

I kept the cup to my mouth and shook my head.

"Come on." He grasped my hand, like it was completely normal to be holding hands with a stranger, and led me down to the water's edge. His hand was cold to the touch and not as strong as Hayden's.

*Ugh.*

I shook away the thought and threatened any future thoughts of him from entering my head.

We reached the water, staying back just enough that the tide didn't reach us.

"Hold on."

Cameron watched in amusement as I dropped to the sand, slipped off my flip flops, and rolled the bottom of my jeans. When I stood up, wooziness caused me to stumble back a step.

"Whoa there." Cameron grabbed hold of my elbow and steadied me.

"Sorry." I glanced into my nearly-empty cup. I wasn't usually such a lightweight. "I guess I just stood up too fast."

"No worries. I've got you." He linked his fingers with mine and tugged me along the beach.

It felt nice to have someone paying attention to me. It had been a while. And though Cameron didn't make me feel safe the way Hayden did, he made me feel excited. Like a girl getting attention from the most popular guy in school. I would've been a fool not to enjoy the attention from such a hottie.

*Hottie?*

"So, as promised, I'm going to show you the sights the coast has to offer."

Cameron walked alongside me, his bare feet on the damp sand while mine were covered by the icy water—such a bitter contrast to the warm flush settling over my skin.

He swept out his arm dramatically. "So to your left, we have the exquisite ocean. Fierce and majestic."

I snickered. "Fierce and majestic?"

His goofy smile spread wide. "Absolutely. Don't you know how vast the ocean is? How far it extends? How deep it is?"

I shook my head.

"Well, it's very vast, extends very far, and is very deep."

I laughed. So did he. It was nice. He was nice. There was no wondering what he was thinking. No long silences. No questions deflected. He was just nice.

"And over there if you really look…" He pointed up the coast to a speck of light in the distance. "You can see the Seabring Lighthouse."

Beads of sweat clung to my hairline. "I think I see it."

Cameron swallowed deeply. "Maybe we could get a closer look sometime? My family docks their boat nearby."

I hesitated, unsure if he'd asked me on a date or was just being kind to the new girl. "That sounds nice."

He grinned as we strolled further and further away from the crowd.

"So, have you and Taylor been friends for a while?"

"Yeah, since we were kids."

I nodded, but my head felt heavy. And stiff. Like I needed to work to nod. What was going on with me? I glanced to Cameron. Could he sense it? His heady gaze told me no.

I looked away, finishing off my beer. I hoped to God it moistened my cotton mouth *and* he didn't try to kiss me.

He let the moment pass, tugging me further down the beach. The sounds of the bonfire faded to a distant memory and the crashing waves became the soundtrack. "So, how do you like SSC?"

It was a loaded question on so many levels. One I really needed to consider. But a bout of exhaustion took hold of my body. My knees wobbled and if I didn't stop walking, I had a feeling they'd buckle.

"It's good." My tongue stuck to the roof of my mouth like I'd been snacking on chalk.

"You're from Austin, right?"

I nodded, unable to formulate the words I wanted to say.

That was the last thing I remembered before my head spun and everything turned black.

# CHAPTER ELEVEN

## HAYDEN

I pulled into the parking lot a little after one, hating the fact that I turned down Sydney. She'd been throwing herself at me all night at Baxter's. I just wasn't feeling it. I guess I hadn't been feeling the liquor either. Because hopping out of my truck, I found myself unusually sober.

I crossed the quiet lot. The small light over the back door of the building cast a faint glow over the property. I glanced to the picnic table where everything seemed to get more complicated. And maybe because I couldn't shake the image of Alex in that black bikini, I checked out the pool.

My feet stopped.

Squinting across the property, I could've sworn someone occupied one of the lounge chairs.

Curiosity pulled me to the surrounding fence. I spotted the silhouette of a person. A small person curled into a ball. Wavy dark hair peeked from the hood of her black sweatshirt.

What was she doing?

I moved through the gate and dropped to my knees at the side of the chair. I waited a moment, taking in Alex's flawless skin. She looked so peaceful. I almost didn't want to disturb her. But it was late and getting cooler.

"Alex," I whispered, gently shaking her tiny arm. Had she been too exhausted to drag herself inside? Or, had she forgotten her key again and locked herself out? I'd seen Katherine leave earlier with a suitcase.

"Alex." I shook her arm a little harder. "Wake up."

She didn't stir. Not even a little.

No one slept that soundly.

*"Mom. Wake up."*

I blinked back the vision, burying it deep inside like I'd been doing for the past eleven years, and yanked Alex's arm to me. It was an ice cube. I dug my thumb into her wrist. Her pulse was there, but it was slow and faint.

*Dammit.*

I scooped up her tiny body. Holding her tightly to my chest, I ran to my truck. I threw open the passenger door and laid her inside.

Suddenly, I went cold.

Her jeans were unbuttoned and the shirt under her sweatshirt was inside out.

*Fuuuuuck.*

I wouldn't let my mind go there. I couldn't.

I jumped into the driver's side and sped through the deserted streets with my heat blasting and my head pounding. I pulled a blanket from behind my seat and threw it over Alex's body, rubbing her back to generate more heat. "Stay with me, beautiful. Just stay with me."

*"You're gonna be alright, Mom. I love you. Just stay with me."*

I shook off the memory.

The hospital was only five minutes away. I made it in three. I didn't park, just pulled in front of the emergency room and jumped out.

I scooped up Alex and ran through the sliding doors. Two nurses in pink scrubs rushed toward us. "Put her down on that stretcher," the young blonde instructed.

"What happened?" the older redhead asked while checking Alex's vitals.

"I have no idea." I stepped back, gripping my hair with both hands wishing I had answers. "I just found her like this."

The blonde attached a device to Alex's finger. "Does she drink? Take drugs?"

I shook my head and gave an indecisive shrug. "She drinks casually. I don't think she's into drugs. I don't know."

"Any idea how long she's been unconscious?" the redhead asked, her eyes showing concern.

I shook my head, wanting to punch a wall or whoever let this happen.

"Are you her husband?" the blonde asked, spying Alex's unbuttoned jeans.

"Fiancé." The lie left my lips readily. They'd have to take pity on the poor fiancé and allow me in the back. I scrubbed my face with both hands knowing what I needed to ask. "Do you think she was—"

"We'll know more once she undergoes a portion of the sexual assault exam," the blonde explained.

"A portion? Why not the whole thing?"

"It's extremely invasive. The victim must give consent for the full exam."

Victim? I dropped my head. I couldn't believe this was happening. I mean, I knew this shit happened. But not to someone I...knew.

The redhead signaled to the blonde. "Let's get her into an exam room." She looked to me regrettably. "You're going to have to wait out here. I'll come and get you as soon as we know anything."

I nodded. They needed to take care of Alex. Not worry about hurting my feelings.

They wheeled the squeaky stretcher through two metal doors. The doors closed behind them, leaving me standing alone in the deserted waiting room feeling beyond helpless.

I dropped down onto a cold plastic chair. A twenty-four hour news station played on a television in the corner of the room, but I couldn't hear a sound. My mind was a jumbled mess. I had no idea what to do to quiet it.

I rested my elbows on my knees, burying my face in my hands.

Why had I let my fears get in the way of getting to know her better? Why had I wasted so much time pushing her away? If I hadn't, I would've been with her tonight. Wherever she was.

Seconds turned into minutes. Minutes to hours.

Each time the metal doors swung open, I jumped up, expecting a nurse or doctor to emerge in search of me. But they always sought another patient's relative.

Sometime after the sun had risen, the metal doors opened again. The redheaded nurse stepped out, searching the nearly empty waiting room. When she spotted me, her breath whistled through her lips. I had no idea what that meant, but I jumped to my feet and met her halfway.

"How is she?" Time stood still as I awaited her response.

"She's still unconscious, but her vitals are getting stronger." She lowered her voice. "Do you know who would've given her Rohypnol?"

My eyes widened. I figured it wasn't just alcohol, but hearing the truth made it real. Made the hell she'd been through while unconscious real. Made me want nothing more than to get ahold of the sick motherfucker who did it and—

"I'm sorry." The nurse interrupted my escalating rage. "I should've broached the subject differently since she's someone you obviously care about."

"No, it's just, I have no clue who would've done it." But when I found out, I'd kill them.

She nodded, obviously realizing the odds of me knowing was a long shot.

"Did you find out...if she was..." I still couldn't say the word. I couldn't fucking say it.

The nurse placed her hand on my arm. I tensed at the contact, but it didn't deter her. She kept it there and shook her head. "We're still waiting on the results of her tests."

I nodded. I knew it took time.

"Sweetie, I know you're not her fiancé. But I'll tell you what. Why don't you go back and sit with her for a little while. She could wake up at any time, and I'm sure a familiar face would be nice."

I made no attempt to deny it. I just followed her through the swinging doors, passing multiple exam rooms separated by light blue curtains. "How'd you know?"

The nurse turned to me with a knowing smile. "A guy like you buys a girl a rock, which she wasn't wearing. And he doesn't let her out of his sight. If you were engaged, she never would've been away from you tonight."

I nodded because she nailed it. I protected what was mine.

And in some part of my messed up brain, I thought staying away from Alex would protect her. From me. From my secrets. From my job. From my fucked-up life.

The nurse stopped and pulled back a curtain on the right. Inside, Alex looked so small tucked under the blankets in the hospital bed. Her dark curls were a stark contrast to the white pillowcase and sheets concealing her partially reclined body.

To an outsider she appeared to be sleeping peacefully. With her insomnia, being unconscious might've been a blessing in disguise. As long as when she awoke, she remained the sweet sarcastic girl I'd come to know.

I sat down in the faux leather chair beside the bed, pulling it right up to Alex's side. Reaching underneath the sheet, I grabbed hold of her hand. Warmth had returned to it. *Thank God.*

I should have released it. I knew I should have. But instead my thumb traced small circles over her delicate knuckles. I wasn't sure who I needed to soothe more, her or me. But I didn't stop. I couldn't.

I examined the platinum band on her middle finger. The one surrounded by small diamonds. The one she toyed with on our way to Jake's.

I took inventory of the private area around us. Wires and tubes from numerous monitors and machines ran under Alex's sheets. A drip bag attached to an IV had been inserted into the back of her right hand, pumping her full of fluids.

I closed my eyes for a long moment. How had this happened? What had she done to deserve it?

That was the messed up thing about life. It hurt people who didn't deserve it and let screw-ups like me exist. Let us live out our shitty existences.

As the minutes crept by, the sterile hospital smell brought on a throbbing headache. The monotonous beeping of machines gradually drove my already anxious mind reeling. And if another nurse poked her head in and didn't have test results, I'd go batshit crazy.

Thoughts of what might've happened to Alex messed with my head, creating images I didn't want to consider. I lifted her hand to my lips and pressed them softly to her smooth skin. "You're going to be okay, beautiful. I'll make sure of it."

I lowered her hand, grasping it between both of mine, concealing it entirely. It was so tiny. A blatant reminder of how fragile she really was. Not only physically, but emotionally.

She hadn't explained the days of crying on the picnic table. Her difficulty sleeping. The reason she'd moved across the state to live with her aunt. But that's what I got for pushing her away when we were just getting to know each other.

As time ticked by, and morning transformed to afternoon, exhaustion overtook my body. I'd been up for over twenty-four hours. And my heavy eyelids weren't going to stay open much longer—no matter how hard I tried to keep them that way.

I leaned forward, resting my forehead on our joined hands on the side of the bed. Maybe I could recharge if I just rested my eyes for a few minutes.

The beeping of the machines, once annoying as hell, lulled my exhausted body and mind into a much needed sleep.

"My hand's asleep," Alex whispered.

My head shot up, my eyes blinking repeatedly, trying to push away the sleep commanding me. The humming machines and sterile smell yanked me back to reality.

Alex lay in front of me, her eyes cracked open. She wiggled her tiny hand still in my grip.

I immediately released it. "Sorry."

"What's going on?" she asked, raspy and barely audible.

My breath left me in a hiss. Terrified to tell her the truth, I jumped to my feet. "I'll go get the doctor."

"Please, Hayden." Her sad eyes pleaded with me. "I want *you* to tell me."

I paused between her and the chair, hating the position I found myself in. But if there was ever a time to man up, this was it. I dropped back down into the seat and grasped my knees. "What do you remember about last night?"

As if needing all her strength to recall, Alex squeezed her eyes shut. "I went to a bonfire with Taylor…I took a walk with Cameron."

"Who's Cameron?" I growled, wanting to break every bone in his fucking body.

Alex cracked her eyes. "Taylor's friend from TSU."

I had a pretty good idea who the guy was. Football player slash surfer. Worked at a taco shop a few towns over. My teeth gritted at the thought of his hands anywhere near Alex. "Did he touch you?"

"What? No. We just took a walk. But I'm pretty foggy on anything after that."

I shoved my hands through my hair, anything to stop from punching something. "Were you drunk?"

"I had a beer, but it felt like ten. I got light-headed and tired. *So* tired."

I stared into her exhausted eyes, not having the balls to explain it. To say it out loud. To break her heart. But when she still hadn't grasped it, I tilted my head to the side and twisted my lips regrettably.

She searched my face, her eyes sweeping over my features. Then her eyes expanded, and her entire face dropped. "Oh my God." Her devastated gaze held mine, begging me to deny it.

Though I did a piss-poor job of hiding my regret, I nodded.

Her eyes glistened with unshed tears as they shot around the small area. I could see her trying to organize her thoughts. Trying to make sense of the senseless situation. "It must've been Cameron. He's the one who gave us our drinks."

"Us? Who's us?"

"Me and Taylor. I can't believe it." Her shock exemplified her naivety.

I wanted to say, "Yes, Alex, bad people do exist in this world." But that hit too close to home. On so many levels.

She noticed her phone and license on the nightstand. "I need to call her."

"You think he drugged *both* of you?"

Her voice sounded so small, so innocent. "Why wouldn't he?"

Hell of a question. "I'll call and check on her."

Alex's brows slanted in. "You'd do that?"

Didn't she realize what I'd be willing to do for her? Wow. Did I really just think that? I jumped to my feet. "Let me get the doctor." I pushed aside the curtain.

"Hayden?" Alex's soft voice immobilized me.

I glanced over my shoulder.

Her eyes stared into mine. "Why are you here?"

Breath whooshed through my lips. Definitely a loaded question. One I wasn't ready to answer. To her. To me. To anyone. I tried avoiding her crestfallen eyes, but they lured me in like sailors to those damn sirens. "I found you by the pool when I got home last night."

Alex nodded, her sadness crippling. "I'm glad it was you."

ALEX

Even before Hayden stepped out to retrieve the doctor, my mind spun like an out-of-control carnival ride. One that makes you vomit on those unfortunate enough to be standing near you.

Why had this happened to me? Was I a victim of circumstance? Was I at the wrong place at the wrong time? Was I being tested to see how much I could handle in one lifetime?

Waking up in the hospital had been shocking. Finding Hayden seated beside me had been equally shocking. But who knew what would've happened if he hadn't found me?

It wasn't just Hayden finding me and taking me to the hospital. Most decent people would have done the same. It was the intangible safety net he afforded me by simply entering a room. It was inexplicable. Something I couldn't understand even if I tried. It just was.

A pretty blonde nurse in pink scrubs stepped inside the curtain. Hayden followed her, his hands buried deep in the pockets of his jeans. Normally, I would've assumed he just had his way with her in a supply closet. But today, knowing he'd taken care of me—saved me—the thought couldn't have been further from the truth. "Well, good morning," she greeted me with a smile.

I nodded. It was the best I could do given my current situation.

She checked the readings on the machines. "You had your fiancé here very worried."

Hayden stood in the corner looking mortified by her words. I needed to ease his discomfort. "Sorry I worried you, babe."

That slow sexy smile that indisputably turned girls to mush slid across his face. "No worries, sweetheart. You're awake now. That's all that matters."

A long moment passed between us as we stared across the small space, neither backing down from the other's eyes. My mind flashed to the picnic table, the pool, the movie. All the moments Hayden had shown a true glimpse of himself. And as much as I wanted to focus on the fact that he'd come to my rescue, I couldn't stop from remembering the hurt he'd knowingly inflicted outside the coffee shop.

How could he be so frustrating, yet put me at such ease? How could he hurt me, yet be the only one to protect me?

"Your fiancé tells me you don't remember much," the nurse said, interrupting our moment.

I broke eye contact first and shook my head, wishing I didn't like the way fiancé sounded each time she said it.

She frowned. "But he told you that you were given a drug?"

I nodded, still stunned it happened in the first place. I'd seen things like that in Lifetime movies. Not in my real life. Then again, nothing over the last month and a half had happened before in my real life.

The nurse glanced to Hayden, gauging his reaction. "What he probably neglected to mention was when you were brought in, there were concerns."

My eyes jumped between the nurse and Hayden. "Concerns?"

She nodded regrettably. "About what occurred while you were unconscious."

My stomach dropped. My hand shot out from under the sheets. Searching for comfort. Searching for reassurance. Searching for Hayden.

Without hesitation, he moved to me, grabbing hold of my hand. He squeezed it just enough to let me know he had me. "Was I tested?"

The nurse nodded. "The results just came back."

My heart thundered in my chest. I squeezed Hayden's hand and swallowed down the large lump lodged in my throat.

"You're clean," she explained. "You weren't assaulted."

I let out a long shaky breath.

"Thank God," Hayden whispered, dropping into the chair beside me, still clutching my hand.

A whirlwind of emotions flooded my body. Anger. Relief. Foolishness. Loneliness. I wished my body could settle on just one. But it was par for the course that was my life.

Tears tumbled down my cheeks. I wiped at them with the hand Hayden wasn't holding, but I couldn't stop their fervent descent.

"Hey." He leaned closer, his eyes leveling with mine. "You're okay." He lifted the back of my hand to his mouth, gently pressing his lips to it. "Nothing happened. You're fine."

I wanted to believe him. Wanted to hold onto the tingle his lips left on my skin. Wanted to grasp onto the sincerity in his voice. I really did. But I wasn't fine. I was nowhere near fine.

"Would you mind doing something about these?" I gestured to my tears, feeling like an idiot for crying in front of him *again*. God. I was so pathetic. "You wouldn't want to witness them for another four days, would you?"

Hayden scooted to the edge of his chair. His minty breath the only thing between us as he inched closer.

I stilled.

He obviously didn't realize I wasn't serious.

He lowered his soft lips to my cheek, pressing slow gentle kisses to my salty tears as they slid down, one after the other.

The beeping of the heart monitor accelerated quite ceremoniously. He had to have heard it. And if I wasn't so lost in the sensation of his lips on my skin, and the glorious tingles left in their wake, I might've been mortified. But what could I do? Hayden was kissing my face.

Once he reached the corner of my mouth, his lips hovered dangerously close. Did the thought of kissing me cross his mind? If so, he didn't let on. With his feet planted firmly on the ground, he placed his hands on either side of my hips and rested the weight of his body on them. Then he leaned over me, his lips touching down on my other cheek, trailing the same slow gentle kisses over my tears from my eye down to my chin.

He pulled back an inch, his eyes dropping to my lips.

In my head, I begged him to kiss me. To make me forget my circumstances, my sadness, my name. I knew there couldn't be a worse time, but the emotions bouncing through my body thought otherwise.

Instead of indulging me in my ephemeral wish, Hayden pulled away and sat back down in the chair beside my bed, leaving me breathless.

I expected him to look away. To avoid my eyes. To pretend he didn't just kiss my face. But he didn't. The fire in his eyes, a fire I hadn't seen before, blazed.

My lips moved before I could stop them. "A tissue would've been fine."

Hayden snorted, before dropping his head and shaking it from side to side.

Over his shoulder, the nurse stood in the corner wearing an envious grin.

Oh, she had no freaking idea.

# CHAPTER TWELVE

## HAYDEN

"I told you, you didn't have to do this," Alex pleaded.

I looked down at her small body cradled in my arms. "Quiet." I pressed the button for the second floor and the elevator doors slid shut with us inside.

Carrying Alex was completely unnecessary. But having her arms linked around my neck felt amazing. And even though I wanted to say I did it to be a gentleman, all the inappropriate thoughts moving through my head with Alex's body tucked into mine, made me anything but.

And given the last twenty-four hours, that made me a total dick.

"Why don't you normally take the elevator?"

How could I not be honest when she gazed up into my eyes like I singlehandedly saved the country from a terrorist invasion? "I don't like confined spaces." Or the things forcing you inside them.

Alex nodded in understanding. But did she really understand? *Could* she ever understand?

The doors to the elevator finally split. I blew out a breath, hoping Alex didn't notice. With minor difficulty, I unlocked the door to my apartment and carried her inside.

"Wow. I thought you were only kidding."

I glanced down at her grinning face.

"The whole fiancé thing. Now you're carrying me over the threshold. People are definitely going to talk."

I laughed as I kicked the door closed behind us.

I made my way over to the sofa and placed her down gently. I never entertained girls in my living room. So I stepped back and admired how at home Alex looked on my large sectional. I liked it. I really liked it.

"Seriously, Hayden. I can't thank you enough."

"I can see that. You've thanked me like thirty times."

She flashed me a condescending smirk. "I'm serious. With my aunt out of town, I have no one. I don't know what I would've done without you."

I shrugged. "Just being a good neighbor." I should've slapped myself for being such a dumbass. But I didn't have to.

Alex shot me a knowing smile as she stood from my sofa. "I should probably head home."

I jumped in front of her, blocking her escape like a crazy person. "No."

Her brows bunched together as she gaped up at me. And even though she'd been through hell, and her day-old clothes were crumpled and her hair a wild mess, she still looked so damn beautiful. "What?"

"Stay with me tonight." The idea definitely sounded better in my head.

Her eyes widened. "Why?"

"I…" I knew I looked like a total bastard debating whether or not to lie, but that's exactly what I was doing.

Alex searched my face, waiting as I waged my internal battle. A battle I had no chance in hell of winning. After more indecisive minutes, her shoulders dropped with an audible sigh.

Yup. That's me. A royal disappointment. And for some reason, I hated that Alex witnessed it firsthand.

*Ah hell.*

"I need to know you're okay," I blurted.

Alex crossed her arms and sassily tilted her head. "And how will you know I'm okay if I'm here?"

She had me there.

I lifted my head to the heavens, praying a higher power took hold of my mouth for the next few seconds so I couldn't screw it up. But when no divine help came, I did the only thing I could. I lowered my eyes to hers. "There's no way I'll sleep if you're across the hall beating yourself up over something some asshole did to you."

Alex stared up at me, her eyes filling with tears. It was definitely not the response I'd been hoping for.

I moved closer, shrinking the distance between us. My fingers flexed at my side, itching to touch her. "Stay with me tonight, Alex. You can sleep in my bed and I'll sleep out here."

Her eyes jumped away. I could see her taking inventory of my apartment. The small kitchen and its empty countertops to the right of the living room. The closed doors leading to the bathroom and my bedroom to the left. She took it all in. Likely pondering my bare walls and wondering what kind of person didn't have pictures.

"Okay," she whispered.

I leaned closer, not trusting my ears. "Okay?"

She skirted around me and grabbed hold of the front door knob. "I just need to go shower first."

"Want me to come with you?" The second I said it, I winced.

She glanced over her shoulder, flashing an amused grin. "I think I can manage. But if I need help reaching my back, I'll give a shout."

I couldn't not smile back at this amazing girl who, after everything she'd been through, still retained her wit.

## ALEX

Sobs tore through my body on the shower floor. The gushing water had nothing on my tears. They started the second I left Hayden's apartment. I tried to be strong in front of him. But the truth remained. I needed my parents. I needed my friends. I needed to understand why terrible things kept happening to me.

I didn't know Cameron. From our first encounter, he seemed nice. Why would he drug me? Did he plan to rape me? Hayden told me my clothes were undone and inside out when he found me. Maybe we'd been interrupted.

And what about Taylor? Why didn't she stay with me? She must've been the one to drop me off. Didn't she realize what happened? Was she the one who interrupted? The one who initially saved me? If so, why hadn't she called?

It was all too much.

Too much on top of everything else I'd been dealing with.

When the hot water cooled and my body began to shake, I knew I needed to get out. Besides, if I didn't make it over to Hayden's apartment soon, he'd probably come looking for me. And finding me falling apart on the shower floor would be a glaring contradiction to the tough façade I tried to assume.

With pruned skin and a wet head of hair, I padded across the hall to his apartment a few minutes later.

Outside I hesitated, wishing I didn't feel uneasy approaching his door. I needed to get over the hurt I'd felt. He'd swept in when no one else had. He'd comforted me with butterfly kisses in the hospital. He'd held my hand through the test results. And he'd carried me to his apartment and demanded I stay. What more could I ask for?

With one last breath, I tapped on his door and twisted the knob. Thanks to the open pizza box on the coffee table, the spicy smell of marinara sauce filled the room.

Hayden lounged on the left end of the sectional with his bare feet up. His hair was wet from a shower, and he'd changed into gray basketball shorts and a white T-shirt. As he bit into his slice of pizza, his eyes followed me to the opposite side of the sofa where I sat down, tucking my feet underneath me.

"Feel better?" he asked with his mouth full.

I shrugged, noncommittal.

He gestured to the pizza on the table. "It just got here. Have some."

I watched his slice disappear in three giant bites. When had he last eaten? He stayed with me all night at the hospital. And never left my side once I woke up. He must've been starving. "I'm not really hungry."

He studied my face, long and hard. Like the longer he stared, the more he'd understand me.

Good luck with that.

"Don't make me come over there and force you."

I held up my palms. "I promise. I'll eat when I'm hungry."

"Fair enough." He reached into the box and grabbed another slice.

Being in his apartment, surrounded by him and that amazing aloe scent, made me feel better. At least better than my pitiful shower display.

"You wanna watch a movie?"

"Whatever you want."

A sexy smile spread from ear to ear. "I like the sound of that."

I couldn't help but grin as he put down his pizza and jumped up, scanning his movie collection on the shelf below his flat screen.

With his back to me, I drank in his muscular form. I knew what lingered beneath that T-shirt, so broad and ripped. Like nothing I'd ever seen before. And even after all I'd been through, I couldn't stop my mind from wondering what he'd feel like. Taste like. Be like behind closed doors. "Hayden?" His name slipped out before I could stop it.

He glanced over his shoulder, his blue eyes popping thanks to the white T-shirt. I'd always been a sucker for blue eyes and his put all others to shame.

I gnawed on my bottom lip, knowing I couldn't turn back now that I'd opened my big mouth. "I don't want you to sleep out here."

He arched a brow. "Where should I sleep?"

My eyes flashed to the twin doors to the side of the living room.

Hayden's eyes narrowed. "Alone?"

After breaking down in the shower, I knew I shouldn't be left alone for a very long time. So I shook my head slowly.

## HAYDEN

*Thank God.*

The credits scrolled across the screen after the longest fucking movie in the history of movies.

Knowing Alex wanted to share my bed played with my head and wired my body. Sure, we stayed on opposite ends of the sofa, but a two-hour movie gave me more than enough time to focus on the palpable electricity whizzing between us.

Never before had I spent so much time with a girl and not taken it to the bedroom. I knew Alex had just endured a traumatic experience. I wasn't that much of a douchebag. But I really wanted her in my bed. At least for the night.

I glanced across the sofa. Alex watched me. "You ready for bed?" I tried to sound nonchalant, but it came off cheesy.

Seemingly undeterred by my cheesiness, she nodded, her eyes locked on mine, waiting for me to make the first move.

I tipped my head toward the two doors. "If you need the bathroom, it's the one on the right. My room's the one on the left."

Alex nodded before sliding off the sofa and moving to the bathroom. Did she need to wear those tiny shorts? Good God. Restraining myself was hard enough when her ass cheeks weren't hanging out.

I grabbed the remote and switched off the television, shrouding the living room in darkness. I stood up. Then sat back down. Then stood up again.

What was I supposed to do? Wait for her to come out, or just go in my room? If I went in, was I supposed to get in bed or sit and wait for her?

Girls usually stripped off their clothes before we even made it to my room. Everything with Alex was so new. It was just a matter of time before I screwed it up again. And I *would* screw it up. I'd become a real pro at that.

"Ready?" Alex's soft voice snapped me out of my head.

Nodding like a pre-pubescent fool who'd never been alone with a girl before, I moved toward my room. I could feel Alex on my heels and smell her vanilla scent. But I didn't turn around for fear of coming face to face with her.

Being that close would only send my body buzzing and hands twitching.

I moved to my dresser and switched on the small lamp, casting a dim glow over my bare room. No pictures sat on my cherry nightstand or dresser. No posters or pictures junked up my white walls. The focal point was the king-size bed. With its black comforter and mound of pillows, it was the area that got the most attention.

And the one place Alex and I couldn't escape each other.

Having no idea if I even had a side, I moved to the right and removed the extra pillows, tossing them to the floor. I usually just slept in the middle. And since I didn't let the girls I took home stay, I never had to tell someone which side to sleep on.

I sat down, contemplating my next move. I heard Alex's soft footfalls padding to the left side. Oh, this definitely had the makings of an interesting night.

I grabbed the hem of my T-shirt, pausing before lifting it. It wasn't like Alex hadn't seen me at the pool with my shirt off. But concealing my tattoo trumped comfort. Too many potential questions there. Instead, I pulled off my shorts, leaving me in my boxers and T-shirt.

The opposite side of the bed dipped slightly as Alex sat down. "Is this okay?"

I looked over my shoulder. She held onto my sheets, pausing before sliding underneath. "What?"

"Me taking this side?"

I smiled. "You can have whatever side you want. If it's the middle you'd like, we can work around that, too."

Alex grinned as she slid under the sheets, turning onto her side to face me. Her hands slipped under her head on the pillow and her eyes zoned in on mine, challenging me to get in. To move closer.

Like I'd really back down.

I slid under the sheets, fluffing my pillow before lying down and facing her. I could sense her nervousness. But she had no reason to be. Not with me. She was the purest thing I'd ever had in my bed. And I liked it. A hell of a lot more than I thought I would.

Alex's shallow breaths were impossible to ignore and so damn adorable I could've listened to them all night. Preferably beneath me and nuzzled right into my neck.

Girls normally couldn't keep their eyes off my body once they were in my bed, anticipating what I'd be like when the lights went down. But not Alex. She stared into my eyes. Not the silver flecks other girls used as a pick-up line to get my attention. Right *into* them, like she saw all the way down to my soul.

Talk about scary shit.

"You really have no idea, do you?" she whispered.

My eyes fell to her pouty lips, contemplating what they'd taste like. She hadn't eaten, so I surmised mint with a splash of strawberry from the fruit punch we drank. "What?"

She reached over, gently brushing a fallen piece of hair back from my forehead. The contact sent shivers rippling through me. *What the hell?* I didn't do shivers, trembles, or any other cliché shit that happened when making contact with the opposite sex. At least I never had before.

Alex tucked her hand back under her head, her tired eyes timid. "What you mean to me. You have no idea."

What could I say to that? Because all I really wanted to say was, *Please don't go getting deep on me right now. Please.*

Her eyelids fell into long drawn-out blinks. Her over-exhaustion and determination to stay awake jockeyed for control. "I'm sorry. I don't want you to feel weird or anything. It's just…you're the only person I have in this town. And I'm not trying to pressure you to spend time with me or anything like that. Because I know…"

My heart hammered at her unspoken words. What couldn't she say? What wouldn't she say? "You know what?" It came out too quickly to be indifferent.

"You don't want to know me," she whispered, catching me in her sad gaze.

*Well, hell.* How could she even think that? After last night? After today? Now? I flexed my fingers beneath my pillow, stopping them from reaching up and cupping her cheeks.

"Alex. What happened at school had nothing to do with you and everything to do with me." I closed my eyes for a brief moment, knowing I sounded like every other douchebag out there who'd hurt someone they shouldn't have hurt. Once I gathered my thoughts, I opened my eyes. Her sad eyes broke my fucking heart. "I just wish I could've warned you."

Genuine interest flickered in her eyes. "Warned me of what?"

My life had become so damned complicated. I'd never had to explain myself to anyone. I'd never had to feel guilty over something I said. I'd never had to apologize for my actions. This was uncharted territory for me.

"It's okay. You don't have to say anything. I just thought you should know you're the only person I trust—which I know sounds crazy since we barely even know each other."

And there it was.

The truth.

I always got the truth from Alex. And strangely, it didn't send me fleeing the room, state, or country. "What about your aunt?"

She shook her head, her lips twisting in regret. "I've known her just about as long as I've known you." My brows slanted in, prompting her to elaborate. "My parents weren't close with her. Actually, they acted as though she didn't exist. I always got the feeling they didn't trust her."

My eyes narrowed. Not trust Katherine? She was the only one who trusted me at eighteen to rent an apartment in her building. "How do you know it wasn't the other way around?"

Alex looked away. "I guess I don't. Not really anyway. My mom said they had a fight before she married my dad, and they stopped speaking." She looked back at me. "So for twenty years, they hadn't spoken. Actually, I spoke to her more than they did. She called on my birthday, but I never met her."

"What changed?"

She closed her eyes, pulling in a deep breath. "My parents died in a plane crash last month. She's my only living relative."

*Fuuuuck.*

My mind tried to sort through the thoughts whipping through it. That definitely answered the *what makes someone cry for days* question. She'd lost her parents. She'd been sent to an unfamiliar place to live with a virtual stranger. And now people were messing with her. "You haven't mentioned them."

Her eyes snapped open etched deep with pain. "Because then it makes my nightmare real. If I don't talk about them, I can pretend I'm away. Like I'll see them again as soon as I get home."

I knew exactly what she meant. I did the same thing in the foster homes. Always believing my mom would show up at the door one day looking for me. But inevitably, the truth caught up with me. And I was still alone. Alex would find that to be the case sooner rather than later. And the pain would be just as harsh. If not harsher.

"My boyfriend's parents were on the plane, too," she continued.

I must've winced because she nodded, wiping away a tear that slipped down her cheek.

"It was my parents' plane. I asked them to invite his parents to our vineyard." More tears trickled down. "I don't even think my parents wanted to go, but they did it for me. *Me.* Their wonderful daughter who sent them out of town so she could spend the weekend alone with her boyfriend." Tears replaced her words.

Jesus Christ.

She blamed herself.

I reached over and lightly rolled one of her soft waves of hair between my fingers.

"No one could determine who was flying the plane. The news claimed it was my dad because he's—he was—a licensed pilot." Alex brushed more tears off her cheeks.

"So after the accident, my friends chose to be there for Preston, not me. They stopped taking my calls. My texts. It's like they erased me from their lives." A humorless laugh slipped from her lips. "Preston was the one to break the news to me. He actually ended the call with 'This is all your fault.'"

My body stilled.

Those words.

That weighty accusation.

Misconstruing my appalled face, Alex shrugged. "I wasn't lying when I said I have no one."

I had no idea what to say. She'd just unloaded...everything. The hell she'd been through. The shitload of guilt she'd been carrying.

If anyone knew guilt, it was me. I knew its far-reaching capabilities. I knew its endless power. I knew the intolerable pain it dispensed. "I'm sorry."

Alex's eyes flashed to the ceiling, allowing my words to hang in the air as she purged her tears.

I placed my hand on her shoulder.

Her eyes dropped to it.

"I know it's no consolation..." I needed her to hear me, to believe me, so I waited for her to lift her eyes. "But you've still got me."

A sad smile slanted her lips. "I didn't give you much choice, did I?"

"There's always a choice."

Her eyes cast down.

"Hey." I lifted her chin with my index finger so she had no other option but to look at me. "You said it yourself at Jake's. You're a survivor."

"I've cried every day since they died. A survivor deals with it head on. I'm not dealing. I'm pretending it never happened. And failing miserably."

"Everyone deals with death differently."

She raised a brow. "So now you're a shrink?"

I hesitated, choosing my words carefully. Unwilling to divulge more than I needed to. "I've had my fair share of loss. Don't let the fun-loving personality fool you."

Alex smirked.

*Thank God.*

Her sharing something so personal scared the hell out of me. I needed to move us away from the serious shit before she thought question time was a free-for-all. "Seriously, Alex. Don't underestimate yourself. You're pretty amazing."

She averted her gaze, glancing around my room for no other reason than to avoid my eyes. "Thanks. Even if you are just saying it to get in my pants."

Something between a gasp and a laugh burst out of my mouth.

She finally looked at me, blinking away the film of tears coating her eyes. "I mean, come on. *Amazing. Survivor.* You're pulling out all the stops tonight."

"Tell me about it. I've never had to work so hard."

We shared a laugh. A comfortable laugh in a place that never saw any conversation. It felt good to share something real with another person. And strangely, a person I wasn't in a rush to throw out of my bed.

"But you've got to know, it's not gonna happen."

I flashed her my cockiest grin. The one that sank my dimples. Girls loved the dimples. "Oh sweetheart, I know the effect I have on women. If I wanted in, I'd be in."

Alex cocked her head. She didn't buy it. And I kind of liked that she didn't. She saw through my bullshit. And if I wasn't careful, she might actually see me. "So you're saying you don't?"

I shook my head. "I'm saying, timing's everything. And tonight, time's not on our side." What could only be described as disappointment stretched over her features. *Well, hell.* "I never said tomorrow it wouldn't be."

Her lips spread into a short-lived smile that faded as her eyelids grew heavier, drooping before my eyes. "Hayden?"

"Yeah?"

Her voice lowered. "Do you snuggle with those girls you bring home?"

I swallowed hard. "What girls?"

"Come on. I'm sad and lonely, not stupid."

I couldn't even think of other girls with this beautiful and vulnerable girl in my bed. I was completely screwed. "No, Alex, I don't snuggle with those girls I *used* to bring home."

She arched her brows. "Used to?"

"Seems my priorities have recently changed." I watched the lump in her throat drop. But there was no way I'd let her off the hook that easily. "Why'd you want to know?"

She shrugged her shoulders. "Just wondering."

Just wondering my ass. "Just wondering if I snuggle with those girls or if I'll snuggle with you?"

Her eyes nearly closed. "Is that your way of asking me to snuggle, Hayden?"

"Oh, I don't ask." I moved closer, sliding my arms around her tiny waist and gently turning her away from me. "I just take what I want." I pulled her back to my front, inhaling her intoxicating scent and loving the feel of her in my arms.

Her smooth hands slid over mine, linking our fingers together. "Good night, babe," she sighed, using the same term she'd used to push my buttons at the bar and relax me in the hospital. It worked then. And it worked now.

"Good night, sweetheart," I whispered.

# CHAPTER THIRTEEN

## ALEX

I opened my scratchy eyes, struggling to get my bearings. The curtains were pulled snug, but the early morning sun still snuck its rays into small crevices casting dim light over the dark furniture in Hayden's bare room.

His scent filled my subconscious. So crisp and fresh. Something I'd forever associate with only him. With his arms wrapped tightly around my waist, his rhythmic breathing told me he was still asleep. His strong front pressed firmly to my back, while his right hand splayed on my bare stomach, under my shirt.

*Hmmm.*

Being in Hayden's bed, with his arms holding me in place, felt like home. If I could stay that way forever, I'd die a very happy girl. Unfortunately, the fluids the hospital pumped into my body caught up with me.

I wiggled my body, hoping Hayden would let up his grasp. But it only caused him to tighten his arms.

God, I'd never felt so safe. Like nothing could touch me. It was irrational. Totally absurd to know him for such a short period of time and feel the way I did. I knew it was. But it was still the truest thing I had.

I grazed my fingertips over his hand—the one on my bare stomach. His fingers twitched, so I kept at it, this time sliding my other hand over my shoulder and around his neck, threading my fingers through the soft almost-curls at the back of his head. "Hayden," I whispered, continuing to move both hands.

He grunted, but made no move to release me.

I had to bring out the big guns. I wiggled my rear end right where he couldn't ignore it. Preston explained the morning male anatomy to me years ago. And from what he said, I should've been insulted if I didn't garner the reaction Hayden sported. Like, *really* sported.

"Morning, sweetheart," Hayden's raspy voice hummed, his warm breath tickling my neck.

*Preston who?*

"Is there a reason you feel the need to rub your cute little ass all over me so early in the morning?"

My hand dropped from his neck. "I need the bathroom."

His grasp tightened. "First tell me how you're doing."

I paused, considering my response. Words like *scared, shocked,* and *unsettled* came to mind. It had been an eye-opening experience to say the least. But being in Hayden's arms made the nightmare fade. Made the pain tolerable. Made the sadness dissipate. So I answered truthfully. "Better than expected."

"Yeah?" He sounded surprised. "Why's that?"

There was no way I could tell him the truth. I'd said enough the previous night. So instead of using words, I reached for his hand resting on my shirt and slid it across my bare stomach with the other, loving the feel of his rough hands on my skin.

His body tensed.

I waited it out, pushing him past his comfort level.

After a long moment, his body relaxed. His fingers twitched slightly before tracing slow circles over my stomach. The tingles left in their wake nearly branded my skin, making me forget my ordeal. Forget my pain. Forget everything.

His hands slid from my stomach to my sides, delicately trailing his thumbs up and down my skin in a slow sensual path. Chills rippled through me. Glorious, wonderful chills. "Is this okay?" he whispered.

"Uh huh," I murmured, because it was all I could muster.

He smiled into my neck as his innocuous thumbs continued moving, never venturing too high or too low. But it didn't stop the delicious sensations from spreading down to my nether regions.

His strong hands sent every one of my nerve endings into overdrive. I couldn't focus on anything but the heat traveling from my arms to my legs and everywhere in between. I never knew someone's touch could elicit such a mind-blowing effect. Add to it his breath on the back my neck, and I was about to self-combust.

Deep in the back of my throat I groaned, unable to stop the low primal sound even if I wanted to. I had a mind to spin around in his arms so I could look into those intoxicating eyes and offer myself up to him on a silver platter.

But my rational side reminded me he never had the same girl over more than once. This moment in his bed might've been all I ever got if I took it any further. And though I wanted nothing more than to surrender to Hayden and the sensations of his magical hands, I couldn't risk losing him. He was the only one I had.

I sighed. "I really have to go."

Hayden chuckled at my indecisive tone. "You can run but you can't hide."

## HAYDEN

*Holy shit.*

I rolled onto my back and scrubbed my hands over my face. What was happening? All night I'd slept like a baby with Alex in my arms. I think she had it all wrong. The only miracle worker around these parts was her.

She had no idea what nightmares plagued my dreams every night—except the two nights I'd slept next to her.

I scrubbed my face again, my morning stubble prickling my palms. What the hell was I doing? She'd just lost her parents. Everything she'd ever known. She'd been drugged and abandoned. She was too vulnerable. Too lost. And as much as my body was telling me it could work, I knew better.

"What are you thinking?" Alex asked.

I dropped my hands and linked them behind my head, marveling at her sweet little body leaning against my door frame. "Just wondering what was taking you so damn long."

Coward.

Alex moved to the bed and slipped back under the covers. This time, instead of staying on her side, she snuggled into my side and rested her head on my chest. I instinctively went rigid. I knew she felt it. But she didn't let go. She held on tighter. "This is new for you, huh?"

I gave my body a minute to relax before nodding.

"Why do you think you sleep with so many girls and not take it any further?"

"Who said I sleep with *so* many girls?" I couldn't help feeling a little embarrassed. Even if it was the truth.

"Well, my aunt might've mentioned it. Then your friend mentioned my expiration date. And I've seen—"

"You've been spying on me?" I looked down at her coffee-colored waves spread over my chest like they belonged there. It took all my willpower not to tangle my fingers through the soft locks.

Alex smiled into me. "Maybe."

I rolled onto my side, wrapping my arms around her waist. I couldn't hold off any longer. It was the first time we'd been this close for an extended period of time. It was the first time the front of her soft body pressed against my chest and I didn't want to jump out of my skin. It was the first time I seriously considered crashing my mouth down on hers.

When her eyes lifted, a longing I hadn't expected filled them. How could I not be honest with her after everything she'd shared with me? "I hardly see them."

Alex's brows squished together. She had no idea what I was talking about.

"The girls I sleep with," I clarified. "I hardly see their faces. It's their bodies I lose myself in for a few minutes, not them."

"A few minutes, huh?" she teased.

I smirked. "Oh, you want to go there?"

She shook her head with a snicker.

But the gravity of the conversation sobered me. "Seriously, they're a place for me to forget what I've got going on. They mean nothing." I could see the sarcasm in her eyes morph to disappointment. Like she finally saw me for the asshole I was. "Believe me, I'm up front with them. They know when they come over here, that's all I've got to offer."

"When'll it stop?"

The question took me aback. I'd never even considered stopping. I'd never had a reason to. "I guess when I finally see her face."

Alex nodded, seemingly understanding.

But could she ever fully grasp the emptiness? The nothingness? The void within me? It was a black hole.

"Why'd you sign me up for the audition?"

Whoa. Talk about a one-eighty. "Because you wouldn't have done it yourself."

"Bullshit."

"What?"

She cocked her head. "Have you ever signed up any of your girls for something without them knowing?"

"I just told you, they're not my girls." I couldn't decide if I was frustrated or amused. "And, no. I've never signed them up for anything."

She lifted a brow. "Not even a wet T-shirt contest? Because the ones I've seen, definitely seemed the type."

I choked out a laugh. "Not even a wet T-shirt contest." Alex had this uncanny way of weaving levity into our conversations when they became too serious. Like she knew when I got uncomfortable and needed a breather. Like she really knew me. "Seriously, I signed you up because you're good."

I could practically see the sarcasm leave her lips. "I believe you called me amazing."

My gaze dropped to her parted lips, so lush and inviting. "I think you might be right." We were dangerously close. She knew it and so did I. Her minty breath drifted over my face. She'd used my toothpaste. Had she expected something to happen between us? Had she hoped for it?

I couldn't stop myself. I inched closer. Her breath hitched in her throat.

*Knock. Knock.*

"*Fuuuck,*" I groaned, dropping my forehead to hers.

"Expecting someone?"

The way she said *someone* told me she assumed it was a girl. Why wouldn't she?

But what she didn't know was whoever lurked outside the door could've been so much worse. "Listen." I pulled back, evening my eyes with hers. "I need to answer this." For the first time, I cupped her warm face between my hands. Her cheeks felt so damn soft I didn't want to let go. Under normal circumstances, I wouldn't have. "Please stay in here. No matter what you hear, do not come out of this room."

"Hayden, you're scaring me."

"*Please.* Just stay in here." I jumped out of bed and hurried out of the room, closing the door behind me.

I leaned against it, pausing for a long moment. My old life and new life were seriously close to colliding. If I could just keep them separate, things might be okay.

I moved to the front door, wishing I didn't have to answer it. But my truck was parked in the lot. No big secret I was home.

I checked the peephole, finding exactly who I expected.

I barely opened the door before Remy burst in looking like he hadn't been to sleep yet. "Dude, where've you been? I've been calling." He dropped onto my sofa and opened the pizza box on the coffee table.

"My phone must've died." The truth was, with Alex around, the outside world disappeared. Most girls would break into a chorus of *Awwws* over the sweet notion. But it wasn't sweet. It was stupid. In my life, losing focus was dangerous. It could get people killed.

It could get *me* killed.

Remy's eyes assessed my apartment like he hadn't been in it a hundred times before. "So…" His eyes landed on the two empty glasses on the coffee table.

*Shit.*

"Have some company last night?"

I shrugged.

His eyes shot to my closed bedroom door, before he flashed me one of his devious grins. "Is she still here?"

"Shut up, man. You know I don't let 'em stay."

Remy stared at me, long and hard. Given the surly look in his narrowed eyes, he questioned my words. Questioned my story. "So, was it Sydney?"

"Nah. Just some bitch. Couldn't even tell you what she looked like."

A sly smile slid across his face. "Yeah. What was I thinking? Totally not your style, bro." He grabbed a slice of cold pizza and bit into it. "So, Cooper called. We got a job tonight."

I nodded. I didn't need to know the logistics. Remy took care of that. As long as I drove and supplied backup, I just showed. The less I knew the better.

"I'm on my way to meet the boys for some grub. You in?"

"Got some shit to take care of."

It may have sounded vague, and most would've questioned it, but not Remy. If it didn't interfere with our job, he didn't question it. Not seriously, anyway. "Pick me up at Baxter's around nine. Unless you wanna get hammered with me first."

I shrugged. "I'll see how the day turns out."

He jumped to his feet, grabbing another slice and stuffing it in his mouth on the way to the door. "Later."

"Later," I said, locking the door behind him. And only then, with him out of my apartment and away from Alex, did I exhale.

## ALEX

Hayden's bedroom door swung open. Still in his boxers and wrinkled white T-shirt, he stood in the doorway looking down at me nestled in his bed.

"Everything okay?"

He nodded, but his eyes were distant. Troubled. Uneasy.

I sat up, keeping the blanket wrapped tightly around me, like that would shield me from his sudden distance. "Should I go?"

He shrugged, then dropped down on the foot of his bed with his back facing me and his head hung low.

Nothing I'd overheard—except maybe his heartlessness when discussing the girl he brought home—explained his indifference. This Hayden was the one I couldn't understand. The one I struggled to keep up with. The one who changed moods like girls changed outfits before a date.

Did I even want to invest time in someone whose personality switched at the drop of a dime? Or was having him in my life, in whatever capacity I could get, enough?

I dropped the blanket and crawled down to the foot of the bed. I sat beside him the way we'd sat on the picnic table. Both silent. Both in our own heads. Both soothed by the other's presence.

"I need to stay away from you," he mumbled into his chest.

Unsure if he was serious or not, I turned toward him. "You do know you're quoting a super famous novel-turned-movie, don't you?"

"I'm serious, Alex. It's not a good idea."

I stared at his bowed head, trying to make sense of the situation. Moments before hadn't he been ready to kiss me?

"There's so much you don't know about me. Things I do that I'm not proud of. Things I've done. Things I don't tell anyone."

"I'm not following."

A sardonic laugh left him as his eyes finally slid to mine. "Exactly. There are things I can't talk about. Blanks I can't fill in."

"Okay. Then I won't ask."

He scoffed. "You don't get it. There are more things I can't tell you, than I can."

"Can or will?"

His jaw clenched. "Both."

I nodded, thinking back to the cemetery. Thinking back to my aunt's warning. Thinking back to his own warning only a few minutes before. I knew Hayden had secrets. Secrets I'd probably never know if I waited for him to tell me.

Could I control my curiosity for a chance to get to know him better? Could I resist the urge to follow him when he didn't tell me where he was going? Was he even worth all the trouble?

I huffed out a long breath. "Fair enough."

His brows arched.

I leveled my eyes with his. "Since I can't seem to stay away from you, I'd say we're just getting started."

His shoulders sagged in defeat. The complete opposite of the relief and happiness I'd hoped for.

I reached over and placed my hand on his solid thigh, attempting to comfort him from whatever displeased him. Sure, it could've been me, but I wouldn't allow myself to believe that. "What is it?"

He stared down at my hand on his skin, like the first time we met. But now I knew him—as much as he'd let anyone know him. And he obviously kept too much locked inside. It wasn't healthy. I should know. He needed someone to talk to. Someone to confide in. Someone who would listen and not try to solve his problems. I could be that someone. If only he'd let me.

"I need you to stay away from me when Remy's around."

I almost didn't need to ask. "Mr. Piercings and Tattoos?"

Hayden nodded.

"Is that who was here?" My thumb moved back and forth over his bare leg, the fair wisps of dark hair softer than expected.

He nodded again.

"Can you tell me why?"

My question was met with the swift shake of his head.

"So, we can hang out, just as long as Remy doesn't know?"

He twisted his lips and nodded.

"He goes to our school."

Hayden shook his head. "He just hangs out there." His eyes flashed around his room, at the bare walls and empty furniture. "This is all I can offer. This apartment, this building, bars and restaurants in other towns. Anywhere Remy won't find out."

I withdrew my hand from his leg and crossed my arms, contemplating his offer for me to be his dirty little secret. "Why does he care who you spend time with?"

"I don't know if he cares, so much as he controls what I do when I work with him."

"You don't strike me as the type to let anyone control you."

He made a low, choked sound. "If anything stands in the way of work, Remy won't tolerate it. And when that's you..." His eyes fixed on mine, almost softening. "I'm willing to try this. But it's all I've got to offer."

My belly rippled with a series of Olympic style backflips. He was willing to *try this*. Whatever *this* was I really wasn't clear on. But he wanted something with me. And I really needed him to want something.

Unfortunately, as soon as the elation settled in, so did the truth. A truth I couldn't ignore.

The reason I felt so drawn to him was because I could trust him. Now he claimed he couldn't reciprocate that trust. He'd keep secrets.

His eyes searched my face. For the first time they looked hopeful. "What are you thinking?"

As much as I wanted him and whatever he could offer, I knew for my own well-being, my own state of mind, my own shattered heart, it wouldn't be enough.

I needed someone to want to be with me. To seek me out and show me off. I wasn't high maintenance like he presumed at Jake's. I just needed a real connection. Not one that only existed when Remy wasn't around.

"I'm thinking..." I knew what I wanted to do. But I also knew what I needed to do. I deserved more. I'd been through hell. Now the guy who saved me couldn't be seen with me. I needed distance. I needed to straighten out my head. "I should probably head home."

Hayden nodded, like he already knew my response.

I stood from his bed.

He reached out, his warm hand grabbing hold of mine. His normally strong hold was gentle. But I could feel his unwillingness to let go.

I didn't turn. Turning would've caused me to stay. And I needed to leave. I needed time.

"I'm sorry I can't be what you need me to be."

I closed my eyes as his words struck something deep inside me. Something fragile. Something teetering on the balance of happiness and despair.

And in that moment I knew…his words weren't only the truth, but also goodbye.

# CHAPTER FOURTEEN

## HAYDEN

Dark storm clouds loomed overhead. Rain sat ready to burst from the sky. I'd waited in my truck outside the Taco Barn for over an hour staring at the front doors of the cantina-style building.

Finally, Cameron stepped outside.

I jumped out of my truck and jogged to him. Before he even saw me coming, I grabbed the back of his neck and slammed his face into the brick building.

"What the fuck?" he cried as I yanked his startled body to the alleyway beside the building and slammed his chest into the wall. With everyone avoiding the impending storm, the area was deserted and his pleas went unheard.

I leaned into his ear, my teeth gritted in disgust. "What did you do to Alex?"

"Alex who?" he cried.

With my hand pressed firmly into the back of his head, I scraped his pretty boy face against the wall.

"You mean Taylor's friend?"

I spun him around, squeezing his shoulders so hard he had no other option but to look at me. Bloody dirt-filled scratches marked up his cheeks. A giant gash split his bottom lip. He deserved so much worse. "Tell me what happened."

His eyes widened once he realized who I was. He'd heard the rumors. But he didn't know the truth. If he did, he would've been even more terrified. "Nothing. Nothing happened. I swear."

I tightened my grip on his shoulders, digging my fingers in deeper. "Did you slip her the drug?"

His eyes shot away.

I slammed him back. His head bounced off the wall like a rag doll. But rag dolls didn't talk, and I needed him talking. I reeled in my anger and eased up my hold. "Did you drug her?"

His eyes shot down. "It was Taylor. She made me—"

My tempered anger was short-lived. I slammed my fist into his stomach with such force his body folded, air abandoning his lungs in a giant whoosh. "Did you touch her?"

He groaned, his shaggy blonde head moving from side to side.

"I said did you touch her?"

With his body still slumped, he screamed, "No! Taylor wanted it to look that way. But I swear on my baby sister, I'd never touch a girl who's unconscious."

"Did anyone touch her?"

"I don't know, man. I don't think so."

The sight of him whimpering like a bitch made my stomach turn. I slammed my fist into his side, needing him to feel my anger. My disgust. My need for vengeance. "You didn't have to do it."

His body slid down the wall, drawing into a ball on the concrete.

*"Fuck, Hayden. You probably killed him."*

I shook off the all too vivid image.

I needed to get out of there.

With clenched fists and my head spinning, I stalked toward my truck.

"With Taylor, you don't have a choice," Cameron muttered.

I looked over my shoulder at the pathetic mess I'd left behind. "You always have a choice."

I drove in circles for almost an hour, trying to get my head in check. After all Alex had been through, how could I tell her that her friend had her drugged? Wouldn't surprise me if she never trusted anyone ever again.

Inevitably, I stood outside her apartment. I'd seen her car in the lot, so I knew she was home. I stared at the solid structure separating us for a long moment. I wished it wasn't just a stupid door that separated the two of us.

I sucked in a deep breath and knocked. When Alex left my apartment earlier, she made it clear whatever was going on between us—my promise to try—wasn't enough for her.

I knocked again, then stepped back. My eyes dropped to the bottom of the door. A shadow lingered underneath.

I felt ridiculous speaking to a closed door, but it was easier than seeing the disappointment in Alex's eyes. "I talked to Cameron today."

I paused, giving her time to open the door. But she didn't.

"He fessed up. Said he did it. But the whole thing was Taylor's idea."

Still no sound. No movement.

"Just thought you'd want to know who you're hanging out with."

Even as I turned and walked to my apartment, I expected her to open the door.

But she didn't.

At least I'd done what I could. I'd gotten her the truth. What she did with it was up to her.

## ALEX

I gripped the doorknob, wanting to pull open the door. Wanting to see the face of the guy who only hours before had held me in his arms, protecting me from the world around me.

But I couldn't.

With my back to the door, and my mind spiraling with the news he delivered, I sank to the cold hardwood floor.

Taylor.

I should've known.

There was no way she would've just let that opportunity slip through her fingers.

Now what was I supposed to do? Confront her? Tell someone?

Being on the receiving end of her vengeance told me one thing. Mess with Taylor and expect a fate worse than death. Acting oblivious could buy me time. Time to drop out of the competition. Time to distance myself from her.

Unfortunately, the only real friend I had just walked away, and I did nothing to stop him.

## HAYDEN

Taylor stood alone outside the student union texting on her phone. I hadn't called her like I told Alex I would. I needed to see her eyes when I called her out on what she'd done.

Taylor's entire body jumped as I grabbed hold of her arm and dragged her inside the building without a word.

Her phony, sugary-sweet persona slipped off her face. "What the hell, Hayden?"

"That's what I want to know." I swung her around the corner into the commuter lounge. I didn't care if people stared. Let them. It took everything in me not to inflict the same pain on her that Cameron got. But I'd *never* touch a girl. Not even a selfish conniving bitch like Taylor. "Have you talked to Alex?"

She looked me dead in the eyes. Admitting no wrongdoing. Displaying no remorse. She actually puffed out her chest. Did she think she was tough? Did she think she'd get away with it? "Not since Friday night."

"You the one who dropped her off?"

Taylor rolled her eyes on a huff. "Since when are you concerned about anyone other than yourself?"

I slammed my palm into the wall beside her head, likely cracking some of the paint. She flinched. "Answer the fucking question. Did you drive her home?"

"Yeah." The tough girl mask slid back in place. "She was plastered out of her mind. I thought she could handle her liquor, but she was falling all over the place. It was embarrassing."

Blood rushed violently through my veins. The thought of Alex drugged, with no one to take care of her, pulled at something deep inside me. Something I didn't even realize still existed.

And knowing the bitch who did it stood in front of me, and there wasn't a damn thing I could do to make her pay, amplified my rage. "Why'd you leave her? Why not bring her into her apartment?"

Taylor crossed her arms and sighed, like my inquisition was a waste of her precious time. "She said to leave her outside. She didn't want to wake her aunt or something."

Lying bitch. "Her aunt's away."

She shrugged. "That's what she said."

I wasn't satisfied. "What happened with Cameron?"

"Cameron? I don't know. He took her for a walk."

"Come on, Taylor. You're boy was more forthcoming than that."

Her bored façade slipped for just a second as she fought to maintain her composure. Then, as if I hadn't just bagged her, her lips parted, a cunning smile sweeping across her glossy lips. "Wait a minute. Are you jealous?"

I scanned the faces of the students occupying the seats. If there weren't witnesses, I would've forced her to tell me the truth. I tried my final hand. "She was drugged."

Taylor's eyes expanded. "For real? Is she all right?"

Oh, her acting chops were stellar. If I didn't know any better, I would've believed her myself. "She said she only had one drink. The one Cameron got for the two of you."

Taylor shrugged. "I was fine."

"No, shit." I evened my eyes with hers, moving in so our noses nearly touched. I lowered my voice to just above a whisper. "I know what you did."

She didn't even blink. "Prove it."

I'd never felt more inclined to snap someone's neck in my entire life. If I stayed a second longer, I would've ended up in jail. I spun away from her and got the hell out of the building.

My heart pounded harder than it had in a long time. Someone needed to take Taylor's ass down. But I couldn't risk the ramifications for Alex. She'd be the one who'd suffer.

Philosophy was a waste of time. I couldn't focus on Aristotle's *Metaphysics*. Who was I kidding? I couldn't focus on anything. Anything but Alex. The girl who'd been avoiding me since the previous morning. I couldn't blame her for not wanting to get involved with someone like me. Someone with nothing to offer. I'd put myself out there the best way I knew how. And it backfired.

The classroom clock seemed stuck on eleven forty. At least in five minutes, I'd have a break for lunch. I needed something to snap me out of my pissed off mood. Not sure if that meant running into Alex or downing some much needed carbs, but both would help.

My phone vibrated in my pocket.

Even though last night's job went better than most and I didn't even have to get out of my truck, I prayed it wasn't Remy. Not today. Not with my mood.

I glanced at my professor before sliding the phone from my pocket. Oddly, everyone else in the classroom checked their phones at the exact same time.

I swiped my finger across the screen. It wasn't from Remy, but the school's alert system. Maybe they were cancelling afternoon classes. I wouldn't argue with that. But it wasn't a voice message. It was a text. No, a photo.

Whispers and snickers erupted around me.

Like a detonated bomb, the photo flashed across my screen.

*Fuck me.*

My stomach dropped out from beneath me.

Bile crawled up the back of my throat.

My pulse pounded in my ears.

I jumped to my feet and bolted out the door. I needed to find Alex. I needed to get her off campus before she saw it.

I rushed through the empty hallways of the psych building, not even sure it's where she was. I thrust my face in classroom windows like a madman. There were brunettes of all shapes and sizes. But none of them were Alex.

Visions of the photo flashed in my mind as I jogged to the arts and sciences building and continued my search. Alex's naked body. Her closed eyes. Her seductive pose. The hungry look on her face.

I wished I hadn't seen it. I wished *no one* had. It didn't depict the real Alex. It depicted someone who consented to being stripped bare and photographed. They wouldn't know she'd been drugged. They wouldn't know what she was really like. What she'd been through. They wouldn't realize the photo existed out of jealousy.

As I stalked the hallways, I reminded myself she hadn't been raped. But it didn't stop the adrenaline from gushing through my body.

I needed to find her.

Classroom doors flew open. People emptied into the hallway from every direction. I maneuvered around bodies, shoving people out of my way. The crashing of my heart and the perpetual ringing in my ears muffled the sounds around me.

I pushed through the building exit, coming to an abrupt stop on the top of the concrete stairs. I scanned the crowded quad. Students crossed the crisscrossed paths in a hurry to their next classes, while some congregated in groups, tossed a football, or sat on the grass. But no Alex.

Had she already seen the photo? Had she gone home? Was she hiding?

There was one place I needed to check, hoping to God she was nowhere near it. I jogged across the quad to the student union and right into the busy dining hall.

My head twisted around, my eyes scanning the faces of the people who'd seen the picture.

*Oh, fuck.*

Alex stood on the opposite side of the room, handing her money to the cashier. She turned with her drink and walked over to Taylor's table.

What was she doing? Hadn't she heard me? Didn't she know what Taylor had done?

She looked so innocent, almost angelic, in her white sundress flowing with each step. She didn't notice all the eyes on her. She didn't know what they'd all seen. At that point, every person in the dining hall stared, pointed, or laughed. It was just a matter of time before she knew it.

I needed to get to her. But too many people with filled lunch trays obstructed my path. I pushed closer, edging around bodies while straining to hear Alex and Taylor's exchange over all the noise. But as hard as I tried, I couldn't get to her fast enough. It was like a bad dream. A nightmare where everything happened in slow motion.

Taylor whipped out her phone and held the screen up to Alex.

Alex's jaw dropped.

Her hand shot to her gaping mouth.

I just about reached her when her knees buckled. I threw out my arms, catching her before her body hit the floor.

A giant hush settled over the room as I lifted her into my arms. "I've got you, sweetheart."

She hadn't fainted. *Thank God.* She wrapped her arms around my neck, burying her face in my chest. "Please don't let me go," she whispered into my black shirt, concealing her quiet sniffles.

I carried her outside into the bright sunlight, making it across the quad and to the parking lot in record time. I needed to stop the photo from spreading around. I needed to stop any others from rearing their ugly heads. I needed to bring down Taylor once and for all.

Déjà vu hit when I placed Alex inside the cab of my truck. At least this time she was conscious. She curled her body into a tiny ball. So small. So fragile. So broken. "Why would she do this to me?"

"I don't know, Alex. People suck. Especially when they feel threatened. You were her biggest competition. You stood in the way of what she wanted."

Alex closed her eyes and rolled toward the back of the seat, covering her face with her arms to block out the rest of the world. Who could blame her? The world had done nothing but shit on her for the past two months. No one deserved that—except Taylor. She deserved it a hundred times over.

I wanted to pull Alex back into my arms and make all her pain go away, but I couldn't. I needed to put a stop to the pounding in my head. And there was only one way to do that.

I leaned down and whispered over her quiet sniffles. "I need to run back in for a second. Will you be okay?"

She nodded beneath her arms.

Under normal circumstances, I would've never left her alone. But something needed to be done.

I stormed into the dining hall, slamming the heavy metal doors closed behind me sending a vicious rumble throughout the room.

All noise ceased.

Every head turned my way.

With my body quaking, I stalked over to Taylor's table. I wanted to grab her by the back of her hair and drag her out in front of everyone. But I needed to be smart.

She glared at me, holding up her phone so the photo was displayed. "Face it Hayden, everybody knows you'd screw anything that walks. Upset you didn't get to her first?"

With a massive roar, I threw out my arms, sweeping the table bare. People jumped back as trays flew across the room. Food splattered on clothes and faces. Metal silverware clinked and bounced to the floor. I glowered at Taylor, who stood unfazed, still donning her bored face. "If you weren't a girl, I'd kill you."

I yanked her phone from her hand and hummed it across the room. It smashed against the wall into hundreds of tiny pieces.

Taylor let loose a string of expletives and shoved my chest with her clenched fists. "You should be locked up for the rest of your pathetic life, you asshole."

I jerked toward her, unsure of what I'd actually do if I got a hold of her. But the guys at the table jumped between us. They had major balls intervening, especially when crimson blurred my vision.

I drew a deep breath. Praying for the strength to walk away. I had a girl in my truck who needed me. A girl I'd do anything for.

I scowled at Taylor's bodyguards, before glaring at her. "If I see that photo anywhere else, or hear you've been spreading it around, there will be hell to pay."

I twisted around and faced the room. All eyes were on me. "Do you hear me?" I screamed at the room. "There will be hell to pay."

## ALEX

Uncontrollable shudders rocked through my body. My teeth chattered something fierce. I couldn't tell if I was having a seizure, a heart attack, or if hyperthermia was about to set in. Being ninety degrees outside, the latter seemed unlikely. But I was just so freakin' cold. I snuggled into the stiff leather seat, trying to soak up its warmth.

The passenger door squeaked open at my feet. Hayden's scent filled the cab, momentarily easing my grief. The truck dipped as he knelt on the floor behind me, his strong hand resting upon my arm. Heat rolled off him in waves as he leaned in, resting his forehead against my side. "Please tell me what you need me to do."

"I'm so cold," I said through chattering teeth. "I just need to be warm."

Hayden moved away, leaving me void of the warmth his body provided. I wanted to ask him to stay, to never let me go, but the door closed before I could utter the words.

Within seconds, the driver's door opened, the truck dipped, and the engine roared to life. A blast of heat shot from the vents. Hayden scooped me into his lap like I weighed nothing and wrapped his arms around me. "You're in shock. But you're gonna be okay." His hands moved up and down my back to warm me up. "I promise. You're gonna be okay."

My parents were dead. I'd been drugged and hospitalized. The whole college had seen me naked and posed like a porn star. And I didn't have a single friend—unless I counted Hayden who needed to stay a secret. But sure. I'd be okay.

"I'm gonna make her pay for this," he murmured into my hair. "I swear I will."

"She won't go down without a fight."

"I'm not scared. You've seen my muscles."

I nuzzled closer, wishing I could smile at his attempt to lighten the mood.

His hands continued their soothing massage all over my back while his rapid heartbeat bounced in his chest, echoing my own.

"I don't know what I'd do if you didn't keep saving me."

Hayden said nothing. Probably thinking I was so much more trouble than I was worth. He definitely had to be over my issues. Most likely wishing he never approached me that first day. "Is your aunt back yet?"

See? Already trying to pawn me off on my aunt. "Not until Wednesday."

He pressed his lips to the top of my head. "Stay with me tonight."

"At the rate I'm going, I should probably just move in," I mumbled into his shirt.

His body tensed and he didn't respond.

*Shit.* "I was kidding, Hayden. Wouldn't want to cramp your style."

He pulled back, looking into my puffy eyes. I must've been a horrific sight, but it didn't deter him from lifting his thumbs to my cheeks and wiping away the tears. "That the only reason you don't want to play house with me?" His penetrating eyes bore into mine.

"Well...I don't know your last name. I have no idea how old you are. Your best friend can't know I exist. And my aunt would probably evict you, but not before sleeping with you one last time."

His lips quirked at the corners, but in true Hayden-fashion, he didn't utter a single word as his thumbs continued brushing away my tears.

# CHAPTER FIFTEEN

## HAYDEN

I cracked open my bedroom door and peeked inside. The lights were off, but I could still make out Alex's chocolate curls spread over my white pillowcase. She'd been asleep since we got home, and it was after eight. She had to be starving. But knowing the trouble she had sleeping, it didn't seem right to wake her.

"Hayden?" Alex whispered.

"Sorry." I pushed open the door and stepped inside. "I didn't mean to wake you."

"You didn't."

I moved to the bed and sat down beside her. She rolled onto her side and looked up at me with swollen eyes. "How you doing?"

She raised her eyebrows.

"Sorry." I averted my gaze feeling like a complete tool.

Alex placed her hand on my forearm.

Before she could do what I knew she'd do, I stopped her. "Don't."

"What?" she asked in her sleepy raspy voice.

"Thank me."

She pulled her hand back, and as if I wasn't even there, she rolled away from me, scrunching her entire body into a tiny ball that fit under the T-shirt I gave her.

"Hey," I whispered. "Don't get upset. Not with me."

"Do I need to run through the reasons my life sucks right now?" She sounded so defeated. So lost. "And add to it the fact that the only person I can rely on is you. *You*. Who can't even trust me. Or be seen with me. I've never been so confused and alone in my entire life. It sucks. Majorly sucks." She dispelled a deep breath. "And just so you know, if I want to thank you, I'm going to thank you."

I didn't move. I didn't speak. I got it. Her confusion. Her loneliness. Her sadness. I just didn't know what I was supposed to do to fix it.

How had it gotten to this point? How had *I* become her protector? Being anyone's seemed laughable. But here I was. Here *we* were. Alex and me against the world. For so long my life solely revolved around me. My wants. My needs. My anger. My problems.

I sat for a long while staring at my bare walls. What would my life be like if my mother hadn't been killed? If I hadn't spent almost eight years in foster care bouncing from house to house? If I hadn't met Remy? If I hadn't sat down at that picnic table?

It had been eleven years since I had anything real in my life. Eleven years since I knew what it felt like to care about another human being. Eleven years since I truly smiled.

*Ah, hell.*

I pushed off my sneakers and slid under the comforter behind Alex. Like the last time we slept in bed together, I wrapped my arms around her tiny waist and buried my nose in her vanilla-scented curls. She didn't seem to mind the intrusion, but she made no attempt to give my bigger body more space. "Martin."

"What?" she mumbled into my pillow.

"My last name."

She shook with silent laughter. In the midst of such a shitty day, I liked knowing I caused it.

"I just turned twenty-two."

Her soft hands covered mine, linking our fingers together. "Happy birthday."

"Thanks."

"You look older."

"I've been through a lot."

Her body tensed. She wanted to ask what I meant. What I'd been through. What I kept hidden from everyone. But instead, she relaxed on an exhale. "Maybe someday you'll tell me."

And there it was. The difference between Alex and everyone else in my life. She expected nothing. And while I was pretty certain I'd never be able to share my personal shit with her—with anyone for that matter—it was getting easier sharing the smaller stuff. And it clearly made her happy when I did. "I've never slept with your aunt."

"Thank *God*," she groaned.

The relief in her voice did crazy things to my head. Did she intend to sleep with me? She had to realize me being there for her wasn't about that.

Time stretched on as we lay in silence. It gave me time to think about all the time I'd spent alone. About all the nights I wasted getting drunk and sleeping with insignificant girls. About the last time I actually felt happy.

Alex's breathing evened out, teetering on the precipice of sleep.

"Alex?" I whispered.

"Mmm," she murmured softly.

"I don't know what this is. This thing going on between us." My voice came out hushed for fear of her reaction—make that rejection. "But I really need it."

Her breath caught in her throat, disappearing completely for a long beat.

Then she squeezed my hands tightly and sighed. "Me, too, Hayden Martin. Me, too."

## ALEX

Sunlight squeezed through the gaps in Hayden's curtains. I'd been awake for a few minutes, enjoying the warmth of his body, and his vice grip holding my back to his front. His steady breathing at my ear indicated he hadn't woken yet, so it gave me time to get my wits about me.

*This thing going on between us...I really need it.*

His flutter-inducing words replayed on a constant loop in my head. Sure, he didn't say anything after his confession, but it didn't erase the fact that it happened.

I glanced to the alarm clock on his nightstand. I only had an hour to get to campus. But could I do it? Could I face everyone knowing what they'd seen?

Was I tough enough to endure their whispers? Their judgment?

Was I strong enough to pretend it didn't affect me?

Not even close.

I wiggled my rear end, knowing how well the approach worked last time. Hayden's receptive body didn't disappoint.

"Morning, sweetheart," he whispered into my ear, his warm raspy breath a balm on my neck.

"Morning." I couldn't stop my grin. It was crazy. My entire world had crashed down around me. But in the little bubble Hayden and I shared, the place where his ability to protect me and comfort me encompassed me whole, everything seemed like it might be okay. Like *I* might be okay.

"You're not planning on going in today are you?"

I spun in his arms and wrapped my arms around his waist. He tensed a bit, but I didn't care. "If I don't go, she wins."

Hayden looked down at me, his gorgeous eyes gentle. "You sure?"

"Nope. But someone once told me I was a survivor."

That slow cocky grin slipped across his face. "That someone must be very smart."

I looked him dead in the eyes, without even a hint of a smile. "And a hottie."

His brows arched. "Oh, yeah?"

I bit my bottom lip and nodded slowly, knowing exactly where I wanted the moment to go. Where I needed it to go.

But Hayden's eyes squeezed shut, as if in unfathomable pain. "We should probably get up then."

Seriously?

If any other girl had given him the same subtle go-ahead, it would've led to some serious stripping. But since it was me, super fragile me, he wouldn't go there. But he had to feel our palpable chemistry, so charged in such close proximity.

*Bastard.*

"I'm gonna do this alone."

"Al—"

I shook my head. "My battle. I'll fight it." My eyes flashed around his room. "And you know, I've been thinking. If this is all I can have…" I met his gaze. "I'd like to have it."

The tension around his eyes dissolved, and he smiled a dimple digging, teeth showing, wide as a canyon smile. Then, as if it were happening in slow motion, he inched closer until our noses brushed. My tongue shot out, moistening my bottom lip in anticipation.

Hayden's hands gripped my hips, holding on fiercely as he closed the distance between us. Our lips collided in an explosion of sensations. His delicious kisses, gentle yet firm, consumed me. He wasn't rough or hasty. I wasn't those other girls. I was something special, and he planned to savor every second he got with me.

My fingers trailed up his muscular back and wove into his hair. Pressing my fingertips to the back of his head, I pulled him closer, molding myself into his solid chest and sucking his bottom lip into my mouth. I couldn't stop myself. I opened my lips slightly on a moan. That was all the encouragement he needed. His tongue plunged inside, caressing and moving with mine in a rhythmic dance. *My God.* It was sexy as hell.

I melted into him. The steady racing of his heart against my chest ignited tiny goose bumps all over my body. I deepened the kiss, needing more. So much more.

Hayden's hands slipped up the back of my T-shirt, his fingers caressing my bare skin. Warm ripples swelled deep in my belly. I didn't want him to stop. I wanted to stay like that with him and never leave. I wanted the outside world to just slip away as he brought every one of my fantasies to life.

But slowly, he pulled back, breaking the kiss. Our heaving chests and panting breaths mirrored one another. His eyes zoned in on my swollen lips. I assumed it meant he wasn't done with me, but his eyes lifted to mine. "If we don't get up—"

"We're never getting up?"

His lazy smile said he was trying to do the right thing. But his thumbs tracing tiny circles all over my back said what's a few more minutes?

With only seconds to spare, I pulled into the campus parking lot nabbing the last available spot. Even though the mystery of what lay beneath my clothes no longer existed, I still covered as much of my skin as possible, donning jeans and a long-sleeve black top.

I hurried across the vacant quad, up the three flights of stairs in the English building, and slipped into Lit 350 as the professor began her lecture.

The girl with the razor-sharp bangs beside me shot me a remorseful nod. I wanted to tell her she wasn't to blame, but why bother talking about it. It just reminded me it happened.

Unfortunately, not everyone appeared apologetic. Girls glared like I'd stolen their boyfriends, and guys stared like they wanted to ravage me. But I wouldn't let their unwanted attention ruin my amazing morning. I held my head up and kept reminding myself I needed to be there. If I stayed home, Taylor got exactly what she wanted.

Sadly, half-way through the lecture, the whispers and stares began to eat away at me. So when the professor dismissed class thirty minutes later, I stuffed my books into my bag one at a time, in no rush to endure more judgmental eyes and unsympathetic snickers.

"So, you and Hayden, huh?"

My head shot up. The room had emptied except for the girl beside me who appeared to be stalling as well. "Excuse me?"

She flashed a wide grin. Her red lipstick such a stark contrast to her jet black hair. "Oh, come on. Who can resist the strong silent type? Am I right?"

Recalling all too vividly what occurred that morning, I couldn't hide my smirk.

"And those dimples. What girl doesn't drool at the sight?" She burst into a fit of adorable giggles. There was something about her retro look and big smile that instantly put me at ease. "You've gotta see the way girls around here throw themselves at him. It's downright pathetic."

I lifted an inquisitive brow. "You?"

She shook her head. "I'm a realist. He's too much man for little ol' me."

I smiled. She had no idea how right she was.

"Poor guy. You can tell he wants to keep his private life private, but these girls make it impossible. If you ask me, he'd rather have nothing to do with any of them. Especially since you showed up."

Her words elicited an unspoken satisfaction.

"People say he's this underground boxer." She lowered her voice, unnecessarily since the room remained empty. "But no one's ever been able to find out where he fights. We just see the cuts and bruises after a match."

I raised a brow. Boxer?

"Now, he's like this knight in shining armor over you."

I wanted to tell her she had no idea, but I let her continue, appreciating any information she'd willing share about the elusive Hayden Martin.

"Don't get me wrong, what happened to you sucked. But I think most of us would've traded places in a heartbeat if it meant Hayden would've carried us out of the dining hall in front of half the school. And then watching him storm back in and threaten Taylor—"

I nearly dropped my bag. "He what?"

"Oh, yeah. You didn't know?"

I could only shake my head as students filtered in for the next class.

She lowered her voice again. "He threatened her, then smashed her phone against the wall. It was classic. And he didn't stop at her. He turned to the rest of the room and threatened anyone who had the picture or intended to share it."

My eyes widened, unable to do anything but stand utterly dumbfounded. I should've realized when he left me in his truck something had happened. But at the time, I was so distraught I couldn't think of anything but my own humiliation.

"I'm Sophia by the way."

"Alex."

Her bright lips slipped into a crooked smile. "Yeah. I know. Come on. You're sticking with me today, girl. My friends are good people. They probably didn't even open the message. And if they did, you'd never know."

"Thanks." It sounded so insignificant. Like it wasn't enough to express what I really felt.

After my final class of the day, I lagged behind to speak with the professor about his lesson. By the time he was done, the building had cleared out. Okay, so maybe it had been cowardly, but cut a girl some slack. The day had been difficult enough.

A beam of sunlight shone through the exit door into the empty first floor hallway. I hurried toward the light. I was almost home free.

"Alex."

Tension grabbed hold of my body, stopping me cold. I closed my eyes, hoping to God it wasn't who I thought it was. I pulled in a deep breath, then twisted around.

Nervous laughter fled my lips as I watched Professor Smith approach, her clasped hands twisting.

"Just wanted to let you know rehearsals start tomorrow."

"I don't—

She shook her head. "Please don't do it."

My brows shot up.

"No, that came out wrong," she explained. "Please don't feel like you can't stay in the competition. You gave the best audition this year. You earned your spot."

I chewed on my bottom lip. While Professor Smith would've been horrified by Taylor's duplicity, I couldn't tell her the truth. It wouldn't help. I wasn't sure anything would. "Can I let you know?"

"I wish you wouldn't think too hard about it. You're already in."

## HAYDEN

I sat in the parking lot on the open tailgate of my truck, my foot bouncing like it had a mind of its own. Alex should've been home thirty minutes ago.

Down deep I knew her delay was only partially to blame for my nerves. After the way things got intense in my bedroom, I had no clue what to expect. What to say. How to act. She'd been through hell. Could I really expect her to make rational decisions?

I followed her lead at school, keeping my distance. But I stayed close enough to know if she needed me. She handled herself like a champ, ignoring the stares and whispers. That took major balls. Some of the toughest guys I knew would've snapped under such scrutiny. But not Alex.

I just wished she wasn't so stubborn and set on doing it alone. I would've driven in with her. Stayed by her side. Told off the masses.

But I got it. She needed to prove she could do it.

I suspected her courage and show of independence had a little something to do with me. More like me telling her we couldn't be seen together.

The purring of an expensive car's engine sent my head twisting. Alex's BMW zipped into the lot, taking the spot next to mine.

Flashing me a big goofy smile, she stepped out. Her sunglasses concealed her pretty eyes. I didn't like not seeing them. They were always so expressive, telling me what her words wouldn't.

My tailgate dipped as she hopped onto it, bumping her shoulder into mine. "Hey."

I matched her grin. "Have a nice day?"

She lifted the sunglasses to the top of her head. "The morning wasn't so bad."

I arched a brow. "Wasn't so bad, huh?"

She shrugged. "Mediocre."

I laughed, deliberately eyeing her up and down. "Well, you made it through the rest of the day unscathed I see."

She nodded, her eyes lifting to the cloudless sky. It must've been the first opportunity she had all day to escape the chaos. "But, as you can see, Hayden *Martin*, the day isn't over yet."

Loving the way my name rolled off her tongue, my smile widened. Since meeting Alex, I'd never smiled so much in my entire life. She brought it out of me in spades. That and some other things that were completely new for me.

"I did run into a little problem on my way out of school."

The muscle in my jaw tightened, my molars grinding. Who did I need to hunt down? "That why you're running late?" My fists clenched at my sides.

She nodded, her eyes narrowing. "Were you out here waiting for me?"

"Maybe."

Her smile stretched wide. "Good."

Her excitement over something so small caused my fists to unclench, my anger to ease, and my body to relax.

"Anyway..." she bumped my shoulder again. "Professor Smith really wants me to stay in the competition."

"You should."

Her head pulled back, jarred by my agreement. "I'm not so sure about that." Her attention moved to the shifting trees. The late September days had grown slightly cooler, and the coastal breezes had given life to the landscape. The wind stole a few of her waves and whipped them across her face. She let them blow, her eyes still focused on the scenery. "Taylor must have other pictures, huh?"

I couldn't lie. Especially when trust and honesty were what Alex needed most from me. So when her eyes shifted to mine, I twisted my lips and nodded regrettably.

"So if I don't do what she wants, she'll keep sending them out until I'm driven back to Austin." She wasn't asking. She knew the chances were high it could happen. She gnawed on her bottom lip. I could practically see the wheels turning. "How much worse could they really be?"

*No. Fucking. Way.*

I stared at the ballsy girl seated beside me. If anyone could pull off the gutsy move, Alex could. She'd already faced everyone at school knowing what they'd seen. And here she sat. In one piece.

"I mean, what are they gonna get next time? A different angle? They've already seen all of me."

The severity of her words jolted me in the center of my chest. Looking her dead in the eyes, I shook my head, not wanting her to feel any more exposed than she already did. "They'll never see all of you, Alex."

She stared back with narrowed eyes. I couldn't decide if she believed me or not. She probably thought it was another attempt to get in her pants. But if she only knew how truly amazing I thought she was, she'd realize something completely foreign was happening to me.

Then, as if snapping out of a trance, she blinked. "Spoken by the ever elusive Hayden Martin."

I grinned. "Elusive, maybe. Honest, absolutely."

Alex tilted her head, eyeing me in what might be described as admiration. Her eyes were so expectant, eager. They took my breath away. She inched closer. I hoped she was giving me the green light to continue where we left off that morning.

My eyes dropped to her lips. I couldn't wait any longer. I needed to taste them.

The phone buzzing in my pocket stopped both of us.

Alex's face drained of color as her eyes widened.

I pulled back, my eyes locked on hers. The intensity present seconds before had been replaced by fear. Fear of what awaited us on the phone.

Alex nodded, giving me the go ahead to look.

I inhaled a deep breath as I slipped the phone from my pocket. Alex stared down at it, undoubtedly sending out a silent prayer.

I swiped my finger across the screen. *Oh, thank God.* A text from Remy. I never thought I'd be so glad to get a text telling me I had to hit up some scumbag.

My eyes lifted to Alex's. She let out a long shaky breath.

Then, at the same time, we burst into laughter.

Alex fell back into the bed of my truck. I followed her lead, stretching out beside her. Our chests bounced in relieved amusement as we lay there with the sky above us even brighter than normal. I guess relief did that shit to you. Made you appreciate the little things a tiny bit more.

Or, maybe it was just the Alex effect.

I waited a long time before letting my head fall to the side. I hated having to blow her off. But I had no choice. "I've got to run out for a little while. Will you be around when I get back?"

Alex nodded as her head fell to the side.

I hoped like hell my words weren't the cause of the disappointment in her eyes.

# CHAPTER SIXTEEN

## ALEX

The heels of my boots echoed all the way down the steep theater aisle. Everyone in the seats turned to stare. I hoped they were simply sizing up their competition. But the way their probing eyes examined me, I'd say they were seeing the picture instead of me.

If that wasn't bad enough, Taylor sat in the front row, looking me dead in the eyes like she didn't single-handedly destroy my reputation in a matter of seconds.

*Bitch.*

She probably expected to steal my spot when I didn't show up. But I did. And I flashed her a grin as I dropped into a seat on the opposite side of the theater, letting her know my presence was payback. Nothing but payback.

"Hey, girl." Sophia dropped down beside me

"Hey. I didn't see your name on the list," I whispered, trying not to interrupt Professor Smith who began spouting off instructions.

Sophia shrugged, sending her black ponytails bouncing. "I'm a woman of many talents." She dropped her heavy backpack onto the floor with a thud.

Professor Smith paused, searching out the distraction.

Sophie wiggled her fingers at her before whispering to me. "No, actually, I'm not. Smith roped me in this morning. I'm in her script analysis class."

"Do you sing?"

"Hell no. I'm a stagehand—whatever that is. But I can add it to my ever-expanding resume. Works for me."

I smiled, meaning it more than Sophia could ever understand.

Maybe the whole situation wouldn't be so bad after all.

Friday's late afternoon sun sat on the horizon while Sophia and I sat fully clothed on lounge chairs by the pool enjoying the light breeze and each other's company. She may have only been five-foot-two, but she turned out to be my very own bodyguard, sticking by my side whenever she could.

"Hey," a deep voice greeted us.

I sat up and glanced over my shoulder, knowing exactly who I'd find. What I didn't expect was him to be shirtless with white and blue board shorts hanging low on his hips. But I wasn't complaining. Neither was Sophia whose mouth hung in her lap.

"I've gotta go." She jumped to her feet as if Hayden's presence was too much to handle.

I grabbed hold of her arm. "It's okay. You don't have to leave."

Sophia winked. "Yes, I do." She slipped free of my hold and raced through the gate, shimmying around Hayden who passed through at the same time.

She probably thought she was doing me a favor by giving us some time alone, since I mentioned how he'd disappeared over the last few days. "Talk to you later," I called.

She gave a quick wave over her head as she jumped into her powder-blue VW Bug and zipped out of the lot.

Hayden sat down on the chair beside me smelling of fresh shower. He shoved back pieces of wet hair that poked up all over. "Was it something I said?"

My cheeks heated, likely flaming on the outside. Would I ever get used to him? His masculine scent? His body? "No. She had to get going."

It was difficult to remain composed when I knew how it felt to have my body wrapped up with his, pressed against it, consumed by it. And how it felt when his tongue explored my mouth with long luscious sweeps. Sensing my body temperature rising, I shook off the image.

"Sorry I've been MIA this week."

I shrugged like it was no big deal, though nothing would have pleased me more than to know where he'd been and what he'd been doing.

"How was rehearsal?"

I shrugged, hating how quickly he changed the subject.

"So, has Taylor tried offing any of the other contestants?"

I choked out a laugh.

## HAYDEN

I sat mesmerized by the laughing girl beside me.

Most would've dropped out of the competition knowing the leverage Taylor held. But not my little survivor. She faced the bitch head on.

I felt like a total dick not being around for most of the week. But Remy had my ass working. Not only shaking down deadbeats, but moving money between Cooper's businesses like we did back when we were younger.

Once I started college and Remy was released from juvie, Cooper gave him more responsibilities. It wasn't like he had anything else occupying his time. He loved his new duties. He wanted more. His ultimate goal was to work his way up the ranks in Cooper's organization.

That definitely wasn't a long-term goal for me.

Alex waved her hands in front of my face. "Hayden."

Her voice snapped me back to reality.

"I asked you a question."

My face must've shown my confusion because she continued.

"I asked if you'd heard about tomorrow night's formal?"

I scoffed. "If you hadn't noticed, I don't really do school functions."

Her eyes cast down. Her fingers played with the hem of her striped shirt. "You just sign other people up for them."

My eyes narrowed. Had I missed something? Was she pulling some female shit where she expected me to read her mind? And what was so interesting about her damn shirt she wouldn't look at me?

"I think I might go." She said it so softly I had to lean in to hear her. "A bunch of the contestants and stagehands are gonna meet up there. I don't really know anyone, so—"

"You should go." I sat up so my legs straddled the chair. "You'll have a good time."

Alex nodded. "I wasn't sure what to tell them..." her voice trailed off as she sat up as well. "Like about you."

*Jesus Christ.*

She wanted *me* to go. But she had to know. I wasn't that guy.

My eyes shifted to the idle pool—my destination until I got distracted by Alex.

Since moving in, that's what she'd become. A major distraction. It wasn't her fault. She didn't even know it. Or maybe she did. Who the hell knew? But I wasn't used to distractions, and it was just a matter of time before she got me into a shitload of trouble.

My eyes moved to the parking lot. Was that Remy's Mustang pulling out? I watched until the silver car disappeared from view, then slipped my phone from my pocket. He would've called if I didn't answer my door. And he hadn't.

A soft hand settled on the back of my shoulder. My body stilled. If I wasn't so fucked in the head, I would've left it there. Instead, I jumped to my feet leaving Alex's hand dangling in the air.

"I've been wondering what that was," she said casually. But as she settled back into her chair, disappointment shone in her eyes.

"Now you know." It came out harsher than intended. But I was pissed she saw it.

She tilted her head. "It's sad."

I glanced to my bare feet. She was right. My tattoo was sad. I'd gotten it when all I knew was darkness. Loss. Anger. Guilt.

"Mai Più?" she inquired.

I nodded at her reference to the words scrolled in black through the image.

"Maybe someday you'll tell me what that means."

I shrugged, hoping I could change the subject. But I didn't need to. Alex stood up and walked to the building, disappearing inside without another glance.

So that's how it felt.

## ALEX

I lay awake all night wondering what provoked Hayden to get a heart pierced with a dagger forever inked on his back. And what was the point of the Italian words for *Never Again* scrolled through it?

When I told him I hoped he'd tell me what the words meant, I wanted him to tell me the significance. Never again what? But the way he pulled away when I touched him told me one thing. I'd never find out.

I was *so* stupid. I made the ridiculous agreement. I agreed to be friends, or whatever we were, and not ask questions or be seen together. That's why when I gave him the perfect opportunity to ask me not to go to the formal—or to join me—he didn't. He followed his rules.

Why did I ever think I'd be able to do the same?

Maybe I was stupid for bringing up the dance. Truthfully, I felt like he'd abandoned me the last few days. *Needy. I know.* Sure, he'd apologized, but not seeing him made me question what was going on with us. Maybe mentioning the dance had been my pathetic attempt to get a reaction.

I huffed out my confusion. I'd never fall asleep with my mind such a mess, so I headed into the kitchen. It was after one when I settled on the sofa with my warm glass of milk. Again.

Just as I lifted the remote to find something to watch, laughter trickled in from the hallway. I jumped up and moved to the door, lowering my eye to the peephole.

Hayden stumbled by with two bottle blondes giggling at his sides. I watched in shock, as their hands traveled all over his body as he struggled to unlock his door.

Why were they touching him? Why was he *letting* them?

My heart sank.

He got the door open, and the blondes slipped inside. Before following them in, he glanced over his shoulder and eyed my door.

Did he want me to see them?

Anger fused with embarrassment.

I'd been so stupid. Leopards didn't change their spots. I should've seen it coming. I'd been played for a fool. There was no misconstruing it. The truth slapped me across the face, and it was time I paid attention. Time I saw Hayden for who he really was.

My knees wobbled as I turned from the peephole. With my emotions in complete disarray, I sank to the floor.

Maybe I was to blame.

We didn't even have a real relationship. I'm the one who let myself believe we did. Believe there was something else there. Something that could grow and turn into more. I'm the one who became too involved. The one who let him in. The one who let him rescue me when I should've been rescuing myself. The one who'd been fooling myself.

Hayden never promised me more. Sure, he said he needed *this*. But maybe I mistook that for needing *me*.

I'd read somewhere that after traumatic experiences, people did crazy things like latch on to things that could potentially make them happy. Potentially erase the pain. Potentially replace the sadness. Some chose drugs. Some chose liquor. I chose Hayden.

I ignored the warning signs. The unanswered questions. The secrets. I held onto the good moments that were few and far between.

A soft tapping pulsed against my back before I even heard the knocking. My eyes shot around my aunt's dark living room. Had I imagined it? I'd been doing that a lot. Imagining things that weren't there.

But when the tapping continued, I crept to my feet and checked the peephole.

With my anger beyond the boiling point, I threw open the door. "What?" I spat.

Hayden glanced up, his bloodshot eyes secured on mine.

I waited for him to speak. To explain his actions. To apologize for leading me on. But he just stared at me.

In the past the sensation accompanying that heady gaze sent my heart racing, but now, as he stood no more than two feet away, it was as if miles separated us.

This time the unspoken words spoke volumes.

I wouldn't play his game any longer. He needed to actually say the words.

But his silence stretched on.

I waited him out. I wasn't going to sleep after what I'd witnessed. What I knew lingered behind his door. I had all night. Besides, he's the one who showed up in the middle of the night at my door.

His long sleeve gray Henley over his strong arms and faded jeans low on his hips showed a man. His defeated expression showed a sad little boy I could almost feel sorry for. *Almost.*

"I don't want you going to that dance."

I blinked hard. "What?"

He grasped both sides of the door frame and leaned in. His words were slurred, and his breath reeked of cheap beer. "I don't. Want you. Going to that dance."

"Hayden, you're drunk. Why don't we talk in the morning? After your guests leave. Where are they anyway? Naked in your bed?"

One corner of his mouth lifted, but not in amusement. The anger in his eyes made that abundantly clear. But why was *he* angry? If anyone had the right to be, it was me. "You're driving me fucking crazy," he growled.

*Oh no he did not.* "Me?" Okay, so I knew it was useless to argue with a drunk person, but it needed to be said. "I'm driving *you* crazy? Let me tell you what, buddy. You're on the crazy train. Actually, you're driving it." I threw my arms out at my sides. "I'm right here. I have been since day one, and you've done nothing about it. Oh, wait. You brought home two skanks whose faces you won't even see, *after* you said you didn't do that anymore."

His glassy eyes stared me down, his voice just above a whisper. "You're not going to that dance."

I dropped my head in frustration. "Okay, so you clearly didn't hear a single word I said." I grabbed hold of the doorknob. "Good night, Hayden." I swung the door shut, but the toe of his shoe stopped it.

He pushed it open, causing me to step back. He sauntered by me like I'd asked him in and dropped down on the sofa, extending his legs and crossing them at his ankles.

I stood in the doorway looking down at him in utter bewilderment. "First of all," I whispered. "My aunt's sleeping. Second, you have two girls in your apartment waiting to make your night."

He spread his arms over the back of the sofa. "Come sit down."

"You're crazy."

"Yeah, I think we already covered that. Something about me driving the train."

I closed the door and walked over to the loveseat across from him, avoiding close contact at all costs. But without warning, Hayden flew off the sofa and yanked me down beside him, wrapping his arm around me and drawing me into his side.

"Hayden?"

He tightened his grasp, preventing me from escaping.

Why, beyond all common sense, did I like it? Why did I feel at home with his scent filling my senses and his strong arms wrapped around me? *Ugh.* He was so damn frustrating. *And* he brought two girls home! Two girls who were still in his apartment.

The thought sobered my temporarily shaky judgment. "Well this was nice. But I'm sure you don't want to keep your girls waiting." I tried pulling free.

I could feel the slight bouncing of his chest in silent laughter as he held me tighter. "Why do you do this?"

I huffed. "Do what?"

"Make me feel things."

"Things? What kind of things?"

"Things I'm not used to feeling."

My traitorous heart sputtered. Why was he doing this *now*? Did he even know what he was saying? Would he even remember come morning? I couldn't stop myself. "I didn't know I was doing that."

Hayden dropped a soft kiss to the top of my head, letting his lips linger for a long while. So long I assumed he passed out. "Oh, you know alright."

I huffed out a breath, partly because he was cutting off my circulation and partly because I was so damn exasperated by his Jekyll and Hyde behavior I couldn't take it any longer. "Then why? Why'd you bring them home?"

The silence was deafening.

Then he sighed, a long drawn-out sigh reserved for no-win situations. Battles you could never even dream of winning. "It's what I do. I screw up everything good in my life. Everything worth holding on to."

# CHAPTER SEVENTEEN

## ALEX

I jolted up, my eyes shooting around my aunt's sunny living room where I was sprawled out the length of the sofa. Hayden was gone. There wasn't any sign he'd ever even been there.

Had he?

"Fall asleep on the sofa again?"

My head whipped around. My aunt stood in the kitchen dropping slices of bread into the toaster. "I guess so."

"Can I get you something to eat?"

She wore yoga pants and a T-shirt, so I knew she was on her way to the gym. I could fend for myself. "No, thanks."

She walked into the living room and sat down on the arm of the sofa. "Can I ask you something?"

"Sure."

The uneasy look in her eyes told me she was treading lightly. "Would you like to come next time I go up to your parents' vineyard? Or maybe Austin?"

The mere mention of the vineyard and Austin brought on an onslaught of anguish. The memories. The pain. The people. The heartache. How could I ever be expected to return to places that were no longer home? "I don't think so."

She nodded, like she already anticipated my response. "Well, you just tell me when you're ready. Obviously, there's a lot to be done. I was going to grab some of your things, but I didn't want to go riffling through your personal effects."

"Thanks." That word again. This woman single-handedly took charge of not only caring for me, but running my parents' vineyard, settling their estate, and maintaining their home—after what they'd done to her. And all I could say was thanks.

Unfortunately, her broaching the subject at all gave me the sinking feeling that once I turned twenty-one in a couple weeks, she expected me to take over those responsibilities. I wished she'd realize that nothing involving me getting dropped back into my old life, surrounded by people who hated me and memories of my parents at every turn, was part of my plan.

But where did that leave me?

In an apartment with a woman I barely knew. Waking up on a sofa after being abandoned by a guy I barely knew. A guy who probably regretted his drunken confessions.

He was probably with the sluts right now. Unless, of course, I constructed the entire night in my head. Then I just walked the fine line between stable and crazy.

Could things get any worse?

I fell back onto the sofa and closed my eyes, needing time to regroup. Time to get my head back in check. Time to slip away from the here and now.

The moment was short-lived, interrupted by a persistent knocking on the front door. A gust of wind accompanied my aunt as she moved by me.

"Oh, good, you're up."

My eyes snapped open. Hayden, with damp hair and board shorts on, stood in the hallway eyeing me over my aunt's shoulder with a devilish grin.

My aunt twisted toward me with inquisitive eyes. I wanted to shrug my confusion, but waited to hear what Hayden planned to say.

"I hope you don't mind, but I'm taking Alex to the beach."

"You are?" my aunt and I asked.

Hayden flashed that slow sexy grin. "I am."

I stared across the room into the depths of his blue eyes, like they spoke something only I could understand. Maybe I had it right. Maybe he really was crazy.

## HAYDEN

We hit minimal traffic on the highway to the coast. Though we'd been in my truck for ten minutes, Alex hadn't spoken a single word. She just gazed out her window at the passing scenery like I wasn't even there.

Picking the perfect time to break the silence, my stomach growled like a caged bear.

"What? No greasy feast this morning?" Alex's eyes remained out the window.

I peeked over, taking in the strapless cotton dress she wore over a teal bikini that tied behind her neck. I couldn't wait to see the rest of it. "Why would I need a greasy feast?"

"Oh, I don't know. To help your hangover."

I laughed. "I'm not hung over."

She scoffed.

"I'm not."

When I woke in Alex's apartment, with her snuggled into my side, my head felt foggy. But when I found those two girls in my bed, the haze wore off and the night's events came flooding back.

I guess I couldn't blame Alex for her silence. I would've given me the cold shoulder, too.

At least I had one thing going for me. If she really hated me, really thought there was no redemption for my dark soul, she never would've agreed to come along with me.

Out of the corner of my eye I could see her watching curiously as we passed the beach entrance without turning into the lot. I drove another hundred yards then turned onto the dead end road at the end, parking my truck by a solid oak fence that blocked the view of the beach.

"What are we doing?"

I slipped my truck into park. "Erasing your memory."

"Once wasn't enough?"

I held back a smile. I knew the girl I'd met back in August, the one I'd come to know—come to care about—was in there somewhere. I'd take a small glimpse if that's all I got. "We're gonna replace those bad memories with some new ones."

Alex turned toward me. And for the first time that day, her features softened and gratitude shone in her eyes.

"Don't say it." I jumped out of the truck.

She slipped out the passenger side, calling over the bed of my truck. "I wasn't going to."

I cocked my head.

"I swear. I'm working on an alternative phrase."

I furrowed my brows. "An alternative phrase?"

She nodded. "One that means more."

I grabbed the small cooler from the bed of my truck. "How 'bout you're swell?" I offered like a true smartass.

She arched a brow. "You're swell?"

I flashed a smile, the one that never failed to get girls to come home with me.

Alex looked unfazed, swinging her beach bag over her shoulder. "It has potential."

"Is that your way of saying it sucks?"

She shook her head. "I appreciate you trying to help. You're swell."

## ALEX

The ocean glistened like a magical paradise as I stood up to my waist in the water. The sun blazed down on my shoulders as my fingertips grazed the calm surface. Hayden was right. I needed to make new memories at a place that now held so much darkness.

Out of nowhere, water splashed into my face, causing me to gulp down a mouthful of disgusting salt water. My eyes jumped around, seeking the sound of Hayden's laughter. "You jerk," I choked out, wiping the briny water from my eyes and mouth.

Before I could retaliate, he ducked under the water and disappeared. I spun around, searching the surface. Though the water stretched as far as the eye could see, the water around me was clear enough to see both sea life *and* human predator.

But where was he?

I got my answer by means of a drenched back. I spun around, laughing at Hayden's playfulness, but he'd disappeared again.

My eyes scanned the surface as I spun in a slow circle. There was no way I'd let him surprise me again. But like a fish, he stayed under far longer than most humans could.

Suddenly, goose bumps scrambled up my arms.

I froze.

Warm breath traveled over the wet skin on the back of my neck. Even with salt water everywhere, Hayden's aloe scent overpowered it.

This time he didn't splash me. This time he placed his hands on my wet hips, gliding them up and down my skin. Then, without warning, he locked his arms around my stomach, pulled my back to his chest, and yanked me down into the water with him. I let out a yelp before being tugged under.

I loved the fun, carefree Hayden. He'd been like that since we arrived—scratch that. Since he had his hands on my ass to boost me over the fence to our own private beach. He claimed to know the guy who owned the property. And since he'd gone away for the weekend, we had the beach to ourselves. But I wasn't a fool. We scaled a fence and didn't have a key to the house. We clearly weren't invited guests.

I finally escaped Hayden's clutches and hurried out of the water and over to our towels spread out on the hot sand. I sat down, reclining on my elbows so the sun could soak up the beads of water covering my body.

Hayden stayed in the water, swimming laps and floating on his back. I wondered if the beach held fond memories for him. Or if the tranquil setting just relaxed his serious side.

As much as I appreciated the view, appreciated watching him unwind, appreciated him trying to help me forget, I'd waited all morning for him to mention the previous night.

Maybe he didn't remember. Maybe he'd been too drunk to mean what he said.

Hayden finally emerged from the water, strutting toward me with innate confidence. The sun sparkled down on his soaked hair, and the water clung like a second skin to every ripple in his chest and indentation in his arms.

"You thirsty?" he asked, sitting down beside me.

I faked a grimace. "You planning on serving me something in a red cup?" With a grin, he reached inside his small cooler and handed me a sealed bottle of water. I unscrewed the cap and took a long refreshing sip. "You're swell."

He flashed a crooked smile. It had to be the panty-dropper smile. "It does have a certain ring to it, doesn't it?"

I turned my attention back to the beautiful view. Last time, the beach and its inhabitants were cloaked in darkness. I remember thinking it was so peaceful, when I couldn't even see fifty yards out. Now I could see for miles where the shimmering surface met the blue horizon.

Cameron had pointed out a lighthouse, but I could only see a faint light. Now I could distinguish the tall white structure in all its glory, protecting sailors on their long journeys. At least today I didn't need a lighthouse to protect me. I had Hayden. "Nothing's going to ruin how much I love the beach. I could stay here forever."

Hayden pointed down the shore. "We could probably set you up a nice little tent down there."

"Yeah, right. You'd be lost if I didn't live across the hall."

He reclined on his elbows so our shoulders were even. "Oh, you think so?"

"I know so. Where else would you show up drunk knocking?"

"Drunk knocking?"

My eyes squeezed shut. I wanted him to remember on his own. There goes that. "Yeah, some people drunk dial. You drunk knock." I glanced to him. His eyes, with their damp lashes clumped together, were locked on mine. It seemed like the perfect moment to discuss what occurred the previous night or make out until we were both delirious.

My eyes dared him to make the first move, but his seemed to be doing the same. We stayed in a stare down, our chests rising and falling, for a long intense moment.

"So, how'd you get the girls out of your apartment?" Sarcasm spewed from my mouth so casually sometimes it surprised even me.

His lips tightened. His eyes broke from mine and stared out at the horizon. "You weren't supposed to see that."

"Why not?"

He shrugged.

"That's not much of an answer."

He looked back, his eyes searching my face.

"Say it," I urged.

"What?"

"Whatever it is you want to say. I'm here. I'll listen. I'll tell you you're stupid. I'll make revolted faces. I'll disagree with you. Just say *something*."

He sat up, wrapping his arms around his knees. It left me with a view of his back and that disturbing tattoo. "I don't want you going to that dance tonight."

A frustrated breath whooshed out of me. We were back to that? "Seriously, Hayden. You can't tell me not to go."

He clenched his fist around his water, crackling the plastic bottle. Then with a scary roar, he hurled it down the beach.

I sat up, pushing myself back on my towel. Sure, his temper unsettled me. But the fact that he ignored my question about the girls, and then had the nerve to get mad at *me* for going to the dance, gave me the green light to unleash my own anger. "What are you so upset about? You didn't have to see me bring two guys home."

His eyes remained on the horizon, but his jaw clenched, his teeth grinding together. "I slept with *you*, didn't I?"

"Did you? Because you weren't there when I woke up." It took everything in me not to get up and leave, liked he'd done to me on more than one occasion. But for some reason, some reason I couldn't control, I needed him to understand. "Hayden, you can't not want me, but get angry when—"

His eyes shot over his shoulder. "I never said I didn't want you."

A tidal wave swelled in my belly. And while I loved his vulnerability, his words had the opposite effect on my head. Confusing me. Frustrating me. Infuriating me. I couldn't take anymore. "Stop it. Just stop it."

Vertical lines creased between his brows. His damn puppy dog eyes were enough to send me over the edge. "What?"

I threw my hand out at him. "Stop looking at me like that. Stop saying nice things to me. Stop being possessive over me. Stop treating me like I'm something precious then ignore me at school. And stop *rescuing* me." The last I wanted to take back the second it left my lips. Because if he didn't rescue me, who would?

He looked hurt. *He* looked hurt. The irony.

"I was stupid to agree to your terms. Agree to not ask questions or be seen with you. Because that's just not me."

He looked genuinely perplexed. "Then why did you?"

I drank in his beautiful face. Sometimes he looked like a lost little boy in need of love. This was one of those times. "Isn't it obvious?"

He shook his head, his eyes staring blankly at me for a long moment. Then, as if I'd explained it to his satisfaction, he sat back on his elbows. His attention shifted back to the water. "I'm taking you."

My head recoiled. "What?"

"To the dance."

"Now I know you're crazy."

He shot me a sidelong glance. "You don't want to go with me?"

I watched the seagulls swoop overhead, as my mind worked to keep up with his split personalities. I looked over at him. "Why would I?"

His incredulous gaze told me I wasn't at all convincing.

"You'd have to get dressed up."

His eyes swept over my body in a slow seductive sweep. "I own a tie."

A traitorous shiver rolled through me. "People would see us."

He shrugged, his eyes studying my legs. "So?"

I swallowed, his inspection causing ripples in my stomach. "You'd have to dance with me."

He nodded, though his eyes zoned in on my stomach. "You don't think I can dance?"

"I'd have to touch you."

He nodded while his eyes moved over my chest. "I hope so."

*Sweet Jesus.* "You might have to kiss me goodnight."

His eyes focused on my lips. "Oh, sweetheart, you can count on that."

A smile curved both our lips.

His eyes finally met mine, blazing with amusement.

And for the first time all day, the silence wasn't uncomfortable at all.

# CHAPTER EIGHTEEN

## HAYDEN

I stared into my bathroom mirror, tying my navy tie—the only one I owned. I still couldn't believe I agreed to go to the lame-ass formal. It didn't start for another two hours, but since it usually took me that long to tie a tie, I figured I'd get it out of the way.

Unable to calm my damn nerves after returning from the beach, I'd taken off, clearing my head one of the few ways I knew how. Now my shoulder was throbbing like a motherfucker.

My phone vibrated on the sink. I let go of my tie and grabbed it. *Shit.* I had a job.

Telling Remy *no* would cause too many questions. But telling him the truth would be worse. It would put Alex on his radar. A place she didn't need to be.

I dialed his number, speaking before he had the chance to. "Can we do this tomorrow? I have plans."

"Plans?" I could hear the irritation in his voice. "What plans?"

"Plans I can't break."

Remy paused. "What time?"

"Seven."

"Tell whoever she is she can wait. I'll have you back by eight." He hung up before I could respond.

*Dammit.* He knew I'd show. I'd never let him down.

## ALEX

My red sequin dress hung from the bathroom door, sparkling in the fluorescent lights. I'd spotted it in a boutique window a couple weeks before, never imagining I'd have any use for it. But after the beach, I drove over and bought it.

I applied the final touches on my face—a little pink blush, some mascara, and gloss. I checked the time on my cell noticing a text from Hayden. Ripples attacked my stomach. I wished the mere thought of him didn't make me such a stupid girl.

**Gonna be late. Eight the latest.**

My body deflated. Why weren't things ever easy with him?

I walked into the living room and dropped down onto the sofa, preventing myself from redoing my makeup or messing up my hair.

I guess I couldn't be too disappointed. What was an hour when I had all night to be seen with him? Dance with him? Touch him?

At seven thirty, I changed into my dress. It stopped well above my knees and clung to all the right places. It made me feel beautiful.

Since it was strapless, I slipped the diamond and ruby necklace my parents gave me for my eighteenth birthday around my neck. My eyes welled.

If my parents were still alive, they would've insisted on meeting Hayden before the formal. Sure, I would've been living off-campus with my friends, but they would've made a special trip for the event.

I could see the whole scene playing out. Them greeting him at the door. My mother taking lots of embarrassing pictures. My dad pulling him aside to give him "the talk." It would've been hilarious to watch Hayden squirm under my dad's perceptive dark eyes. My mother on the other hand, would've been gushing over his good looks and telling me what a cute couple we made. She never liked Preston, so she would've been pushing for Hayden.

I inhaled a deep cleansing breath, giving myself a moment to mourn what could have been for a little while longer. Then I dabbed my eyes with a tissue, reapplied my mascara, and headed out to the living room to wait for Hayden.

Alone.

## HAYDEN

My dashboard clock read seven forty-five. Remy wasn't ready when I showed up at his house. The next thing I knew we were headed to some pool hall in another town, a good half hour from my apartment.

Alex was gonna *kill* me.

We walked into the seedy dive. All eyes turned our way. Fucking great. Bikers. Their snarls indicated they didn't appreciate us on their turf. And to make matters worse, the scantily clad girls huddled on the bar stools watching them play pool ogled us like fresh meat.

Ignoring the unwanted attention, we sauntered over to the bar in the center of the room like we just stopped by for a beer. The burly bartender in the wife beater stepped up to us.

"Two Buds," Remy ordered, his eyes scanning the room.

I settled on a stool, figuring Remy would tell me which guy we were there for. But instead, he grabbed his beer from the bartender and took off, stopping to talk to different groups as he circled the room. Some of the guys clearly knew him, and others probably knew of him because of his ties to Cooper. But none of them looked happy to see him.

A redhead in a low-cut black top and tiny jean skirt slid onto the empty stool beside me. "Hi," she purred. "Haven't seen you here before."

I took a long pull of my beer, keeping my eyes on Remy. "Haven't been here before."

"You looking to have some fun?"

"Nope."

She ran her fingertips up and down my forearm. "You've got no idea what you're missing."

Ignoring her and her damn hand on my arm, I watched Remy follow a lanky bald guy in a leather vest out the back door.

"Erica," an angry voice shouted across the room, sending my head snapping in its direction.

A guy with a shaved head and snake tattoos wrapped around both arms advanced. He looked about ready to kill the woman beside me.

"What the hell are you doing?" he asked her, but his eyes slid to mine.

"What's it look like?" she responded.

*Oh, no fucking way.* I leapt to my feet and headed to the same door Remy exited through.

"Smart move, pretty boy. Get out before you need to be carried out," he shouted.

I shoved open the back door, sending a gust of cool air wafting inside. *Shit.* Remy twisted on the ground, shielding his head from the bald guy who stomped relentlessly on his chest.

I bolted toward them, grabbing the guy from behind and pinning his arms to his sides. His long legs kicked out in front of him in an attempt to escape my hold. "Relax, man. Relax."

Remy struggled to his feet, staggering back a foot or two. I tightened my grip on the guy, knowing he wasn't finished with Remy yet.

Out of nowhere, pain ripped through me like nothing I'd ever felt before. Shards of broken glass rained over my head, splitting my scalp in two. I released the guy and cradled my throbbing head. As I sank to my knees, broken bottle crunched beneath me.

I brought my hands around to see how much blood gushed, but a heel to my back sent me face-planting into the concrete. I braced my hands on the glass-covered ground, but heavy boots kicked me from all directions, preventing me from getting up.

I covered my head, steeling myself and enduring the attack on my body until I could find a time to take out their legs. But that just left my throbbing shoulder unprotected.

My attackers showed no mercy. Their blows alternated between the right and left. They were unyielding, beating every inch of my body. Their voices were muffled, all meshing together. I caught *my girl* and *Cooper.* Then something inside my body literally snapped.

*Holy fuck.*

Like a vacuum, the air sucked right out of my lungs.

Stabbing pain shot through my sides. My shoulder burned as if on fire. I groaned loudly, but it didn't stop them. They were driven. Angry. Psychotic.

After a fierce blow to my head, I felt myself slipping. Fading. Teetering between consciousness and darkness. If they kicked one more time in just the right spot, they'd surely kill me.

*"Fuck, Hayden. You probably killed him."*

I couldn't shake off the image this time. It's what my life had come to. I'd taken a life and now mine sat on the brink. I deserved their rage. Their hatred.

I deserved to die.

"Hey!" a distant voice shouted.

Feet shuffled. Footsteps withdrew. Sounds grew further and further away.

Until nothing.

Thunderous roars whooshed through my ears. My pounding chest heaved. Sweat drenched every part of me. Pain engulfed me whole.

I cracked open my eyes. Black spots clouded my vision. I could see enough to know Remy and I were alone in the alley. Both on the ground. Both writhing in something worse than pain.

Blood covered Remy's face. His shredded T-shirt hung off his skinny body. We needed to get the hell out of there. My head whipped around seeking an exit. Déjà vu stopped me cold. A concrete wall surrounded the alley.

"You alright, bro?" Remy climbed to his feet and spit out a wad of blood.

With as much effort as I could manage, I pushed myself to my knees. Sharp pains ripped through my sides like I'd been stabbed repeatedly. With every motion the stabbing increased and everything spun.

I keeled over, warding off the inclination to heave.

My legs were pure jelly, so I began crawling toward the wall. I didn't get far, before dropping my head in exhaustion.

"You just gotta make it to the gate," Remy said.

My head shot up.

A gate?

Remy wrapped his beaten arm around me and lifted me to my feet. As my heavy body hung on his, we struggled through the gate and toward my truck, barely making it there without collapsing.

I half expected it to be surrounded by men with bottles or weapons. But the lot was empty.

Remy slid behind the wheel. I collapsed in the passenger seat. I tried to sit upright, but the pain made it impossible. I leaned against the window and prayed for the pain to be taken away.

Moments passed, but they could have been hours. Noise alternated with silence. Darkness with light.

"I know who'll make you feel better," Remy said.

## ALEX

I stood from the sofa, needing to change out of my dress. I had no idea why I still wore it. I guess it took some time to realize I'd been stood up. I know. Stupid, right?

I tried Hayden's cell once eight o'clock came and went, but my calls were sent to voicemail. I wondered if a family member needed him, because why else wouldn't he have called?

But when hours passed and he still made no attempt to contact me, I grew angry. Angry I'd given in to him so easily after the stunt he pulled the previous night. Angry he'd do something so terrible after all I'd been through. Angry I believed in him in the first place. I didn't force him to take me to the dance. It had been *his* idea. How could he leave me sitting home alone without so much as a call?

Then realization hit. A punch to the gut type of realization felt only after being made to look like a complete fool.

He'd apologized for not being what I needed him to be. He'd said no one could know. He'd brought two girls home.

Did I really need it spelled out for me?

*Ughhhh.*

Why was I so naïve? So stupid? So hooked on the fairytale that wasn't?

Shuffling in the hallway snapped my attention to the door.

Call me a glutton for punishment, but I hurried to it, aligning my eye with the hole. Hayden passed by slowly, being held up by a short brunette.

With every bit of strength and every remaining ounce of pride I possessed, I blinked back the tears that sat ready to fall. He wouldn't see me cry. I was too angry for that.

I threw open the door.

Hayden leaned against his door frame while the girl unlocked his door. He glanced over his shoulder, wincing when he found me standing there. I didn't look away. I wouldn't. He needed to see what he did. Who he hurt. Who he'd never hurt again.

Whatever we had, *this thing* he needed, it was over.

## HAYDEN

"Just give me a minute," I growled at Marisol as I rushed into my bathroom.

*Rushed* might've been pushing it. I found it difficult to even walk. My ribs were definitely broken, and I suspected one of them had punctured my lung, hence my difficulty breathing.

I grasped the sides of the sink and examined my reflection in the mirror under the bright overhead bulbs. Except for some minor scrapes and cuts on my cheeks and chin, my face survived mostly unscathed. My body, which took the brunt of the attack and stung with broken glass, didn't fare as well.

It was strange. I could endure the physical pain. The broken ribs. The punctured lung. The cuts and bruises. But the emotional pain— what I felt seeing Alex in her doorway—not so much.

The devastated look on her face when she saw me with Marisol was one of the most heartbreaking things I'd ever seen. And I'd seen my fair share. She still wore her dress. She held out hope I wouldn't disappoint her. But of course, I had.

I closed my eyes tightly. I'd blown my chance at a normal life. With a girl who saw something in me others didn't. And for what? To have the hell beaten out of me by guys who owed someone else money.

This wasn't the life my mother wanted for me. Hell. This wasn't the life *I* wanted for me.

But how could I explain it to someone like Alex? How could I explain why I worked with Remy? How could I tell her about all the evil things I'd done?

I couldn't unleash my demons on her innocent soul. I wouldn't. She was better off believing I was a selfish lying dick.

"Come on, Hayden." Marisol tapped on the bathroom door. "Let me in."

I reached back and unlocked the door, careful not to exacerbate my injuries.

Marisol pushed it open and stepped inside, all five feet of her squeezing in behind me. "Take off your shirt."

"That's usually my line," I choked, having a hell of a time getting the words out.

"I'm glad to see you've still got your sense of humor. Wait. Since when do you make jokes, Mr. Serious?"

"Fuck off."

"That's more like it." Marisol lifted my shirt, dragging it cautiously over my head before tossing it to the floor. She ran her hands gently along my sides. Then moved them around to my front, inspecting my ribs. I could see in the mirror they were black and purple.

"Owww," I growled through clenched teeth.

"They're definitely broken."

"No shit."

Ignoring my grumbling, she continued her examination. "Let me clean up the cuts and then wrap the ribs."

With my hands white-knuckling the sink, I leaned forward and carefully dropped my head. Any movement still hurt like a son of a bitch.

Marisol plucked the pieces of glass from my skin with tweezers, and cleaned the cuts on my sides with antiseptic. Each touch sent a fierce bite tearing through me, sucking the air right out of my lungs. "What do you think about my lung?" I asked through gritted teeth.

"Do I really need to say it?"

"I'm a big boy."

"You need to be checked out by a doctor."

"Not happening."

"You're a stubborn ass, you know that, right?" She huffed a long drawn out breath. "Hypothetically speaking, if you were to go to the ER and they thought it was only a small puncture, they'd send you home to wait it out. See if it got worse."

I wanted to nod, but thought better of moving.

"Just promise me you'll call me if it's not healing or your breathing's still labored."

I'd lost count of the number of times Marisol swooped in to take care of my sorry ass over the years. Her family had been my last foster family—the only caring one. Marisol commuted to nursing school while I lived there. Unfortunately for her, she didn't get the foster brother she'd hoped for. The type that hung out and went places with her. It wasn't that I'd been a prick to her. I just already worked for Cooper at the time and was biding my time until I saved up enough cash to move out on my own.

My head whipped up at the same time Marisol ripped the bandage off the back of my left shoulder. "It's so much prettier than the other one."

"Can you put that back on and just wrap my ribs, please?"

"Don't angels usually have blue eyes and blonde hair?"

I dropped my head, squeezing my eyes. "Marisol, I swear to God if you don't shut up and help me, I'm going to—"

Her hands disappeared from my back. I imagined them planted on her pear-shaped hips. "You're going to what?"

I shook my head, defeated and in a hell of a lot of pain.

"So you gonna tell me who that girl was out there?"

I shook my head again, wincing at the sharp pains accompanying the motion.

"She looked really pretty in that dress."

"I didn't notice," I muttered, lying through my teeth.

"I saw the tie and shirt on your chair. Were you going somewhere?"

I shook my head. And down deep, I wondered if *that* lie had actually been the truth all along.

## ALEX

I'd spent the last twenty-four hours buried under a blanket on the sofa.

But once the cushions at my feet sagged, I knew my aunt was done respecting my privacy. "You want to talk about it?"

I peeked out and shook my head.

"Alex…" She sighed. "I've been trying to give you space. Please tell me if I've been wrong to do that." When I didn't answer, she expelled another breath. "Tell me what you need and I'll do it. If it's counseling, I'll get you the best counselor in the state. If it's school, I'll get you tutors. If it's money, I'll get it for you. It's all yours soon anyway. Just talk to me."

I understood her frustration. I'd been in the same situation with Hayden. He didn't tell me anything. It was a huge mistake to believe any relationship could work that way. People actually needed to open up. Talk. Share.

"I'm just sad," I whispered.

My aunt leaned down and wrapped her arms around me. "Oh, honey, of course you are. It's to be expected."

"I feel so alone." The flood gates opened and nothing could be done to stop them. "I miss them so much. I try not to think about them because then it doesn't hurt as bad. But then I feel guilty for not thinking about them. Then there're my friends. Who aren't even my friends anymore. I'm not sure they ever really were. But I miss…having friends." I couldn't continue. The tears were too much. The hurt too great.

My aunt could have said something to console the blubbering mess beside her, but she didn't. She sat there, comforting me with her gentle touch as I sobbed in her arms. She understood I just needed her presence. Because nothing she said would take away the pain. Nothing she did would bring my parents home.

My sniffles were the only sounds in the room for a long time.

Maybe the distance between my aunt and me was all my fault. I'd made conversations difficult, sticking solely to the superficial. I hadn't confided in her. I hadn't asked her for help when clearly I needed it.

I wiped away the tears lingering on my cheeks. "Why'd you and my mom stop talking?"

Her sharp intake of breath told me I caught her off guard. "Why do you think?"

"I have no idea. She never said."

Her lips twisted in contemplation as she sat up, settling into the spot beside me. "Your dad."

"He wouldn't let her talk to you?"

She shook her head. "No, no. Nothing like that. Your dad and I had…well, we had history."

"You dated?"

She nodded. "For almost two years."

My head recoiled. "I didn't know that."

"Of course you didn't. It was a long time ago."

"How'd he end up with my mom?"

Her eyes shot away, clearly averting my inquisitive eyes. "Oh, sweetie. No use drudging up the past."

"Please, Katherine. I need to know." Whining hadn't been my intention, but in that moment I needed to understand. Katherine had shown me nothing but kindness. Why had my parents kept her out of my life?

She took in as much air as humanly possible before expelling it. "He cheated on me with your mother. Nine months later you were born."

My eyes widened on a gasp. "Oh my God."

She nodded. "My exact reaction."

"But they always seemed so in love?"

"Oh, sweetie. They *were* in love. You just sealed the deal for them." She closed her eyes for a long moment, the memory visibly paining her. "I wasn't stupid. I saw the way he looked at her when he'd come to our house. And I saw the way she looked at him. The way she loved his attention. I was the one stopping them from being together. But I loved him so much. I needed him to let me go. Because I would've held on to him forever." She forced a sad smile. "But, had they never gotten together, there wouldn't be you."

"You didn't want anything to do with them after that?"

An insincere laugh left her. "Oh, it took me some time. That's for sure. But when I tried to reach out—forgive me for saying this—your mother didn't want to reconcile. Mutual friends claimed she felt threatened. So I kept my distance. Only making contact with you, or at least trying to. You were the innocent party in our tangled mess."

"I'm so sorry that happened to you. No one should be deceived like that."

"We were all so young." She shrugged. "You do stupid things when you're young." She sounded so nonchalant, but her pain was real. And for over twenty years, it lingered.

"Doesn't make it right, though." I turned to her, hoping she saw the sincerity in my eyes. "I'm sorry I'm here. I must be a terrible reminder. I must be making your life—"

"Stop," she cut me off. "Having you here is the most excitement I've had in years," she laughed.

"Well then you missed a boatload last night while you were out," I mumbled.

Katherine's head whipped around, her eyes searching her apartment for signs of damage.

I tightened the blanket around me. "I didn't throw a party." Who would I have invited? Sophia went to the formal. "Hayden asked me to a dance."

Her head pulled back. "Hayden? I didn't think he went out with college girls."

I shrugged. "I guess he doesn't. He blew me off. Then came home with another girl."

My aunt cringed. "Oh, Alex. I'm so sorry."

I expected the tears to gush again. But they didn't. Maybe my body had finally learned to only shed tears over something sensible.

"You know…you and Hayden really aren't so different."

"I'd never stand someone up and make them look like a fool." I didn't mean to sound defensive, but comparing me to the guy who'd broken my already battered heart didn't sit well.

"No, obviously you wouldn't do that." She ran her hand gently over my hair, the same way my mom had when I was a little girl. "But maybe you should talk to him. Hear him out. There may be more to the story than meets the eye."

I tilted my head not buying it, but appreciating her efforts.

"I'm serious."

"I'm going to need a little more than that."

She worried her bottom lip. "I told you before, it's not my story to tell. But if you were to learn of it on your own, say online under his full name and hometown of Beaumont, I wouldn't be telling you now, would I?"

I stared dumbfounded, wondering why I hadn't thought to do that. Then again, I only learned his last name recently. I jumped to my feet and gathered up the blanket.

"It's no good having regrets."

My eyes narrowed.

"I should have done something to stop the standoff with your mom. I should've forced her to talk to me. Now it's too late."

I nodded my understanding before heading toward my room. Halfway down the hallway I stopped and turned back around. "Thank you, Katherine."

The glint in her eyes as she smiled told me she understood the depth of my words.

# CHAPTER NINETEEN

## HAYDEN

I'd parked my beaten ass on my sofa for a solid week. And while the bruises had faded and the cuts had begun to mend, the pain still lingered. Marisol had stopped by to check on me and confirmed my ribs were healing. Slowly.

A soft knocking on my front door drew my attention away from *SportsCenter*. Careful not to move too quickly, I pushed myself up and moved to the door, feeling as if I'd aged fifty years in a week. If Remy thought for one second I'd go anywhere with him in the shape I was in, I had news for him.

I lowered my eye to the peephole, then staggered back.

It wasn't Remy.

Not even close.

I slowly pulled open the door.

Alex, in torn jeans and a flowy red shirt, clutched a folder to her chest. Instead of looking at me, her eyes peeked around me, checking to see if she'd interrupted anything. Once she determined I was alone, her eyes flashed to mine. "I noticed you haven't been to classes."

I shrugged non-committal.

A watched her swallow down a sassy comeback or her anger. Either one I deserved.

"Well anyway, Sophia works at the registrar. She got me a list of your professors. I stopped by and picked up all the notes and in-class assignments they didn't post online."

My eyes narrowed in confusion. "Why?"

Holding the folder out to me, she forced a smile. "Just being a good neighbor."

I struggled to suppress a grin, especially when she threw my own stupid words back in my face. I reached for the folder, wincing at the sharp pain that ignited in my side.

"What's wrong?" She jerked forward like she wanted to help, but quickly stepped back.

I couldn't tell her I needed to lie down without her expecting an explanation. So I braced myself against the door frame and clutched it for support.

Alex gnawed on her lip. I could see the internal battle playing out in her eyes, but I really needed to sit. "So, I appreciate you bringing this by," I said, prompting her to leave.

She didn't move. She stood waiting for something. Something specific. I could see it in those expressive eyes.

My lips twitched in the corners as it hit me. "You're swell."

Her smile split in two before she turned and disappeared into her apartment.

*What the hell just happened?*

## ALEX

The following day when Hayden opened his door, still sporting scruffy stubble on his face I wasn't used to, I held up the container of hot chicken soup I'd spent the last two hours making. "Just thought you might be hungry."

Hayden stared at me for a minute before stepping aside so I could enter.

I didn't move. "It's already hot. If you've got a spoon, you just need to eat it."

He cocked his head. "Maybe I don't want to eat alone."

I cocked my own. "Maybe I have a hot date."

"Well, he's gonna have to wait 'til I'm finished with my meal." He arched a brow.

*Damn him.*

No matter what he'd done, that intangible pull still existed between us.

Sure, it took a week for my hard feelings to ease, but they had. Somewhat. I mean, he lived across the hall. I couldn't avoid him forever.

Okay. So I'd be lying if I said the story about his past didn't sway my decision to try to forgive him. It absolutely did. Who could stay mad at someone who'd seen what he'd seen? I didn't *see* my parents die. I couldn't imagine the pain and nightmares accompanying that memory.

I blew out a breath and entered his apartment. My eyes took in the rumpled blanket on the sofa and the unlabeled prescription bottles littering the coffee table. "So what's the diagnosis?"

He closed the door behind me. "Besides being an asshole?"

I smiled. "That should've been my line."

"Beat you to it," he grinned, like we hadn't been avoiding each other for the past week. Then he sat down, like an old man trying not to pull a muscle "I've got a few broken ribs."

I walked into the kitchen, searching cabinets and drawers for a bowl and spoon. "That sucks."

"Yup." Of course he didn't elaborate. That would've been asking too much.

Unable to find a ladle, I poured the soup from the container into a bowl, trying not to spill any on his countertop. I carried it out and placed it into his awaiting hands.

"Secret recipe?" he asked as he lifted the spoon to his lips.

I shook my head. "No, mine would've contained cyanide. It's my mom's."

Despite the threat, Hayden smiled and tipped the spoonful into his mouth.

I dropped onto the opposite corner of the sofa, the same place I'd sat the first night I'd been to his apartment.

After he found me unconscious by the pool.

After he brought me to the hospital.

After he stayed by my bedside all night.

After he asked me to stay with him so he could keep an eye on me.

Yeah. No matter what he'd done since then, I couldn't forget he cared for me when no one else had. He looked after me. He rescued me.

When had anyone rescued him?

*That's* why I brought his homework and the soup. Not because I was a pushover. A doormat. A glutton for punishment. But because he needed me. Whether he realized it or not.

"It's really good," he said. "She must've been a great cook."

I hadn't purposely conjured up memories of my mother in a while. Sure, memories of her flooded me on a daily basis, but they were uninvited flashes of moments I hadn't expected.

Now Hayden wanted me to recall a specific detail. Something that made her special. Something I'd have to learn to live without.

The backs of my eyes prickled. All at once, a rush of memories flooded me. Her in the kitchen. Her hips swaying to music while she cooked. The spicy pasta sauce bubbling on the stove each Sunday. The freshly baked dinner rolls accompanying every meal. The sweet apple pies sitting on the windowsill. "Yeah. She was."

"What was her best dish?"

I crossed my arms, settling back into the black leather. "Why are you doing this?"

His brows squished together. "Doing what?"

"Bringing up my mom? You know it's hard for me to talk about her."

"Doesn't mean you shouldn't. Just because she's gone, doesn't mean you need to forget her."

He was absolutely right. But I couldn't help wondering if he was really talking about himself. "Chicken parmesan."

He grinned as he downed another spoonful. "I'd be up for trying that next."

"Next? Who said you're getting anything else?" I was trying to remain sassy or aloof, or maybe both. But the odds were in his favor I'd cave and cook it for him.

Hayden's eyes held mine for a long moment. Like he wanted to say something important. Something long overdue. "How are rehearsals going?"

Classic Hayden. Change the subject when things turned too serious. "Okay. Taylor's still waiting in the shadows for someone to quit or get sick."

"She sucks."

I nodded.

"When's the show?"

My head withdrew. "You're not planning on coming, are you?"

"Never know."

"I won't hold my breath," I murmured, finding it difficult to curb my resentment, no matter how hard I tried.

Discomfort flashed in Hayden's eyes before they shot down to his soup. "Just so you know, I had every intention of—"

"Please." I lifted my palm. "I didn't come here to rehash the past."

His brows lifted to his messy hairline, before his eyes narrowed on mine. "Then why did you?"

Hell of a question. Did I pull a Hayden and deflect? Or show him how honesty worked? "To start fresh."

"How do we do that?"

I tucked up my knees and wrapped my arms around them. It wasn't like I had some grand plan. I just knew regardless of the mistakes he'd made, he needed someone in his life as much as I did. And since I had no one but my aunt, I needed him, too. "I'm Alex."

His eyes studied me tucked into the corner of his sofa.

Okay, so maybe had I thought it out, I could've been more creative. But I wasn't finished yet. "I live with my aunt, who I barely know, because as you know, my parents died. Come to find out, my dad cheated on my aunt with my mom and nine months later I showed up. Katherine must *love* having me around."

Hayden winced from the other end of the couch.

"I have no friends except Sophia because my old friends abandoned me and I can't trust anyone at my new school...But some days I'm dealing better than I thought I would. And I think that has something to do with this guy I met when I moved here. This frustrating and kind and infuriating and thoughtful guy."

He stared at me with terror in his eyes. He should've been terrified.

I lifted my chin. "Your turn."

His eyes flashed away, avoiding my gaze at all costs. He stared out the window from his seat. It had been extra windy lately, blowing down a number of limbs. Was he watching the shifting trees? Or was he just afraid to look back?

I almost felt sorry for putting him on the spot, but he was a big boy. If he felt uncomfortable, he'd just change the subject.

After what felt like an eternity, Hayden cleared his throat, breaking the awkward silence. "You once asked me why I live alone." His eyes moved from the window to me. "I live alone because my parents died when I was ten."

My heart slammed into my rib cage. I was scared to react. Scared to move. I didn't want to do anything that would cause him to clam up.

His eyes moved back to the window. "My father used to beat me and my mom."

I gulped down the lump in my throat, aching to be near him. To comfort him.

"I was so small back then. So weak. I couldn't protect us. I wanted to. Man, did I want to...My mom finally had enough. She packed us up. We were gonna run away while he was at work. She was so happy. I'd never seen her so carefree, tossing her things into a suitcase humming along to her favorite songs."

My heart broke knowing they never got their happy ending.

Hayden's eyes abandoned the window, lifting to the ceiling. "He came home early. It was like he knew. Because he never came home early. He did his normal throwing her across the room and beating me thing." Hayden rubbed the scar on the bridge of his nose.

"Then, it was like watching an alternate reality. He pulled out his gun. His fucking gun. And aimed it at me. My mom jumped in front of me. That's when he fired across the room and shot her. Three times. What kind of animal does that?"

Tears fell from my eyes hearing Hayden revisit the horror of that day.

"Not a day goes by when I don't wonder if I could've done something to stop him."

"*Hayden.*"

He shook off my sympathy. "After he'd done it. He looked at me with the gun pointed to his own head and told me it was all my fault. Then he fired."

My heart almost jumped out of my chest, knowing what he'd witnessed. Knowing the depth of those cruel words.

I wanted to go to him. To wrap him in my arms until he knew everything would be all right. But he needed to continue. He needed it out of his head. He needed to be free of the demons.

"I've gotten a little better with people touching me, but obviously he's the reason I get all awkward and flinch when it happens." He finally glanced to me. His eyes so vulnerable. "I don't do it anymore when you touch me."

I smiled through the tears, loving that he didn't.

"As you've probably noticed, I don't have many friends, at least ones I can rely on." He swallowed. "But there's this girl. This amazing and stubborn and beautiful girl who I can't seem to get out of my head even though I know I should."

My heart soared, but I didn't dare utter a word.

"She deserves so much better than me, but she sticks around for some unknown reason. And I wish I could tell her why I had to blow off our date, but I can't. Because letting her believe what she does about me, is so much better than what she'd think if she knew the truth."

Major crocodile tears dropped from my eyes. Obviously there was more he wasn't telling me, but he'd shared so much more than I ever imagined he would. I couldn't hold back any longer. I crawled across the sofa and tucked myself into his side, careful not to disturb his ribs. I slipped my arms around his waist and rested my head on his shoulder. "I'm so sorry that happened to you, Hayden. No one should have to go through something so terrible. No one deserves that."

He shrugged it off, but I knew he agreed.

"It wasn't your fault."

He nodded. "I know."

"If you could've done something to stop him, you would've." It wasn't a question. It was an assurance.

He nodded, but I wasn't convinced he believed me.

"Me."

"What?"

"You said you didn't have anyone to rely on. But you've got me. You can rely on me. Even if I'm angry as hell at you, you can still rely on me."

He didn't respond, just dropped a kiss to the crown of my head and let it linger.

# CHAPTER TWENTY

## HAYDEN

Thick fog hovered over the dark road. Heavy rain bounced off the windshield. Both made it impossible to see more than ten feet in front of my truck. I pulled up the hood of my sweatshirt and sank into my shell. After being out of commission for over a week, I needed to mentally prepare for the job I loathed.

Remy's leg bounced wildly beside me as he chewed away at his pinky nail. Something was up with him. But I had no desire to find out what it was. I just wanted to get the job over with and get the hell home.

That's where I needed to be.

With Alex.

The same Alex who disappeared from my apartment the previous night after I spilled my guts to her. It was insane. Once I got started, I couldn't stop. All the shit I kept bottled up just poured out of me. I knew it's why she left. She didn't want to push me too far. And while her leaving sucked, it gave me time to think.

She was obviously someone I could confide in. Someone I could be myself with. Someone I could care about—*did* care about.

But could I ever let her all the way in?

Could I pick and choose what I disclosed? Could I avoid telling her everything?

Because two things stood in my way.

The huge skeleton in my closet. The one that would send her packing the second she found out.

And my job—my debt to Remy.

But unless I moved away from town, maybe even Texas, I'd never be able to escape the hold Remy had over me. I mean, how could I ever repay the guy who took the fall for me?

I took a deep breath, letting the sad truth seep in. I was stuck in a no-win situation. And there was no end in sight. No way out. Could I really pull Alex into it with me?

The hair on the back of my neck stood on end as I slowed in front of a dilapidated house twenty minutes outside of the town limits. There were no houses on the immediate left or right. They were tucked behind trees in more of a zigzagged pattern you'd find in rural areas. And with the heavy slanted rain, none could be seen from the dirt road.

Remy sat forward, slipping his gun into the back of his belt. When I stopped the truck, he pushed open the passenger door. The crisp October air and a shitload of mist rushed inside filling my body with chills.

"Be right back." He hopped out and tore off toward the front door. The rain drenched him instantly, but it didn't slow down his determined stride.

I unfastened the gun from below my seat and tucked it into my belt. I hated the looks of the place. Only two of the windows possessed shutters. Roof shingles littered the ankle-high front lawn. The screen door hung on a single hinge. And three beaten old cars sat on cinderblocks in the gravel driveway.

My eyes flashed to the front door. The lopsided screen pushed open and the barrel of a shotgun emerged pointed directly at Remy's forehead.

His hands flew up.

*Motherfucker.*

A guy peered around the gun, searching behind Remy. I dropped in my seat, hoping like hell the downpour obscured his view. I was no coward, but I couldn't help Remy if the guy knew I lurked in the darkness.

I slid over to the passenger side and slipped out the door. My adrenaline spiked and shivers overtook my body as the rain saturated my clothes. Luckily, my truck concealed me from the house and its whacked-out owner. It gave me a second to plot out my route. I needed to be cautious not to reveal my presence too soon or move my almost-healed ribs too quickly.

I took a deep breath, then ducked behind tree trunks and crept to the side of the house. Once I made it to the driveway, I crouched between the cars. It sucked knowing nights like these were what my life had come to.

The side door to the house sat ajar. I hurried to it, slipping inside unnoticed. I glided along the empty kitchen wall in my squishy sneakers, pausing to listen for anything indicating there were others in the house.

Except for the rain pinging off the remaining shingles in droning successions, it was unnervingly silent.

I stepped through the kitchen doorway and into the living room. Luckily, it was a hoarder's dream. The junk piled everywhere concealed me from the guy at the front door with his back to me and his gun still on Remy.

Soaked to the bone, Remy babbled from his spot on the front steps saying whatever it took to get the guy to lower the gun. "I'm serious, man. Let's make a deal. I'll make it worth your while. No one ever has to know."

I slid my gun from my belt and stalked over to the owner with the gun extended in front of me. I lifted it to the back of his head, releasing the safety to announce my arrival.

*Click.*

*I closed my eyes with my arms still wrapped around my mom, braced for the impact of the bullet.*

*"This is all your fault."*

*He fired.*

I shuddered at the memory, needing to pull my shit together. Needing to get Remy out of there unharmed.

Everything happened in slow motion. The guy lowered his shotgun. Remy grabbed for it. The guy wouldn't relinquish it. He slammed the butt of the gun into Remy's stomach, sending him folding at the waist.

*Click.*

My body stilled.

The sound hadn't come from my gun.

A gun jammed into the back of my head, snapping my neck forward.

"Say a prayer, motherfucker," a gruff voice declared. A large hand grasped my shoulder and shoved me to my knees. I had no time to react. He ripped the gun from my hands.

My eyes squeezed shut. Visions of my mother at the moment my father shot her flooded my mind. Her fear. Her gasp. Her blood. God, there was so much blood. The gruesome images remained engrained in every blink of my eyes. Every breath. Every nightmare. Even at the hour of my death.

The gun's trigger *popped* behind my head. I flinched. Shivers rocked through me, sending my body into a fit of tremors.

A bellowing laugh rumbled in my ear. "Well how about that. A game of Russian roulette. Someone up there must be looking out for you." Without hesitation, he slammed the butt of the gun into the back of my head. Pain exploded as my body folded, my face hitting the hardwood floor. "Too bad your luck's run out."

A gunshot crackled the air, thundering throughout the room. I shielded my head, tucking my body into a ball.

Had I been shot? Had Remy?

I waited for the darkness to engulf me. To take me to my mother. To absolve me of my sins. To rid me of the guilt and pain I'd carried for far too long.

But the darkness never came.

Neither did the pain of a bullet tearing through my body.

I kept my head tucked down, praying to be put out of my misery quickly. I couldn't bleed out on the floor of this hell hole. This wasn't how my life was supposed to end.

A heavy thud dropped to my right. My body instinctively jumped to the left. My eyes cracked open. The guy from the front door lay sprawled in an unnatural position on the floor beside me. Face down, blood pooling around his body.

My body stayed down, but my head flew up. Remy stood with the dead guy's shotgun pointed at the man behind me. I hadn't seen him yet. But his deep voice had me conjuring a hundred different monstrous images.

"Now why would your buddy go and put a bullet through your head?" Remy asked him, so calm, so cool, so devious.

Another loud blast crackled the air.

I dropped back down, my arms shielding my head. And even though Remy had fired the shotgun, my body shook like a thing unnatural.

"Twice." Remy fired another shot, leaving no doubt my attacker was dead.

## ALEX

The flow of rain outside provided a calming peace in my aunt's otherwise silent living room. The pumpkin-scented candles I'd set out provided just enough light to study by. Most girls would've been afraid to be home alone during a late-night storm, especially with the thunder and lightning claiming their place in the sky and knocking out the electricity. But not me. I enjoyed the darkness and the solace created by the storm.

Soft tapping came from the front door. I snatched my cell from the end table and checked the time. Just after midnight. No wonder why I could barely keep my eyes opened. I grabbed a candle and stood from the sofa, feeling a little hesitant to approach the door, especially with my aunt away at my parents' vineyard. But once I checked the peephole, my fears subsided.

I pulled open the door. Hayden stood drenched with his head hanging down.

"Hey," I smiled, not having seen him since our heart to heart the previous night.

When he looked up with bloodshot eyes and damp flushed cheeks, the smile slipped from my face.

Tears?

*Shit.*

I placed the candle down on the small table beside the door and launched myself into him, wrapping my arms around his soaked body and tucking my head under his chin. "What's wrong? Are you all right?"

He clutched his arms around my shoulders, gripping me as if he needed me for support. His entire body trembled. His choppy breaths caught in his throat.

Were his wet clothes causing the reaction or something else?

I moved us away from the doorway and into the living room, closing the door with my foot to separate us from the outside world. Since Hayden wouldn't relinquish his grasp on me, I maneuvered us to the sofa. When the backs of my knees touched it, I eased us down and just held him. Feeling the tremors tearing through his body, I held him tighter.

After a long moment passed, I pulled back slightly so I could see his face. His distant tortured face. "Hayden?"

His usually gorgeous eyes stared blankly at me, like he wasn't seeing me at all. Like everything except his body was somewhere else. His teeth chattered wildly. I cupped his frigid stubbly cheeks between my hands and searched his eyes for a sign of life behind the darkness. Sadly, the darkness prevailed. "I need to get you out of these wet clothes."

The Hayden I'd come to know would've made some smartass comment, egging me on, calling my bluff. But that wasn't the same Hayden seated with me. The one lost somewhere deep inside his own head. And I had no freaking clue how to reach him.

I tugged down the zipper on his sweatshirt and slipped the sleeves down his arms. His eyes followed my movements, but he didn't stop me.

I discarded his soaked sweatshirt on the hardwood floor, and grasped the hem of his red T-shirt. I lifted it slowly, cautious of his broken ribs. He bore it like the pillar of strength he normally was, never even wincing. I wondered if his ribs had healed, or if the pain in his ribs paled in comparison to whatever troubled him.

I dropped his shirt onto the growing pile, noticing faint bruises covering both his sides. His eyes followed my hands as I gently trailed them over his naked chest. My fingertips skated over the deep ridges in his torso and abs, made more prominent by the flickering of the candles. It wasn't at all how I imagined this experience happening. "Tell me where you're hurt."

His eyes locked on mine, but he didn't speak. He reached his hand behind his head, wincing as he touched it. I ran my fingers under his in his dripping hair, finding the huge egg-shaped lump he'd indicated.

I jumped to my feet, retrieving an ice pack from my aunt's freezer. I scooted in behind him and held the pack to his head. What wasn't he telling me? What was he involved in?

Before I could ask if he had any other pain, my eyes widened.

The dim candlelight made me question my eyesight. Question what I'd seen on the back of his left shoulder. But when I focused all of my attention on that one spot, there was no denying it. A new tattoo covered his skin.

It took everything I had not to trace my finger over the beautiful angel. Her wavy dark hair. Her flowing dress.

"It's you," his raspy voice admitted, startling the hell out of me.

I somehow managed to keep the ice pack to the back of his head and, in what felt like slow motion, shift beside him. I glanced into his bloodshot eyes. "What?"

He searched my face. "It's you."

Before I could stop it, my breath whooshed through my lips. "Why?"

"Isn't it obvious?"

I shook my head, my heart pounding around in my chest like a pinball.

Hayden lifted his icy hands to my cheeks. "It's how I see you. This shining light in my otherwise dismal existence."

I dropped the ice pack and grabbed hold of his hands on my cheeks. Closing my eyes, I savored the moment. Savored his touch. Savored his words. Savored his vulnerability.

"Tonight was a wakeup call for me. A big fucking wakeup call. It reminded me how fast things can change. How fast everything can be taken away from me. Alex, I need you."

My eyes snapped open. Hayden's honesty stared back at me. It was there for the world to see. For *me* to see.

"No more pushing you away," he promised. "No more secrets."

A humorless laugh shot from my lips. I wasn't sure if I should've been ecstatic about his sentiments, or petrified by what brought them on.

## HAYDEN

Was she laughing at me? Or the whole ridiculousness of the situation? Once again I'd shown up at her place late at night. This time, after almost being killed.

*Classic.*

But I'd been serious. I was done pushing her away. She needed to know. She needed to hear it. Really hear it. The fear I felt when the trigger popped behind my head was more than a wakeup call. It was a bellowing siren.

Alex dropped her hands from mine, avoiding my gaze. "You need to get out of these pants."

On a normal night her telling me to drop my drawers would've been the start of something promising. But not now. Not when everything was so screwed up. Not when she'd ignored the fact that I'd spilled my guts *and* got a tattoo of her likeness.

What the hell had I been thinking? I pushed myself to my feet. "I'm gonna head home."

Alex jumped up. "No."

"No?"

She shook her head. "Stay."

I raised a brow. "You sure about that?"

She nodded. "I need to make sure you're okay. You might have a concussion."

For a split second I thought she wanted me with her for the sake of having me there. Not so she could babysit my sorry ass. I didn't need her pity. I didn't need anyone's.

With anger grasping hold of every synapse in my brain, I turned toward the door. I needed out.

Before I could move, Alex's small hand slipped into mine. "Come on." She gave me a little tug, leading me down the dark hallway and into her bedroom. It was amazing how quickly my anger dissipated when it came to Alex. "Hope you don't mind my small bed."

The candle on her dresser gave off just enough light for me to see her queen-sized bed. Compared to my king-sized, it was smaller. But that just meant we'd be closer.

I watched as she pulled back her comforter. It was that awkward moment again, when I wasn't sure what to do.

As if reading my mind, she glanced over. "Why don't you get out of those jeans while I use the bathroom." She walked to her closet and tossed me a towel and a pair of guy's basketball shorts. Jealousy clutched at my gut. Whose were they? Before I could get too worked up, Alex flashed me a crooked smile and slipped out of the room.

In the aftermath of everything that had gone down, she made me happy. She made me forget the baggage that came with being me. She made me see a future. That was something I'd never done before. And seeing as though less than an hour ago I almost didn't have a future, I was pretty damn happy to be there.

I struggled out of my wet jeans and boxers and folded them into the towel. I should've run home to change before stopping over, but I was too messed up to even consider it. I just knew I needed to see Alex. She made everything better.

Before she returned and found me in all my glory, I slipped on the dry shorts and slid under the covers. The massive lump on the back of my head throbbed like a son of a bitch against her pillows. No way I'd be able to sleep lying on it, so I turned on my side toward the center of the bed and waited.

The minutes ticked by and Alex hadn't returned.

Had I misread the entire situation? Did she plan to stay on the sofa?

The more time I lay there alone, the faster the darkness crept in. With each blink of my eyes I saw them. The two men on the floor. The blood. The satisfaction on Remy's face.

My heart began to race and my palms began to sweat.

What the fuck?

Was I having a panic attack?

The bedroom door pushed opened and a sliver of light crept in. Alex slipped inside with another candle, wearing tiny cotton shorts and a tight tank top. Her eyes met mine for a split second before she moved to the opposite side of the bed.

My heartbeat slowed. How quickly everything else was forgotten whenever she entered a room.

She placed the candle on her nightstand. Then slipped under the covers and moved closer to me. We lay there eye to eye for a long time, just breathing each other in. Savoring each other's presence. Savoring the silence.

Alex lifted her hand and ran her fingers through the back of my hair, brushing them lightly over the lump, so gentle and calming, like a mother's hand on a child. She had the ability to lull me to sleep. But sleep would only lead to more nightmares.

"Feels like it's gone down a little."

I nodded, inhaling her just-brushed minty breath.

"Do you want more ice?"

No way I'd let her leave me again. Not with her fingers in my hair. Not with her needing to take care of me. Not with the demons lurking when she left me alone. So I shook my head, careful not to irritate the swelling.

She pulled her hand away, tucking it with the other under her pillow. She looked me straight in the eyes. "What happened?"

I closed my eyes, trying to find the words. I had promised no more secrets. But where did I begin? Where did I end? I wished she would've given me a little more time.

Alex sighed. "Never mind."

My eyes snapped open. "No. I need to do this."

She stared back at me with doe eyes.

Jesus. She was so damn innocent. In seconds that would all be shattered if I told her the truth. Told her the evil things I was capable of. But I promised. And I intended to keep my promises. "I work for a bookie."

Alex didn't even blink. She just nodded, encouraging me to continue.

I blew out a shaky breath. "When he doesn't get paid, Remy and I are sent to collect his money."

"Okay. So why the broken ribs and massive lump? Aren't you any good?"

My lips turned up in the corners. Was she seriously making a joke about it? "I'm okay."

She arched a brow. "Mediocre?"

"Yeah, mediocre."

She was trying to make it easier on me. No one had done that in a long time. But I had more to share, so my grin faded.

"These guys we deal with, these guys who don't pay up, they're scum. They have no desire to pay. They don't see the urgency. So, our visits are rarely friendly."

"Have you ever used a gun?" she asked without blinking.

Way to go right for the heavy stuff, Alex. "I've never pulled a trigger."

"Have you ever seriously hurt someone?"

I nodded.

"How bad?"

"Can I just say bad and leave it at that? At least for tonight?"

She nodded, though the disappointment in her eyes was hard to miss. "What happened tonight?"

I inhaled, letting the giant sigh glide though my nose. "I had a gun aimed at my head. When the guy pulled the trigger, the chamber was either empty or the gun jammed."

She gasped at the same time her hands flew up and cupped my cheeks. Her fingers shook as they ran over my features, delicate and slow. She must've been thinking the same thing as me. *How the hell are you here right now?*

Her fingertips trailed over my skin. From my unshaven cheeks and chin to my lips, over the scar on the bridge of my nose to my eyes. Memorizing my face in case she never saw it again.

I grasped onto her hands at my cheeks and held them there, loving the feel of her warm touch. *Needing* her touch more than I ever needed anything in my life. "I'm gonna make some changes."

Sadness flashed in her eyes. "I'll help you."

I scoffed. "If it were only that easy."

"I'll do whatever it takes, Hayden. I'm serious. You're worth it. You know that, right? You're worth it."

I closed my eyes, feeling tears welling behind my lids. Fucking tears. What was it about this girl that stripped me bare? And how the hell could she make me feel her words? Make me believe they were actually true?

Without another word, she leaned in and pressed her lips to mine sending a warm tremor coursing through my cold body. As difficult as it was to do, I dropped my hands to her hips, letting her set the pace.

Her lips glided over mine, sucking and teasing me like we'd done this hundreds of times before. Her tongue licked across the seam of my lips, seeking access. I resisted, wondering how long I could hold off. How long I could be a gentleman.

Within seconds, my lips parted and her tongue slipped inside. The back and forth sweep sent chills up my spine. She had this innocent way of taunting me without realizing she was even doing it. I was done for.

Alex moved closer, her body curving flush against mine. I felt a shiver roll through her as her warm skin pressed to my chilled body. It didn't stop her, though. Her arms wrapped around my neck. She needed to be closer. Undeterred by the condition she put me in down south, she slipped one of her legs between mine.

I couldn't take anymore. I rolled her onto her back, loving the feel of her small body squished beneath mine. Staying partially on my side, I hovered over her, running my hand down her side and under her tank. I waited for her to stop me from going any further, but she didn't. She kept teasing me with her tongue, hungry and greedy, plunging deeper and deeper. It was almost too much. *Almost.*

I pulled back, enough to catch my breath. But it was no use. Both of us panted like dogs. My lips dropped to the soft skin on her neck and that tender spot below her ear. The one that sent her moaning. I licked and nipped and kissed her skin until she let loose a series of adorable little whimpers. Working my way down the front of her neck to the top of her tank top, I continued my assault on her sweet body.

Her delicate fingers grazed lazy figure eights up and down my spine. From the dip above my ass to the tips of my shoulders, warmth radiated in their absence. Moving higher still, they played with the hair at the back of my neck.

I was more than primed to make my descent to the last bit of exposed skin below her neck when she pushed me back.

With ragged breaths and a heaving chest, I rolled onto my side. Had her mind caught up with her body? Had she finally realized I was more trouble than I was worth?

She sat up and stared down at me with heavy-lidded eyes. It wasn't the look of someone having regrets. It was the look of someone as into what was transpiring as I was.

Alex pulled the hem of her top up over her head, exposing a lacy black bra. My jaw dropped and my body twitched. I all but came undone right there.

She tossed her shirt to the floor, then pulled me by the shoulders back on top of her. My bare chest met her practically bare chest. I couldn't hold back any longer. I leaned down and crashed my lips to hers, savoring the sweet minty taste for a long intoxicating moment. Plunging. Circling. Consuming.

I pulled back from her lips and moved down to her neck, inhaling her vanilla scent as she twisted and coiled beneath me. I kissed and sucked the soft skin around her neck before moving my way down. I swirled my tongue and devoured the smooth swells of her breasts. Running my nose between them, I lowered myself to her flat stomach, seriously unable to get enough of her.

When my lips reached the top of her shorts, I contemplated my next move. I knew what I wanted to do. And growing a conscious at that moment wasn't it.

*Un-fucking-believable.*

I'd hate myself in the morning for putting on the brakes, but I'd hate myself even more if my first night with Alex was forever associated with what brought me to her apartment in the first place.

Almost being murdered was no joke. Add to it, two men died at the hand of my best friend. That shit didn't just go away, no matter how preoccupied my mind was or how much I wanted Alex.

I glanced up from my spot below her naval. She rested on her elbows, her confused eyes locked on mine. I pushed myself up beside her, this time running my fingers over the soft and flawless skin on her face.

"Did I do something wrong?" She sounded nervous. In desperate need of reassurance.

"What? No. You're perfect." I leaned over and pressed my lips to hers, lowering her down from her elbows to her back. I kept my pace slow, trying to reassure her through our connection. Through the way we fit together. "I just want to wait until everything's right."

"So time's not on our side?"

I laughed, loving how she never forgot a thing I said.

Her hand slid slowly down my chest, leaving a tingling sensation in its wake. "Something tells me you may be wrong about that."

As much as I hated admitting it, I'd been wishing Alex would touch me like that for a while. And real life surpassed even my most vivid fantasies.

*Shit.* Her hand hadn't stopped at my shorts. It slid beneath the waistband. I grabbed it with a death grip. "Not tonight, sweetheart." It took more effort than expected to say the words.

With embarrassment in her eyes, Alex pulled her hand away. "Well, this has got to be a first for you."

"What?"

She glanced at my tented shorts. "Saying no."

"Oh, I'm not saying no." I pressed myself into her thigh, letting her feel what she did to me. And how much I wanted her. "I'm just saying not tonight." I leaned down, letting my lips and tongue devour hers. Her groans and sighs were music to my ears and by far the most adorable thing I'd ever experienced. I pulled back, nuzzling my nose gently to hers. "I told you I'm changing. That starts now."

She rolled her eyes. "Oh, lucky me."

# CHAPTER TWENTY-ONE

## ALEX

The ringing phone in the living room pulled me from a sound sleep. I kept my eyes closed, loving both the soft comfort of my bed and the strong arms holding me from behind.

Hayden's steady breathing told me he was still asleep, so I took the opportunity to just be in his arms. Be secure. Be completely content that *he* was safe.

As much as he tried to hide it, what happened the previous night scared the hell out of him. I knew real tears when I saw them. And those were definitely tears on his face when he showed up at my door.

I hoped he meant what he said about changing. Because I wouldn't be able to sleep if he continued working with Remy. The not knowing. The fear of where he was and who he was going to see. The risk he took stepping onto someone else's property demanding money. He didn't have nine lives. One of these nights, he wouldn't be so lucky. And that knowledge would destroy me every time he left his apartment.

"Alex, it's me," my aunt's voice projected loudly from the answering machine. I cringed, hoping she wouldn't wake Hayden. "Just wanted to wish you a happy birthday, honey. Sorry I won't be there to share it with you. But we'll celebrate when I get back on Monday."

"Happy birthday, sweetheart," Hayden whispered in his husky morning voice.

I twisted in his arms and rested my cheek against his bare chest, realizing my bra was the only thing separating us. "Thanks."

"Were you gonna tell me?"

I shrugged as he pulled me tighter. "Careful for your ribs."

He didn't let up his grip. "They're fine."

I inhaled his aloe scent, absorbing it like I needed it to function. "Can I ask you something?"

"Go for it."

I pulled back and looked up into his eyes. Even with his unshaven face which I discovered last night concealed a bunch of small cuts, he was gorgeous. Even more so knowing he planned to change—and I might've had a little something to do with it. "Have you ever called me beautiful?"

His forehead creased.

I laughed. "That didn't come out right. I wasn't fishing for a compliment or anything, I swear. It's just, when I was in the hospital, I had a dream you called me beautiful. It felt so real. I've always wanted to ask."

A sexy smile stretched its way across his lips. "I like you dreaming about me."

I rolled my eyes. "It was just that once."

"Well since we're being so honest," he said, not buying it at all. "I have something to admit."

I raised my brows.

"That night. In the hospital. I did call you beautiful. Probably a hundred times when I was begging you to wake up."

I closed my eyes, loving his honesty, but hating the thought of that night.

"It's how I see you. A beautiful, innocent angel."

I opened my eyes, realizing the gravity of his words. He'd gotten a tattoo for God's sake. I raised my face to his. "*Your* angel."

He met me half way. "*My* angel."

## HAYDEN

I'd never spent a whole day making out with a girl and not getting her naked. I guess I really was changing. Didn't stop me from needing a cold shower when I left her apartment, though.

I hadn't spoken to Remy. A couple of the guys called and said he'd been on a major bender. Alcohol, drugs, women, and more drugs. Remy on a normal day was fucked in the head. Add murder to the mix and you had a volatile Remy.

But I wouldn't let any of my bullshit mess up Alex's night. She deserved an amazing birthday. The first one without her parents. And I was gonna be the one to give it to her.

When she opened her apartment door, I staggered back, floored by how gorgeous she really was. There was something about her flowing brown hair and gorgeous green eyes that stole my breath away every time I looked at her. And who could ignore her strapless red corset-top, black skirt, and knee high black boots? *Hot damn.*

With a wide smile, Alex stepped into me, wrapping her arms around my waist like she hadn't been with me all night and day. She looked up into my eyes, dreamy and content. "Thank you." She didn't have to explain. I knew she meant my clean-shaven face and the white button down shirt I wore with a loose blue tie.

"What happened to 'you're swell'?"

Her eyes hung on mine. "Oh, you are so much more than swell."

I parked outside Ellington's, the fanciest restaurant in town. I'd never been before. Never had a reason to. I wanted to check if we needed a reservation before bringing Alex in, so I pushed open my door.

Alex grabbed my arm. "We're not going here, are we?"

My brows furrowed. Every girl wanted to eat there. "That was the plan."

Alex stuck out her bottom lip. On any other girl the pout would've annoyed the hell out of me. But on Alex, I wanted to pull her to me, suck on her bottom lip until she begged me to do dirty things to her, then give her whatever the hell she wanted. "I thought we might be going somewhere else."

I snorted. "Care to clue me in?"

She shook her head.

I stared out my window watching overpriced cars pull up to the valet as well-dressed couples got out and made their way inside the restaurant. The same restaurant Alex wanted no part of.

But if not something romantic like Ellington's, where? Had she mentioned it and I didn't catch on? "Not even a small clue?"

She shook her head with a smile, clearly finding my bewilderment amusing.

When it finally hit me, I smiled, too.

Of course.

Jake's was beyond packed, but somehow we snagged a seat in the middle of the room. The place echoed with voices of the groups jammed around high-top tables and those butchering songs on stage. And though we needed to shout to speak, Alex didn't seem to mind. She'd worn a giant grin since we pulled into the lot.

I glanced around the crowded room. "I can't believe this is your idea of a good birthday."

"You thought it was a good idea for a first date," she challenged.

"Oh, sweetheart, that was never meant to be a date."

She raised a dubious brow.

"I was trying like hell to keep you away from me."

She threw back her head and laughed. So carefree. So beautiful. "How'd that work out for you?"

Before I could offer up a smug reply, the waitress slid up beside our table. Her eyes immediately locked onto mine.

*Oh shit.*

Without missing a beat, Alex's hand slid across the table, linking our fingers on top of it. "We'll have two bottles of Bud."

Only then did the waitress notice Alex sharing the table with me. "Huh?"

Alex didn't even bother glancing back. She just gazed across the table at me, laying on the enamored eyes big time. "I said my man and I'll have two bottles of Bud."

My man? I liked the sound of that. And the feisty way she uttered it, staking claim and taking names.

The waitress blinked hard. "Yeah. Okay."

"And two tequila shots," I added.

"Sure. Be right back."

With the waitress gone, Alex squeezed my hand. "Maybe we should've already had the talk."

I suppressed a smile, wanting her to say the words.

She lifted her chin toward the bar where the waitress awaited our drinks. "No more of that."

I smiled, loving how possessive she'd become. "No more of what?"

She tilted her head, eyeing me in disbelief. "Don't give me that innocent act. No more girls."

My head recoiled. Did she really think I'd want to be with other girls after I'd tasted her?

Misreading my expression, her eyes flared. "Are you joking?"

She looked about ready to take a swing at me or bolt, so I linked my foot around the bottom of her stool and pulled it to me. With only inches separating us, I took her other hand and held both in my lap. I leaned forward, moving my lips to her ear. "Don't you realize you've ruined me for all others?"

Her soft waves brushed my cheek as she shook her head.

I pulled back slightly, needing to see her eyes. Needing her to see *my* eyes. "I haven't been with anyone since I met you."

She cocked her head to the side.

"I swear."

"Hayden. I've seen them."

I shook my head, determined to make her believe me. Believe the truth. "I'm serious. Anyone you saw was to make you stay away from me. Except Marisol the night of the dance. She was just nursing me back to health."

"I bet she was."

## ALEX

I didn't mean to give Hayden a hard time. I did believe him about Marisol. I just couldn't believe he'd gone to such great lengths to keep me away from him. *Or* that he so willingly stopped sleeping around after meeting me once. The jury was still out on that one.

The waitress returned with our drinks, placing them down one at a time on the opposite end of the table. Was she trying to pry us apart?

When she finally moved to her next table, Hayden lifted his shot without releasing my other hand. "Happy birthday, beautiful."

I lifted my shot with a smirk. I didn't need him to call me beautiful.

Hayden's eyes jetted around the room, ensuring no one could hear whatever he planned to say. His eyes slid back to mine. "Thank you."

My forehead creased. "For what?"

His pretty eyes didn't waver. They held mine. Caressed them. Made sure I believed him. "For coming along when I needed you."

My lips parted as I struggled to process what he'd said. Hadn't he just admitted to pushing me away? Why would he if he needed me?

Tears stung the backs of my eyes.

"You turned me into a creepy stalker who just needed to see you," he admitted, grazing his thumb over my knuckles. "You made me laugh with your smart little mouth." His candor made his eyes drift from mine for a long moment. When he finally looked back, I could've sworn his eyes were glassy. "Bottom line, Alex...you made me feel."

I didn't even bother trying to stop the tears sliding down my cheeks. Hayden's sincerity floored me. "Thank you," I mouthed.

Though his eyes itched to move away, his gaze showed a warmth he saved only for me.

I tossed back my shot and closed my eyes, needing a second to process the moment. To let his words truly sink in.

Hayden's arms slipped around my waist, bringing me to the safe place I associated with only him. Tiny shivers zipped through me as he pressed his lips to my cheeks, stopping the tears as they fell. One after the other.

I wrapped my arms around him, letting him hold me for a long moment. A long unspoiled moment in the middle of a noisy, crowded bar. It couldn't have been more perfect.

"How about a song?" he murmured in my ear.

"What do you want me to sing?"

He pulled me by the hand off my stool. I patted my eyes with the back of my free hand, trying to rid any trace of tears as we moved to the DJ.

Hayden leaned down to speak to him. When his grip on my hand tightened and he led me onto the stage, I did a double take. "What are you doing?"

He flashed me a nervous smile, then pulled the stool forward and sat down. "Giving you your birthday gift."

The guitar intro to Pearl Jam's "Alive" exploded through the speakers. I threw back my head and laughed. Of course he'd pick something so symbolic.

Thankfully, for Hayden, the bar was crowded. Because when the lyrics scrolled across the screen, I could barely hear my own voice over the noise, forget his. But I had to hand it to him. He sang. Whether he was good or bad, it took major guts to get up in front of a packed house and belt out a song. But he did it. And I knew he did it for me, which made me love him even more.

Love?

*Oh, crap.*

## HAYDEN

Singing at Jake's turned out to be the most embarrassing thing I'd ever done. When Alex and I descended the stage, we were met by lots of high fives. I couldn't tell if they were happy the song ended and my ass was off the stage or if I didn't totally suck.

At our table, we ordered more drinks and a heaping plate of nachos. As I devoured half the plate, Alex stared at me with a crooked smile. The same smile she'd worn since we left the stage.

I knew my gift was the cheap way out, but I had this need to give her whatever she wanted. Not because it's what she was used to. But because I got to watch her face light up, her eyes grow big, and happy creases dig into the corners of her mouth.

Pure serenity.

Maybe I couldn't afford expensive things, but I'd make damn sure to come through in the other areas.

"A couple months ago I couldn't even imagine celebrating my birthday. Celebrating anything." Alex flashed me a sad smile. "But this. This has been perfect."

I took a pull of my beer. Alex's candor still unnerved me. It had been a long time since anyone spoke to me with the honesty she did. And just as long since I meant something to someone, the way I clearly did to her. "Glad you're having fun."

Alex leaned closer, her voice lower than normal. "When are we doing the body shots?"

My brows flew up as I choked down the beer in my mouth.

Was she joking? She had to be joking. Because she was too classy to strip down so I could suck shots from her naval in the middle of a packed bar. Not that I wouldn't want to. Because, man, I wanted to.

I shook my head like the standup guy I needed to be. "No way in hell I'm letting anyone see you like that."

Her cheeks flushed to a pretty shade of pink. "I didn't mean here."

*Fuck me.*

I lifted my face to the heavens. I needed strength. Mine was seriously faltering.

I wanted this. And I wanted it with Alex. But I had a feeling, like deep down in places my conscience had no business being, that she'd never had sex before.

I needed to be smart. There was a lot riding on the remainder of the night. I couldn't do anything to screw it up. The old Hayden would've. This Hayden couldn't. "Why don't we finish up here and see where the night takes us."

## ALEX

Had I just been rejected? Because it felt a lot like a rejection.

I didn't understand. After the way things heated up over the past twenty-four hours, I assumed it was a logical progression. It wasn't like I'd asked him to screw me on a table in the middle of the bar. Okay. So maybe the screwing was implied, but come on. He's a guy. What guy wouldn't immediately ask for the check and race back to his place?

Maybe he wasn't planning to sleep with me. Maybe he sensed my inexperience. Maybe it was so glaringly obvious I should've been mortified.

"Hey," Hayden's voice broke through my musings.

I glanced to his blue eyes, such a contrast to his white shirt and navy tie.

"Where were you just now?"

No use lying. I tapped the side of my head.

"Well stay out of there. Our night isn't even close to over yet."

His assurance brought a bevy of flutters to my stomach. God, I was so easy.

"Wait here," Hayden instructed as he turned off the engine and jumped out of his truck.

My feet bounced with nervous energy as he passed the front of the truck. He opened my door and took my hand, helping me out. My nerves kicked into high gear as we set off toward our building.

It was happening. It was really happening.

Hayden pulled me across the leaf-covered lawn. Before I realized what he intended, he stopped. His hands locked on my hips, and he lifted me onto the picnic table I hadn't realized was behind me.

The wood distressed beneath his weight as he sat beside me. Wrapping his arm around my waist, he drew me into his side and dropped a kiss to the top of my head. "This is what I was thinking about doing the day we met."

I smiled into his side, recalling the moment.

"I probably should've. It would've saved us a lot of wasted time."

I laughed. "You would've scared the hell out of me."

His voice became serious. "You were so sad. I knew whatever was causing you pain, I needed to make it go away. I needed to make it better. I just didn't know how."

I stared up into his eyes. Just like his words, they were truthful and exposed—and let's not forget drop dead, melt into a puddle of goo, dreamy. I couldn't believe he saved it all for me. All those other girls got his body. But I got so much more.

Trailing a finger across my cheek, he brushed a stray piece of hair out of my eye. "I've never needed to help someone the way I need to help you."

"Sorry, I'm so pathetic."

He lifted my chin with his finger, leveling his eyes with mine. "That's not what I meant. It's like...I have this need deep inside. It makes me *want* to help you. *Want* to be there for you no matter what. No matter when. No matter where."

With heady emotions whirling through me, I grabbed his tie and pulled him to me. My lips collided with his. He was more than willing, grabbing hold of the sides of my head and unleashing his own lips and tongue. A long moment slid by as we lost ourselves in the sensations we created. *God.* How any girl could settle for just one night with him was beyond me. Our feelings were transferred through our connection. That deep, permeating connection that made Hayden admit things I knew he'd never admitted before.

He pulled away, his tongue grazing his bottom lip as his eyes locked on my lips. He didn't want to stop. And I loved that he didn't want to. "Come on," he said on a sigh, jumping down from the table and holding out his hand for mine.

Instead of going inside, he led me to the pool and sat me down on a lounge chair. I watched with growing anticipation as he dropped to his knees in front of me and lowered his warm hands to my left thigh. He slipped his fingers around the back of my leg while his thumbs massaged my bare skin. Goose bumps scattered everywhere.

*Oh sweet Jesus.*

Stopping his hands at the top of my boot, he lowered the zipper from the back of my knee down to my ankle. His fingers slid inside the opening, running up and down my calf sending ripples rocketing.

Was there a spot on my body that didn't react to his touch?

He glanced up at me through his impossibly long eyelashes as he slipped the boot from my foot.

"Am I getting the usual Hayden Martin treatment?"

A sly smile crept across his lips. "Oh, no. You're getting more than the usual. It's your birthday. Remember?"

"So there's a birthday special?"

"Let's just say I know how to improvise."

I smiled as he repeated his seductive boot removal technique with my right leg, before slipping off his own shoes and socks and rolling up the bottom of his jeans.

He took my hand and led me to the side of the pool. The moon shone down on the still surface as we sat on the edge with our feet dangling in the cool water. Again, he slipped his arm around me, drawing me into his side, like he couldn't get close enough.

"And here, I saw you in that bathing suit. My God, woman. Were you trying to kill me?"

I threw back my head. "Believe it or not, when I came out here, you were the last thing on my mind. Sleep. Sleep was on my mind and my need to do it. Until, of course, you showed up and thrust your shirtless self in my face."

He laughed, squeezing my body as he did. "Liked what we saw, did we?"

"You're so conceited."

"And you love it."

I rolled my eyes, not even bothering to deny it. A distant siren sounded in the quiet night as the cool air tickled my bare arms.

Hayden's voice deepened, growing serious once again. "It was that day I realized there was more to you than just a gorgeous face."

*Gorgeous face?*

Even with the butterflies taking flight in my stomach, I couldn't quell the sarcasm. "So you liked my body?"

"Uh, yeaaaah," he deadpanned.

I nudged him with my shoulder, and his shoulders shook with laughter.

"No, seriously. You were so damn funny and sarcastic and just…real. Not at all like other girls I'd been around."

I stared down at the water sparkling in the moonlight unsure of what to say.

"And if I'm being completely honest, it took all the willpower I had to leave you that day. But I knew if I stayed, I couldn't be held responsible for my actions."

"So, no laundry?"

He shook his head. "Cold shower."

We both laughed for a long time. I wished those deep creases around his eyes when he laughed—when he let himself relax—would stay forever.

He leaned down and his lips sealed over mine, soft and gentle. Such a contradiction to his tough façade—his tough life. And instead of ravaging my lips until they were raw, he tortured them with tender caresses. Like they were something sacred. Like *I* was something sacred.

He pulled away with a smirk, probably because we were both breathless and gasping for air like we'd just finished a race. "That day I so wanted to do that."

"I probably would've let you. And I'm thinking I would've liked it."

He brushed his nose against mine. "Only liked it?"

I rolled my eyes. So damn cocky. "I would've loved it."

"That's better." He jumped to his feet, pulling me to mine. We grabbed our shoes, and he tugged me away from the pool. "Two more stops."

We were half way to the door of the building when I yelped. Hayden yanked me down onto his lap in the middle of the lawn. I giggled, not from his playfulness—which I loved—but from to the awkward way I straddled his hips in my short skirt. He didn't seem to mind because he leaned in, kissing me softly below my ear before nuzzling my neck with a muffled groan.

My God, if he'd just stay this playful and truthful, everything would be beyond perfect.

"Now, if we'd watched the movie this way, I guarantee you wouldn't have fallen asleep."

"You said you wanted me to sleep," I reminded him.

He nodded. "Yeah. I knew you needed it." His eyes grew distant. It happened so quickly. Like a switch went off and the carefree Hayden vanished.

I wasn't about to lose him, so I gripped his chin lightly and made him look at me. "What?"

He shook his head, his eyes drifting away from me.

I gave him a moment, wrapping my arms around him and holding him to me as the leaves on the trees rustled in the breeze.

"I don't sleep much either," he said. "I've got a lot keeping me awake at night. But that night, out here next to you, I slept. No dreams. No waking up in a cold sweat. I just slept." He tightened his grasp on me. "It happens when we share a bed, too."

I smiled a big stupid grin. As much as I needed him, he needed me, too. They weren't just words uttered in a bar. Every second we spent together made that abundantly clear. It was irrational, and probably unhealthy, but it was what we had. What we were. "After all you've done for me, I'm glad I can help you. Even if it's just in a small way."

"So you think your aunt'll let me move in?"

I pulled back to find a hopeful grin on his face. "Not unless you plan on staying in her room."

He laughed. "Oh, no. It's your room or I'm out."

I shook my amused head. "So, where to now?"

He grasped my hips and helped me to my feet. He slipped his hand into mine, guiding me into the building. When we stepped onto our floor, he turned to me. "We already went to Jake's, so that covers that, but something happened after. When we got home. You thanked me for helping you forget."

My gaze dropped to my bare feet, feeling vulnerable hearing my words repeated.

"Instead of letting you walk away. I should've done this." Hayden dropped his shoes and cupped my cheeks. I had no other option but to look up into his piercing eyes. "I will do whatever it takes to make you forget. I'll say whatever you need me to say. Go wherever you need me to go. And I'll be whoever you need me to be."

*Holy hell.*

Dropping my boots, I wrapped my arms around his neck and forced his lips to mine. His words hit deep, and in that moment, with his words filling my head, my body, and my heart, I knew this thing between us was more real than anything I'd ever had before.

I pulled back and looked into his eyes. They were anxious like mine. "I want you, Hayden. I want all you're willing to give."

He said nothing. Just gripped my rear end and lifted me until my legs wrapped around his hips. He kissed me like he needed me to breathe. Fervent and rough. He slammed my back against his door and continued kissing me, consuming my lips, my neck, my ear, my jawline. It was amazing. He was amazing.

God only knows how he unlocked the door, but it swung open and we practically fell inside. But Hayden wouldn't let me fall. He'd *never* let me fall.

My heart ricocheted off the wall of my chest as he kicked the door shut and carried me to his bedroom, gently lowering us to his bed. Neither of us let up our hold, kissing until we couldn't breathe. When we pulled apart, our chests heaved.

He gazed down into my eyes. "Are you sure this is what you want?"

Keeping my eyes locked on his, I nodded. "I've never wanted anything more." I reached for his collar and unknotted his tie, slipping it off his neck.

He immediately went to work on the buttons of his shirt before giving up and yanking it half-buttoned over his head, leaving him in all his bare-chested glory. I wondered if he realized how beautiful he was or if every girl before me had told him so.

His lips crashed down on mine. His tongue slipped inside my mouth, sweet and playful, sweeping in every direction. We were so in sync. I mimicked his give and take, his push and pull.

His lips skated down my neck, kissing and nibbling my skin until I whimpered and groaned beneath him. I had no idea where the sounds even came from. But the quivering sensations he brought out of me definitely merited the primal noises.

Thanks to my corset top, Hayden had full access to my neck and upper chest, and he took full advantage of it, moving over every inch with gentle swirls of his tongue. My breathing quickened as his hands sought access to the skin underneath my top. I hated to break contact, but he couldn't maneuver it off alone. And that's exactly what I wanted him to do.

What I *needed* him to do.

I sat up causing him to sit back on his heels. His eyes, hungry and feral, awaited my next move. I twisted so the clasps running the length of my spine faced him.

He didn't hesitate. His fingers went to work on the small contraptions. His frustrated sighs blew over my back as his big fingers fumbled with the clasps. Finally, one unsnapped, giving way to all the others. I held the front to my chest as Hayden unsnapped the last clasp, revealing my naked back.

He planted a kiss on the back of my neck and his index finger ran down my spine, sending delicious shivers through me.

The time had come.

But could I actually go through with it?

## HAYDEN

*Holy shit.* I'd never been so nervous in my entire life. Having Alex in front of me seconds away from being topless caused me to rethink and regret every stupid girl I'd ever been with. They were a prequel. A waste of time to hold me over until the real deal came along. And Alex was definitely the real deal.

*And* seconds away from being mine in more ways than one.

My heart hammered in my chest as I waited for her to drop the arms holding her top in place. As much as I wanted to rip it off and ravage her, I wanted to take it slow and do everything right. I didn't want to give her any reason to second guess being with me. Or worse, regret it.

Slowly, she peeled the red fabric from her chest and tossed it onto the floor. Now I wouldn't be a guy if I didn't look at her amazing body. But for once I felt guilty gawking. My normal move would've been to grab hold of her incredible assets and make her whimper in delight. Instead, I reached up and caressed the soft skin on her cheeks with my thumbs, holding her eyes. "You are the most beautiful girl I've ever seen."

Alex smiled a small timid smile, probably doubting my words. But it made no difference. I planned to prove it to her. All night long.

I leaned in and pressed my lips against hers, gently rolling her onto her back. My bare chest lowered to hers, skin to glorious skin. She wrapped her arms around me so the soft swells of her chest and the hammering of her heartbeat pressed into me.

Goose bumps scattered over my bare skin. Fucking goose bumps. What the hell was wrong with me? It wasn't like I'd never been with a girl before. I should've been embarrassed by the number of times I had.

It was Alex.

The feather light touch of her fingertips traced patterns up and down my back. I could barely contain myself as they sailed downward, drifting over my ass, sliding to my hips, and grazing up the front of my jeans. She swept her hand over my favorite area, testing the waters. And the waters were more than cooperative, garnering a quiet hiss as sweet sensations rushed through me.

I wasn't sure she knew the hiss was a good thing, because her fingers moved away. But only for a second, before landing on my belt buckle. She went to work, effortlessly unfastening it. If I didn't know any better, I'd think she'd done it before.

Damn. Maybe she had.

She slid the belt from its loops and dropped it off the side of the bed. She unsnapped my button and carefully pulled down the zipper, running her hand inside my jeans and over my boxers.

*Oh, shit.*

Her hand proved a little too much for me to handle, unless I wanted everything to end prematurely. So I broke contact and leaned off to the side of her, giving myself a little time to regroup as I pushed off my jeans.

## ALEX

*Holy crap.* Why'd I feel so self-conscious? It wasn't like he hadn't seen the picture of me. Like the rest of the school, he knew what lay beneath my clothes.

But the idea of slipping off my skirt, now that I'd already lost my top, unnerved me. Like a game of strip poker, I wished I'd worn two pairs of everything to prolong the moment when I lay totally naked.

I sounded like I didn't want this. But I did. I really did. And I wanted it with Hayden. So before he could cover me with his body, I lifted my rear end and shimmied out of my skirt, leaving me in my almost nonexistent black thong.

Hayden gazed down at my body, making sure his eyes didn't linger on any one area for too long. I loved that he did that. Because what guy wouldn't want to stare at a practically naked girl in his bed? I understood the urge. I couldn't stop staring at him, in nothing but his boxers with his muscles rippling with every movement.

Instead of letting him roll on top of me again, I pushed him back and straddled his hips, leaning in so our bare chests touched and I wasn't overly exposed. When he smiled up at me, his eyes were filled with anticipation.

I could feel every hard inch of him beneath me. *Sweet Jesus.* I lowered my lips to his warm neck. It smelled like his crisp scent and tasted bitter like chocolate. His hands moved to my rear end, gently caressing my bare skin as I teased him with my tongue, kissing and sucking along his collar bone.

Getting a little more comfortable with my position, I shifted my lips and trailed down the smooth skin on his upper chest. He hissed when I lowered to his pecs, so I paid them extra attention, sucking and swirling my tongue around and around until he shivered beneath me.

I moved down his torso and licked across the amazing ripples in his abs. The whole experience sexier than all my fantasies. I nibbled the area around his belly button. His body squirmed beneath me, and groans purred in the back of his throat. He'd warned me he groaned. I loved knowing I caused it.

I gripped the waistband of his boxers and slowly peeled them down his sculpted hips. Of course he had the perfect V going on down there. But before I could get a closer look, he caught my hands and stopped them from moving any lower. At first I thought I'd done something wrong. But then he did the honors, slipping off his own boxers.

I tried not to stare, but *holy hell*. Feeling it was one thing. Seeing it was something else entirely.

Before I could tear my eyes away, Hayden had me pinned down on my back. "None of that tonight. Tonight I want you to see how amazing we can be together."

Ripples attacked my belly. Amazing, body tingling ripples that kept rolling and rolling and rolling.

Hayden smiled a dimple-digging smile before his lips sealed over mine. His tongue pushed inside my mouth before I could prepare for it. Powerful and possessive, claiming me with every plunge.

I ran my hands over the inward curve in his spine and up the slope of his smooth rear end. He clenched at the contact. His manhood, in all its glory, stood against my bare stomach, pressing into me like a declaration of things to come.

Even though he was noticeably more than ready to proceed, he stayed at my mouth, devouring my lips and tongue, making me forget everything, including my name. His hand slipped down my neck and over my chest slowly. Agonizingly slowly. His touching, caressing, circling, and squeezing ignited a direct line of pleasure between my thighs. One I didn't even realize existed. But, oh, how it did.

His hand continued its descent, gliding over my belly button and under the minimal fabric of my underwear. His fingers swept lower, gently moving to places no one had ventured before. His middle finger slipped inside my warmth and his thumb stopped on the highest point of pleasure. His light pressure and deliberate movements sent delicious tingles pulsing everywhere.

My head flew back, my eyes squeezing shut. I couldn't keep my body still. It moved with his movements.

*Oh, my freaking God.*

## HAYDEN

Alex's breathy whimpers and obliging body told me one thing. She was more than ready for me. She'd been responsive, enjoying everything I did to her. Everything I made her feel. It was such a fucking turn-on.

In the past, I focused on my needs. A girl's came second. But tonight, it was all about Alex. I'd make her forget any guy who came before me. I'd make her ache for me. Crave my touch. Need me, and only me, for the foreseeable future.

I kept my fingers moving where it appeared she wanted them, adding another digit to the mix. Slipping in and out, up and down, all around. Her body arched in delight. I contemplated letting her go like this, but I wanted to be inside of her the first time.

I withdrew my fingers.

Alex groaned, making it clear I'd left her on the brink.

I opened my nightstand, grabbing hold of a foil packet. I clutched it in my hand, crinkling the wrapper so she could hear it. It was her chance to stop me. Her chance to put on the brakes. Her chance to realize this was a huge mistake.

I looked down at her body tucked beneath mine, waiting for the sign.

She gazed up at me, her chest rising and falling. "I want this Hayden." Her voice came out breathy and sincere. "I want this with you."

Her words sent chills racing up my arms. Never had someone looked at me with such love-filled eyes and meant exactly what they said. Especially knowing what she knew about me. "Just say the word and I'll stop. I obviously won't want to, but I'll stop."

Alex watched mesmerized as I worked the condom on. Once I had it in place, only one thing stood in our way.

I inched my way down Alex's body, my nose brushing over her delicious skin. I gripped her thong with my pinkies. Grasping my intent, she lifted her ass. I inched the piece of string down and discarded it with the rest of our clothes on the floor.

I crawled back on top of her so our chests aligned, her knees cradling my hips. Not wanting to crush her under my weight, I balanced on my forearms, hovering above her. She caught me in her gaze, trusting me with the only thing she had left.

Keeping our eyes locked, I positioned myself at her entrance and gently pressed against her. Her eyes squeezed shut, like I knew they would. I eased my way in, inch by inch, determining my movements by the severity of her wincing. "Is this okay?"

Her head bobbed, but her eyes remained clenched.

She wanted to be strong. I could feel it in her grip on my arms. But I didn't want to hurt her. And while I didn't have any experience with virgins, I knew this would hurt. "We don't have to do this tonight."

Her eyes snapped open. "Oh, you are not getting out of this. You've got me. Now show me what you're going to do with me." Her voice was serious, with a tinge of the sarcasm I loved so much.

Not being able to resist, I flashed my panty-dropping smile. "Your wish is my command."

My words and smile had the desired effect. She grabbed my ass and pulled me closer, urging me deeper inside. As I slid further in, she instinctively wrapped her legs around my waist, making sure I had easier access to my destination.

Smooth sailing ensued. She felt amazing. Tight with her innocence intact. Knowing no one had ventured where I was, made me savor every second even more.

She trusted me.

She'd waited for me.

I never thought that would happen for me. I always thought I deserved what no one else wanted.

Until Alex.

It wasn't going to last long at the rate we were going, our bodies sliding together as one, a mere sheen of sweat separating us. The gentle way she nuzzled my neck, running her tongue up to the sensitive spot below my ear, proved too much for me to handle.

I continued thrusting so nature could take its course. Trying to make it as enjoyable for Alex as possible, I reached between us and pressed the pad of my thumb to her most sensitive spot, stroking small circles round and round.

"*Haydennn*," she groaned.

Her breathy whimpers in my ear, her trembling body, and her inner walls clenching around me sent my own body over the edge. Sensations I'd never felt before rocketed through me.

I froze for a long moment rooted inside of her. Savoring the moment. Savoring the inexplicable feelings she brought out in me. Savoring our physical connection. Savoring the knowledge I could stay like that forever.

My breath escaped me as I rolled us onto our sides so I didn't crush her. The glazed look of euphoria on her face made the moment even more memorable. She blinked multiple times, her eyelashes fanning over her cheeks as she fought to recover.

When her eyes finally focused, they gazed into mine like she'd opened an incredible gift. One she hadn't expected. She didn't speak. She just leaned forward and pressed her lips to mine, soft and slow. She dipped her tongue inside so gently I almost couldn't feel it. Then she pulled back slightly, evening our eyes. "Did you see my face?"

My breath caught in my throat.

A satisfied smile slid across her contented face, as she closed her eyes. "I thought so."

My God. I loved this girl.

Loved?

*Oh, fuck.*

# CHAPTER TWENTY-TWO

## ALEX

I stared at my reflection in the bathroom mirror. I didn't look any different except for my slightly swollen lips. But I felt different. Not my sore nether regions. My clear head. My light heart. And my easy smile.

*Knock. Knock.*

I hurried into the living room and opened the front door. Hayden stood there wearing the same ridiculous grin as me. My God. Was it possible he got better looking overnight? Well seeing as though I slept next to him, I didn't think so. But his light dusting of facial hair, faded jeans, and fitted navy shirt made him perfect in my eyes.

I dug my hand into my hip, shelling out some morning sass. "Can I help you with something?"

He nodded, but didn't answer. He just walked in, causing me to step back. Unfortunately, it wasn't me he sought. He made his way into the kitchen and opened the refrigerator, pulling out a bottle of water.

"You're thirsty?"

He walked back in and grabbed my bag from the sofa.

"You're making sure I stay hydrated?"

He chuckled as he stuffed the bottle into my bag.

"You're kidnapping me?"

He smiled, his dimples digging in. I still couldn't believe he belonged to me—as much as Hayden would let himself belong to anyone.

I walked toward him, giving my hips a little extra shake. I reached up and cupped his cheeks, pulling his face down to mine and planting a nice long kiss on his lips. His minty breath made it easier to dive in, tangling our tongues, consuming as much of him as humanly possible in the middle of my aunt's living room.

Eventually, he pulled back, his chest heaving in tandem with mine. "Okay, okay. I want to drive you to school."

My head retracted. "Why?"

He buried his hands in his pockets, his blue eyes peering out from under his long lashes. "Well, because I can."

I cocked my head. "That the only reason?"

He stifled a grin. "Maybe I want people to know you're mine."

I tried not to melt into a puddle of goo for fear of inflating his already massive ego. "Who said I'm yours?"

He grabbed my hips and pulled me to him. Okay. So I clearly affected his body. "I have it on very good authority that you are very much mine. And I want people to know it."

I gazed up into his playful eyes.

Oh, he was good.

## HAYDEN

I could see by Alex's cute smile, as I helped her out of my truck, that she loved that I'd driven her to school. Loved that I had every intention of showing her off as my own. Especially after initially telling her we needed to keep us quiet.

My eyes raked over her tight jeans and long sleeve peach shirt that flowed when she walked, like the angel's dress in my tattoo. Alex didn't work overtime like other girls trying to snag a guy's attention. Everything about her was so effortless. "Ready?"

"Ready."

When I linked our fingers, Alex's eyes shot to them. Her lips curved even more, but she didn't say a word. She didn't need to.

Given the turning heads as we crossed the quad, we were a huge surprise to everyone. Apparently, they hadn't been paying much attention. I carried the girl out of the dining hall in my arms and threatened the life of anyone who had the picture. Did it really take a genius to figure out we wanted each other?

Alex needed to drop off a psych paper at her professor's office before her first class, so I waited for her outside the building. I hoped Remy didn't plan to drop by campus. I hadn't heard from him or seen him since...well since the other night. I figured he'd be laying low for a while.

I stared out across the bustling quad at the people hurrying to their morning classes. The surrounding trees had begun to transform from green into dark hues of maroon, yellow and orange.

*"Well how about that. A game of Russian roulette...Too bad your luck's run out."*

"Ready?"

My body jolted as Alex slipped her arms around my waist from behind, resting her cheek against my back.

I took a deep breath, clearing the visions from my mind. I could do it. I could push it all away.

I twisted around, but Alex didn't drop her arms. So I snaked mine around her, dropping a kiss on the top of her head as we stood in a relaxed embrace.

After a long moment, she lifted her head and gazed up at me with those dreamy eyes. But something in them shifted. Darkened. "Are you okay?"

I nodded. But it was a lie. A lie after I promised to be honest. My eyes shot away.

Alex sighed, a sigh *I* caused. "Well, I'm here if you need to talk. You know that right?"

My eyes focused on the door and the students passing through it en route to their next classes. I nodded again, knowing full well there were just some things I couldn't bear to share.

After dropping Alex off at her first class, I didn't see her again until lunch. I waited for her outside the dining hall, then we grabbed a couple sandwiches. I led her by hand to a table at the far side of the dining hall—the opposite corner from where I normally sat with the guys and Remy when he showed up. Thank God he hadn't.

I sat down beside Alex and pulled her water from her book bag, handing it to her. "I saw the signs for the competition."

"Yeah?" She twisted off the cap and took a sip. "It's Saturday night. I thought I told you?"

I shook my head. "Where should I sit?"

I noticed her brows slant as she reached for her sandwich. "What?"

"Do you want me right in the front where you can see me or somewhere else?"

She laughed. "First of all, the spotlight is so bright I won't see anyone. *Thank God.* And second, you don't have to go."

I reached for her chin, lifting her face toward me and leveling our eyes. "There is nothing that could keep me from being there."

Her eyes searched my serious face for a long while. "You *were* the one who got me into this mess in the first place."

I smiled, moving in before Alex realized I intended to kiss her. PDA had never been my style, but it definitely added a little something to the kiss as we lost ourselves in each other's lips, neither caring who saw us.

I hung out in my truck while Alex finished rehearsal. When my phone vibrated on the seat beside me, I expected a text letting me know she'd be right out. But when I checked the screen, Remy's name appeared.

*Great.*

Knowing I couldn't avoid him forever, I lifted the phone to my ear. "What's up?"

"Dude, where've you been?"

"Me? I hear you've been hitting it pretty hard these days."

"Yeah, well you know." Remy's words came out rushed and jittery. "So you up for Baxter's tonight? I hear the Webber twins are gonna be there."

My gut twisted at the thought. How had I ever slept with those girls? All enhanced and dirty.

"It hasn't been the same without you."

"Yeah, well broken ribs can really cramp a guy's style."

Remy's voice lowered. "He got you good, huh?"

Remembering the look in both dead men's eyes, my voice came out hushed. "Yeah."

"Not as good as I got him." Remy's maniacal laugh carried through the phone.

My stomach churned. Vomit crawled up the back of my throat. Me almost being killed. Remy killing them. Remy laughing about it. It was twisted and wrong on so many levels. "Look, I gotta go."

"Alright. Think about Baxter's. I'll be there."

I disconnected the call, my mind reeling like a kite's string on a windy day.

I could feel my loyalty to Remy faltering with every breath I took. In every moment I spent with Alex. But very few friends would kill to protect me. Remy would. And had. I just wished he wasn't so hell bent on turning my life upside down with his.

I needed out. And I needed out now.

But what else could I do? If I hadn't been such a screw up, I'd have more credits. I'd be able to get a liberal arts degree like Alex. Maybe I could turn it around next semester. Double up on classes. Maybe it wasn't too late.

I dropped my head back on the headrest, trying to control the erratic racing of my heart.

I knew I was only fooling myself.

I knew too much about Cooper's operations, or at least he assumed I did because Remy did. I was a liability. And a liability couldn't just up and quit his organization.

He'd kill me before he let that happen.

ALEX

I grabbed my backpack and headed for the theater exit. I passed Taylor who, for once, wasn't glaring at me.

"Good luck Saturday," she said, like she actually meant it.

I ignored her. I'd gotten good at it.

"Alex."

*That* voice had me spinning on my heels. Sophia hurried over. We had a test in class, and she'd been working on the set backstage, so I hadn't talked to her.

She gave me a sly smirk as she walked out of the theater with me. "Guess you found a new seat at lunch."

I smiled.

"I so called it."

I laughed. "Yeah, you did."

"Everyone's talking."

I rolled my eyes as we stepped out into the sunlight. "What else is new?"

She shook her head. "No. They're wondering what your secret is."

I arched a brow. "My secret?"

"Hayden Martin does not drive girls to school. Hayden Martin does not hold girls' hands on the quad. Hayden Martin does not walk girls to class. Hayden Martin does not make out with girls in the dining hall. Hayden Martin—"

"Is more unbelievable than I ever imagined." I tried to suppress a smile to no avail. "And, as you've noticed, he's all mine."

She patted my back. "You lucky bitch."

"You have no idea."

Sophia and I parted ways in the parking lot. I walked over to Hayden's truck. Through the window I could see his head resting back like he was asleep. But when I pulled open the passenger door, his head whipped up.

"Sorry. Didn't mean to scare you." I slid into the seat waiting for him to greet me with a kiss. He didn't. He didn't even smile. "Sorry rehearsal took so long."

The roar of his engine was the only response I got.

*Okay?* Were we playing charades again? Was he hoping I'd attack him like I had that morning to get him talking? I wondered if he realized normal relationships didn't work that way. He needed to actually talk to me. He *promised* to.

But given his silence and the vacant look in his eyes as he drove through town, he didn't plan to. And by the time we pulled into our parking lot ten minutes later, he still hadn't uttered a single word.

The weekend had been perfect. What happened between then and now?

I needed to understand, but I didn't want to push him by asking questions he couldn't or wouldn't answer. So where did that leave me? Where did it leave us?

With my sanity holding on by a string, I did the only thing I could. Before he even switched off the engine, I jumped out of his truck. I'd almost made it to the building when his car door slammed shut behind me. The ominous echo sent my body spinning. Okay, so I was pissed. Pissed at his silence. Pissed he didn't explain what was wrong. Pissed he couldn't trust me.

He took his sweet time, but eventually he stopped in front of me. Instead of saying anything, his eyes fell to his feet.

"Talk to me," I urged.

He lifted his head, but his eyes stared over my shoulder, avoiding me like he had earlier when he lied about being okay. "I never promised you I'd be good at this."

"Good at what?"

He motioned between us without looking at me.

"After what happened this weekend, I'd say you're damn good at this." I did my own motioning between us.

A muscle in his jaw tightened. "I get angry and I don't know how to deal with it."

"Did I make you angry?"

His face squished up and he shook his head, like I'd asked a stupid question.

"Then who?"

"I got a call when you were in rehearsal. And I'm trying to figure out what to do about it."

Relief swept over me. I slipped my hand into his, needing to comfort him any way I could. "Well I'm sure whatever you decide will be the right choice."

The comment earned me cold eyes and furrowed dark brows. "Oh yeah, because all the decisions I've made up to this point have been brilliant."

I drew in a quick breath, alarmed by the edge to his voice. "I just meant you'll figure it out."

He pulled his hand free from mine, burying it in his pocket.

*That hurt.* "Look, Hayden, I can't tell you what to do. I'd never even try. But sometimes a fresh perspective can help. So when you're ready to talk, *if* you're ever ready to talk, I'm here." I contemplated walking away, but that would've given him the green light to run from our problems whenever he got the urge.

He pulled in a deep breath. Seconds passed before he exhaled. "I won't bring you into my shit."

I threw my arms out at my sides. "I'm already *in* your shit."

He blinked multiple times before realization flashed in his eyes. *Finally.*

I slid my arms around his waist, fully prepared for him to pull away. But he didn't. "I'm scared for you." I stared up into his distant eyes. "I can see whatever you're not saying isn't easy." His eyes reluctantly dropped to mine. "I don't want you to deal with it alone. I don't want it to eat away at you."

He scoffed.

"Well, I'm here." I rested my cheek against his chest, listening to his heart thumping faster than usual inside. "Just don't push me away."

He slipped his arms around me and held me closer. I melted into his chest, not realizing how tense I'd become. Or how much I craved his touch. I wanted nothing more than to make whatever plagued his mind disappear. I just didn't know how.

"I know I suck at this." His voice was low, tentative. "But you've got to know, you're the only thing keeping me sane right now." He pressed his lips to the top of my head, allowing them to linger. "Without you, I'd be completely lost."

It was crazy how easily my anger disappeared when he admitted things like that.

# CHAPTER TWENTY-THREE

## HAYDEN

I dropped onto my sofa, burying my head in my hands. I saw the hurt in Alex's eyes when I didn't invite her over. I wished she understood how fucked up my head had been since letting her in. One minute I'm on cloud nine because she's around and wants me. The next I'm angry at the world, shackled by the life I'd chosen.

My phone vibrated on the coffee table. I assumed it was Remy checking if I'd be at Baxter's. But the screen read *Restricted*. I lifted it to my ear. "Hello?"

"Cooper wants to see you tonight," a gruff voice informed me. "Alone. Back door of his restaurant at ten. Tell no one."

A chill ran down my spine. A piercing sound rang in my ears. My pulse sped up. Cooper didn't call you in to ask about your day. He summoned you when you screwed up. Then he dealt with you. And in his world, *dealt with* meant made you disappear.

*Fuuuuck.*

Remy and I screwed up one too many times.

This was how it all ended. I *knew* I survived too many bad situations unscathed to make it out of this nightmare alive.

I gripped the sides of my head with shaking hands, thoughts zigzagging every which way. Had Cooper already called Remy? Was he going to do it when we were together? Maybe he'd make Remy kill me. Maybe that's why Remy called.

I stood from the sofa on shaky legs, unable to sit still. I paced the length of the living room trying to calm my nerves. Trying not to pass out. Trying to wrap my head around what inevitably awaited me once I left my apartment.

I rushed to my front door. I needed to pick up Alex and get the hell out of town before Cooper even knew I disappeared. I'd take her up north. Maybe home to Austin. Or maybe somewhere no one knew us.

I stopped with my hand on the door knob.

Then dropped my forehead against the door.

What was I thinking?

I couldn't bring Alex into it. It was my mess. My fucking mess. And as stupid as my decision had been to join Remy in Cooper's organization, I chose it. And seriously, if I thought for one second Cooper wouldn't find me, I was delusional. He'd find me. And when he did, he'd do worse than kill me.

By nine-thirty, I'd downed at least a quarter of a bottle of Jack. I normally had a high tolerance for alcohol, but I couldn't walk a straight line to save my life.

*To save my life.*

I almost laughed at the irony, because there was no saving my life. Cooper *was* going to kill me.

I stepped out of my apartment in a black hooded sweatshirt and jeans. The sweatshirt itself seemed fitting. It's what I wore to Victor's grave. I threw the hood up over my head. It'd be my only protection from the fate awaiting me.

Before I took another step, Alex's door flew open. She dug her hands into her hips. "Going somewhere?"

My eyes raked over her body, so unbelievably hot in her little blue pajama shorts and matching top. I couldn't stop myself. I stalked over, my lips crashing down on hers as I pushed her into her apartment and shoved the door shut. "Is your aunt home?" I asked against her lips.

She shook her head with a giggle as her lips moved with mine.

I picked her up and her legs wrapped around my hips. I loved how light she felt in my arms. How we fit together. Always eager. Always in sync. But we didn't have much time. I dropped down onto the sofa with Alex straddling my lap.

She pulled back, licking her lips with a little grin. "I could get used to hellos like this."

But it wasn't hello. It was a cruel, untimely goodbye.

"Did you leave any liquor for anyone else? Your breath's lethal."

I shook my head. No use denying it.

I stared into her eyes, trying to memorize every little fleck of mint green etched into them. My God, it was going to be hard to walk out that door. Hard to leave the best thing that ever came into my life. Hard to break her heart. "I've got to run out for a little while." I tried for nonchalance, but my shaky, slightly slurred words were anything but.

"When will you be back?" Her brows bounced playfully. "Because that kiss is going to keep me awake all night if you don't finish what you started."

At a moment like that, I couldn't believe I even had it in me to laugh. "I've created a monster." And within seconds, I'd be abandoning her. Like everyone she trusted before me.

The thought sobered my drunk ass.

Alex's fingers played with the hair at the back of my neck. I loved when she did that. I never told her that. I never told her a lot of things. Now it was too late.

"You were pretty upset this afternoon. You feel any better?"

I shook my head. Couldn't she feel my entire body trembling?

"Anything I can do?" She nuzzled into my neck, kissing the sweet spot below my ear with tiny wet kisses that numbed my skin.

"I love you." The words flew out before I could stop them.

Her lips froze. Nope. Every part of her body froze.

"I just thought you should know."

Her head pulled back slowly. Her wide eyes stared into mine. I could practically hear her thoughts. Her fears. Her shock. She thought it was too soon.

It *was*. It was irrational to be in love with someone you hardly knew. It was something I would've given other guys shit for. But with Alex, it was the truth. As dysfunctional as we were, with the messed up circumstances drawing us together, we worked.

And forget about her patience. She'd been enduring my bullshit every step of the way, and here she sat knocking down the very walls I'd created to protect myself from feeling anything. She knew, even when I didn't, it was exactly what I needed. *She* was exactly what I needed.

But given her silence, and the startled look on her face, I ruined the moment. Our last moment together.

Without warning, her lips tipped up in the corners. "You do?"

I could've made up some lame-ass excuse for my momentary bout of craziness, but why bother? "I knew it the second we met."

Her eyes closed and her shoulders relaxed, as if savoring my words. I could almost see the stress in her face disappear before she let out the most adorable little sigh. "Thank you, Hayden."

"Thank you?"

She leaned her forehead into mine and opened her eyes. "For making my prayers come true."

Not the exact response I was hoping for, but one hell of a close second.

Reeking dumpsters lined the dark alley behind Cooper's restaurant. I stood for a long moment staring at the lone metal door. I'd left my gun in my truck. What was the point? The second I whipped it out, Cooper's guards would've used me for target practice.

With my heart lodged in the back of my throat, I stepped forward and tugged on the door. It didn't budge. Maybe I still had time to get the hell out of dodge. I'd leave everything behind. If Cooper found me, he found me. But there was always the off chance that he wouldn't bother looking. He'd just let me go.

But then what?

I'd be alone.

Always alone.

At least in the next few minutes, I'd pay retribution for the things I'd done and the things I'd seen and stayed quiet about.

Fuck it.

I pounded once on the door. A dull thud reverberated off the dumpsters. I stepped back as the door swung open. One of Cooper's suit-clad guards gave me a nod and stepped aside so I could enter. I made my way through the short hallway. He lifted his chin toward a dark stairwell.

My white knuckles gripped the cold copper railing as I climbed the steps alone, stopping every few to slow my pounding heart. At least I attempted to.

I inevitably reached the closed door at the top. I pictured Alex's smiling face after I told her I loved her. Okay, so maybe it took a while for the smile to appear, but when it did, it made everything else happening to me disappear.

I wanted to hold on to that image until Cooper put the bullet through my head. Hopefully he'd do it as soon as the door opened.

My pulse hammered harder than anything I'd ever experienced as I knocked on the door. Immediately, it swung open, causing me to jump back a step. Another guard nodded, stepping aside to let me into the office.

When I spotted Cooper behind his big mahogany desk holding a phone to his ear and not a loaded weapon to my head, I exhaled a slow unsteady breath.

Cooper, in his late forties with dark hair and a hint of gray around the ears, wore a tailored dark suit. Not at all what you'd expect of one of the biggest bookies on the coast.

When he noticed me standing there, he lifted his chin. The small gesture put me at ease. It wasn't the look of a man about to finish me off.

Maybe he was too smart to kill me in one of his establishments. Maybe as long as I stood inside, in a building with people eating dinner downstairs, I remained safe.

It's when I left the building, I needed to be scared shitless.

Cooper switched off his phone and motioned for his guard to leave the room. "Give us a minute." When the door closed, Cooper pointed to the chair across from him. "Sit."

I dropped down into the stiff leather. If I didn't stop trembling, I'd never be able to stand back up.

"Scary situation Friday night."

Not wanting him to notice my shaking hands, I grasped onto the wooden arms of the chair and nodded.

He leaned back in his high-backed chair and crossed his arms across his chest. "Did Remy tell you it was taken care of?"

"I haven't really talked to him about it."

Cooper arched a brow. "Oh? I thought you boys were tight?"

"I hear he's been partying pretty hard." I swallowed. "I'm guessing it scared the hell out of him. You know. His hand in it and all."

Cooper nodded, then leaned forward, steepling his fingers in front of him. He hesitated for a long moment, his narrowed eyes assessing me. "I need to ask you something. And I need to be sure it's in absolute confidence."

"Of course."

"Have you noticed anything strange going on when I send you two out?"

My forehead creased.

"I mean with Remy. Like him taking off alone with no explanation. Or him making deals with the deadbeats."

My eyes jumped away, my mind working to recall what I'd seen. On a good night, Remy was fucked in the head. It'd be impossible to guess why he did anything he did. But I'd heard him trying to make a deal at the house, before the gun jammed into my head. I just thought he was pleading for his life.

"I'll take that as a yes."

My eyes flew back to Cooper. "I swear. I have no clue what he's been up to. I don't ask and he doesn't tell me." I tunneled my fingers through my hair, hoping Cooper didn't mistake my nervousness for guilt. "Is it bad?"

Cooper nodded once.

"Fucking Remy," I mumbled. "As stupid as he can be, he's saved my ass more than once. And now he killed to protect me. You gotta know I owe him my life."

Cooper leaned back in his chair and crossed his arms again. A long moment passed between us where his eyes never left mine. He considered his words carefully. A man like him always did. "Would it help to know while Remy may have killed that man to protect you, he killed his friend because he was trying to cover his own ass?"

My brows furrowed. "The guy had a gun to Remy's head."

"I know. But Remy knew him. Knew he was gonna rat him out."

Huh?

"Remy went there with the sole purpose of killing him."

My head retracted. "I don't understand. The guy came to the door with the gun already drawn."

"He'd already ratted Remy out. So he knew he'd retaliate."

I dropped my head back, wondering what else I didn't know.

"It seems Remy's been embezzling money from me for a while now. Every time you two collect, it's short."

*What the fuck, Remy?*

"Of course he always has excuses. Usually trying to convince me that getting something from these guys is better than nothing. But it wasn't adding up."

I closed my eyes, pushing my palms into them.

"I've known him since he was a kid, since you were both kids. So before taking matters into my own hands, I needed to determine your involvement. It's obvious he's working alone."

I nodded, thankful for his trust.

"With that being said, we're not finished."

## ALEX

Hayden and I sat beside one another in the crowded dining hall. To an outsider, things between us looked fine. But since telling me he loved me two days ago, Hayden hadn't been the same.

I didn't expect roses and chocolates, but he'd been distant. Disappearing without explanation. Quieter than usual. And all displays of affection had ceased to exist.

I found myself asking questions, which only garnered a nod, shake of his head, or shrug. Even when I asked a question requiring more than *yes, no,* or *I don't know.*

I wondered if it was my fault. I mean, my reaction, or lack thereof, to his confession was appalling. Truthfully, it knocked the breath right out of me. And even though he'd been drinking, he'd said it. He'd actually said those words. And liquid courage or not, coming from Hayden, it was a monumental step—and completely insane.

Two months ago, we didn't even know each other. How had our feelings developed so strongly? So quickly? How had our lives become so intertwined? Maybe our misfortune in losing our parents had bonded us. Or maybe the way he kept saving me had cinched our connection.

I looked out over the dining hall envious of the smiling girls whose biggest concerns were what to do Friday night. I stabbed at my salad, trying to process Hayden's behavior. Trying to determine my next move.

"What do we have here?"

Before my eyes even lifted from my food, I knew who the deep voice belonged to.

Hayden's head shot up from his burger as Remy slid into the seat across from us. His jeans and faded black band T-shirt hung off his body. He looked more frail and sickly than I recalled. He reached across the table and stole a handful of fries from Hayden's plate.

"What's up, man?" Hayden's words were cautious, almost shaky.

Remy stuffed the fries into his mouth as he lifted his chin to me. "I meant the bitch."

I answered before Hayden could. "The name's Alex."

"Al. Ex." My name dripped mockingly off his pierced tongue.

Up close, his gaunt face and discolored teeth made the hairs on the back of my neck stand on end. My attention dropped to my salad. If I acted like I wasn't there, maybe he'd forget I'd spoken.

"So, is this who you replaced me with?" Remy taunted Hayden.

Hayden's hand found my thigh under the table. "We're just hanging out. It's nothing serious."

My eyes shot up.

A sly smile wet Remy's lips. "Of course it's not. Bitches can't be trusted."

Hayden's hand stiffened on my leg.

"Did you hear him?" Remy's eyes flashed to mine. "It's not serious. So run along. Me and my boy have things to discuss."

Hayden's grip on my leg tightened, an unspoken directive to stay. "Dude. She's fine."

Remy's fiery brown eyes darkened. He looked about ready to jump across the table. Had Hayden never defied his wishes before?

A strange silence fell upon the dining hall.

Had everyone heard what was transpiring in our corner?

My eyes shot around. All eyes were trained on two uniformed police officers crossing the room. Their dull footsteps resounded as they moved closer and closer to our table.

"Remington Tyler." They stopped behind Remy. "You have the right to remain silent."

A sadistic smile stretched across Remy's face as his head whipped around. Only a lunatic would find humor in being arrested in front of a room full of people.

The stocky officer withdrew his handcuffs, taking Remy's wrists behind his back and pulling him to his feet. The smile never faded from his face as the officer continued reading him his rights.

"Hayden Martin, you have the right—"

My head snapped around, my eyes wide. The second officer stood behind Hayden reading him *his* rights while placing cuffs on his wrists. Hayden's head stayed down. He made no attempt to argue. No attempt to ask questions. No attempt to look at me.

"Wait! What's happening?" I asked frantically.

"Miss, remain seated," the officer ordered as he yanked Hayden to his feet.

"Hayden," I pleaded as the officer pushed him along.

Hayden's eyes remained locked on the tile floor. "Just stay out of it, Alex," he muttered before being led out of the dining hall alongside Remy for all to see.

# CHAPTER TWENTY-FOUR

## ALEX

The late October breeze carried dry leaves across the quiet parking lot where I sat on the hood of my car. My eyes focused on the front door of the rusted brick sheriff's office. The same one that hadn't opened in hours. Darkness had already crept in. Of course it had. Nine hours had lapsed since the police arrested Hayden.

And I'd yet to get any answers.

What could he have possibly done?

Had he even done anything?

I burrowed my fingers into my hair. *Ugh.* What was taking so long?

At nine forty-five, the door finally swung open. My aunt exited first, followed by Mr. Jacobson, my parents' lawyer, and then Hayden. His jeans looked slept in, his white T-shirt was a wrinkled mess, and his hair stuck up like he'd run his hands through it a thousand times.

I slid off the hood. My feet barely touched the pavement as I ran to him. I didn't say a word. I just launched myself into his arms. Thankfully he caught me, only staggering back a couple feet. "Whoa."

I held on as tightly as I could, burying my face in his neck. "Are you okay?"

"Yeah. Thanks to you."

Whatever troubled him and caused his distance over the past two days was forgotten. I squeezed him tighter, never wanting to let go.

Sadly, it wasn't my call. Hayden lowered me to my feet, grabbing hold of my right hand as he turned to Mr. Jacobson and shook his hand. "Thank you, sir. I appreciate everything you did for me in there."

"Well, like I said. They had nothing to hold you on, son. Talk about incompetence."

I gazed up at Hayden's tired face as he shook my aunt's hand. "Thanks for being here, Katherine."

"Oh, honey. I've been here since you moved in. You're just too stubborn to let anyone help you."

"That's for sure," I mumbled.

Hayden shot me a sleepy smile, dropping my hand and wrapping his arm around my waist until I was tucked firmly into his side. "Is it now?"

I nodded.

He leaned down to my ear and whispered, "Take me home, sweetheart."

"Gladly, babe."

## HAYDEN

The hot shower cascaded over my face, giving me more damned time to think. It's all I'd done in that suffocating cell. Cooper's words replayed in my head like a bad song. The things Remy pulled behind my back. The danger he put me in—not only with the deadbeats, but with Cooper himself.

Cooper warned me Remy would be arrested, but he never mentioned I'd be brought in. Or that the shit could hit the fan at school in front of everyone, including Alex. And while I felt confident he would've eventually stepped in to bail me out, it would've just meant I owed him more. Having Alex save my ass meant I'd cut at least one tie with Cooper. And that brought me one step closer to getting out of this life all together.

Ironically, the girl who would've liked to know everything about me, decided she didn't want to know why I'd been arrested. On the ride home, I tried to open up to her, tried to explain what went down, but she blasted her radio and sang along like I wasn't even in the car.

I switched off the shower and wrapped a towel around my waist. I wished I could say I washed off all the filth from the cell, but that would take time. I stepped out of the bathroom and into my bedroom.

My head withdrew and my body stilled.

Alex lay sprawled on her side on my bed eyeing me up and down like candy. "Lose the towel," she commanded.

I raised my brows. In my fantasies, she was naked when she made the request. "You sure you want to go there?"

"You still have those handcuffs?"

Only she could make light of such a fucked-up situation. I slid down beside her, keeping my towel tucked tightly around me, and slipped my arms around her waist.

"You're soaked," she squealed.

I shook my hair like a wet dog.

She squealed even more, burying her face in my chest. She paused for a long moment, trailing her fingers over my back. "You really scared me today."

"You? I was scared shitless." I laughed, though it wasn't funny.

She wove her fingers through the hair behind my neck, playing with it gently. "I know this thing between us happened fast," she whispered. "But I can't imagine being away from you...I need you, Hayden. *So much.*"

"Hey," I said softly. "You've got nothing to worry about. Fast or not, me and you, it's real. I'm not going anywhere."

Her eyes snapped open. I wasn't prepared for the abundance of hope filling them. "Do you know what that means?"

I shook my head. Having high expectations in my world usually got me nowhere fast.

"You're mine. And I'm not letting you go anywhere without me."

My stomach gave way to a giant ripple. If I was a pussy in the eyes of guys everywhere, so be it. This girl—*my* girl—wanted me for the long haul. And that shit made me happy. God damned happy.

Alex's lips collided with mine, pouring everything she felt into the kiss. Relief. Excitement. Fear. I got it. I felt it, too. Her tongue slipped inside my mouth, eagerly sweeping and tangling with mine like it was meant to be there.

I dove in, feasting on her lips. Moist. Delicate. All-consuming. I needed to erase what happened earlier from my memory. I needed to lose myself in Alex for the rest of the night. I needed to remain lost in our own little world for as long as humanly possible.

Before I realized what she was doing, Alex pulled her body away from mine so quickly I fell onto my stomach. She hooked one leg over my hips and straddled my towel-covered ass.

She leaned forward, her chest pressing into my back as her breath tickled my right shoulder, the one with the heart and dagger tattoo.

*Oh.*

She'd never seen the ugly thing up close. I relaxed my body and let her examine it.

Her finger replaced her breath, lightly tracing the outline of the heart over and over again, avoiding the dagger entirely. She eventually abandoned the image and traced the words scrolled through it with her fingernail. Tiny shivers rolled through me as her nail dug into my skin.

I felt her warm breath as she leaned even closer, planting a soft kiss over the words. "Have you changed your mind?" she whispered against my skin.

I turned my face on my pillow. "About what?"

"Never again."

I smiled. "What do you think?"

Instead of telling me, she traced the words with her tongue, licking slowly—maddeningly slowly—over my skin. I fucking loved it. "I asked *you*," she purred into my shoulder.

"I think I was a stupid kid when I got that tattoo."

"Oh? So now that you're so old and mature, what do you think?" She trailed kisses over the length of it.

"If I met you back then, I would've screwed it up. I'd still be the same angry idiot."

She didn't speak, just trailed a line of kisses from my right shoulder to my left. I couldn't believe I didn't tense when her finger traced the outline of the angel. It was so personal. So risky to have done it in the first place. "Do you regret this one?"

"Not a chance."

"Oh, no? Why's that?"

I shook my head. She'd gotten enough honesty out of me for a lifetime.

"I think she needs words."

My smile spread. "Oh, yeah? Like what?"

"I'm sure *you're swell* in Italian sounds much sexier."

"So you think I should get something sexy on me?"

"Oh, babe. You've already got something sexy on you."

I twisted so quickly she had no other option but to straddle my front. "You talking about the angel or you?" I grabbed her face and pulled her down to me.

She smiled against my lips. "Both." She slipped her hand under my towel and grabbed hold of me right where I wouldn't resist. "I wonder if they would've let me visit you in jail."

I couldn't stop the moan in the deep recesses of my throat as her hand slipped up and down, working wonders on my already tense body. "I would've snuck you in."

"Oh, yeah?" she purred.

"Oh, fuck yeah."

## ALEX

Hayden's pinched eyes, furrowed brows, quiet pants, and moans with my name were something I enjoyed almost as much as the pleasure he'd brought me on my birthday.

When he found his release, I snuggled into his chest, listening to his labored breathing. It was one of the sexiest sounds I'd ever heard.

"You are unbelievable."

I giggled, knowing I had no idea what I was doing. I listened to what seemed to please him and went with it. "I'm hungry."

He choked out a laugh. "Is that code for something else?"

"I'm sure it could be. But right now, I'm starving. My lunch got interrupted, and I'm guessing the Five-Os didn't feed you?"

"Five-Os?"

"I'm hooking up with a criminal. I've gotta use the lingo."

He shook his head, probably alarmed by both my dorkiness and the fact that I'd called him a criminal but hadn't asked what happened. He had to realize I was trying to make things easier on him. He'd been through hell.

Half an hour later, I sat with my back pressed into Hayden's side on the sofa, hoping the proximity would settle my nervousness as we ate our pizza.

I *did* want to know why he'd been arrested. But at the same time, knowing what I did about his job, I knew there could be some truth to the accusations. Hayden worked with Remy. Remy hadn't been released. It didn't take a genius to realize Hayden must've been there when Remy committed the crime they were holding him for.

Hayden leaned forward, tossing his crust into the box on the coffee table. I took the opportunity to settle into the spot beside him. When he sat back, he turned toward me. "I promised no more secrets. So tell me what you wanna know."

She paused for a long time, a mix of fear and indecision clouding her eyes. "Why were you arrested?"

He exhaled a long breath. "Two men were killed. Remy's fingerprints were found at the crime scene."

"Did he do it?"

Hayden chewed his bottom lip. His eyes searched the ceiling for an answer that wasn't there. "Next question."

I huffed out an irritated breath. Why couldn't he trust me completely? "Did you do it?"

His eyes widened with a mixture of anger, hurt, and surprise. "I'm here, aren't I?"

"You didn't answer my question."

He sighed. "No, Alex, I didn't do it."

I blew out a breath. It wasn't like I thought him capable of murder, but the way he evaded my question made me wonder what secrets he still planned to keep from me.

"Why'd they release you?"

"My prints weren't at the crime scene."

"Were you there when they were killed?"

He gnawed on his bottom lip, likely drawing blood. "Next question."

I grabbed the pizza box and jumped to my feet, feeling beyond frustrated. With Hayden. With myself. With the whole stupid situation. I carried the box into the kitchen and tossed our garbage, loaded the dishwasher, and wiped down the countertop.

Having nothing left to clean, I crossed my arms and leaned against the sink, staring across the rooms at Hayden who stared back. "Why are we doing this? You clearly don't want to tell me anything."

He took in the distance between us. He wasn't happy about it. "It's an open investigation. I can't say anything that could incriminate me or you. The less you know the better." He tilted his head, his eyes pleading with me to understand.

I knew he'd do whatever it took to protect me. But when he said he'd open up and be honest, I expected more. "The two men who were killed. Did they have anything to do with the gun pointed at your head?"

He stared at me for what felt like forever.

Though we were two rooms apart, the gravity of the situation hit me fiercely in both the head and the heart. "If they weren't killed…" I swallowed down the knot in my tightened throat. "You would've been?"

His stare didn't waver. Even as I walked back into the living room and sat down beside him, his gaze remained impenetrable.

I trailed my fingertips lightly over his features. Features I never would've seen again if those men had their way.

Life had been so cruel to Hayden. So careless with him and his emotions ever since he was a child. What had that done to the man sitting in front of me? How had it shaped him? What had it forced him to do to survive?

I didn't really want to know the answer to my next question. But I needed to know. "Have you ever killed anyone?"

I saw the second my words registered. He blinked and his eyes shot away.

If I didn't care about him the way I did, I would've grasped how disconcerting his reaction was. But I did care about him. And he hadn't admitted any wrong doing.

*So why were his knuckles clenched and his jaw tight?*

Minutes slipped by in deafening silence.

I wanted to scream for him to tell me already. Tell me the truth. Tell me what he was hiding. But I knew if I wanted answers, I couldn't push him. I needed to be patient.

He finally looked back at me.

His eyes slid shut, and his head gave way to a slow painful nod.

Time stood still.

My stomach dropped to the deepest depths of hell.

I'd asked the question, but couldn't have anticipated his response.

I had no time to brace my heart. My head. My emotions. I had no time to think about what the news meant for him. *For us.* How could this guy who saved me, who treated me like a precious gem, who kissed me and handled me so delicately, take someone's life?

I didn't believe it. There had to be more.

With his eyes still closed, Hayden's head fell back against the sofa. "I was eighteen." His voice came out low and raspy. "Remy and I had been working for Cooper for a while. Back then we were both hotheaded and angry and wanted to beat the hell out of anyone who crossed us. That's why Cooper had no problem relying on two teenagers. We got the job done."

His eyes opened, focusing solely on the ceiling, while his ashen knuckles grasped his knees. "We were beating up this guy. Kicking and punching him 'til he was unconscious." A solitary tear slipped down his cheek.

Even after what he'd admitted, it took everything in me not to move to him. But I needed to hear everything. I needed to understand.

"We heard sirens. We knew we needed to get out of there. But we were in an alley. Surrounded by a wall. Only one of us was making it over. Remy didn't blink an eye. He linked his fingers and boosted me to the top." Hayden finally looked at me, staring me dead in the eyes. "He was the only one there when the cops showed and declared the guy dead."

The weight of the secret he'd been concealing released from him and his tears fell freely. He made no attempt to hide them or wipe them away.

I couldn't take anymore. I moved closer, latching onto his arm and holding on tightly. "It was an accident."

They were my words, but I couldn't be sure who I was trying to convince more. Him or me.

My emotions were in total disarray. This guy I needed with every fiber of my being had taken someone's life. How could I ever look at him the same way again? How could I ever justify what he'd done? How could I ever be certain the rage he displayed that night never touched me?

Hayden shrugged. "Doesn't matter. A man was taken from his family. And I did it."

"You said Remy was—"

He shook his head before I could finish. "He stopped. I didn't. He's the one who pulled me off the guy. He's the one who pled guilty to involuntary manslaughter and never once brought up my name. He's the one who spent almost a year in juvie for something I did." He finally swiped at his tears. "I live with the guilt every day. Every. Fucking. Day."

"You owe him." It wasn't a question. It was the realization of why he put up with Remy. And why he jumped whenever Remy called. "But something happened to make you question that loyalty."

Hayden's glassy eyes met mine, startled by my assertion.

"You left him at the sheriff's office. You didn't fight to get him out."

Hayden's eyes drifted to the window, staring out at nothing but darkness. He'd unloaded so much more than I ever expected. So much more than I was equipped to deal with.

"What was his name?"

Hayden's wide eyes shot my way. His tear-stained cheeks such a contradiction to his tough reputation. "What?"

"What was the man's name? The one in the alley."

He paused, like I'd asked a difficult question. The longer I watched him contemplate his response, the more I realized he'd never uttered the man's name before. "Victor," he whispered.

My heart lurched.

Was I heartbroken or relieved?

My mind flashed back to Victor's grave. To Hayden standing all alone in the darkness.

"I'm no better than my father."

My head jerked back. Did he really believe that?

While I obviously struggled to make sense of the truth he'd unloaded on me, make sense of the fact that the guy I'd been falling for with each passing day had killed a man, I knew one thing for sure. Hayden wasn't a cold-blooded murderer like his father.

I could see it in his eyes. Hear it in his voice. Feel it in his touch.

He lived with his guilt. He felt remorse. He wanted forgiveness. He needed absolution for his sins. Unfortunately, no matter how many times he visited Victor's grave, it would never come.

But it didn't stop him.

"Your father was a coward." The anger in my voice surprised both of us. "He took the easy way out. Living with the guilt is the hard part."

His eyes were too much for me to take. He was hurting. His candor had taken everything out of him. And while he may not have explained my questions about Remy, he'd been open. More open than he'd ever been. He deserved a reprieve—at least for the time being.

Pushing aside any doubts I had about him, any trepidations I had about his temper or his past, I leaned up and kissed his cheeks, eliminating the salty tears with my lips.

"You are not your father, Hayden."

His eyes squeezed shut. The truth too much for him to take.

"You're a good person who made a mistake. You didn't set out to kill anyone. It's terrible it happened. For you, for him, for his family. But it can't be erased. You need to let go of the guilt."

His eyes opened, dropping to his knees. "Remy's the only one who knows the truth."

I closed my eyes, letting the reality sink in *and* the fact that he trusted me with his deepest, darkest secret.

"I can't even begin to imagine what you think of me."

I took a deep breath, hoping the words that followed were the absolute truth. "I think you're an amazing guy who survived more than one horrific event in your lifetime. You've been living this existence haunted and alone for too long. It's time you let someone else in." I cupped his cheeks, forcing him to look at me. "Let that someone be me."

"Why?" he whispered.

"Because I love you, Hayden. There's nothing you can tell me that will stop that."

His breath caught in his throat and his eyes expanded.

I pressed my lips to his salty lips and made him feel my words. He slipped his arms around me and collapsed onto the sofa with me clinging to his chest. He held me for silent hours, before we fell asleep in each other's arms.

# CHAPTER TWENTY-FIVE

## ALEX

I hadn't spent the night at Hayden's. I'd woken up—if that's what you'd call what I'd done after he dropped the bombshell—and snuck out. I needed time to think. And I couldn't do it with Hayden near me. I needed distance to put everything into perspective.

I'd spent most of the time trying to grasp the fact that he'd actually done it. He'd actually taken someone's life. It was incomprehensible. And not the news I expected to hear, nor wanted to hear. It had the power to change everything.

But it was an accident. Not pre-meditated.

There was a huge difference.

And what I'd come up with—what I kept reminding myself—was if you cared about someone, then you took the good with the bad. You overlooked their unalterable pasts. You loved them unconditionally. You helped them when they needed help. You were strong when they needed your strength.

Wasn't that what Hayden had done for me?

*Knock. Knock.*

I skirted around my overnight bag beside the front door and pulled on the doorknob.

Hayden stood there, pivoting so I could see the backpack on his back. "Ready?"

I lifted my brows. "You don't even know where we're going."

He shrugged his broad shoulders. "It involves you, me, and a packed bag. I'm game."

It was strange to see him so carefree after he'd bared his soul to me the previous night. I wondered if he donned the mask he'd become so accustomed to wearing. Or if the truth had lifted some of the guilt he'd been carrying.

He moved closer toward me and slanted his head, kissing me gently. If my aunt wasn't in the other room, I would've let the kiss last much longer than it did.

I reached for my bag, but Hayden playfully bumped me with his hip and grabbed the bag first. "Lead the way."

As the local landscapes became a blur in the bright afternoon sun, signs for the airport appeared. Hayden's head whipped to me, his eyebrows lifted in question.

I only smirked, neither confirming nor denying his suspicions.

Ten minutes later I pulled up to a private airport hangar. Hayden's eyes were about to burst from their sockets as he examined the private jet parked inside. "Are we going somewhere in that?"

Feeling more unsure than I had when I made the arrangements on a whim, I nodded. "It's only a half an hour flight, but I need to do this. I haven't been on one since—"

Hayden reached over and took my hand, rubbing small circles over my knuckles with his thumb. "I'm glad you want me with you."

He didn't add *after everything I told you*, but I got it.

And I did want him with me. He wouldn't lie and tell me it would be easy because he thought it's what I wanted him to say. He'd just be there. He'd be my safety net.

The pilot greeted us before we settled into the soft ivory seats. Hayden dove into the wood-faced compartment below the circular window concealing the stocked mini bar while I buckled my seatbelt, needing a moment to focus on what I was about to do.

When the engines whirred to life and the jet started to vibrate, I gripped the armrests for dear life. With a little work, Hayden loosed my rigid fingers and slipped his hand underneath mine, pulling it into his lap. "You can do this."

I met his steely gaze and nodded as the plane taxied onto the runway.

"You know. We could just make out the entire way. Then you wouldn't even have to think about it."

With an appreciative smile, I leaned over and kissed the cocky grin right off his face. He wasn't kidding. He unleashed his willing lips and tongue on mine, luring me into a long, delicious, rum-laced kiss. Maybe the mini bar wasn't such a bad idea. But given the forceful pressure of Hayden's lips and the plunging of his tongue, he had no intention of letting go of me.

And I could live with that.

We spent the thirty-minute flight talking and laughing, making out, and playing cards. Hayden proved to be a good teacher, insisting on teaching me Blackjack since I only knew drinking games.

"We'll be beginning our descent," the pilot announced from the cockpit. "Be sure your seatbelts are fastened."

My stomach dipped and I immediately began gathering the cards and shoving them back into the box. Many of them slipped into my lap. Hayden noticed my struggle and reached over, withdrawing the box and cards from my shaky hands while his distracting lips traveled up my neck.

My eyes squeezed tightly while I attempted to push my fears aside and lose myself in the sensation of Hayden's lips on my skin. "Oh, you're good," I murmured.

His smile pressed against my neck. "Just good?"

I chuckled as he continued attacking my neck, earlobe, and lips.

When the wheels touched down on the runway and the plane bounced as if made of mere plastic, I felt at ease and even more in love with Hayden than I thought possible.

My parents' driver met us on the tarmac and led us to a black town car. He had a new job, but dropped everything to be there for me. "Welcome home, Ms. Montgomery." He held the back door open so Hayden and I could slide into the backseat.

"Morning, Max. Thanks for the pickup."

From the curious way Hayden eyed six-foot Max, clad in a dark suit and sunglasses, this was something totally new for him. I guess, outside my old life, most people didn't have drivers and housekeepers and planes and vineyards.

As soon as we settled into the black leather seat, I snuggled into Hayden's side needing a long nap. It wasn't the short flight that knocked me out. More like the knowledge the plane could've gone down at any time and my life would've been over.

Hayden pressed his lips to the top of my head. "You do know most people skip school and go to the beach, right?"

I nodded. "We're not most people."

He smiled into my hair. "That we're not. So…this is Austin?"

I nodded.

"What do we have planned?"

I shrugged. What I needed to do could be taken care of at any time. My first hurdle was the plane.

"Can I meet your parents?"

I jerked away so quickly, I deserved Hayden's startled look.

He inched closer and cupped my cheeks between his hands. He leaned in so our noses touched. "I want you to take me to where they're buried. They are buried, aren't they?"

*God.* I hadn't even considered stopping by the cemetery. That seemed like a massive step for my first trip back. A step I wasn't ready for.

"I think I should introduce myself." He gave me a heartfelt smile. "You know, explain my intentions. Ask for their blessings."

A small smile tugged at my lips because I knew he meant it. He meant everything he said.

But visiting the cemetery was a big deal. A really big deal.

I inhaled a deep breath, considering the fact that Hayden sat beside me with his strong yet gentle hands on my cheeks.

Loving me.

Protecting me.

When he was with me, I could do anything. "Okay," I whispered.

He rubbed his nose to mine. "Okay."

## HAYDEN

We pulled to a stop in the middle of the vast cemetery. I waited for Alex to say something, make a move, step out. Anything. But she just stared out the window at the endless rows of gravestones, adorned with flower-filled urns, spread as far as the eye could see.

Maybe I'd pushed too hard. Maybe visiting the cemetery wasn't at all what she had in mind for our trip. I reached over and linked our fingers, giving her hand a little squeeze.

With her eyes engrossed in what lay outside the window, she sighed. "Ready?"

"Only if you are."

She didn't respond, just pushed open the door. Before stepping out, she twisted toward me. "You know, you're pretty swell."

My chest tightened. Because me being there, was exactly what she needed. And I really liked being needed.

We stepped out into the seventy-degree air, the swaying trees creating the only sounds for miles. I wondered if Alex had visited after the funeral because she maneuvered around the different sized stones like she'd taken the same path many times before.

The bell in the church tower rang eleven times. On its final chime, Alex stopped and looked down at a polished gray stone with her parents' names engraved in the front.

My body stilled. My eyes locked on the statue carved into the side and top of the stone. A kneeling white angel with its head and arms draped over the top crying in despair.

*Talk about irony.*

Releasing my hand, Alex dropped to her knees. She reached out and touched the smooth stone, tracing the letters of her parents' names with her fingertip.

"Do you want me to give you some time?"

She didn't look up, just shook her head.

My heart ached as I watched her glide her finger along the grooves over and over again. It was as if she hadn't believed they were gone until she saw their names etched in the stone.

I knew that feeling of denial. And I *saw* my mother die.

Alex didn't speak. I assumed she was speaking to her parents in her head. Probably apologizing for what she felt was her hand in their deaths. I wished she realized her parents didn't have to fly that day. Even if it had been her idea, it was their choice. And who's to say it wouldn't have happened the next time they boarded the plane? Or the time after that?

Death claimed you when it wanted you.

Alex reached over her shoulder, holding out her hand for me. I took hold of it and let her pull me beside her. She didn't look up at me. She just stared at the stone. "This is Hayden."

I grazed her knuckles with my thumb.

"He came along when I least expected him." She paused. "But I'm pretty sure you guys had a little something to do with that."

Her words sent a chill coursing through my body. How could she believe there was more to our first encounter than mere coincidence? How could she believe, after I'd spent so long not caring about anyone—not even myself—her parents would send me to her? How could she believe after everything I'd admitted about my past, her parents would see fit for me to love her? I was the last person they'd want their daughter with. How could she not see that?

"Dad, you'd really like him. He loves Pearl Jam just like you."

No wonder she knew the songs. He must've played them around the house like my mother had.

"And Mom, you'd think he was so gorgeous."

I couldn't hide my smile.

"He's got the most beautiful blue eyes I've ever seen. They're like ice. And he's got these eyelashes that go on for miles. Oh, and he's a great kisser."

I laughed, both in surprise and relief that she could joke at a time like that.

"But seriously, he loves me and treats me the way you'd want me to be treated. I just wish you would've had the chance to meet him."

She paused for a long moment. I wasn't sure if she needed a moment or was still talking to them privately. But I knew what I needed to do. "Hi, Mr. and Mrs. Montgomery."

Alex peeked up, flashing me a melancholy smile.

"I hope you don't mind me being here. But I wanted to thank you for sending me your beautiful angel when *I* needed her so much."

She squeezed my hand in appreciation, but I wasn't finished.

"I promise to take care of her for as long as she'll have me. But between you and me, I don't plan on ever letting her leave me."

I knelt down and wrapped my arms around her, pulling her close. Her body melted into me, her arms slipping around my waist. The tears she'd been holding back finally released.

We didn't move. We didn't speak.

Time slipped by and soon the sun ducked behind the trees casting us in shade.

"Have you been to your mother's grave?"

My stomach turned over. Of all the things she could've asked. "Yeah."

"Do you go often?"

I shrugged. "Sometimes."

Alex dried her cheeks with the back of her hand. "Does it make you feel better to be there?"

"A little." Truthfully, anger and regret usually superseded it.

"Did you get your dimples from her?"

I smiled. "Yeah. Hers were even bigger than mine."

Alex gave a silent laugh. "Can I meet her?"

"Absolutely." I wanted nothing more than to introduce the two most important women in my life. Too bad only one would be doing the talking.

Alex said nothing on the ride to our next stop. She lay with her head in my lap, while I gently stroked her waves. The quiet hum slipping from her lips indicated she'd fallen asleep. And after the day she'd had, she deserved it.

My phone vibrated in my pocket. I slipped it out carefully, managing not to wake her in the process. *Galveston Sheriff's Office* lit up the screen.

Apparently, Remy hadn't made bail. He must've been going crazy surrounded by those four walls. But I sent the call to voicemail. I was nowhere near ready to deal with him.

The sun sat lower in the sky by the time we turned into a gated community. My mouth practically hit the floor as we passed mansions of all sizes and designs. I'd only ever seen such wealth when celebrities flaunted their cash on television.

Alex's affluence suddenly terrified me. I'd become involved with a girl who'd been raised with the finer things in life. That's all she knew. I barely managed to support myself.

At the end of the road, we turned, making the half-mile trek up the winding private driveway lined with impeccably-manicured trees. At the end, we were met by a circular expanse. In the center sat a water fountain. Of course she had a water fountain. And the water-spouting-statue was another angel.

I glanced to the heavens. *I hear you, Mom. I hear you.*

When the car stopped, Alex stirred but didn't wake. Like at the cemetery, the driver had the good sense to let us get out at our own pace. Good thing. I needed time to examine the imposing structure before me.

The three-story, white, brick house boasted varying sized peeked roofs. Floor-to-ceiling windows took up the majority of the exterior, with a massive window above the vaulted doorway displaying an enormous crystal chandelier. Perfect landscaping lined the exterior, as did a cobblestone walking path.

I knew Alex was rich. But this was unbelievable.

I leaned down. "Hey. We're home."

She stirred again, but her eyes remained closed.

"Come on. I'm expecting the grand tour of this resort."

Her eyelids fluttered before her eyes finally opened and settled on mine.

"Hey. You okay?"

She nodded, sitting up slowly and gaping out the window at the house she hadn't seen in months. "Well, let's get this over with." She pushed open the door and waited for me to step outside before proceeding to the front door.

To say I was floored once we stepped inside would be the understatement of the year. I called it a resort. I should've called it a museum. With its cathedral ceiling and checkerboard-marble floor, every step echoed like the long walkways of a quiet gallery.

From the formal sitting room to the dining room, statues on marble pedestals sat in the corners of the rooms. Paintings, in gaudy gold frames, hung on the walls.

The only room not requiring a velvet rope sat in the rear of the first floor, beyond the grand staircase. And just because it didn't appear off limits, it wasn't any less impressive. The rows of maple cabinets, stainless steel appliances, and speckled granite countertops came straight from the pages of an interior design magazine—for the rich and famous.

The windows, encompassing the entire rear of the first floor, overlooked a pool and guest house. They gave the house an ocean-view feel without the ocean. I wondered how far their property extended since the emerald backyard seemed to roll for miles.

"It's beautiful."

Alex turned from her spot in front of the walk-in pantry where she stared at the stocked shelves and followed my eyes to the view outside. She didn't say a word.

She was taking it all in. Being back in Austin. Being back in her home. Being inundated by memories at every turn. I needed to be mindful of that.

She grabbed hold of the pantry door like she intended to close it, but she didn't. She reached out and lightly brushed her fingertips over the frilly apron hanging from a hook inside the door. Lifting the fabric to her nose, she breathed it in. "I was starting to forget what she smelled like."

It broke my heart watching her torture herself like that, but I leaned back against the center island, giving her time with her grief. It's what she needed.

After long moments stretched on, I knew I needed to distract her or lose her completely. "Hey you got any honey in there?"

I watched her shoulders shake with silent laughter. "I like honey."

I grinned, recalling our exchange at Jake's. "I don't doubt it, but what do you say we go for a swim, then enjoy the honey?"

She let the apron fall. As she turned toward me, a smile pulled at the corners of her lips. "You looking for a rematch?"

"Do I need to let you win this time?"

She shook her head. The almost-smile faded as she closed the pantry door. "Maybe later."

I walked over and wrapped my arms around her, holding her to my chest. Breathing in *her* warm scent. "Whatever you want. Whatever you need. I'm not going anywhere."

She nodded into me, letting me hold her for a quiet moment. "Want to see the upstairs?"

"Are you asking if I want to see your bedroom?" I pulled back so I could see her face. I flashed my 'proven to win over even the toughest crowds' smile. "Because I absolutely want to see it."

Thankfully, she smiled back.

## ALEX

Standing in the kitchen in Hayden's arms proved one thing. I never would've been able to return home without him.

I needed him.

We didn't share memories in Austin. We didn't share anything that would've brought me back to the sad place I'd escaped months ago. Every moment would be new. We'd create our own memories.

I led Hayden up the grand staircase. We took the right toward my bedroom. I had no idea of its state. When I left, I grabbed a handful of clothes and didn't bother to clean up. I just needed to be out of the one place I associated most with my parents. I just needed to breathe.

Hayden and I stepped inside my suite. Clothes hung off my desk chair. The down comforter on my unmade four-post bed hung on the floor. Shoes were kicked into the corner of the room. And the pillows from my sofa in the sitting area were tossed all over the floor.

I fell back onto my messy bed and giggles erupted.

"What's so funny?" Hayden asked.

I looked up at him towering over me and shook my head like the crazy person I appeared to be. "I don't even know. It just feels so good to be here and not feel like I can't touch my own stuff."

His brows furrowed.

"We had this ninja housekeeper," I explained. "If I left my room for more than two minutes, she'd sweep in undetected and clean anything I left out of place."

The bed sagged as Hayden sat down beside me. "Ninja, huh?"

I grinned, the recollection bittersweet.

He glanced around my room, taking in all the girly accessories strewn about. "Is it weird being back?"

I nodded.

His eyes flashed to mine. "Is it weird having me here?"

I shook my head. "It's like bringing my two worlds together."

He picked up a framed picture from my nightstand. "Who's this?"

"My ex."

He examined the picture of Preston and me at his frat's formal last year. Me in my strapless green dress and Preston in his tux, complete with the dorky bow tie. I begged him to wear a normal tie, but he didn't listen. "Looks like a tool."

I snorted, which lead to a long cleansing laugh.

Hayden placed the picture face down on my nightstand, then reclined beside me. We both stared up at the ceiling. "Why don't you have a picture of us next to your bed back home?"

I glanced over, expecting to see amusement in his eyes. Instead I found sincerity. "We've never taken a picture together."

He contemplated the thought. Then pulled his phone from his pocket and tapped the screen a couple times. He leaned his head into mine and held his phone out above us. "Smile."

I did. A big goofy smile because I was home. In a place I never thought I'd step foot again. In a town I never thought I'd return to. And I was surviving. Because Hayden was by my side.

He snapped the picture then checked it. "Your eyes were closed."

"Were not." I grabbed for the phone, but his long arm held it away from me.

"Let's try again."

Instead of staying still when he snapped the picture, I turned my head and kissed his cheek. He laughed, but it didn't deter him. He took at least ten more, claiming something was wrong with each one. I assumed he was trying to lift my spirits, but a small part of me hoped he just wanted pictures of us together. And since he didn't have a single picture in his apartment, the thought elated me.

"You've got enough for both of us to have a collage by our bed," I teased.

He didn't laugh. He just turned on his side with his head in his palm. "If you stay with me, then we'd only need one."

*Wha-huh?*

The way he stared down at me with those smoldering eyes, I would've thought he was serious.

"You know...I have an aunt who'll have your neck if she thinks you're coercing her niece to live in sin. You sure the two of you never—"

I squealed as Hayden rolled on top of me, pinning me to the bed. "What's it gonna take, woman? I swear to you, since you showed up, you're the only one I've thought about." He brushed his lips below my right ear sending tiny shudders surging through me. "You're the only one I've dreamt about." He brushed his lips below my left ear eliciting the same tiny shudders. "And you're the only one I've been naked with." He leaned down and brushed his lips to mine.

I slipped my arms around his back lost in the sensation of his lips now nibbling their way down my throat. "Is that your way of avoiding the question?"

He laughed, but when he lifted his head and his eyes met mine, I could see his exasperation. "Yes, Alex, I had a life before you showed up. But I *never* touched your aunt."

"But you've been with older women?"

He closed his eyes and growled. "Why do girls do this? Why do they insist on torturing themselves with their boyfriends' pasts?"

My eyes expanded while my stomach summersaulted. "You're my boyfriend?"

His eyes snapped open. "I sure hope so. I don't go around telling just anyone I love them."

I couldn't fight off my smile, though I kept my lips tight for fear of laughing aloud like an idiot. "And you love me?"

He smiled, those amazing dimples sinking in. "Now you're just fishing."

I couldn't hold back my laughter any longer. "Damn straight I am."

Hayden leaned in and kissed me, intoxicating me with his possessiveness. His tongue licked across the seam of my lips and dipped inside, sweeping and circling. His lips were so soft. So moist. So hungry. It made all the kisses before pale in comparison. This one carried the feelings associated with what was happening between us. The trust. The love. The future.

I pulled back, catching my breath while he nibbled down my neck. "You were my first, you know."

He stopped his attack, nodding into the crook of my neck.

I gasped. "It was that bad?" He'd slept with tons of girls—women. How could I ever compare?

He rolled onto his side, resting his head in his palm and staring down at me with apologetic eyes. "I know it's impossible, but if I could, I'd erase everything I did before we met. Those girls, they didn't mean anything to me. Being with you..." His thumb traced my bottom lip. "It meant everything to me. It still does. And you trusting me to be your first was such a damn turn on, I can't even begin to explain it."

I reached up and ran my nails through the back of his head. "A turn on, huh?"

He brushed his lips to mine, speaking against them. "Big time."

"Well, what do you say we pretend it's the first time all over again?"

His mouth sealing over mine was the only response I got.

# CHAPTER TWENTY-SIX

## ALEX

Waking up naked in my childhood bed with Hayden twisted around me like a pretzel was something I almost couldn't comprehend. A few months ago, the only future I envisioned had Preston in it. Life without him seemed impossible.

Until Hayden.

Being with Hayden felt right. Like the stars aligned to bring us together. I knew he wasn't perfect. Far from it. But neither was I. We were two people trying to maneuver through life after the crummy hands we'd been dealt. And we were surviving.

I tried to slide out from under his warm body, but he held on tighter. "Hayden. I need to shower."

"No," he grunted into my neck.

"We've been in bed for almost an entire day. I'm sweaty."

"I like you sweaty."

I eyed the container of honey on my nightstand. "And sticky."

He dragged his tongue up my neck, ensuring he hadn't left any honey on my skin. "Mmm. I love you sticky."

"You can come with me."

His eyes snapped open. "Seriously?"

I nodded, biting my lip in anticipation.

Hayden jumped out of bed in all his naked glory. A magnificent sight I could go on and on about. But why bother? It was what it was. And it was all mine.

I wrapped the sheet around my body and padded to my bathroom. He followed closely behind, not even attempting to tug the sheet off like other guys would have. But then again, Hayden wasn't like other guys.

I reached inside the two-person shower and flipped the knobs. Through the glass, Hayden's eyes took in the four powerful jets shooting out from various angles.

I dropped the sheet to my feet and stepped inside. Hayden followed, pressing his naked front to my back. I leaned my head against his shoulder, feeling every hard inch of him as the water soaked the front of my body. He wrapped his arms around my waist, caressing my stomach with tantalizingly delicious circles, while he pressed open-mouthed kisses down the side of my neck.

I couldn't stop the rumbling in the back of my throat as my head fell to the side, giving him easier access. He grabbed a bar of soap and lathered up my body as his lips continued their assault.

When I was nothing more than a useless pile of mush, and the throbbing between my thighs was almost too much to bear, Hayden spun me around so my front pressed into his chest. I slipped my arms around his neck as the shower jets soaked the back of my head.

He stepped forward, causing me to step back. The warm water rained over our faces. Hayden licked his way up the side of my neck, making his way to my lips. When I opened to let him in, the water mixing with our tongues made everything more incredible.

I needed him. I wanted him. I'd do anything for him.

Hayden shifted, moving our faces away from the spray. Our lips were still connected—moving as one. As the water hit the back of my head again, another jet hit the back of his. Yearning to be closer to him, I lifted my leg to his hip. I needed to feel him. Needed to feel his pleasure.

Grasping my need, he caught me under the knee and lifted me so I straddled his hips. He twisted and stepped forward, moving my back against the wet shower tiles. "You never stop amazing me," he purred into my lips.

Burying my fingers in his hair, I smiled and pulled him as close to me as possible.

I knew then that I would do anything to have moments like these with him forever.

## HAYDEN

Alex let me drive her father's Maserati to breakfast. A fucking *Maserati*. Would I be a total pussy to admit showering with Alex surpassed driving the car? Because it had.

Apparently, my promiscuity had rubbed off on her. And I loved it. Loved that she couldn't stop touching me. Loved that she couldn't stop kissing me. Loved that she'd become so comfortable with me. She had no reason not to be. Her body was amazing. *She* was amazing.

The overhead bell on the café door jingled when we stepped inside. Heads turned and whispering ensued. Alex handled it like a champ, taking my hand and leading me to a corner table tucked in the back.

I glanced around the crowded room. All fifteen tables with freshly cut flowers in small vases had a view of the swank shops and overpriced restaurants lining the street.

Thanks to the breakfast aromas wafting through the room, my stomach growled like a caged lion. I chanced a peek at Alex, figuring she'd be amused by it. With her hands folded on her closed menu, she gazed across the table at me, seemingly lost in thought.

I shot her a crooked smile, bouncing my eyebrows for effect.

She smiled.

"What are you thinking about?" I asked, rolling up the sleeves of my white button-down shirt.

Her smile expanded before she mouthed, "You."

"Care to share?"

She shook her head.

I sat back and crossed my arms, admiring the beauty before me. In the café, in her hometown, Alex looked like a true Southerner in a blue sundress with a thick leather belt. But instead of cowboy boots, she rocked her flip flops. "Alright then. I'll guess."

"Go for it."

My eyes settled on hers, so green and brilliant. "You're sitting there, admiring the fine male specimen in front of you, thinking you can't believe this gorgeous guy—make that hottie—is here with you when he could be off breaking hearts and taking names all over the great state of Texas."

She stifled a smile. I wished she wouldn't do that. I loved when she smiled.

"You're thinking the dimples are amazing and the body is a thing of dreams. How am I doing so far?"

She laughed. There wasn't a finer sound in all the world. "Not even close."

I mouthed. "I don't believe you."

She rolled her eyes and shook her head in amusement.

"You know what you're getting?"

She nodded.

"Are you gonna make me guess that, too?"

She nodded.

I glanced around the room, checking out the heaping dishes of other diners. "Pancakes?"

She shook her head.

"Eggs?"

She scrunched her nose.

"Waffles?"

She laughed, finally taking pity on me. "A panini and chocolate milkshake."

"For breakfast?"

"Sure, why not?"

An older waitress dressed in a bumblebee costume, complete with bouncing antennae on her head, approached our table. "Happy Halloween, kids. What'll it be?"

Alex flashed the waitress an adorable smile, like she was asking Santa for a special gift. "I'll have a chicken and roasted red pepper panini and a chocolate milkshake."

The waitress jotted down Alex's order. "And you, honey?"

I closed my menu. "I'll have the same."

The waitress nodded before hurrying off.

*"For breakfast?"* Alex asked behind a big smile.

I leaned back and extended my legs, crossing them at the ankles. "If it's good enough for my girl, it's good enough for me."

Her smile remained. "Am I the only one who forgot it was Halloween?"

I shook my head. "But now that we know, I'm hoping for a treat. Preferably one with honey."

She laughed, her eyes sparkling. "I love having you here."

"I love being here."

"Yeah? Why's that?"

"You fishing again?"

Her head bobbed eagerly. But before I could indulge her in the hundreds of reasons I loved being there with her, the smile slipped from her face. As did the color in her cheeks and the sparkle in her eyes.

My head whipped over my shoulder. A tall brunette and the guy from Alex's picture strolled into the café. "Fuck."

I turned back to Alex. Her eyes shot to her lap. It took no more than a second, but gone was the girl who seduced me in the shower. Gone was the girl fishing for compliments. Gone was the girl excited over having a damn panini for breakfast. In her place sat a sad timid girl defeated by life. Defeated by the mere memory of her past.

I reached across the table and grabbed her limp hands, holding them tightly in the center of the table. "Hey."

Her eyes remained in her lap.

"Alex, look at me."

Her eyes lifted the slightest bit.

"Let's get out of here."

Her eyes shot back down. "I need to be here."

It was as if she decided she'd done something wrong and needed to pay the price. It broke my damn heart.

My head shot back over my shoulder. The two stared from across the room, whispering to one another. My skin buzzed as my adrenaline kicked in. I jumped to my feet, but Alex held onto my hands so tightly her knuckles whitened. "I'm fine. We're fine. Let's just stay and eat."

My pulse pounded in my ears as I dropped back down into the chair.

Her ex was hurt. I got that. He'd lost his parents. But Alex had, too. How long did he expect her to take the blame? To be his punching bag? I hated the looks they'd given her. Hated the fact that my strong girl had transformed into a shell of herself. But what could I do? I didn't want to upset her any more than she already was.

And as much as I wanted to help, it wasn't my battle. I needed to let her handle it her way.

When our food arrived, Alex didn't say a word. She focused on her meal, taking a few sips of the milk shake and barely touching the panini. It was torture.

When the waitress brought the check, I grabbed it and threw down some cash. I seized Alex's hand and pulled her to her feet, evening my eyes with hers. "I love you."

She nodded, but not in a way that said she believed me.

So while it might've been childish, I didn't care. I wrapped my arms around her and kissed her in the middle of the crowded restaurant. It wasn't a passionate kiss by any means, but it made my point to her and everyone else in that room. Someone loved her. Someone cared about her. Someone knew what an amazing person she was.

I linked our fingers, keeping a strong hold of her hand as we made our way to the door. When we passed her ex, I stared him down, stopping him from even thinking about uttering a word.

As quickly as her flip flops would carry us, Alex tugged me away from the café and down the sidewalk. Once we were a safe distance away, she exhaled a giant breath, like she'd been holding it in the whole time we'd been inside.

"You did good in there."

She stopped in the middle of the sidewalk and looked up at me. "How can you even say that?"

"I'm serious. You didn't run. You stayed."

"Yeah, but I obviously didn't—"

"Alex," a deep voice shouted from behind us.

Alex's shoulders tensed.

Her ex made his way toward us, his hands buried in the pockets of his jeans. "Hi," he said from a distance.

Alex turned to face him. "Hi."

He inched a few steps closer. "I didn't know you'd be coming back."

She shook her head. "I just had some things to take care of."

His eyes shifted to me, giving me the once over. It wasn't malicious, more out of curiosity. But I still wanted to give him the finger then pummel him.

"This is Hayden." Alex moved her hand between us. "Hayden, Preston."

"Nice to meet you," the idiot said, like he actually meant it.

I didn't say a word.

Alex crossed her arms. "Did you want something, Press?"

He shrugged, his face uneasy. "Just wanted to see how you were doing."

She scoffed. "I'm guessing just about as good as you."

He nodded, a slow pathetic nod.

"But at least you had people to lean on. People to mourn with. I'm guessing no one stopped returning your calls."

*Nice one, Alex. Go right for the jugular.*

"I…" Words abandoned him as his eyes jumped around, searching for something to say.

"Don't. Nothing you say will make it better. But know this." Her voice was stronger. Forceful. "It was *not* my fault."

His eyes creased in the corners as it hit him. As it finally occurred to him what he'd done. Who he'd hurt. What he'd lost in all of this. Alex could've been the one thing he held onto, but he chose to blame her and push her away instead.

## ALEX

After leaving Preston speechless on the sidewalk, I dropped Hayden off at the house to relax by the pool while I ran out. He offered to tag along, but didn't force the issue when I told him I'd rather go alone. He probably assumed I was doing something personal. Which I was.

I'd been thinking a lot about my parents' vineyard. It had been in my father's family for over seventy years. Being the only living heir meant it belonged to me. So did the restaurant, banquet facility, spa, and hotel.

I hadn't spoken to Hayden about it, but I'd been considering moving into the hotel and learning the day-to-day operations once I graduated. I could go to grad school at night and eventually earn my MBA. It's what my parents always wanted. And now it was one of the only things I had left of them.

I had no intention of hiding my plan from Hayden, but from everything he'd told me, the only constant in his life over the years, the one who'd stuck around, who hadn't abandoned him—intentionally or not—had been Remy. And while I wanted nothing more than for Hayden to come with me, he had a life. And though things seemed strained between Remy and him, he had a friend who stood by him. And a job that paid his bills.

Could I ask him to leave that behind?

Heartfelt declarations aside, everything between us was still so new. There was no assurance we'd even be together eight months from now.

Besides, I had a feeling the only thing Hayden would hear when I told him my plan was goodbye.

# CHAPTER TWENTY-SEVEN

## ALEX

By Saturday morning, nerves had overtaken my body. I'd never been so nauseous in my entire life. Hayden tried to relax me, but nothing worked. And he tried *everything*.

"You need to eat something," he insisted from his sofa where my head lay in his lap.

"I'll eat if I'm hungry." But there was no chance I'd ingest anything knowing it could reappear during the competition.

Hayden leaned down and pressed a kiss to my temple. "Well, just don't go passing out on stage."

I turned my head so I could see his face. "Nervous you'll need to carry me off in front of everyone?"

He shook his head with a grin. "More worried they'll make me take your place."

I laughed. "Yeah, but then you'd have to fight Taylor for the spot."

He laughed as he slipped his hand beneath my head to support it while he slid out from under me. "You sure you're gonna be okay if I—"

"Go." I turned onto my side and watched him grab his jacket from the closet. "It's important." I had no idea what sparked the sudden fire under him, but the second we returned from Austin the day before, he started searching for a job. "I'll just see you at the show."

He walked back over to the sofa and stood over me. "I'll be there." He bent down, placing one hand on the cushion in front of me and one behind me so he hovered over me.

I twisted beneath him so I lay on my back. "Don't be late. I sing first."

"I won't." He leaned down, his lips lingering over mine. "I wouldn't miss it for the world." He kissed me soft and gentle. "Have your aunt save me a seat."

I nodded.

"You're gonna be unbelievable. No worries." He stood up and grabbed my hands, tugging me to my feet. "Let's get you home so you can get ready." He draped his arm around my shoulders and walked me across the hall.

I hesitated with my hand on the doorknob. Then spun back around. "I'll see—"

Hayden moved in, pressing me against the door and sealing his lips over mine. He dove in like he'd never see me again. Hungry and deep. Forceful and endearing. Our tongues a glorious tangled mess.

He eliminated the nerves. The nausea. The fear. It was only the two of us. And our crashing hearts.

When he pulled back, I struggled to find my breath and my footing.

I caught a glimpse of his crooked smile before he turned on his heels and walked off. "See you later," he called over his shoulder, knowing exactly the condition he'd left me in still pressed against the door.

An hour later, I applied the finishing touches on my makeup. I knew Sophia would do me up with a boatload of stage makeup when I got to school, but my mother always taught me to leave the house looking the way I wanted to look if I saw an ex-boyfriend—or Channing Tatum.

Impatient knocking came from the front door. I hoped it was Hayden stopping by to tell me he got a job. I threw open the front door and stumbled backwards on a gasp. "What are you doing here?"

## HAYDEN

I searched the crowded foyer for Alex, feeling ridiculous carrying around a huge bouquet of pink flowers. I maneuvered around enthusiastic parents and anxious singers, but couldn't find her anywhere. She'd been so nervous. I hoped she wasn't off puking in the bathroom.

Inside the theater, I dropped into the aisle seat beside Alex's aunt who snagged us seats in the center of the room. She eyed the massive bouquet in my lap, giving me an impressed nod.

The lights flickered on and off and a voice announced the show would begin in five minutes.

"Was she nervous?" Katherine asked.

"A little. But she's a natural. She's gonna be amazing."

Katherine reached over and placed a firm hand on my knee to stop it from bouncing. "Then why are you so nervous?"

I glanced from her hand to her probing eyes. I'd never realized how similar they were to Alex's. "I'm not sure if she told you, but I'm the reason she's in the show."

Katherine shook her head, but her stare indicated she wanted me to explain.

"I signed her up for the audition without her knowing."

Her brows lifted as she removed her hand from my leg. "Gutsy move."

I nodded. "I knew she could sing. I just figured she needed a little push. So, I guess I'm just nervous *for* her."

"You really care about her, don't you?"

I nodded, suddenly feeling uncomfortable and needing to look away.

"Well, she's lucky she found you."

I kept my gaze averted, never feeling so unworthy in my entire life. People poured into the crowded room slipping into seats until there wasn't a single empty seat in the theater.

"I'm serious. She was lost when she came here. She'd lost everything, including her spunk. I didn't know if there was anything I could do to snap her out of it. That is, until she met you." She laughed. "She'd kill me for telling you this, but she couldn't keep her eyes off that peephole for more than a couple minutes at a time."

I smiled, my stomach doing a fluttering thing I thought was reserved for preteen girls. But man, I'd been at that peephole just as often.

"Just take care of her, Hayden. She's so very fragile."

I finally met Katherine's eyes. "I promise you. I'd do anything for her. Absolutely anything."

With that, the lights in the theater lowered. We sat in silent darkness for a long moment until music from the sound system filled the room. The emcee's voice broke through the music. "Welcome to SSC Voice."

The audience erupted into wild cheers.

"Tonight we have a phenomenal lineup of singers performing some of today's hit songs. Be sure to keep track of your favorites. You'll be voting during intermission."

The intro music to Alex's song replaced his voice.

When the curtains parted and the spotlight shined, Taylor stood at center stage.

I flew out of my seat, up the aisle, and into the empty foyer. My head twisted around. I spotted the deserted hallway running adjacent to the theater. The echo of my soles pounded in time to my pulse as I bolted down it, stopping at the door that read *Contestants Only.*

I threw it open and burst into the congested room. People raced around. Applied makeup. Rehearsed. Sat nervously

Where the hell was Alex?

Sophia paced in the corner with her phone in her hand. I rushed over and grabbed hold of her arm. "Where's Alex?"

"Jesus, Hayden," she gasped. "I have no clue. I've been trying her for the past hour. But it goes straight to voicemail."

I dialed Alex from my phone, hoping she'd answer if she saw my name. But it went straight to voicemail. I gripped the sides of my head trying to make the pounding stop. "Fucking Taylor."

"I hate her, too," Sophia assured me. "But when Smith told her she was going to have to step in for Alex, she was shocked. She's a good actress and all, but she looked genuinely stunned."

I knew what Taylor was capable of, so I didn't buy it. I wedged my way into the area beside the stage, doing everything in my power to stop myself from rushing it in the middle of the song.

My heartbeat thundered as I watched Taylor sing like the spot in the competition actually belonged to her. As if she had nothing to do with Alex not being there. I glanced to Sophia who'd stepped up beside me. "How much longer?"

"Under a minute."

I nodded.

"Do you think—"

"She's fine," I cut her off. "I just need to get to her."

It seemed like hours before Taylor stepped off the stage. She only made it two steps before I grabbed her skinny arm and yanked her into the empty hallway. I harnessed every bit of reserve I had not to slam her head against the wall. "Where is she?"

Taylor's eyes widened. "You think I had something to do with this?" My grip on her arm tightened. Her eyes squeezed in pain, but she shook her head adamantly. "I have no idea where she is."

Not sure how long I could hold off before really hurting her, I gritted my teeth. "Tell me where she is."

She shook her head even more vehemently, her eyes frantically flying around. "I swear, Hayden. I don't know. I had *nothing* to do with it."

The way her damp eyes glistened under the bright hallway lights scared the hell out of me. Because if she didn't know where Alex was, no one did.

## ALEX

I sat in the center of a dark room, my hands and legs bound to a wooden chair, my body shaking uncontrollably. The only window was covered by a thick curtain, and I couldn't even see my lap in the pitch black. I strained to hear outside the room, but with the door closed, I could only hear the faint sound of a distant television. No actual voices.

I couldn't imagine what Hayden and my aunt thought when I wasn't at the competition. They had to know something had gone terribly wrong.

And what about Taylor? She got exactly what she'd hoped for. Me gone. She couldn't have planned it better herself.

A loud crash resonated in another room. Goose bumps shot up my arms and legs. Please don't let him come in here. *Please.*

The door swung open. The bright hallway light blasted inside the dark room. Having been in darkness for far too long, my sensitive eyes squeezed shut.

Heavy boots staggered in.

*Please God, don't let him touch me.*

I cracked my eyes a pinch.

Remy carried the gun he'd held to my head at my apartment. *Before* threatening Hayden's life if I didn't go with him.

He was still strung out on something, acting all jittery and paranoid like the whacked-out lunatic he was. I didn't think it was possible for him to be more terrifying. But he was.

He shoved his emaciated face in front of mine. Only a few inches separated us. He lifted the gun and jammed the cold barrel into my temple.

I held my breath, squeezing my eyes—as if it would somehow ease the pain of a bullet.

I knew Remy's capabilities. Hayden hadn't come right out and told me Remy killed those two men, but his silence did. Remy was a murderer. A cold-blooded murderer. I doubted he made any late night visits to *their* graves.

A portentous *click* filled the silence.

A quiver rocked through me, jolting my body to attention. I squeezed my eyes even tighter as I cringed away from the pressure of the gun. "Please don't do this," I whispered.

"What did you say?" he shouted.

Tears leaked out of my closed eyes. My body trembled violently as thoughts of all the things I loved inundated my mind.

Hayden who stole my heart and put it back together. My aunt who took me in when I was a constant reminder of the life she'd never have. Sophia who befriended me when it could have made her a social pariah. All the good in my life. All the things I'd never see again.

Then my parents' faces flashed before me.

They gave me my strength. My determination. My will to live this existence without them. They made me the woman I'd become. And that woman wouldn't give up, even with the odds stacked against her. She'd fight. Like she'd been doing every day since they died.

"I didn't think you'd be stupid enough to speak," Remy's voice snapped me back to hell.

Every inch of me trembled as he ran the barrel of the gun down my cheek. "I've been wondering why Hayden's kept you his dirty little secret." My eyes flew open as he pulled my shirt's V-neck open with the gun and looked inside.

"Please don't do this, Remy."

With gun in hand, he struck me across the face thrusting my head violently to the side. *Holy shit.* Pain exploded with the force of his blow. Somehow I remained upright, but a severe throbbing travelled from my forehead down to my chin. No doubt he'd broken bones. Maybe even teeth.

"Don't ever use my name again, you bitch." He stood up and paced the floor. "I can't believe Hayden trusted you with our shit."

I wanted to explain he hadn't told me anything. That he wouldn't defy a friend's trust. But I couldn't risk it. The repercussions could be too great.

Tears streamed down my throbbing cheeks as I stifled my whimpers. I needed to be patient. I needed to wait it out. I needed to suck up the pain taking over my entire face if I had any chance of escaping alive.

# CHAPTER TWENTY-EIGHT

## HAYDEN

My elbows dug into my knees while my head pounded between my hands. I'd been in the same spot on my sofa since realizing searching for Alex was like trying to find a needle in a haystack on a cold dark night during a downpour. I'd nearly driven off the road twice out of pure exhaustion.

The last time I'd felt that helpless was the night I couldn't stop my father from putting a bullet through my mother's head.

I closed my eyes and shoved down the memory.

I wanted to help. I *needed* to help. But I had no idea what else to do. I'd called everyone I thought may have seen her or heard something. I even considered fronting Remy's bail so he could rally the troops and help me find her. Yeah. I quickly rethought that idea.

I'd told the detectives anything I thought might lead them to Alex. Including what Cameron and Taylor had done. Taylor might've been surprised by Alex's disappearance, but it didn't hurt to question her. And finally bag her for drugging Alex and hacking the school's alert system.

Katherine wasn't too thrilled to learn about that one.

Alex's ex-boyfriend also got a visit. But they'd come back with nothing.

They checked airport logs and visited her family's vineyard. But neither turned up anything.

"Hayden?" Alex's aunt called from somewhere nearby. "Would you like something to eat?"

I shook my head, not even bothering to look up. I knew what I'd find. Katherine's dark circles mirrored my own. As did the exhaustion and worry overwhelming her every breath.

The detectives didn't want her tainting possible evidence in her apartment, so she'd been staying on my sofa, wanting to be close by if Alex returned.

As if she just up and walked away.

We'd bonded over the last three days as investigators breezed in and out of her apartment searching for any little clue they might've missed. My apartment served as their home base. And as much as I hated cops, them being there ensured I got information I otherwise wouldn't have.

What I knew. Since Alex's car remained in the parking lot, her phone remained on the bathroom counter, and there was no sign of a struggle, they deduced she went willingly with her abductor. That meant one of two things. She knew the person. Or, she'd been forced to leave under duress.

Both thoughts scared the living hell out of me because either way, Alex was alone and terrified.

I hated to admit it, but my hope had begun to fade. I'd seen the detectives' faces. I'd heard their whispers. Hell, I'd seen enough television to know most abductees were killed within the first twenty-four hours.

It had been *three* days. Three torturous days. And still nothing.

Needing to be away from the noise—away from the constant reminders Alex was gone—I headed into my room and fell back on my bed. I didn't turn on the television for fear of seeing another news teaser about her disappearance. They called her The Missing Millionaire.

Apparently, she'd collected her inheritance while we were in Austin. The investigators were optimistic a ransom request would surface. But it hadn't. And her bank accounts and credit cards remained untouched.

I couldn't understand why she hadn't mentioned her inheritance to me, especially since she dealt with it while I was in Austin with her. But I guess it didn't really matter. The only thing that mattered was that she offered every penny she had to her abductor. Money could be replaced. She couldn't.

I glanced to my nightstand. The night we returned from Austin, Alex printed one of the pictures I'd taken of us and framed it for me. Though it hurt to look, I grabbed the picture from my nightstand and forced myself to look at it.

Our heads were pressed together. Our smiles matched. *God.* She was so beautiful. Those gorgeous green eyes. That shiny dark hair falling over her shoulders. Those stunning features.

Then there was me. What did she even see in me? What made her overlook all my bullshit and see the guy she knew I could be?

My eyes welled, a common occurrence over the past three days.

Having tortured myself long enough, I placed the picture back on my nightstand and draped my arms over my eyes.

*Please bring her back to me.*

# CHAPTER TWENTY-NINE

## ALEX

A whoosh of air left my lungs as my head got thrown to the side with another vicious blow. Black spots clouded my eyes. One more time and I'd be out cold. I could feel it. I welcomed it. With my hands still tied, there was no protecting myself. I could barely open my eyes. Fresh blood slipped from my nose, dripping over the dried blood from the previous strike.

But I was still breathing.

And though the weight of my head pulled my body forward, I still sat upright.

I'd tried with every ounce of energy to escape the ropes keeping me a prisoner. I hadn't taken Remy for a Boy Scout, but the knots were tight. And as the days waned, so did my energy and the strength necessary to escape.

I tried reasoning with him, explaining I had money. Lots of money I could transfer to his account without anyone discovering the source. But that's what elicited his latest blow.

He didn't care about money. That wasn't what this was about. That, in itself, made everything worse. Because then, I had nothing left to offer.

"What did he tell you?" Remy demanded, squatting to look up into my bowed face.

I tried lifting my head up, but it was too heavy. It wasn't the first time Remy asked the same question. But my answer remained the same. "Nothing."

"Then why'd he leave me in there?" He moved so close his spit sprayed across my face. "Why'd he leave me to rot in that cell?"

"I don't know." Trying to talk to him or calm him down proved useless. Anything I said set him off. So I refrained from saying much.

Remy stood and paced the stretch of floor in front of me, the damn gun glued to his hand. He mumbled to himself, but that was nothing new. Most of the time he made no sense. Maybe the pills he kept popping were finally killing him. Or maybe it was just me losing consciousness. Again.

It was odd. I no longer feared Remy. Or his gun. I'd become numb to them. Numb to the pain. Numb to the fear. Maybe exhaustion, hunger, and dehydration did that to a person.

Since I hadn't been permitted to leave my spot, I'd soiled myself days ago. But having been deprived of food and drink, I had nothing left to dispose of.

I really just wanted to be put out of my misery.

"You stole him from me."

I closed my eyes. What could I say? I did. I stole the one person Remy counted on. Unintentionally. But I stole him nonetheless. "I needed him, too," I whispered.

Remy flew in front of me, bending to meet my swollen eyes. His stinking breath invaded my senses. "What could you need him for? He's *my* best friend. We'd die for each other."

I had no response. Nothing I said would make him understand what Hayden and I shared.

"Then you came along with your expensive car and lawyers and weaseled your way into his life. We were fine without you. You fucked everything up. He never would've lied to me before you. He never would've left me rotting in that cell unless you were chirping in his ear."

I shook my head, but barely.

"We had a job last week. Did you know that?"

Why would I know? Hayden didn't *tell* me anything about his work.

"Do you know what he did?" He raised his voice to a scary level. "I said do you know what he did?"

Terrified of what he'd say or do next, I shook my head. I might've been numb, but the unknown still scared the hell out of me.

"He didn't answer my God damned calls. He knew I called and didn't answer. My best friend would never drop me for some bitch." His teeth clenched and his words dripped with hate. "Some no-good piece of replaceable ass."

Remy jerked away and continued to wear out a path in front of me. It gave me a moment to breathe. A moment to assess my surroundings. I raised my eyes. He was getting sloppy. For the first time, the door behind him sat open a couple inches. A television played, but I couldn't see it. I couldn't see much in the dim light or with my cheeks swollen into my eyes. But I glimpsed freedom—if I wasn't still bound to a chair.

"So how do I plan on getting my friend back you ask?" He didn't look at me. He just paced with his gun. "I take away the distraction."

When his words registered, my heart stopped. It actually stopped. And as much as I wanted Remy to end it for me, the thought of never seeing Hayden again became real.

He'd blame himself. I'd be another person he cared about who was killed.

The whole situation wasn't fair.

It was *insane*.

"I'm sure while Hayden was running his mouth he told you I have no problem handling a gun." He released the gun's safety. "And someone as meaningless as you will be easier than most to dispose of."

There wasn't a thing I could do to stop it. A sob exploded from my lips. Because it finally hit me.

Hayden wasn't coming to save me.

# CHAPTER THIRTY

## HAYDEN

"You sure, Hayden?" Alex asked in that sassy little way only she could.

We were in her room in Austin. For some strange reason, I turned down her offer to share another shower. But it worked in my favor because she set about changing my mind in a variety of interesting ways involving her stripping down to her underwear.

Pounding on the door sent my body jack-knifing. My chest heaved from the sudden intrusion as I struggled to get my bearings.

I wasn't in Austin. I wasn't with Alex.

She was still missing.

My chest constricted.

"Hayden?" Alex's aunt called from behind my bedroom door.

I scrubbed my hands over my unshaven face, trying to keep my tears at bay. "Yeah?"

"You have a visitor."

Running my hands through my hair, I suddenly realized my room was aglow with sunlight. How long had I been out? "I'll be—"

The door swung open. Cooper's suit-clad body filled the doorway. Why the hell was he in my apartment? In my bedroom? He didn't make house calls. People were brought to him.

I jumped to my feet like a lowly recruit before the general.

"Sit down, son."

I did as told and nearly shit when he closed the door and took a seat beside me on my bed.

His dark eyes assessed my empty walls and furniture, the same way Alex's had the first time she'd been inside. "Sorry to hear about your girl."

I nodded. Was that why he'd come by? To offer his condolences? She wasn't dead. She couldn't be.

"They have any leads?"

I swallowed around the lump in my throat and shook my head.

"Listen, I came by to tell you something." My eyes lifted to his face, but his eyes stared at the picture on my nightstand. I wondered if he could see how in love Alex and I were—are. "And I know once I do, you're gonna be really angry with me. I don't expect anything less."

I gripped the comforter at my sides, bunching the fabric tightly in my fists. "You're scaring the fuck out of me right now, sir. Please just tell me what you know."

He shook his head. "I don't know anything. It's just a hunch."

Beads of sweat formed on my forehead.

Cooper avoided my probing gaze. He stared straight ahead, his eyes creasing in the corners. "That night in the alley. Did you ever wonder if that guy was still alive?"

"What?"

He shot me a sideways glance. "When Remy lifted you over the wall? You think the guy could've been alive?"

Having no clue why he'd bring that up—especially with my life in shambles—I shook my head.

"Why not?"

"Because I was there. I saw him." My voice rose, never having spoken to anyone about it but Alex. "I saw his lifeless body. I've seen his grave."

He nodded. "Oh, he died that night alright." He stared at me long and hard, considering his words. "But you didn't kill him."

I sucked in a sharp breath. "What?"

"You didn't do it. Remy did."

My stomach dropped as my jaw hung to the floor. He wasn't talking about the story Remy told the cops. He was telling me something I didn't know. Something I couldn't have known.

"He didn't want the guy talking, or going to the feds about me, so he kicked him in the head until he took his last breath. *After* you scaled the wall."

My head spun with images of that night. I'd been there. I'd seen him with my own eyes. Hadn't I?

*Jesus Christ.*

All this fucking time.

All the guilt I lived with.

All the choices I made because of it.

"I never understood why Remy wanted you to believe you did it."

Anger welled inside of me, deep and fiery. I scrubbed my palms over my face. "So he could hold on to me," I hissed. "So he'd have my unwavering loyalty."

"I'm sorry. I should've told you sooner."

I nodded, my mind still whirling.

"In our world, respect is key. You've earned mine ten-fold." He patted me on the back and stood up. "You've still got a job if you want one. But I won't stand in your way if you don't after what I've kept quiet about."

I watched speechlessly as Cooper walked to my door and stopped.

He turned back with repentant eyes. "Remy made bail."

## ALEX

Being tethered in the same spot for days had turned my body cold and limbs numb. My heartbeat had slowed to a distant thumping. My breathing was labored. And my cotton mouth barely opened.

I couldn't understand why Remy didn't just kill me. I guess he wanted me to die a slow death. Torture me for stealing his best friend. Drive me completely insane.

Hallucinations had taken over my reality. Dreams mixed with my nightmares. I often mistook Remy for Hayden. In those brief moments, I attempted to smile or speak. Until being tugged from my delusion when he opened his mouth.

Everything was so hazy.

So distant.

So dark.

In the beginning I tried to stay awake. I didn't try anymore. I found it easier to drift off to a place where visions of Hayden kept me safe. His smiling face when I fished for compliments. His strong arms when he wouldn't let me go in the middle of the night. His dimples when he smiled. His vulnerability only I got to see.

Those images kept me sane in the midst of my darkest hours.

I was close. So close to no longer existing. So close to joining my parents. Preston's parents. Hayden's mom. Victor. I could feel it with every fiber of my being. Hopefully, I'd fade away the same way I'd spent most of my last hours. Unconscious.

*Pound. Pound.*

My ears perked at the distant sound. Was someone building a house nearby? Hayden would be good at construction, so strong and talented with his hands. I wondered if he found a job. Anything to keep him away from Remy and the evil life he lived.

*Pound. Pound.*

Maybe it was a kid playing basketball. Hayden mentioned he'd played when he was younger. He also dispelled the rumor about boxing, but thought it was a good cover for when he got blindsided on the job.

*Pound. Pound.*

Was the noise solely in my head? Because if so, why was it becoming increasingly louder?

Clearer?

Closer?

There was no use trying to lift my head. Remy was probably in a drunken stupor again. I wouldn't use my last bit of energy on him. He wouldn't get that.

A door thrust open rattling the wall behind it.

"Oh my God, Alex."

My Hayden dream again.

"I'm here, baby, I'm right here," his rushed voice promised.

His hands always went to work on the ropes around my ankles first. He'd get to my hands after I lifted my head and we exchanged a tear-filled exchange.

Hallucinations could be so cruel. Because each time I came to and realized it wasn't real, devastation hit and the nightmare I found myself in was actually reality.

"I'm here. I've got you. You're gonna be okay. I swear to you, you're gonna be okay."

Even in my hallucinations Hayden soothed me. Protected me. Saved me. Who knew the mind could be so callous?

My eyes remained closed. I wasn't foolish enough to believe the mirage, even if I did allow myself to indulge for a little while.

"I found Alex. She's at Remy's on Ocean Road."

Hayden calling in my whereabouts always ended my dream. It was the painful moment I discovered it really wasn't him. The moment I discovered without a shadow of a doubt, I was completely alone. Secured to a chair. Surrounded by darkness.

"Step back," Remy's voice ripped through my delusions like a vicious tornado. Always destroying my dreams.

## HAYDEN

My head flew up from where I crouched at Alex's feet, attempting to untie the ropes. *Ropes.* My beautiful girl was tied up in fucking ropes. The sight of her almost unrecognizable face, so bruised and swollen, gutted my heart and fucked with my head. I was seconds away from going ballistic.

Remy stood in the doorway of his spare room. The room he'd kept Alex a prisoner in for four days. *Four fucking days.* I was gonna tear his head off and then kill him. *Hate* and *disgust* weren't strong enough words for what I felt. "What have you done?" I couldn't even look at him as I worked on the knot at her right ankle.

In my peripheral, I saw him saunter in, like he hadn't kidnapped my girl and done God knows what to her. I couldn't even consider the possibilities. It'd distract me from getting her out. And she needed medical attention. Fast.

But I knew Remy. And no matter how calm he appeared, there wasn't a chance in hell he'd let us both leave.

My shaking fingers somehow unknotted the knot, pulling the rope free from Alex's ankle.

"So, my long lost friend reemerges. What brings you here?" Remy asked as if it were some kind of joke.

"I see you made bail." I needed to keep him talking. Keep his attention off Alex.

"No thanks to you," he growled as he lifted his boot and shoved his heel against Alex's chair. The force sent the entire chair flying backward.

"Oh, my God." I dove to stop its fall, but my hand only made it behind her head as the chair landed. Thank God she was already unconscious.

I couldn't take anymore. I was beyond the point of thinking rationally. My anger superseded reason. My adrenaline shot through the roof. My savage side erupted. I lowered my shoulder and charged at Remy with a giant roar.

He had no time to brace himself. He flailed back as I tackled him to the floor, his head bouncing off the floorboards like a beach ball. His gun slipped out of his pocket. I swept it across the floor toward Alex. Fuck his gun. I wanted him to feel the pain. I wanted him to suffer.

"Get off," he growled through gritted teeth, but he didn't shield himself.

Did he think I wouldn't hurt him? Because I wanted to kill him with my bare hands. I let my fists loose. First my right then my left. Then I alternated. Blow after blow.

Blood sprayed from his nose, covering his face, me, the floor. I was going to kill him. I was really going to do it.

My vision blurred. Tears mixed with the sweat dripping down my face. Ragged breaths were all I could manage as the rage within me escalated to epic heights.

My blows were relentless. Incensed. Unrestrained.

I wanted him to feel what Alex had been through—what he'd put her through. I wanted him to feel the hate I felt for him.

I glanced over my shoulder at Alex, still unconscious. Still bound to a chair. Still beaten and broken. I needed to reel in my anger. I needed to pull myself back from the edge.

She needed me.

Pushing off Remy's heaving chest, I stood. My eyes didn't leave him as I backed away. "Why would you do this?" I squatted at Alex's left ankle, working on the ropes. "How could you fucking hurt her?"

"I needed you. I needed you and you blew me off. For *her.*"

Jesus Christ. He sounded like a scorned ex. He was even more delusional than I ever imagined.

"You owed me."

It was like being kicked in the gut. Abused for too long by the one person who had something to hold over me. Something to cinch my loyalty. Something that was a complete lie. "I owed you nothing," I spat. I couldn't believe he had the balls to keep up the charade after everything he'd done.

"I protected you. I always protected you," he screamed as I sat back on my feet watching him lay there a bloody mangled mess.

"You protected *you*. It's only ever been about *you.*"

"No, man. It was supposed to be us. We were supposed to start our own organization. One that rivaled Cooper's. You're the only one I'd ever trust to do it with me."

I shook my head at his delusional ramblings. Cooper would've killed Remy before he ever let him lure business away from him.

I'd heard enough.

I pulled the rope free from Alex's left ankle and went to work on her wrists. I needed to get her out of there. "What you did was fucked up. You're fucked up." The skin was raw around Alex's wrists like she'd fought to get free. My God. How hard had she worked to escape? "If I find out—"

*Click.*

Oh fuck.

*"He got your time. Your affection. Your love. It was all supposed to be mine!"*

I shook off the echo of my father's voice as I turned slowly, bracing myself for the barrel of a gun in my face. But it wasn't aimed at me.

Remy stood with the gun aimed at Alex.

My heart leaped to my throat as I threw my body in front of her, shielding her from the gun. From Remy.

I glanced over my shoulder. He hadn't lowered the gun. Darkness clouded his eyes as he stared across the room at me. God, I knew what he was capable of. I wrapped my arms tightly around Alex, like it could somehow protect us from his insanity.

Burying my nose in her hair, I closed my eyes and sent up a silent prayer to whoever might be listening. *Please don't let him do this.*

"You were my family, Hayden."

*Oh, God.* I squeezed my eyes tighter, braced for the bullet.

"You were the only person I ever trusted."

Maybe if he saw my face, he'd be unable to do it. I lifted my head and looked up at him.

Something flashed in his heartless eyes. It wasn't anger, more like understanding. Understanding that I'd do anything to protect the girl beneath me. This wasn't about him anymore. He no longer had my unyielding loyalty. He'd lost that all on his own.

He lifted the gun to the side of his head and pressed it into his temple.

I sucked in a breath.

"Now I don't even have you."

Behind him, the living room door opened. Cops in swat gear with guns drawn inched their way in. But they were too late.

Remy's finger squeezed the trigger.

The fatal shot echoed throughout the house stilling everyone. This time, I prepared myself. This time I closed my eyes so I wouldn't have the vision forever etched in my mind, replaying in my nightmares.

And there *would* be nightmares.

Because I knew the truth.

This happened to Alex because of me.

I didn't even bother looking when the cops and medics surrounded Remy's body. I untied Alex's arms and lifted her lifeless body. EMTs rushed in and led me to the stretcher in the driveway. I placed her down and followed them into the back of the ambulance.

They hooked her up to IV's, pumping her full of fluids while treating her external wounds. She looked so small. So swollen. So broken. I gripped her cold hand and didn't let go.

I wouldn't.

No one would take my beautiful girl away from me.

*Never* again.

# CHAPTER THIRTY-ONE

## HAYDEN

Sitting beside Alex's hospital bed, grasping her frail hand for dear life, was the worst type of déjà vu. I glanced around the room. The red and orange glow outside the window signified the end of another day. Another day of speaking to her and getting no response. Another day of hoping her dreams weren't nightmares. Another day of longing to hear her laugh.

She'd been unconscious for three days, after being gone for four. It had been a full week since I'd seen her smile. Since I heard her voice. Since I breathed normally.

Katherine begged me to take a break. And I would. When Alex woke up.

Sometimes her eyelashes fluttered like a hummingbird—which the doctor assured us was a good sign. But she hadn't opened her eyes.

I lifted her frail hand to my lips and pressed softly. "I love you so much. All the way down to my bones."

Katherine and I had been taking shifts talking to her. Even when it wasn't my turn, I slept in a chair in the corner of the room in case she woke up. I meant it. I'd never leave her side again.

Katherine had just run home to shower. So I had Alex all to myself.

"So, I've been thinking about something pretty important…how I'll propose. Before you say it, I know what you're thinking. We're too young. But I didn't mean next week. I meant I *will* propose someday and you *will* say yes."

Steering clear of her face, I leaned in and kissed the top of her head gently, not wanting to disturb her breaks and bruises. "I swear to you, I've never been more sure about anything in my life."

I thought I knew nightmares, but nothing compared to the uncertainty surrounding Alex's disappearance. Four days of not knowing where she was, what she was enduring, or if she was even alive, proved to be my worst nightmare.

Now that I had her back, had her within reach, I knew what I wanted. And I'd be damned if I didn't get it. I wasn't scared anymore. I wanted her to know how I felt. What I thought. What I wanted. Frankly, I just needed her to wake up so I could tell her to her face.

"And by the way, I want kids. Lots of them. Like a whole soccer team of them running around with their mother's brown hair and green eyes."

I pressed my lips to her hand, keeping my eyes from venturing to the darkened rope burns around her wrists. "And they better have my dimples. Girls love the dimples."

I could hardly look at her swollen and discolored face without breaking down. It took every ounce of strength I had to sit there and talk to her like the whole situation wasn't my fault. From Taylor to Remy, none of it would have happened if she hadn't met me. If I hadn't approached her.

Maybe she wouldn't even want anything to do with me when she woke up. Maybe she couldn't forgive me. Maybe I caused her too much grief. Too much pain. Too much sorrow. Like Remy had for me.

The waterworks began yet again. I couldn't control them. I was consumed by guilt. Consumed by anger. Consumed by the fear of what she must think of me. "I'm so sorry this happened to you, Alex. I'm *so* damn sorry."

I still couldn't wrap my head around it. How could Remy ever put a hand to her? Keep her tied up? Starve her? The thoughts were too inconceivable. I always believed him to be a threat to our happiness, always having such a strong hold over me. But never could I have imagined he'd do something so sadistic to the girl I loved.

Alex's hand twitched in mine.

My head shot up.

I leaned in closer, still grasping her hand like I'd ceased to exist without it. "Alex. I'm right here. I'm not going anywhere."

Her eyelashes fluttered.

"Open those pretty eyes. Let me see them."

Her doctor said dreams caused the eye movement. I hoped whatever she dreamt about was peaceful. Like a vision of her parents. Not a nightmare about Remy. She already lived that.

I exhaled a disappointed breath. I knew I needed to be patient, but patience sucked.

"Okay, so I know you're probably sick of this story, but it's the best one I've got. Besides, you *are* the one who's always fishing." I pressed my lips to her hand for a long moment wishing she'd just put me out of my misery and wake up.

A giant multi-colored balloon embossed with Get Well shifted below the air vent as I thought back to the first day we met.

"It was late August when the most beautiful girl I'd ever seen stepped into my life. She was this little thing driving a killer car and carrying a huge suitcase. Even back then, I knew she was out of my league. So I waited four long days before I worked up the nerve to talk to her."

I kissed her hand again, but when I looked back to her face, her lashes had stopped fluttering.

My shoulders dropped on a sigh. But I wouldn't give up. Not when she needed me.

"I know what you're thinking. How could I, God's gift to women, be nervous to talk to a girl? But I was. I was terrified. She wasn't like the others. She was sweet and innocent and sad. So damn sad. And don't ask me why, but I wanted to make it all stop. I needed to."

I ran my free hand through my hair, trying like hell not to focus on the bruises and swelling covering her face.

"When I finally talked to her, she blew my mind. She was exactly what I'd been waiting for. Beautiful, funny, sarcastic, stubborn. So stubborn. And even though I fought to keep her away, she wouldn't let me. She wormed her way into my life. My head. My heart. Eventually, I had to stop fighting it. And when I did, when I let her in, let her know my demons, I knew I'd found my match. My perfect match."

Tears fell from my eyes so freely it should've been disconcerting.

"By her birthday, I was a goner. So far gone it wasn't even funny. She thought she was the only one experiencing something for the first time that night. But she was wrong. I was getting to experience something, too. An all-consuming, rip-your-heart-out-of-your-chest-if-you-were-rejected, kind of love. And once it hit me, once I could plainly see that's what we had, I knew I'd do anything to keep her. Because in my eyes, she was finally mine. It was that moment I promised whoever was listening upstairs, I'd protect and treasure her for the rest of my life."

As the words left my lips, the knowledge that I hadn't protected her crushed me. I scrubbed away my tears, closing my eyes to regain my composure in case someone walked in.

"I love you, too," a soft voice whispered.

My eyes snapped open, but Alex's remained closed. I looked over my shoulder at the empty doorway.

I knew wanting something to happen badly enough could make you believe it happened. But that wasn't it. I knew what I heard. I'd know that voice anywhere.

"Alex?" I leaned in, careful not to get too close for fear of startling her if she opened her eyes.

I watched her swollen lips move. "You saved me, Hayden."

A cross between a gasp and a sob broke from my lips. I missed her so damn much. I wanted to spread kisses all over her beautiful face. But I couldn't risk hurting her with so many broken bones healing underneath her bruises. Instead I lifted her hand already in mine and kissed it over and over again.

"I missed you," she whispered.

My tears were a God damn waterfall spilling everywhere.

"I knew you'd come for me."

I closed my eyes, unable to believe she'd finally woken up *and* she didn't hate me. "Oh, baby. I'm so sorry I didn't find you sooner."

"Do *not* blame yourself." As weak as she was, she was determined to speak her mind. "This is *not* your fault."

I couldn't speak. I couldn't do much of anything but wipe at the tears falling down my cheeks.

Alex's head fell to the side. Her eyes cracked open enough so she could see me. "You did *not* do this."

I nodded, knowing she truly believed that. "I'm gonna spend the rest of my life making it up to you."

I could've sworn her lips twitched. "Promise?"

# EPILOGUE

## ALEX

### *EIGHT MONTHS LATER*

"You got everything?" Hayden asked.

I looked around the empty purple bedroom. It took me less than a day to pack everything. I picked up the only remaining evidence I ever lived there. The latest framed picture of Hayden and me on my nightstand.

Our squished faces usually made it difficult to see where his face stopped and mine began, but not in this one. Hayden sported facial hair and I wore my graduation cap. Hayden didn't get to wear one yet. He had a few more credits to earn. Sophia had taken the picture on the quad after I crossed the stage, and our wide smiles matched.

Hayden's strong arms slipped around my waist from behind. His chin rested on my shoulder. "I love this picture."

I twisted my head so I could see him. This guy I'd grown to love more and more every day. And not just because he saved me. Because I knew I saved him as well. "You say that about every picture of us."

Hayden spun me around until I could do nothing but look up into his amazing blue eyes, the ones that knocked me off balance the first day I looked into them. The ones that held my future. "That's because you're in them."

I rolled my eyes as I tossed the picture onto the bed and linked my arms around his neck. "You know, you don't have to keep working so hard to get me. I'm already yours."

He lowered his lips to mine, his soft and tender kiss forcing me to feel his love. I wished he got the memo. Everything he did, day after day, accomplished that already. He pulled away, his eyes locked on mine. "I need to keep it that way."

"You do realize I'm going to be your boss, right? I'm going to get to tell you what to do, whenever I feel the urge."

His dimples sank in, framing a full-blown smile. "I'm counting on it."

I leaned in and kissed the smile right off his lips. "Can we stop by to see your mom before we leave?"

His eyes softened. "Yeah. She'd hate it if I took you hours away without a goodbye."

"She does love me, doesn't she?"

"It's all those damn flowers you bring her."

I smiled, but deep inside I couldn't curb my apprehension. He was taking a giant risk uprooting his whole life for me. This was his home. The only place he called his own after everything he'd endured. "You sure this is what you want?"

He tightened his arms, and I could feel his heart deep and steady against my chest. "I would follow you to the ends of the earth if it meant we'd be together."

A smile slid across my lips. "Hayden Martin, corny? No one would believe it."

"Who cares what anyone else thinks? I only care what you think."

"How long do we have?"

"Forever."

I smiled up at him, knowing that was the truth.

Since saving me from Remy, he said things like that all the time. That whole experience changed him. It changed us both. We were open and honest with each other. And it worked. We worked. We weren't perfect, and we accepted that.

Hayden lowered his voice to that husky tenor I got when I woke up next to him. "My life began when I met you. What happened before is a memory. Something that'll never happen again."

"Better not," I teased.

"This." He nodded between us. "Me and you and this adventure we're about to embark on. This is my reality. And, from where I stand, it's a pretty amazing reality."

I couldn't resist. I was a sucker for romantic declarations. I jumped up so he had to catch me and wrapped my legs around his hips. "I love you, Hayden. I love you so much it seeps right down to my bones."

Hayden's head recoiled. "You heard me?"

I couldn't be positive I'd heard everything he uttered at my bedside in the hospital, but I heard enough. I pressed my lips to his. This time it was me who took it soft and gentle so he knew just how true my words were and how deep my love ran.

I pulled back and nuzzled my nose to his. "Now I just can't wait for the proposal. It better be freaking amazing."

"Not mediocre?"

"With you?" I shook my head. "Never again."


THE END

# Acknowledgements

Thank you, wonderful readers and bloggers, for taking a chance on my debut novel. I cannot express my gratitude for the time you invested reading, reviewing, and spreading the word about my story when there are so many amazing novels out there. I hope you enjoyed getting to know Alex and Hayden as much as I enjoyed writing about them.

Thank you to my parents for instilling in me both a love of storytelling and the notion that anything is possible. To Heather and Kim for loving all the same teeny-bopper television shows and sappy romance movies I love. To my husband for putting up with my laptop in front of me at all times. I really am listening when you're talking. I swear! And to my son for still napping so I have time to write during the day.

Thank you to the wonderful Stephanie Elliot for editing my first draft. Not only did you motivate me to actually put it out there, but you also gave me so many great suggestions to help make it the best it could be. Thank you for helping me throughout this journey!

Lastly, thank you to LJ at Mayhem Cover Creations for your beautiful cover. It really captured the tortured essence of the story and the will-they won't-they feeling between Alex and Hayden.

If you'd like to get in touch with me or learn more about me, check out my website www.jnathan.net or my Goodreads page. I look forward to hearing from you!

## About the Author

J. Nathan resides on the east coast with her husband and son. She is an avid reader of all things romance. Happy endings are a must. When she is not curled up with a good book, she can be found spending time with family and friends, teaching high school English, and working on her next novel.

Made in the USA
Lexington, KY
22 July 2014